DEAD AIM

Center Point
Large Print

Also by Dusty Richards and available from Center Point Large Print:

Rancher's Law
The O'Malleys of Texas

This Large Print Book carries the Seal of Approval of N.A.V.H.

DEAD AIM

The O'Malleys of Texas

Dusty Richards

CENTER POINT LARGE PRINT
THORNDIKE, MAINE

This Center Point Large Print edition
is published in the year 2018 by arrangement with
Kensington Publishing Corp.

The text of this Large Print edition is unabridged.
In other aspects, this book may vary
from the original edition.
Printed in the United States of America
on permanent paper.
Set in 16-point Times New Roman type.

ISBN: 978-1-68324-724-1

Library of Congress Cataloging-in-Publication Data

Names: Richards, Dusty, author.
Title: Dead aim : the O'Malleys of Texas / Dusty Richards.
Description: Center Point Large Print edition. | Thorndike, Maine :
    Center Point Large Print, 2018.
Identifiers: LCCN 2017060360 | ISBN 9781683247241
    (hardcover : alk. paper)
Subjects: LCSH: Large type books. | GSAFD: Western stories.
Classification: LCC PS3568.I31523 D426 2018 | DDC 813/.54—dc23
LC record available at https://lccn.loc.gov/2017060360

DEAD AIM

CHAPTER 1

Lying on his belly beneath the covered wagon, he squinted as the gun smoke from the barrel of his Winchester burned his eyes. He stared through the buckhorn sights at another of the many war-painted bucks charging around the wagon circle. Long John O'Malley damn sure felt angry by their savage attack on this wagon train. He fit the next war-painted brave in his gun sights, then squeezed the trigger, and one more screaming warrior bit the dust.

Levering in a fresh cartridge, he took aim through the wavering dust and dropped another campfire buddy of the attackers off his racing horse. A woman in her twenties slipped in on her hands and knees beside him underneath the wagon and set down a fresh box of cartridges. Then on her stomach she feverishly tore open the thick paper box. Her face bathed in sweat, her blue eyes wide open in a feverish fear, she whispered, "When will they ever quit?"

"When they all get sent to the gates of hell."

"How many have you picked off?" She was still on her stomach, searching the scene of the attackers racing around screaming while they poured both arrows and rifle balls at the wagon train's circle. An arrow thudded into the wagon box right above her head and she jumped. His .44/40 took out another war-painted pony, and the rider went flying through the air.

"I have not kept count. Thanks for the ammo." On his side, he began rapid reloading of the rifle with the fresh rounds. Then he rolled back and spotted the prize of the day coming on the same route that his own men had taken. The trailing war bonnet showed off the measure of this man's rank. And his screams were to encourage his men to fight even harder.

Long bore down on him with his sights and squeezed. The chieftain, hard struck in the chest, went off the butt of his horse in a backward somersault.

She screamed, "You got that son of a—"

Her hand caught the swear word on her lips.

Their war cries fell silent. Their guns no longer barked. The shocked, loud, body-painted riders warily crowded around on horseback and afoot where their leader lay on the ground.

The woman scooted back next to him and kissed the unexpecting Long hard on the mouth. He blinked in shock at her actions. When she rose off him and backed away, he rolled back in position and began in rapid fire to drop those braves gathered around their fallen leader. Three more went down under his hot bullets, and the rest of the Indians hurriedly hauled the chief's limp body off by his arms out of sight.

A cheer went up from inside the wagon ring. "We've whipped them! Yeah! Yeah!"

Still on her knees, her blue eyes bored a hole into him. She shook her head. "Not them. You whipped them. I am not a brazen woman, but I owe you my life and so do all these people in this wagon train."

He nodded he heard her and she backed out. With newfound hope that this fierce attack might be over, he reloaded his Winchester, picked up the box, and with them and the gun in his hand, he eased his way out. Clear of the wagon, he straightened to find himself surrounded by the excited men and women of the wagon train.

"Mister, you single-handed killed half that damn Indian Nation. But by getting that head chief you sure shut them down." After Long set the rifle down, the wagon master, Tucker, shook his hand. "Where did you learn how to fight Injuns before?"

"My father." He took a deep breath of the fresher air. "My brother Harp and I grew up on the Texas frontier. My father went after Comanche to get captives back. We rode with him because all the other men were gone to war. We fought them and managed to trade for some. But I've been warring with Indians since I was twelve years old."

Tucker frowned at his words. "You're part Indian?"

"Yes. My father was a Cherokee. He was killed in the Outlet before I was born. I know only a little about his people. But yes, I have fought Indians."

"You told me you sold lots of cattle in Abilene, Kansas. Big herds, weren't they?"

"Over six thousand head this time. We sold eight hundred head in Sedalia, Missouri, last year right there at the end of the war."

"What is a man that rich doing out here with a wagon train load of sod busters?" Tucker laughed, amused.

"That money is in the bank. I wanted to see the Rocky Mountains and what was out here, but I had no desire to fight all these warring plains tribes."

Several others laughed and Tucker frowned. "It's how you talk, O'Malley. You sound like a Texas professor. No one's ever saw a man half Indian who talked like that before."

"My mother taught me most of that. I can read and write, too."

"Oh, no doubt. Sometime tell us about that first cattle drive you made?"

"It was almost as bad as this Indian war you all are fighting out here."

Tucker made a face.

"See, General Lee signed a peace treaty back

east. The war didn't end that easy in Arkansas and Missouri last year. We took our herd right through them."

"I understand. Men, we have a job to do. There's wounded Indians lying out there need to be sent to the happy hunting grounds. Some of our own stock needs to be treated for wounds. The oxen and horses need to be put out to graze to keep their strength. And sadly enough, there are three of our own dead we must bury. We roll west in the morning. And, Mr. O'Malley, we thank you and we thank God for sending you to help us stave them off."

"Yes, you all are welcome. One question, Tucker."

"Yes."

"How much more ammo do you have left in case you have another attack like this one?"

"We'd have enough. But yes, we are low. I thought we had enough forever. But I didn't expect this much fighting."

"Keep that in mind when you find a source to secure more."

"Oh, I certainly will."

Long went with a few men, outside the circle, to send any downed Indians to their end. Several wounded warriors were still alive, so the grizzly job continued on the bloody battlefield of scattered bodies of the braves and their injured mounts as well as on the ground surrounding the wagon ring.

A young married unarmed man named Hennessey walked beside him across the battle-strewn field of dead horses and Indians. "Do you think there are more war parties ahead of us?"

"They tell me there are thousands of Indians camped out here. We are invading their country. They even fight with each other over the land ownership. Yes, you may have more fights and then, too, you may go unscathed."

"Invading?"

"I don't know what the hell else to call it." Long shrugged his shoulders.

Hennessey laughed. "I just want to find a good farm in Oregon to raise my family."

"I bet you'll have to fight them up there."

"I guess you are right. I better learn how."

Long drew his Colt revolver. "That Indian lying over there is not dead. Can you use a pistol?"

"Sure."

"Cock it and shoot him in the head."

"I-I never shot anyone."

"That buck would have killed and scalped you and raped your new wife."

Hennessey nodded.

"Here, shoot him." He handed him the Colt. "Keep your eyes open."

The man's hand shook as he extended his arm

and cocked the hammer back. The revolver spit the bullet and gun smoked. His whole body shivered as he stepped back two steps and dropped his gun hand to the side of his leg.

"He's dead. Don't ever hesitate to kill your enemy. It will be him or you that survives." He took back his six-gun and holstered it.

Hennessey folded his arms, shuddered, and nodded. "I am going to have to get a damn sight tougher than I am. Won't I?"

"If your family and you can ever survive in Oregon, you damn sure will have to."

"You about have them all kilt. I better go back and check on my wife."

"Get a smaller caliber pistol than mine and shoot it till you get damn good."

Hennessey nodded. "Thanks, Long. I know what I've got to do. I will."

Long wondered if the boy really had the deep down nerve to do it.

He met with one of the older men on the battlefield doing the same job.

"Name's Hurley."

"Long O'Malley."

"I know you. I saw you trying to teach that boy what he needed to do."

"He better take my word or he'll be sprouting daisies."

"You ever think some of us came from a different source?"

Long nodded he did and swept up a dropped .30-caliber Colt from the ground. Some Indian lost it. He polished the dust off it on his sleeve, then he spun the cylinder to be certain the chamber was empty under the hammer.

This might be the gun that boy needed. He stuck it in his waistband.

"How long you going to ride with us at this snail pace?" Hurley asked.

"Oh, probably not much longer."

"I appreciate your leadership. I served in the war and I thought it was all over, but it ain't, is it?"

"These red men won't sign an armistice like Lee did if that's what you thought."

"Hey, here's a brand-new Winchester." Hurley swept it up and checked the barrel to be sure it wasn't bent. "How in the hell did he get this rifle?"

"Probably bought it with furs."

He lowered the lever and ejected the cartridge. He caught the shell and smiled. "Bet he never got to fire it." He handed it to Long.

The gun in Long's hands, he examined it. "I bet you're right."

"Hey, guys, get all their arms," Hurley said to the others. "We may need them later."

"I need to go back and clean my rifle. You have enough help out here."

Hurley agreed and thanked him. The final count

was thirty-six dead Indians just in the field. The count did not include the chief or others, either dead or injured, who were taken away when the able-bodied ones fled the area.

In camp, out of his packs, Long found the ramrod and unloaded the rifle to use the brush to clean the bore. He was busy with a rag on the ram to further clean up the traces of spent powder out of the rifle barrel.

A tall blond, attractive woman came by and stopped. "Mr. O'Malley, do you have a woman at home in Texas?"

He looked up and smiled at her. "No."

With a smug look at him she said, "My sister in Saint Charles would make you a great mate."

"How is that?"

"Oh, she likes flashy men."

He chuckled. "I don't consider myself flashy."

"Well you damn sure are." She gave him a high sign and went on her way with a cute swing to her backside.

If the sister was as pretty as her he might ride back there and find her. He went back to finish cleaning his rifle. Instead of poking along with these friendly folks, much as he liked them, he better get to riding west if he was ever going to see the Rockies and then get back to Texas to be of any help to his brother Harp on the family ranch.

Later that night asleep in his bedroll, someone

whispered in his ear, "Don't scream. I don't have any ammo. Let me in there with you."

It was his ammo lady and he raised the blanket. She hadn't come there to read his palm about his future. It was too dark for that.

CHAPTER 2

Dawn broke the hold on the eastern horizon. Long had dressed and decided to go see about some breakfast. At her wagon a middle-aged woman, Mrs. Yarborough, each morning served oatmeal with some sugar and cream, if there was any available, and coffee. Not the greatest brand but it was coffee, and all of that for twenty-five cents. Several bachelors ate there with her. She dished him out a metal bowl full and told him to get seated and she'd have the tin coffee cup he handed her filled.

"Thank you, ma'am," Long said to her.

"You don't have to thank me. You paid for your breakfast. These others are going to owe me lots of labor when we get to Oregon." She laughed and set his cup of steaming coffee beside him.

"Oh, Mary Margret, my mother would beat me if I didn't say thank you to you."

"Heavens to Betsy she must have been strict on you."

"It did not hurt me or my brother Harp. In fact it helped. He was less than eighteen when we took our first cattle to Missouri and he was the ramrod. He had good manners and he was firm, but through him and his leadership we took those

17

cattle through a land of people that really hated us and sold them."

"I never thought about that. Manners do impress people. Where is he?"

"He's home with his neat wife Katy and new son Lee buying up the state of Texas and gathering more cattle to take back to Kansas next spring."

She laughed. "How much land is he going to buy?"

"One big place I hope. I plan to leave tomorrow for the West. I need to get out there to see those Rockies and get back home."

"Well, you did show us how to circle up and fight them Injuns. I say we sure needed you. You know they are planning the three funerals to be held shortly."

"They won't need me for that. I have my horses ready. Thanks for feeding me." He finished up his oatmeal, downed his coffee, then gripped her shoulder and kissed her forehead.

"God bless you, lad, and I hope you get back to your family."

"You are an angel. I plan to do that very thing." He shook a few more hands, mounted his stout bay horse, and took the chestnut packhorse with him. Many shouted good-bye to him and thanked him.

The great road was one of many of the paths busy with the westward movement even this late in the season. He was a little concerned about these folks, who in the opinion of veteran travelers were not far enough west for late summer and they would have to winter somewhere in less than survivable conditions. His own two horses were stout ones and in the cooler air he short-loped them to put miles under their hooves.

He passed more wagon trains and freighters. Lots of trade goods were being borne westward by oxen. Railroad rates were too high to pay, and the high raw costs of lying rails deeper and deeper into this unsettled land had slowed its expansion. So oxen did the work until the rails caught up.

The birds of the plains scattered at his approach. He'd seen lots of prairie chickens and their barely feathered new brood. Killdeer and others scurried after bugs. Several buffalo herds detoured him, though they were not as numerous as he heard about, but he knew the pressure of hunting them was driving them west.

He made miles across the plains, which was an endless track following the sun westward. Long stopped to camp with wagon trains and freighters, to talk to people, eat some woman's sweet dessert, and then push on. His separation from Harp he found was the hardest part of his exploring adventure. His brother was home building the O'Malley family ranch, maybe an empire after their last big cattle sale in Abilene, and he wasn't back there in Texas to help him. His conscience bit him over his self-centered plans to satisfy a whim.

A week later he rode up on a small family wagon outfit in late afternoon and spoke to the gray-haired man who was in charge. They wore shabby clothes, looked poor, and their outfit was patched.

"My name is Long O'Malley."

"Get down. Set a while. We have no coffee but we're friendly."

"You have a coffeepot. I have coffee we can boil."

"Woman, this fine man has coffee to share."

A blank-eyed teenage girl appeared and smiled. "I kin fix it."

"Well boil some water and get things going," the man said as three young men came in, sat down, and stared at him.

"Boys, this is Long O'Malley."

They nodded.

"He has real coffee to share. Ain't no burnt barley. Nice, ain't it?"

They only nodded.

"Them his horses, Paw?"

"Yes, he rode in here a short while ago."

"Nice horses you ride."

Long agreed. "They're good enough."

The oldest one stood up. "You must be rich."

"I'm a rancher in Texas."

"Paw, I think we need them horses."

"Why, don't insult our guest, son."

"I think—"

His words stung Long. His back up, he said, "Go sit down. You're not taking my horses or threatening me."

"Why, mister—"

"Sit down or I'll fill you full of lead. Move." The Colt in his fist, Long slowly backed up. He lifted his rein and stepped in the saddle. His gun ready for any move they made. Then he guided his saddle horse with his knees so he could get the lead rope and throw it over his packhorse's neck. All the time he kept them in his sight. Then he whirled the bay with his body and holstered his gun and left. The packhorse broke to go with him and galloped beside his stirrup. They went west.

There were all kinds, good and bad people, on the road west. Next time he'd look them over better before he stepped off his horse. This open country certainly could be dangerous. All the scum of the earth rode the western expansion wave. What did they say? No law, no restraint west of Abilene. He was beginning to believe it.

He met three travelers two days later; two of the men wore suits. The other was a cowboy who was their guide and camp cook. His name was Theo and said as he shook Long's hand that he originally came from Fort Worth. The other two men were Pinkerton detectives.

Atmel Hunter was the head guy, and he talked very eastern. Kenneth Loren was the younger suited man with him. Around the campfire Hunter told him their purpose and showed Long a couple of sketches.

"This guy, Arthur Chapman, set up this cattle drive down in Texas no doubt much like you and your brother did. Folks around Waco where he lived obviously thought he was another drover who could deliver their cattle to the Kansas market and cash in their livestock, then pay them. Arthur and his brother Kenneth and a man named Miles McCracken made up the Brazos Cattle Company. They took two herds of steers north . . . most all were cattle they had contracted to sell for others. Approximately four thousand head. They sold them and then gave each cowboy twenty bucks to go get drunk on. And that night while the hands partied they took a powder. Isn't that the word they gave us?"

Amused by the story, Long nodded he understood. "Yes. And no doubt they had over three hundred thousand dollars in their pockets."

"Exactly. One of those punchers stranded in Abilene without his pay wired home. The ranchers got the word and hired the agency to find the felons. You haven't seen those men's faces we showed you?"

"No. I never saw them. They must be smiling though."

Hunter frowned. "What do you mean by that?"

"Lordy, I had that much money I'd smile all the way to San Francisco."

The other two laughed.

"I am sorry but I find nothing funny in thievery. But I figure that must be one of the richest robberies in history," Long said.

"It very well could be."

"Are there traces of them being on this road?"

"Yes, we have evidence they passed this way."

"How much reward will be paid for them?"

"If you can recover any of their money, it will pay one quarter of the amount recovered."

"Hunter, you know if some hardcases learn they are that valuable, they will do them in and keep the money."

"Oh, no doubt. That is why we are on horseback. Other agents from our Denver-based office are coming this way to head them off."

"Well good luck. I bet they aren't the only ones absconded with cattle proceeds in Abilene."

"No. The agency caught two such men a few weeks ago in Saint Louis and recovered half the proceeds remaining."

"That much money and only half of it remained in that short a time? What did they do with the rest?"

"Obviously spent it on wine, women, and song."

Long shook his head. "That must have been some party."

"I'd enjoy being there," Loren said.

"My brother and I took a herd to Sedalia last year at the very end of the war. At the time that country wasn't even over fighting the war. We had the cattle sale money transferred back to a Texas bank, and we paid all the people involved. But I could see how someone could slip off with that money and be gone a long ways from home in no time."

"Exactly. If that cowboy had not wired home and told what happened, they would still be scot-free. They could have been to the west coast before anyone discovered them missing."

"You think you will run those three thieves down riding horses out here?" Long asked them.

Hunter nodded. "Yes, we might pass them riding in a coach."

"Hey it makes work for me," Theo said with a grin.

Long nodded he understood. "I see any of them; I'll try to get word to you."

"Being part Indian, do you belong to a tribe out here?" Hunter asked.

He shook his head. "My father was a Cherokee. He died before I was born. My stepfather raised me. He's Irish. We lived on the edge of the Comanche lands down where I grew up in Texas. I know little about the Cherokee except their reservation is in the eastern part of the Indian Territory."

Hunter nodded. "You sound like you are well educated."

"My mother saw to that. My half-brother is a real businessman."

Hunter shook his head. "When you first spoke I expected broken English, not an educated southern drawl."

"Lots of people are surprised at my speech. Thanks for sharing your meal with me. If I may I'll bed down here tonight and go on in the morning."

"Sure, go right ahead. What is it so important for you to see the Rocky Mountains?"

"Have you ever had something you really wanted to accomplish in your life? That's my desire. To finally really see them."

"I have been to Denver several times. They are just mountains usually snow-capped."

"Good. Then they are still out there waiting for me."

They laughed and Long did, too.

Nice to sleep near some real people and talk with them about intelligent things. He shared his coffee with them. They had another brand and it didn't taste as good as his Arbuckle.

Loaded and saddled, he left them and rode west. He had to detour mid-day for a passing buffalo herd. Then he returned to the road that ran parallel with the Platt River. Rolling hills lined the roadway, and signs of homesteaders in newly erected shoddies could be seen along the way.

His plans were to later return east on the Arkansas River route, which lay south of there. This route had begun showing the wear and tear of a much used way west. In late summer most of the land boomers were already out west. The late ones faced harsh wintering somewhere on the plains. That worried him every time he thought about their future. Not a problem for him but they had a place in his mind—he would never forget, as a boy, his family's hard long wagon move from Arkansas to Texas.

He stopped mid-day at a road ranch trading post named Logan's Ranch and Post. Such places had several buck skinners hanging around. These were the men who dealt with the Indians in fur trade, whiskey, and arms sales. They carried Bowie knives and liked Pennsylvania-made single-shot rifles, feeling they were more accurate than cartridge ones. Most of them had squaws for wives. For fun and entertainment they held wrestling matches, and hatchet and Bowie knife toss competition.

Long could sink an ax in a tree at a good distance. In Texas he'd won his share of contests. So when he rode up to Logan's Ranch and Post he saw the setup of such a contest opening and about to start. He wanted into the competition.

"How much to enter?" he asked a bystander.

"Ten bucks. You got it?" another man said, holding a handful of money.

"Here." He handed the man two five-dollar bills. "I need to hitch my two horses."

"I can hold them for you." The barefoot boy in short overalls held out his hand.

"Good," he said, and dismounted. "What is your name?"

"Stanley O'Connor, sir."

"Long O'Malley. They're gentle. Don't let anyone steal them, and let them graze."

"Oh, I'll take good care of them."

"I trust you." He left the youth and went through the crowd of onlookers and nodded to the bearded men lined up for the contest.

A few competitors shook his hand and welcomed him.

"Pick you a hatchet," one guy said, indicating the crate full of shiny new axes.

He hefted a few. They were lighter than he liked, but they were sharp edged for manufactured ones. But all the competition had to use them, so they were equally at no more advantage than he would be.

"From the looks of your clothes you must be from Texas?" the buck skinner standing beside him asked.

"Yes. Camp Verde west of San Antonio."

The man chuckled. "Man, you are a long damned ways from home."

27

"Yes."

"Line up. Watson is the judge. Get in line. Give your last name to the clerk when it is your turn."

"Wilkins," the first man said as he stepped up to the line drawn in the dirt. He drew back and the ax swished through the air and bounced off the large post set up as the target.

"Next?"

"Arnold."

His hatchet was deflected.

"Cole."

His ax barely stuck and then fell off. The crowd awwed.

"Newland."

Long expected this next big man to split the post into two.

The giant reared back and roared like a mad grizzly bear. His ax stuck solidly in the post. A cheer went up and the onlookers grew in numbers.

"Dawson." His ax went wild.

Another struck the post by Newland's and fell away.

It finally came to O'Malley.

He gave his name, stepped up, and studied the post and where to hit the post to not strike the already sunk-in hatchet. With a step forward the ax flew with all his might, and it made a responding clunk and was inches hard sunk next to Newland's in the post. There was applause.

"We have a tie and three more men to toss."

"You Injun?" his large competitor asked him.

"Part. But my father died before I was born."

The big guy laughed. "Hell I knew right off when you said your name you wasn't raised in some old tepee."

"No, I wasn't. What will they do next?"

"Take our axes out and step off five more feet."

"Good luck," Long said, and walked back behind the new line.

Several shook his hand and they told him Newland usually won these contests. He nodded and smiled. In Texas he usually won such competitions. But anyone with luck and the skill on his side could win at any time.

He chose another ax and Newland won the coin toss to go first. The big man reared back and the hatchet swooshed through the air. It barely caught in the top of the post but held.

Long nodded at his competitor, then he reared back and flung his ax. It sunk hard in the post's center and they applauded.

"Newland, you want another toss? Your hatchet is in the post . . ." the man judging the contest asked.

The big man shook his head. "Texas here won."

The crowd cheered.

Long went over and shook his hand.

"Texas, if I ever get in a nasty fight I want you on my side." Newland's blue eyes twinkled.

"Newland, if I am close I will be at your side."

"Get your cup," one guy said, elbowing his way in the group. "We got us some real lightning here."

The man carried around a gallon-size crock, pouring some liquor in each cup. Long had his ready and knew it was respectable to taste some though he wondered how many severed rattlesnake heads they had put in the batch making the hooch?

"Here's to the West," someone toasted.

"Yeah!" went up the shout.

After some cheers, a woman dressed in buckskin came and pulled on his sleeve. "I gots some fresh buff roast, mister. These louts will drink till they fall down. Come and eat with us."

"Thank you, it sounds great. My name is Long." Tossing the rest of his drink, he hooked his cup back on his belt.

She had his arm and hurried him along. "Mine's Ruthie."

"Wait. Wait. I have your money," the official said, calling after him.

He accepted the money and counted it out. One hundred eighty dollars.

"Is it all there?" she asked, looking closely at the exchange.

"Yes. And thank you," Long said to the man, folding the money into a stack to shove in his pants pocket. He asked her, "What is your name again?"

"Ruthie."

"Mine's Long."

The sharp-faced woman in her twenties looked him up and down. "You told me that already, and you damn sure are long."

He chuckled and then joined her hurried steps to the cooking area.

"Sit down. I'll cut you some good slices."

Another attractive brunette was in his face. "Coffee or water?"

"Coffee." He unhooked his tin cup from his belt for her.

He sat down and soon was served a heaping wooden slab piled with great smelling slices of rib roast. A hot French bread loaf soon joined it. That and a steaming bowl of meat juices to dip torn off pieces of the bread in. Long shook his head in amazement. "This is wonderful. Thank you so much."

"Eat it then," a chubby white woman said.

"Won't you all join me?" He swept his arm for them to sit with him.

"Damn right," his guide Ruthie said.

"Where do you live?" one asked him as if anxious to know more about him.

"Texas, west of San Antonio."

"What are you doing out here?"

"Just looking around."

"You have a wife?"

"No wife."

Hands on her wide hips she demanded, "Are you telling us the truth?"

"I swear I have no wife."

"I have a daughter," another said to get it in.

"Oh, I better not get one right now. I may have a hard time getting myself back down there let alone to have a wife along. Thanks."

They laughed.

"Ladies, this is the best meal I have had since I rode out of Abilene."

One of the darker skinned women asked him with one eye shut to stare hard at him, "Do you have a ranch?"

"Yes. I imagine my brother has bought me a lot more land since he got home."

"Is he married?"

"Yes. Harp is happily married and has a new son."

"When will you go back to Texas?"

"After I see the Rocky Mountains are my plans now."

"You need a cook to go along?"

"No, ma'am."

So he whiled away the afternoon talking to these wives and daughters, and they grilled him hard. Hard enough he wished he had Harp there to talk for him.

Full of good food, he and his young helper

unsaddled the horses. He had let them graze and drink. Then they hobbled them for the night nearby and he paid him a quarter.

Later he spread out his bedroll close to his animals and at sundown he crawled in his bedroll to sleep. The half-moon was hung high when one of the camp females whispered in his ear, "Let me in."

"Does your husband know you are here?"

"He died six months ago."

"Then he can't kill me."

She giggled. "You're funny." With that said, under the starlight she shed her dress and he let her quickly under the covers.

CHAPTER 3

The Denver-destined road split in western Nebraska. One route went to Denver, the other to Fort Laramie. He decided to take the Denver route. He'd been traveling over three weeks and met many forms of people on the trail as well as some generous women. Not to have Harp to talk to left him a big space in his being alone as an individual in this prairie world. No woman had turned his head though he found some comfort in the volunteers' conversation and their individual nocturnal sharing.

That evening he was camped by himself on the Platt River. With his survival skills, plus some gut line tied on a willow pole with a small iron hook and a fat grasshopper, he caught some trout earlier and fried them. His camp was set up well off the main road, and when he noticed his nearby grazing horses look up at something, he saw, on the far bank, two riders preparing to ford the river directly across from him.

One wore a felt hat and the other rider had braids. Her horse was on a lead rope. The Platt there was swift and deep enough at that spot he decided the horses might have to swim the middle to cross it. Both riders made the ford and soon had their dripping mounts shaking water on the gravel under them. The second horse found his footing and came up beside her companion. The braid-headed girl could sure ride. She stayed on, bareback, during the crossing.

Surprise was written all over the stranger's face, like he had not expected to find anyone, when he saw Long stand up. He booted his horse up onto the bank above the beach. The second horse came, too.

Dripping wet to his knees, he reined up and set his horse down. After a glance over at the one he led, he turned back to Long. "You need her?"

"Who is she?" Long reset his near windswept Stetson to settle it on his head.

"A big Sioux chief's daughter. He'd pay you a hundred buffalo hides for her safe return."

What in the hell would he do with that pile of hides? He moved around to inspect her. She turned her face away from him.

"You speak English?" he asked, deciding she was only a teenager.

She sullied for a moment, then turned to him and in perfect English she said, "Only to polite people. My father would pay more than that for my return."

"Damn you, bitch. She ain't said one damn word in English to me in two days."

"How did you get her?"

"I found her out picking wild flowers and decided there was a reward out there for her."

35

"I think he was spying on me."

"There's two sides to everyone's story. What do you want for her?" he asked her captor.

"Five hundred dollars."

"I only have about a hundred and seventy dollars in my pocket in real money on me."

The stranger dropped off his horse and used the mount to steady himself while he removed one boot at a time to dump the water out of them. "That ain't enough."

"Well you will have to go find a more prosperous customer. That is all I have."

"What does that mean?"

"That means I have no more money than that."

"Pay me," he said in defeat. He held out his hand. "I am sick and tired of putting up with her."

Long counted the paper money out into his hand. It was most of the hatchet contest prize he'd won at the outpost.

"What's your name?" he asked.

"Jack Bromley."

"That includes her horse?"

"Hell, yes. That's some dumb Indian broomtail. You got a thing to eat?"

"Nope." Long shook his head.

"You're an Injun, too, huh?"

"Part Cherokee."

"Well you can have that bitch." Took him two tries to get back in the saddle in his soaked boots. "Oh, she says she's a virgin. I doubt that."

36

"Bye, Jack. Travel safely." Good riddance of that dumb guy. The man rode away. He walked over . . . got out his jackknife. She drew back.

"Hold out your hands. I'll cut that rope."

"Good." She held her hands out and he cut the rope that bound them.

She lay down on the horse's neck to catch the lead rope. Once up she booted him to leave.

"Wait," he said. "I lied to him. I do have food."

Like she didn't hear him, she didn't rein the horse up to stop until she was down at the water's edge. Then she twisted and looked back at him.

He spoke to her over the river's rushing by. "I don't want your body or any rewards, but you should stop and eat. Then you can go find your people."

She reined around. "You serious?"

"I bought you didn't I?"

Still on horseback she made a sour face. "I wish I knew why."

"I hate to see anyone be a prisoner that doesn't deserve it."

"That was lots of money."

"It saved your life. So what is money for anyway?"

"But I am an Indian, you are mostly white."

"No, we both have hearts that pump our blood, and we both should care for one another."

"Why should I care for you?"

"Because we are both human beings."

She shook her head as if she couldn't figure it out, then slipped off the horse.

How old was she? A teen. No matter she was a real pretty girl. But after their meal she would disappear like smoke in the rolling land beyond that river. No matter. He would feed her and, maybe, she would answer some questions about her people he, himself had no answers for.

He cooked her the other fish he'd saved for breakfast. She sat cross-legged across the fire looking very fixed on leaving as soon as his meal for her was over.

"We get through eating, I need to catch more fish for breakfast."

"You have a bow and arrows?"

"No, I use a grasshopper."

She made a face like she thought he was crazy. "How does he catch fish?"

"After you eat I can show you how."

She shook her head about the possibility of it happening.

He watched her eat the cooked fish with her small fingers a piece at a time. Second bite she smiled. "He is very good. I never ate one so tender."

"Most people cook them too hard."

She laughed and pointed at him. "That is it. They do."

"How far are your people away from here?"

"Maybe three to four days' ride. They hunt for

buffalos to have food this winter. So they move a lot."

"Can you find them?"

"I will."

"There are lots more men out there like him."

"I know."

"Have you ever seen the Rocky Mountains?"

"I saw lots of mountains. Which ones are they?"

"They told me there are some great mountains that run north to south across the land."

"Oh, yes, but you have to be at the foot of them to see them."

That was different from what he thought it would be. He reached forward and poured her some coffee."

"What is this?" she asked when he handed her a cup.

"Coffee."

She handed the cup back. "I don't like coffee."

"Try it. You didn't like hard fish."

She stopped, looked at him, and laughed when she reached for it back. "I will try it."

She put her lip on the cup.

"It is hot. Only sip it."

She did and smiled. "It is good and it is hot."

"See I have not lied to you."

She nodded.

"I need to get back to Texas. But I came to see those mountains. After I see them I can try to take you to your people. Or you can go back alone and try to dodge guys like him."

She gave him no answer.

"Can we ride there in a week?" he asked.

She shrugged. "I don't know. I have been out there but I never counted how far it is."

"Well, wait until morning and I won't bother you and we can go find them."

She was drinking her coffee. "That was very good. Show me the grasshopper trick."

"Let's go." He took off his boots and socks, then he rolled up his pants. Armed with his pole, he led her to the water on the way catching a fat hopper in his Stetson for a net.

She stood close by while he threaded the bait on a hook. When he finished she snickered and shook her head at the joke he'd pulled on her. He waded out and cast the hopper upstream. The hopper traveled down the current, and, immediately, a trout took it. The pole bent and the girl joined him, wading in the stream, to cheer his fight on until he managed to corral a nice-size fish and toss him on the gravel.

He rapped him on the head with a rock before he noticed her skirt and britches were neat-like, lying on the bank. He knew Indians didn't take being half naked as seriously as white people. Then she handed him another fat grasshopper.

"Thanks, I needed more bait. Get out there in the water. I can show you how to catch them."

She obeyed him. He was grateful she still had her blouse on. She tossed the hopper. But not where he felt it should be. He made the next cast for her and handed her the pole. It was swish and the pole bent into a U. She had a real fish on her line, and he caught her by her slender waist to hold her from being drug downstream.

"We—got hi—him."

"Yes, we did, girl. Lead him to the shallows and I'll toss him on the bank."

He moved around, bent over, and scooped the slick large fish up onto the gravelly beach.

When he rose he saw three tough-faced men seated on their horses facing them.

"Not a bad catch. Huh, guys?"

CHAPTER 4

"Well ain't she a real pretty bitch, boys?" the big man with the mustache asked the two saddle bums with him on horseback. They nodded and grinned like some greedy dogs about to feast on guts at a cow killing.

"What's your business here?" Long asked.

"The Indian princess."

"She isn't free to go."

"We ain't asking you—"

It was his time to take action. Long roared so loud that he spooked two of their horses backward. Then with his gun in his fist he shot at the leader fighting to draw his pistol while trying to control his horse, but he was already half out of the saddle. Another one tried to shoot over the struck man's spooked horse, but Long's bullet cut him down.

Number three was whipping his horse to escape. During his scramble to get up the bank, Long shot at him three times but missed and he was gone in the brush. Long's gun arm dropped in disgust.

She was shaking there beside him and hugging him.

He petted her on her back and wondered how to settle her down. "I'm sorry but I had no choice.

They would have killed us or killed me and took you."

"I know. I am not a child. Are there more?"

"Lord, I don't know. But I imagine they are only the first ones."

"How did they find us?"

"I bet they found Bromley and he told them."

"What should we do?"

"I'll clean the fish while you dress. Then we'll load up our horses and head west. Find us a safe place, tomorrow, down the road and sleep."

"I know that you chose me over your own life. I will go with you."

"I hope I can protect you. If we move fast, I think we can shake them, but it will be tough going at times."

He was back at the water's edge washing out the big trout he had gutted, and she had put on her clothing. Next he dressed the other fish and told her to take them to camp. He'd clean up the mess, take the dead men's guns, and be along to load up.

The big dead man had little identity. Long was about to give up when in the man's saddlebags he found a letter written to Wallace Odom. The address was Omaha, Nebraska. The other man had nothing but a worn-out cap and ball pistol. He dragged their bodies down to the water one at a time and then he put their corpses out in the river to float downstream. He unsaddled their mounts and tossed their wornout saddles in the stream. Next he sent the two horses into the river shouting and waving his arms, making them go across the river. They struggled up the far bank under a barrage of rocks thrown at them to make them hurry off.

He had two well-used handguns, two knives, and twenty dollars in change and went back to camp. She had it all packed and he began to load the packhorse. Then he saddled his own horse. They were on the road as the sun sank beyond the far horizon.

"I am so sorry that intervened in our talking. What do they call you?" he asked.

"It is the Sioux word for a flower. You can call me Rose."

"Rose." That is what he'd call her. "Their saddles were not worth a damn. I will find you one that fits you."

"I can ride a horse without one."

"I will find you a suitable saddle."

"You are very made up in your mind."

"What is that?" He frowned over at her.

"I wanted to leave you. You stopped me. You want me to ride a saddle and you won't listen."

"Trust me I know. You will need a saddle if you ride with me."

About dawn, they found some brush cover down by the riverbed, unloaded the horses, and slept in the shade until past noon. He awoke drowsy. She was still sleeping in a blanket he gave her.

His holster strapped in place, he put his hat on and checked on their horses.

They were grazing and fine. When he came back she sat up under her blanket.

"Are you awake?"

"Oh, I am fine. I couldn't start the fire."

"I bet I can. You look peaked."

"What is that?"

"Worn out?"

She made a disappointed face at him. "I am at that time when I need to be alone."

"I can try to find us a hideout today."

"Alone?"

"Whatever. Will you be well in two or three days?"

"It should go away by then."

He cooked the fish. She barely ate anything. They moved west without any interference. Her pale face made her look ready to faint. His greatest concern was she might faint, fall off her horse, and hurt herself.

Four hours later in the moonlight, he led them down into the brush and cottonwood trees along the river to find a place where they could camp. There was grazing there for the horses. He set up her blanket and then carried her there from where she dismounted.

"I am not a baby."

"I didn't call you that." He hauled her small body in his arms and gently laid her down on the blanket. "I am going to cook some beans. Sleep."

"Long?"

"Yes."

"You are a very sincere man."

"Where did you learn English?"

"*Padres*."

"They come out here?"

"They came from Canada for three summers to our camps. I learned French, too."

"Well, all I ever learned was English. My mother was a great teacher. Me and my brother, Harp, did lots of bookwork, and when we'd get a little sloppy talking she'd twist our ears. Guess it didn't hurt either of us."

"Harp is your brother?"

"Half anyway, but I call it all. Mom had me after she learned my father was killed off on the Outlet. My stepfather's first wife drowned and he found Mom, took her to a dance, and married her there. Harp's nine months younger than I am. Oh, he's a dandy."

"You miss him?"

"I've never been separated over a day or two in my life from him. I let him talk for me when we needed a voice on the trail. I got this big crazy idea to see this country when we started home for Texas. Told him I'd go see the Rockies and then come home."

She shook her head. "I didn't do this sick business on purpose."

"I didn't think you did. I'm just proud you stayed with me."

"Can you afford to lose a few days here?"

"I can. But I wish I had a better place."

"I am a Sioux. We live out here."

Long shook his head. "How old are you anyway?"

"I have been here for fifteen winters. My mother has them notched on a stick. She can't count."

"A fine way to know things."

"She told me she had these same problems, too, as a girl. She promised me I would outgrow it."

He stood up. Were they through chasing her? He doubted it. Damn, if only he had Harp there—

"Have I ruined it?" she asked.

He whirled around. Her dark brown eyes looked sad in the fire's light. "Ruined what?"

"When I told you my age, did that worry you?"

He dropped his chin and put his hands on his hips. "I had hoped you were older. You sound older. I'll be twenty-one."

She shook her head. "That is not old."

He snickered. "I need to tell you a story. One day last year when Harp found his woman it was some kinda magic. Her man at the time was going to be hung shortly for murdering another man. So she had no one. She stayed around that store in Arkansas and he came by, bought two cans of peaches, and they went off up on a creek to eat them and they were set forever."

"That dumb man caught me away from the main camp. I was really feeling sorry for myself when he found you."

"Tell me something from your life before. When you were at home. Did any warriors bring horses to your family tepee to marry you?"

She nodded her head. "I untied them. Then I shooed them away."

"Why?"

She shrugged. "They weren't for me."

"You never saw me until Bromley brought you to me?"

"You were the first white man he met since he kidnapped me. He said he wanted lots of money for me."

"I won that money throwing hatchets at a post the day before."

"That was all you'd paid for me?"

He nodded his head, sat down beside her, and hugged his knees. "Rose, you get to feeling better. I don't know our enemies. I don't have any horses to send to your father. No canned peaches to feed you . . . but I figure we can work all that out between us."

She put her hand on his knee. "I will get better I—promise." She drew up in pain.

He sat up and nodded. "Willow leaves tea."

"What is that?"

"Stay here."

"Where are you going?"

"To find some willow leaves."

She looked at him, peeved. "You were about to get serious and you are going away."

"Rest easy. We've got lots of time to talk."

In a short while he had several limbs of leaves he had gathered off the willows down by the river. His arms full, he dropped them on the ground and built a fire. Then with his jackknife he began slicing up the leaves and bark.

He soon had them in his boiling water and sat back.

"What is that going to be?" she asked.

"An elixir."

"What is that?" She held herself in pain.

"Stops pain. I don't know how long it has to boil."

He took the cup from his belt, dipped out a half full cup of steaming water, and set it down. "It's too hot."

When it was cool she sipped it. "Not as good as your coffee."

"Wait until it cools."

In a short while she nodded after drinking the cup of his potion. "I feel much better."

"Good. If you feel like that in the morning we will ride on."

"Do you think those men have quit trying to get me?"

He shook his head. "For some reason they want you. I can't imagine why."

"What would that be?"

"Does your tribe have lots of money or gold?"

She shook her head.

"The only reason I can figure out for all these bad guys wanting you, they expect to make some big money. If you don't have any more pain get some sleep. Maybe in the morning we can continue west."

"Where did you learn about willow tea?"

"My mother. She used it for toothaches, broken bones, headaches. I had almost forgotten it. It must be a painkiller."

"Oh, it is." She rubbed her lower stomach under the buckskin dress.

He tucked her in and went to check on their stock. The animals were sleeping on their feet as he watched the moon drop below the horizon. What would he do with her? Return her to her people? Could she survive in his world? In Texas people might snub her for being an Indian. He'd felt some resistance himself being shown toward him in the past. Harp would not put up with it. But she was almost still a child.

After a meal of oatmeal the next morning, and more of his tea, they saddled up and continued on their ride west. They pushed hard, and when he looked for her reaction she nodded she was all right and they rode on.

They found a store on the rolling prairie. He told her to stay with their horses and he'd find them something to eat inside the store. There were only two or three loafers around when he went inside. The store had few food items on empty shelves. No *frijoles*. No peaches. Some canned tomatoes and rice he bought, paid for, and went outside.

There were two scruffy men out there beside her horse and demanding her name. He crossed the space. "Get the hell away from her."

"Who are you?" one of them demanded.

"The guy that's going to shoot you if you don't get away from her. Now get."

He fumed as those two went back toward the store. "What did they want to know?"

"What my name was." She winked at him, looking half-amused at his anger.

He frowned back at them. "What did you tell them?"

"My name in Sioux."

"Good. I bet they couldn't translate that." He flipped back the diamond hitch to put the rice and tomatoes in the panniers. Those packed inside, he was disappointed over the poor quest for something to eat. That wasn't a store. Just a depot for white lightning—he recovered the canvas and put the hitch back on.

They rode west.

He had not seen any wanted posters for her in there. There were many wanted outlaw ones.

In late afternoon, he could at last see the outline of the mountains.

"Another day we should be there," she said.

"Yes. Have you ever been in them?"

"Not here."

"I guess they run north and south."

She smiled at him and turned up her palms for him. "I have to guess so."

He shook his head. "I am pleased to have you with me. When I am satisfied I saw them, then you must tell me if you wish to go home or go to Texas."

"You wish to go home, don't you?"

"Yes. I have a ranch there and my brother."

She booted her horse in beside him. Then she held her fingers up apart a small space. "Is there that much room for me?"

He nodded. "There is lots of room there. My mother would smother you. She never had any girls. My father would, too. After this year Harp and I will have some real large ranches."

"I never lived in a house."

"It is not hard. You shut out the cold and rain."

She shrugged. "If you are not ashamed of me, I would go there."

"I have never been ashamed of you."

She nodded. "I have tried to figure where I

belonged. I have been at peace with you these days we shared. My life was not easy with my own people. How will they survive?"

"These people who passed through here have no end. Now you have chosen I want to buy you a saddle, some clothes, and we can find a wagon train going east."

"We need a train?"

"It would be safer. We can go back perhaps on the Arkansas River route. Trading wagon trains use it to go back and forth to Saint Louis."

"I am pleased to ride with you."

"So am I to have you." He leaned over the horses and hugged her.

Long studied the spectacular snow-capped mountains riding toward them all day. Two days later they made Denver. He found her the right size saddle, and they put their horses in the livery.

The livery owner stopped them before they left to find a room. "I have a better horse for her to ride if you want to look at him."

"How much does he cost?"

"Look at him first."

He turned to her for an answer.

She shrugged.

"Show him to us."

He sent a boy after him. The roan horse led easy, looked excited, and walked on his toes when the boy brought him. He checked his mouth—a four-year-old.

"Give her the lead."

She looked at Long. He said, "Try him."

She began to talk in Sioux to the compact red roan horse. Then she grabbed a hank of mane and swung swiftly aboard. When she gave him slack he raced out back, and when she pulled on his head he slid to a stop in the dirt. She patted his neck, then turned him around to come back.

"How much?" Long asked.

"A hundred fifty."

"A hundred and her horse."

The man shook his hand.

"What do they call him?"

"Powder River."

Long nodded and paid him.

They were refused admittance to the first dress shop they stopped at. She told him laughing, "They do not want your money."

He was not laughing. "We will find someone needs the business."

The next two ladies were delightfully friendly. They tried several dresses on Rose to get to see how she looked in them. Some were too fancy, but they found some nice-looking dresses that would work for her.

Then the younger one of the ladies said, "Why don't you buy her some boy clothes to wear when she is riding?"

"Why is that?"

"She will be more comfortable and who cares . . . she is an Indian girl."

He about laughed. "I guess she's not confined to anything in her dress is she?"

"I am not being disrespectful to her race. But riding she will feel much more comfortable."

"No disrespect. You two ladies have been patient and generous with us. We were barred from buying anything up the street. They must not need business huh?"

The older woman said, "They are too snooty. Mr. O'Malley, you and this girl are welcome here any time you are in Denver."

He ordered the three dresses they chose.

When they were alone, Rose said, "Why three? I can only wear one at a time?"

"That will come to you later. Don't worry . . . I am not a poor man."

They bought two sets of boy clothes that she tried on at the mercantile in a closet to be sure they fit her. He bought her some boy-size suspenders for the pants and she smiled. Then he bought a suit coat for himself, and the night the first dress was done he took her to an opera.

She was awed by the music, and, while he understood little, it was an intriguing evening for both of them.

Walking back to the hotel in the cooling night air, she asked him where he learned about such things.

"A school teacher told me that if I ever got a chance in my life that I should go to see an opera."

"I loved it. The music and the singing. What are your plans now?"

"Ride back to Texas."

The desk clerk when he gave him the room key also handed him a note.

It read:

> Long, there were some tough men here today asking about you and the girl with you. I told them nothing but felt you should know.
>
> The liveryman
> Hinkle

"What is it?"

"Time to check out and ride south."

"Why?"

"Men were at the livery asking questions about us."

"Go now?"

"We better. Get our things from the room and go."

"Is there a place to be safe anywhere?"

When at the top of the stairs, he whispered to her, "Texas."

She nodded and in the room she hugged him. For a long moment the two of them treated themselves to a moment of rest and assurance in their clutch. She was his ward and he was her shield from harm.

They headed south in the night. Camping before dawn at a rancher's windmill off the road. There they slept a few hours and rode on.

Long bought some more food for them to eat in Pueblo. There he met Clem Sparks, a freighter out of Missouri who was headed east to St. Louis with Mexican woven cotton blankets, pottery vessels, and other items he found in Santa Fe. He'd come up there to Pueblo in hopes of finding some more freight to haul east but found nothing to take back with him there. Sparks owned two dozen wagons and extra, long-eared mule teams that he drove along in case any died or was crippled. Also he had six tough guards to defend it besides the drivers.

Long and Rose took the Arkansas River Trail east with his outfit. To most it was the Santa Fe Trail, but some folks didn't want to give the Hispanics credit for anything. Two Mexican women, wives of the drivers, also went along. Sparks's outfit bristled with Winchesters and Colts. Sparks repeatedly warned them the Indians along the way this time could be treacherous and for them to stay close to camp at all times.

In the case of an attack they'd circle the wagons and hold them off. But as summer turned toward fall most Indians were too busy laying in food supplies and the train moved east safely, at a snail's pace. Sparks had them put Long's panniers in a wagon so there was no loading or unloading of the packhorse. Long and Rose rode their saddle horses at the head of the column with Sparks or one of his lieutenants.

The days dragged along at twenty-mile stretches or less per day. Rose helped the other wives fix meals. Her women problems returned in three weeks and she rode in the lead wagon and drank willow tea the next few days. She assured Long she would overcome it and be back to ride with him shortly.

He grew impatient, by the day, with the train's slow pace. They passed out of Colorado into western Kansas where, at the time, most of the warlike tribes were situated. She was back on horseback and her old self.

Sparks took a day to rest and repair things when he and his scouts thought it would be safe to do so. Long and Rose went off a short distance to a place on the river and talked freely about Texas and his plans for their future.

"When will I become your wife?" she asked.

He knew she was growing much more anxious over the matter of their pairing. He wasn't resistant to the idea, but he wanted things perfectly right before they entered into it. They could wait until they were alone in a safer place like being at home.

"When we can find a place to be alone and safe," he promised her.

She nodded, seated on a fallen cottonwood log. "I am ready to be your wife."

"There is so little privacy in camp. I want to save it for a special time and place."

"The days are so long. The nights are worse not sharing my body with you."

"Our time will come. I promise you that we will have a dreamlike union."

She agreed and he hugged her. Then he kissed her. He kissed her a lot, but still held out for the right moment—not some quick flash in the pan affair. This would be for their lifetime.

Two days later farther east on the road, their scout Jules Hambee rode in late one afternoon, where they'd parked for the night, and talked to Sparks. Then the two men, looking very serious, came over and talked to Rose and Long.

"Jules thinks a band of Cheyenne are gathering to attack us. He thinks she should ride in a wagon for her safety."

Long looked over at her. "You heard the man. What are your wishes?"

"I would rather ride with you, but I know you will want to fight them if they come, and with me in the wagon you would be free to do that."

He nodded. "I want you safe. I thought we were about past the mean ones, but Jules has no reason to fabricate."

She smiled and shook her head. "What is that word?"

"Means he did not make up something."

She nodded. "Tell Woolley I will join him. There is no need to stop."

Sparks agreed that for her safety it would be best. The next morning Long helped her up with the jolly driver, Woolley, who welcomed her riding with him again.

While they were stopped the night before, Sparks and Jules told the drivers, guards, and the rest of the wagon train the situation, and said they would go ahead, find a good site, then circle and stand them off. Long put Rose's horse in the herd of loose mules and horses, telling the herder boys what the deal was about the Indians.

On the move, Long started watching the northeast horizon closer. This was where he figured they'd come from. He hoped those Indians didn't think they were sodbusters that they could easily swarm over.

Every man on the train, he knew well, was an experienced driver or guard and with it went training and knowledge of how to hold off an Indian attack. They were not inexperienced Indian fighters. Those bucks would soon learn these guys could shoot them off their horses. They had lots of ammo and real lever action–fighting weapons, not single-shot muskets.

Long first saw their dust boiling over in the

east when he started back to the front of the train. Woolley was already bringing his lead wagon around in a circle. The herders brought the loose extra mules and horses to be inside that ring. Helpers were being sure each man had enough ammo and good weapons in working order.

They were unhooking the teams and putting them in the center with the loose ones. There was no time to unharness them. The distant drum of the war ponies' hooves could be heard as they thundered toward them still beyond the horizon. Men refilled their water bags from the water barrels in the side of the wagons. This could be a long battle, no telling, except someone he heard say that the Indians were getting desperate. All summer long endless wagon trains of land seekers had plodded west, shot their buffalo and other game, making their source of food much scarcer. Few of the tribes still stayed out there on the plains, but it would only be a short matter of time until they must move. Long knew it and so did the Indians. These white invaders would soon fill all of their country.

Riding at the front that morning, he began to hear their distant war cries. It was time to circle the wagons. Orders were given and they militarily-like began to form the circle. The loose animals were driven into the middle.

The Indians' cries would soon deafen everyone's ears with their screaming. His horse in the herd, Long went to find Rose. She piled out of the wagon at the sight of him coming through the great-circled fortress.

"Rose, stay over here where they piled these crates. It is intended for a hospital. The other two women coming?" Long looked around for sight of them.

"No, they told me they fought with their men. They say they can shoot."

"You get in that hospital. You may have to help bandage the wounded."

"I can. Protect yourself." Then she stood on her toes and kissed his mouth.

"I will come for you when it is over. I will . . . I promise."

And she was gone to hide in the center place where they would treat the wounded. He went with his rifle and two boxes of cartridges to where Sparks stood giving orders.

"I think they will charge right at us and try to get inside the circle. We need to keep them out and make them circle us. We have to mow that charge down so they will be forced to ride around their own dead horses. We can kill them as they ride past us."

"When your rifle is empty use your pistol. That initial charge must be turned," Long added.

"When Long's rifle is empty, have him a spare one loaded," Sparks told one of the horse boys named Dale, chosen to reload rifles for Long.

"Yes, sir."

"Any Indian inside the circle must be killed immediately."

The sounds of their approaching fight grew louder, and Long knew they were coming at a breakneck speed. He waved at Dale to be ready with the second rifle. He stood beside the front of the wagon he figured would be their main target. He could see them now.

"Shoot their horses. Cut them down," he shouted to the others, and he began taking down approaching horses.

In an instant he swapped rifles for a loaded one. More horses went down under his and the other men's bullets, and that made the field impassable for the Indians in the back to charge over the downed, dying, but still kicking horses. Fleeing bucks tried to escape all the hot lead being shot at them. He'd swapped rifles four times, and the boy always had the next one loaded.

Sparks shouted, "We've stopped them."

Long nodded at him and went to picking off either horse or rider he could see in his iron sights through the thick gun smoke and dust on the scene. Without any wind, visibility had become a serious problem. But guns continued to crack whenever a mounted fighter came out of the fog.

Sweat ran down his face in streams, and if the gunpowder smoke didn't burn his eyes the sweat did. He mopped his face on the kerchief around his neck. He feared using it for a mask in case he might not see everything going on.

There must have been a dozen Indian drummers out there somewhere beyond the riders' track still beating on their drums the whole time. He'd liked to have gone out there and shot some of them to shut them up. A warrior came out of the smoke trying to control his spooked horse. Too late and he was blown off his horse screaming from the bullets making a sieve of his body.

Long was satisfied the Indians, by this time, knew these teamsters were not simple farmers. And they would, despite their small numbers, be able to fight to the end.

The drums finally went silent and the howling quit. Too quiet for him. Then Woolley came over and shouted for Long to come quick to the center area. Long had to duck the frightened mules bolting around him and others kicking some unseen enemy in their panic inside the circle. Plus their honking so loud he could hardly hear a thing when Woolley shouted for him, "It's Rose. She's been shot by a stray bullet."

He came up to one of the other men holding her half on his lap. Too much blood was on her dress. Long dropped on his knees and took her gently into his arms.

"Rose, Rose don't die."

She coughed and then managed to say, "I love you so—much—"

So did he. But at that very moment every drop of life went out of the body he held.

"Men! Men!" Sparks shouted. "They're coming back to try us again."

"She's dead," he said to the man who'd found her. "Cover her and I'll get back to my gun." He stood up and ran through the mules, took the Winchester from his loader, and began dropping all the Indians that came into his rifle's range. His jaw hurt; he had it clenched so tightly it ached.

Tears, not from the smoke and dust but rather directly from the internal feelings over the heavy loss of her on his mind. She was dead. He'd never get to have the wedding he promised her that they'd planned. Nor have the wedding night to share with her in a fine bed and her virtue. *Damn you, red devils . . . I'll see you all in the fires of hell and re-kill every damn one of you down there.*

After their second try the Indians left, carrying some of their fallen brothers off the field of death. Many corpses were too close to the accurate riflemen in the wagon circle for them to recover and were left among the dead and dying war ponies.

There was silence in the wagon camp. Two men had minor wounds and were doctored.

Sparks and his top men circled and squatted around Long to comfort him.

"This may not be where you wish to bury her.

But there is no way to take her body with us. I am sorry," Sparks said to him.

"She would understand. But when we bury her I want her body so concealed that no damn Indian can dig her up to disfigure or rape her."

Sparks looked half-sick back at him. "Would they do that?"

"Damn right. It would be as big a deal for them to do it as tramping on my soul for killing so many of their brothers."

"We can bury her tonight. Real deep. Damn it, Long, we loved her as much as you did. There's not a dry eye here. She was an angel walking among us. All of us were so damn jealous that she was your girl, and we'll make damn sure they can't get to her."

Long nodded. "I've lost some things in my life. My cow dog that got bit by a rattler, a horse, who went down in a badger hole that I wouldn't have sold for a thousand dollars. I had to shoot him. But Rose was so special in my life—that I wouldn't touch her until we were married. That concerned her, but I held her that great in my heart and mind to be square with her.

"God sent her to me up on the Platt. A worthless man brought her to my camp and he offered to sell her—I gave him all the money I had at the time. It is not the money I lost but her gentle spirit. Boys, this is hard."

They all agreed.

"I told her when he left her with me, I told her that she could go back to her people. She wasn't sure. I said that I was going to see the Rocky Mountains and she could come with me—"

Concerned, Tucker said, "Sit down before you fall over."

He did so on a crate. "I told her, then, 'Rose, if you still want to go home I will take you.' After that was settled we went to Denver, and I bought her that horse, saddle, and some new clothes. Then the stableman—hell, fellows, I didn't tell you how three hardcases came to us right after Bromley sold her to me. They said they were taking her." He rubbed the side of his hand on his forehead. "I fed two of them to the fish in the Platt River. Anyway the Denver stableman told me some tough guys had come around there asking about me and her at his stables. So we left in the night and found your outfit down by Pueblo. We planned to be married at Christmas at our family ranch in Texas."

"Why did they want her?" one of the men asked.

"Maybe because her father is a big Sioux chief. I never pressed her about that. I knew she was homesick. Now my entire life has fallen into a pile of fresh hog shit."

"Long, I've been out here for near twenty years. I've fought beside some of the toughest men anyone ever heard of, but you are the toughest

Indian fighter I have ever known. I knew when they charged you that they were tackling the hardest, toughest Indian fighter I ever met. We can't heal your loss, but ain't a man here tonight don't think that about you."

"Boys, if Harp and my dad had been here there'd been a lot less of them that would have ridden home."

One of the men held up something. "I've got a bottle of whiskey. Good stuff. If you want it you can have it."

"No, but thanks. I am so mixed up now that whiskey would really put me spinning."

"We can stay and talk all night and the others can dig that grave."

"I've said about all I need to say. A drover would say to his partners I'd cross the next river with any of you any time. *Gracias*."

He rode his horse, took hers and the packhorse away from them the next day. In two weeks pushing himself hard he was at the trading post of the half-Cherokee John Chisholm on the Salt Fork. He'd met John that summer going north and they laughed about being alike—both half-Cherokee.

He told John he'd seen the Rockies. John had been there before, too.

"Mighty tall hills," Chisholm said, and they both laughed.

He talked to John about Rose and losing her.

And his friend told him, "The maker in the sky treated you to her. But he had more work for her in that final place. I, too, have lost such perfect women. They never complain. Never nag you and bring sparkles into your life. But instead the others always survive."

They both laughed.

Among Chisholm's trading goods he found a well-made, sheep wool–lined, long-tailed leather coat like new. It fit Long perfectly and he bought it. After he paid for it, John told him that the man who owned it last was still alive when he sold it. That the damn fool had sold it to buy whiskey and the next night froze to death without it.

Long was never sure if he was teasing or right about it—but he knew, headed south, as long as he had it on he wouldn't freeze to death.

On the Texas Road he met up with an outfit returning home from Abilene and going south. Long met Grover McCarthy, who owned the Plains Cattle Company that was situated west of Austin, on the road. He and his dozen boys, his remuda, and chuck wagon made up their outfit, and Grover told him he was welcome to come along with them going home. There were enough worthless bums on the road south looking for a single man to prey upon that Long was grateful for their company.

Long, right off, liked Grover and his men, mostly boys who were a fun bunch, so he brought along his packhorse and Rose's pony and joined them. They loaded all his gear in the chuck wagon, put the extra two horses in the remuda, and headed south leaving behind the Salt Fork Trading Post of John Chisholm.

The rivers were all low in the fall, and some of the boys asked if he could swim.

"I sure can. Harp and I were raised in western Arkansas, and as young boys my dad made us learn to swim. His first wife drowned, so Mom and us all learned how to swim. When we got to Texas we didn't have enough water but we had learned how, and you don't forget it."

One of the boys said, "Where I was raised we didn't have any water 'cept in a well deep enough to swim in."

They all laughed.

Those boys wanted to stop and party in Fort Worth. So Long shook their hands, loaded up his gear, thanked them, then him and his ponies headed southwest. He wanted to be home for Christmas, and partying at the moment didn't have an appeal to him.

Late that next night, across Brazos River, he'd not found a site to camp before dark. Then he discovered a loose-saddled horse in the road and caught him. The good gelding must have gotten loose and was dragging his reins. Long decided he'd have to make a camp and try to find the owner in the morning. Maybe they'd been thrown or were hurt. He had a candle lamp in his things. He'd need some light while he tied up the horses, so he unpacked that. Then he began to unload things under the lamplight. It wasn't that big a help, but it beat the moonless darkness. The saddle horse had a brand but he couldn't read it.

He found some wood and had a fire going to cook some *frijoles* and make some coffee. It brightened up his rough campsite among the post oak and cedar along the wagon tracks someone called a road that supposedly went south to Kerrville. He knew it was still several long days' ride from home.

When involved at last in pouring himself a cup of coffee, he heard someone cock a pistol behind him.

The sound chilled his blood—all the care he took and this might be the last moments of his life.

"Get your damn hands in the air or I'm blowing daylight right through you, mister."

He set down the cup and rose to his feet all careful-like. It was a woman's voice but she sounded tough.

She reached in and jerked his Colt out of the holster. "Now get over there."

"I'm sorry. What are you so mad at me about?"

"I figure you work for that gawdamn Orem Cates. I ain't going to be his whore."

"I'm sorry. I don't know him or you for that matter."

"Don't lie to me, you big sumbitch. Why, you guys doped me tonight or I'd got somewhere's safe. But—I got—dizzy."

He knew in an instant she must be fainting and tried to catch her, but in his effort to save her she rode him to the ground, her limp form on top of him. She was six feet tall and not fat but a very big woman—a real nice enough looking one, too, from what he could see in the fire's light. He set the gun aside from her and rearranged her body to be more comfortable, putting his saddle under her head.

Then, sipping coffee, he wondered how to revive her. Man that sure was a lot of woman there. Who was this Orem somebody? Obvious someone had doped her. But what could he do? A twenty-some-year-old woman he had no name for was passed out cold in his camp. Someone was trying to enslave her or she thought so anyway.

How in the blue blazes did he get caught up with these women? Her and Rose had both been dropped in his lap. Of course he loved Rose and they'd made—would've had a good life together. This woman was an Amazon. He read a book somewhere about them.

He almost laughed out loud about how he had been nearly crushed to death by a storybook character.

Still amused about that, at last he went about fixing a bowl of steaming beans to eat. She'd tried to come around once, but didn't make it. He finally hid her gun in a pannier, put his own back in his holster to have it at hand should he need it, and got ready to sleep on the ground across the fire from her.

The temperature had dropped so he put his heavy coat over most of her and kept his own blanket for himself to sleep in. She still puzzled him, but maybe she'd sleep it off, and when she woke up maybe she'd explain. He sure hoped so.

When the sun tried to rise he woke up. The temperature had dropped even colder. When he got water on the fire for coffee she stirred. He glanced over where she had pulled herself up into a sitting position huddled in his great coat.

"Oh, my God. What in the hell did you do to me?"

"Not one damn thing, lady. You came in here accusing me of something I had nothing to do with—doping you or poisoning you. I simply found a loose horse, saddled, in the dark on the road and made camp."

She shook her head. Her brunette hair was in her face. She looked a mess, and a large one at that.

"First tell me who in the damn blazes are you?"

"Long John O'Malley from down by Kerrville. I've been from Abilene, Kansas, to Denver to see the Rockies and dodging fighting crazy wild Indians to get back here. My business is driving cattle herds to Kansas."

She parted her hair and tossed some back. "And you've got a damn nice thick coat I am loving this cold morning. Me, well six weeks ago I had a husband. He got into a gun fight with a man who came by and told me to leave my husband and for me to come be his concubine."

Smiling, Long said, "He had lots of nerve to tell you that, didn't he?"

"Oh, he had the gall of a real billy goat. That old sumbitch riding a stud horse like he was Napoleon telling me that I needed him." She made a repulsive face and shook her head over her situation.

"Well here's what happened next. Rory, my husband, got so mad over it he went to town and got in the damndest gun fight with those sumbitches. Ended up wounding some of them and got kilt his-self."

"I'm sorry about that."

"Well I buried him. Bless his soul and went to running my ranch. Next they went to running off my hired help. I told the sheriff but him and Orem Cates, the bastard that told me to leave Rory, are as close as brothers."

"So what happened next?"

"I told you. Cates's boys run off my help, and yesterday they come to forcibly take me to

74

their paw. Well I fought them hard as I could and they got me down and about choked me to death giving me laudanum. Then loaded me onto a horse. I fooled them acting groggy and I got away in the night. But the drug struck me and I got dizzy, fell off the horse, but remember stumbling down the road. When I found your camp I thought you were more of them Cates."

"What is your name?"

"Janet Holcroft."

"I'll make us some breakfast, Janet, and then we can go see what can be done for you."

"Hey, you must have family, a wife, a ranch, too much for you to worry about my ass."

"The woman I was to marry was killed by Indians in Kansas six weeks ago. My brother's been running the H Bar H ever since I left. I would like to settle this horrific war for you before I go home."

"Well I wouldn't turn down any gawdamn help. You got a brush? My hair is a damn mess."

"How big a ranch do you have?" he asked her.

"Oh, a section. Rory's daddy fought in the Tex/Mex war and he earned it as a sixteen-year-old boy."

"Wow."

"We lost him last year to the fever. But he was a great guy and he left Rory with the ranch. His dad's second wife had a baby after him but they both died at the birth. Rory's mom had died earlier from snakebite." She paused. "Where did you come from?" she asked.

"My Cherokee father died out hunting buffalo. I never met him. My stepfather married my mom before I was born up in Arkansas. My nine-month younger brother Harp and I are very close. We took six thousand head of cattle to Abilene last year."

"Why hell, Long, you've got enough money to burn wet mules on a wet damn rainy day and have some left."

He laughed. "I never thought about it like that."

She got up and put the coat on. "I've got business to take care of right now. I swear I'll come right back and I won't shoot you."

"Don't take too long . . . these eggs and ham I have here will be done soon enough."

She nodded and strode off in his coat into the brush.

He shook his head after her. Why, she might even up and claim it for her own.

They ate his cooking. She bragged on his Arbuckle coffee and then she gathered dishes to wash them and his pan.

"I'll saddle the horses. Anywhere you want to go, or home?"

"Won't do any damn good to go to the sheriff. Told you, him and Cates are like brothers."

"Fine. Your place?"

"If they ain't burned the son of a bitch to the ground."

He stopped. "I know you're mad, but cussing like a sailor won't bring your man back or stop these bullies from attacking you."

"Hmm, my cussing bothers you?" Her blue eyes stared a hole in him.

"It does. You're a pretty woman and it comes out of place for me."

"You may have bad eyes, too."

"No, my eyes are fine. Your cussing, aside from bothering me, does nothing but distract from you."

"Well." She wet her lips. "Not one man ever told me that in my life. How did a half Indian learn so much and so many words I never heard of, ever, before in my life?"

"My mother, and I hope someday you meet her."

"Long, I want to meet her."

"We can go down there. You'll like her."

"And from here on, I will try not to cuss around you."

"Don't do it for me. Do it for yourself."

"Go pack. I'll have these—dishes done in no time."

He tossed her a hairbrush that she caught.

"Thanks. I'll try to look better wearing this fine coat and talk more like a lady."

Horses packed, they rode for her ranch. He

felt better when they found the place was still standing.

She dropped off her horse. "Long, this is all I have from a wedding and three years of marriage. Rory worked hard. We sent two hundred head of cattle, we had big enough, with a drover and got eight thousand dollars. Paid off the longest standing ranch loan in Texas and I have the rest in the bank.

"I guess Cates thought I was free game for no reason I could give. I swear I never as much as smiled at him. I met Rory up at Cleburne at a dance. He was like you, six feet tall and it was nice. I'd danced with midgets since I was sixteen or younger.

"He told me he'd marry me if I'd move to his ranch down here. That wasn't hard. I figured I'd be an old maid if I didn't. No, that's not so. He was very gracious and respectful of me. We were married two weeks later. His paw was still alive and he was a good old man until he later died.

"After we got the loan paid off, Rory got serious and we went to branding mavericks that were all over the place. The Cates got pushy about us taking their cattle, but we never did one blame thing about rounding up any of theirs. Why, we branded five hundred head, Rory, I, and two cowboys in the past three months."

"You've been busy."

"Right. Now I can go hire me some gunnies and wipe that bunch out."

"Not so fast. They can put you in jail for doing that."

She made a sour face at him and shook her head. "You're so straitlaced. I figured that you'd want to do it the right way."

"I don't want to be put in jail, either. Let's see if they come back for you. We can defend your house and that is not a crime. If I can hold off Cheyenne and Sioux war parties, we can do the same with the Cates."

She smiled. "I'm game. But before we get to be too serious I need to warn you about my failings. Him and I have been married three years and I have not been pregnant once. So I am not much of a prize for a wife. Now I've warned you."

"If we come to that river, we will cross it."

"Another thing . . . you are pretty flat honest about things. I like that."

"Amen."

"How many women have broke your heart?"

"A few."

She made a face at him. "That ain't a number."

"Two. One was a widow with children. One was an Indian princess."

"The widow?"

"She had children and decided she didn't want to remarry. The princess was killed in a wagon attack a few weeks back."

"I am sorry. That is so sad."

"Well let's unsaddle and see what happens."

She came over and hugged him, then kissed his cheek. "Thanks for staying to help me. I sure hope your plan works."

He stood still for a long moment, then nodded. He about lost it and kissed the fire out of her. But instead he kept it all inside. There would be time for that—later. He hoped.

They took turns sitting up on guard shifts that night in her house and no one came. He carried a rifle and cartridges anywhere he went doing chores. The next night they had a heavy rain at sundown and still no one came.

The day after that a neighbor woman came by in a buggy, asked how she was and said she was going to town and did she need anything. He remained out of sight until she left.

When she was gone, hands on her hips, Janet said, "That woman has affairs going on with them boys of his. Only reason she came by was to report I was here alone."

"Good. Maybe they will try something."

"I bet they do now."

"How old are those boys?"

"Twenty on down. All of them. One of them younger ones was drunk and told Rory, in the saloon, that he should try that woman's body. He said he told them he wasn't interested. He was faithful. I believed in him."

80

That night, awake, sitting on the dark living room floor on guard duty, Long heard a harsh whisper. "Shut up. I get her first."

They were coming on foot from the west. He moved across the dark room to quietly open the window. Two were sneaking up in the ghostly starlight from, as Long figured, the west side. He took aim out the open window, shot both of them, and they crumpled to the ground. Quickly he ran for the front door and saw two more running madly north toward the road in the night's inky light. He took another down with a quick shot, and his effort put spurs on the last one who managed to escape.

"Long? Long? Are you all right?" she cried, rushing outside with a pistol in her hand.

He caught and held her back from going to the downed raiders. "I am fine. Three are down. One got away."

"What can we do now?"

"Sun comes up we will ride to town. Have the sheriff and justice of the peace come out here and decide."

She hugged him in her nightgown. He lightly kissed her. When they stepped apart she nodded. "Anyone ever tell you that you are the meanest man in Texas?"

"No."

"Well you are."

"What does that mean?"

"When we get all through with all this I am going to prove to you I am the meanest woman in Texas—bar none."

"And?"

She slapped him. "You know da—good and well what I mean."

Working hard to control his amusement he said, "We will have to see about that."

CHAPTER 5

Mid-morning, the two of them brought everyone back to her ranch. Justice of the Peace Adam Walker, Sheriff Alton Baker, two deputies, two undertakers, and about two dozen curious men and women on horseback and in buggies as witnesses accompanied them.

When they got back to her house she pointed out Orem Cates, seated on his stud horse, in the front yard. The two living brothers had drug their kinfolks' bodies up to the yard gate.

Cates swung his horse around. "Sheriff, arrest that bitch and her lover for killing my boys."

"I can't do that, Orem. Those three were obviously trespassing on her ranch. I am sorry, but I may have to arrest you for aiding and abetting them on this raid. Orem, you can't exceed the law. It is up to the JP to make sure it is kept. Men, arrest them."

Orem went for his gun but Long beat him to the draw, and the old man's last bullet struck at the feet of the JP's horse. That spooked his horse backward, unseated Justice Walker, and, in the confusion, Cates's other two boys went for their guns. But by then the deputies were armed and shot each of them twice and they fell out of their saddles.

The JP scrambled around after his hat, the wind scooting his out of reach. Someone caught his spooked horse for him.

His Honor brushed the dust off his suit coat, restored his hat, and said, "My decision is this was all in self-defense. Undertaker, take them all to town."

"Why did Orem do this?" The sheriff had his hat off and looked shaken that his friend could do something like this.

"You just can't tell, Sheriff." Long shook his head at the man. "Cates was here telling her she should cast aside her husband, and be with him, and that's what got her husband killed. Then they came here and tried to drug and kidnap her. I came here to protect her and did just that."

"Who really in the hell are you anyway?"

"Long John O'Malley, a rancher and cattle drover out of Kerrville."

"Didn't I read somewhere about you delivering the first Texas cattle to Sedalia last year?"

"Yes. Me and my brother Harp did that."

"Why Orem was a damn fool to even think about messing with you."

Long put his arm around Janet's shoulder, with her standing beside him like she belonged there, and he laughed. "I thought so, too, but he didn't know who he was up against."

"Sorry about Rory, too. Thank you, ma'am, for

finding this man." He and the others rode off. The funeral wagon was loaded and left.

The two of them did not wait until dark. The battle between the meanest woman and man competition went on for the rest of the day and long into the night in her feather bed. Next morning they set out to find a buyer for her ranch. They sold it two days later, all of her branded stock and the ranch for fifty thousand and that, with her bank money, they sent by Wells Fargo to his family banker Jim Yale in Kerrville.

They hired a cowboy to drive the loaded wagon with her things, including her feather bed, to the H Bar H in south Texas. They took three of her good horses, his outfit, Rose's pony, and headed south.

He sent a wire saying they were coming and that they wanted to be married on Christmas day.

While there he bought himself a good canvas long tailcoat, 'cause his bride-to-be wasn't about to give up the wool-lined one. Two days later going south it tried to snow on them, then it turned warmer. Along the way he had to tell her all he knew about his family and all the stories of moving from Arkansas to Texas, fighting Comanche, and branding mavericks.

The day before Christmas Eve, about dark, they drove up into his folks' yard.

The stock dogs barked, someone fired a gun off, and the Injun warning bell rang loudly. Harp, his wife Katy with the baby Lee, Long, Janet, Hiram, and his mom all danced in the yard.

"You two are getting married Christmas day?" his mother asked after getting bits and parts of their plans.

"If we can?"

Harper clapped him on the shoulder. "Well, brother, I already have it arranged for that afternoon at three p.m."

"That's good. It will be before the baby is born anyway."

Janet threw her head back and frowned at him. "That's not so, you big clown."

"Oh, that's not right." He tried to clean it up but everyone was laughing.

"Long, don't pick on her. She might whip you."

Jan laughed. "Damn right, Mom. I bet I can, too."

"If there is any betting, gal, I am on your side."

"Long, you taking that?" Harp asked.

"After what I have been through I have had it all happen to me."

Mom herded them for the house. "Well, let's all go inside and we can settle it in there. Janet, where did you get that lovely coat? It sure looks warm."

"It really is. He bought it in Kansas from some famous trader named John Chisholm."

"You met Long up there?"

"No, closer to Waco. It is long story but I kept the coat and him both."

"Wait until I tell you, bro. We have way over fifty sections of our own ranch land south of here," Harp said. "In one big wad, too."

"Is that all?"

"Hell if I'd had some help I'd bought a hundred. What did the Rockies look like?"

"Damn tall hills." He'd found it was sure good to be back home again.

Later while Janet took a bath, he and his mom talked alone in the kitchen.

"She's some woman. But you know that don't you, Long?"

"She is. They shot her husband about two months ago. Then they doped her and were going to take her to be their father's slave. She got away, barged in my camp, and tried to shoot me for what they did, but she passed out."

Her mother was chuckling. "Sounds like a war to me."

"Mom, she cussed so bad when I met her it was a bad distraction."

She frowned at him. "She's sure got over it."

"Oh, yes. She said damn the night we came here, but she was worried about the meeting with you is all."

"Oh, I see. She's a real woman. I think you two will make it fine."

"She sold her ranch up there to come down here

with me. She is a very rich woman. We put it all in the bank down here."

"She spoke about roping cattle?"

"Yes, she can do that, and I believe she could outride me on a bronc."

She hugged him. "I think she'll be fine. Getting married Christmas day, huh?"

"Unless she decides to shy out."

"No. No, she won't do that. I saw how she fit under your arm, like me and your dad did when he took me to that first dance."

"And married you, huh?"

"And me as pregnant as a cow."

"Well, knowing that, I couldn't resist my comment, last night, about her non-condition."

"She has a good sense of humor. She doesn't fly off the handle easy. That is a real attribute in a woman."

"I agree, Mother Love."

"Every one of us missed you. Was it worth it? Your side trip?"

"My reward for going was getting my bride Janet."

"Then, Long O'Malley, you did very well." She kissed him good night on the forehead.

They both laughed.

The next morning he and Harp talked about the "ranch."

They went over the Texas bargain deal on the vast amount of ranch land they bought.

His brother said he figured the carpetbaggers' government needed money and discounted the so-called rangeland sales to cover their shortage.

"What else?"

"There are some small ranches inside the area, and I am trying to buy them out. Most, I bet, are thinking about it since the rangeland they use is now ours and not belonging to Texas."

Long nodded he understood. He also saw how their ownership would cause some friction with landlocked property owners.

"How is the rest working?"

"Good. Of course we have things to settle. Everyone is gathering the mavericks, but we are getting our share of the ones that we can find. The next thing is for us to replace the longhorn bulls with British breeds that fatten easier and make better meat carcasses."

"I've heard that all over."

"The Indians are all upset up there?"

"Who wouldn't be? The buffalo numbers are going down fast. Their way of life is being squeezed out. These are nomadic wanderers, and to be put on a reservation does not appeal to them. It is not how they have lived, and settling down and becoming farmers doesn't suit these horseback-riding warriors."

"They've pushed the Comanche back, but they are still out there and no doubt getting tougher by all the pressure on them. The army surprised a large camp of them and they fled, leaving lots of great horses. I took some men and we rounded up lots of the geldings, so we got most of the cream—the best of the lot."

"It's a big shame that in all this fighting they will lose those great strains of horses."

Harp agreed. "But we'll have a colorful remuda."

"I understand you are the supervisor over at the Diamond Ranch, too?"

"With you included, too. That was the deal I made with the sisters. We share the supervision. I made Doug Pharr the foreman over there. Red helped him at first because he was better at Spanish, but Doug now runs the main ranch. I sent Chaw down to the CHX Ranch I bought from old man Erickson in trade for a small nice town house down on the river and a forty-dollar-a-month payment while he lives. Dad's old friend Hoot runs another new place that we bought."

The Erickson agreement story shocked Long so much that he made Harp start all over and tell him about the deal from the beginning. "Erickson had lots of land, didn't he?"

"Ten sections. He wanted a simpler life. His age had really slowed him and the business part started confusing him. He has no family. I promised that we'd look after him the rest of his days."

"That sounds fair. Then you bought the rest of the new land from the Texas government and that with the rest we own gives us a fifty-section ranch?"

"Yes. Takes in all we had before, but we have some landowners inside that ring. I am planning to try to buy them. Some have no real claim and only squatted on their places. Texas law makes no place for squatters on that land. If they didn't file, then they can be moved by the law."

"Who is handling that?"

"You want the job?"

"Hell, no. But if you need me to do that I will."

Harp turned his palms up. "Some will accept a buyout. Others it may be a life and death situation for them. If they are old settlers let them stay out their life on the place. What can that hurt?"

"I agree. Do we have a list?"

"Yes. The tax collector has those deeded places circled on my map. A deputy clerk saw most of these places and counted livestock for tax purposes in the past year, so we have some names and places. Others we will have to find."

"Who will help me?"

"Our accountant Reg Hoffman. He's crippled, but he can do the paperwork for you here at the house. He is at his home now for the Christmas holiday. The real homesteads have a description as well as their location on the map. As I said, the rest we will have to scout out. Some of our ranch

91

hands know where these places are, and they will tell either their foremen, or you, so you know where to find them."

"That sounds good. I am taking a week or so honeymoon, and I am sure my wife will want to go along on this job. Maybe I can talk her out of it, but I doubt it. And I don't always have your patience, but I promise to try to control it. We can talk about what value these places have if we must buy them."

"I will ride with you anywhere you think you need me."

"Thanks. Now I have to explain it to her." Damn he dreaded this, but she needed to know and understand the whole thing and the repercussions.

"Long, thanks. Together we will iron out our problems."

"Harp, I thought that first cattle drive was the end of our problems. I was wrong. It only started them all. I can say one thing between you and me. I really love her and feel she is the one I needed. At first I merely wanted to help a nice woman who had lost her husband—murdered by some bad men. But I fell in love with her and am very glad I found her."

"Mom told me she suspected that, too. She is a real pretty woman."

"A big pretty woman." Long left it that way and headed for the house. Tomorrow he'd be married to her and they could live their life out as ranchers—he hoped.

Later in their bed upstairs they talked softly snuggled together.

"You sure that you don't want off this train of ours?" she asked him.

"Yes, I am sure. I look forward to sharing my life with you, Jan."

"You know I get bossy at times, but I will try to bite my tongue when I get upset."

"We both need to be respectful of each other."

She kissed him. "I'm learning lots about you. You talk a lot to me. Your mother said you held things inside. Whatever you do, don't hold things back from me. I am a big girl and I am in this to support you and our life together."

"I promise I will. I talked to Harp today. On all this land we bought, there are squatters who have no rights to be there. Others have homesteads and they own the land, but we can shut them off from the range around it, which is our land. We need to buy them out if we can. It will be touch and go."

"And?"

"Well I told him I would take that job. It needs to be done."

"You will ride out and talk to these people?"

"Yes."

"They may shoot you?"

"I hope not. Will you help me?"

"Of course, but it won't be easy, will it?"

"No. It could be dangerous. The listed land is marked on our map. I plan to do them first. The others are squatters and have no rights, but we intend to resettle them if they let us. Older settlers can live out their lives out there on their land if they wish to."

She snuggled against him. "I can help you. This is our last night living together as sinful people. Tomorrow we will be man and wife. Let's enjoy it."

Hmmm—they did that very thing, and in his book that was okay.

CHAPTER 6

Christmas morning, they opened gifts. Jan cried when she opened an envelope from his mother.

"What does it say?" Long asked her.

"She said she'd help me fix up the house we choose." She dabbed at her wet eyes with the kerchief he handed her. "And I thought I'd be pushed aside for marrying her son."

Both women in the room ran to her aid.

"Why would you think that?" his mother asked.

"I didn't know you—"

"That is not the case, Jan. We're so glad he found you. You are one of us," Katy said.

"I know. But I have lived among spiteful people who resented anyone intruding in their world. I can't believe everyone's acceptance. I could not believe all the concern you have shown me. My deceased husband's own cousin came and told me, at his funeral, that he and his family would be taking over my ranch. He demanded I give them the ranch."

"Oh, Jan, you never told me about that," Long said.

"I was so ashamed of them demanding it that I didn't share it with anyone, but a lawyer told me they couldn't do that. I knew they'd try something before it was over. Long did enough for me, insuring I wasn't taken as a slave. He didn't need to know my sack of problems with Rory's family. I worried they'd do something when I sold the ranch. But we sold it so fast they had no time to stop it. I think they planned to take my ranch by claiming in court that I was mentally unfit to run it."

His mother began hugging and rocking her. "Jan, we will all stand with you. You are one of us now and always will be."

"Hey. This is no time to be sad," Hiram said. "This is your wedding day, me girl. That worthless lot up there will never realize what a treasure they've lost."

"See? You are in a safe place," Long said.

She agreed with a nod.

Hiram asked her if she knew where her parents were.

"My father is dead. I lived with an aunt from my tenth year on. She died last year."

"You don't know where your mother is at?" Katy asked her.

"I don't think about her. When she left me with my father she never even said good-bye."

"Who did she leave with?"

"I never knew his name. I never tried to find her." She shook her head, and the nice hairdo that they'd fixed for her event later that day swung loose.

"I heard once she worked in a house of ill

repute, but I never looked into it. My aunt, my father's sister, was a ship for me to survive with. I attended school. I never had any nice clothes, but she tried her best. I attended school in overalls most of the time. Between my height that I hated and my sorry wardrobe I struck back to survive. My husband, God bless him, Long has heard my story about my life with him. He lifted me up from being the poor too tall girl who wore hand-me-down clothes and very used shoes."

Hiram said, "Don't shrink. The O'Malley men appreciate your height, me lassie."

They all laughed.

The noon meal at the ranch had been like old reunion days as Long met all the men who made the first run north with Harp and him to Sedalia. He laughed at the sight of Chaw, recalling the guy in a tattered confederate uniform, who on this day wore a big Boss of the Plains Stetson, white shirt, tan pants, and a businesslike jacket. The rest looked nice, but that Johnny Rebel sure turned respectable looking in Long's book that day.

Hiram had told her earlier he'd be real proud to give her away. The three women drove one buckboard. Baby boy Lee was left home with a nanny. Hiram drove Long in another one. Their ranch foreman, Red, rode to town with Harp. All the crew plus their families were either on horseback, in buggies, or in rigs headed for the ceremony in town.

On the way into town Long asked his dad, "Mom said you rented a fancy coach and team to take her to the dance where you two got married?"

Hiram flicked the horses to pick up their pace. "I did for a fact. Your mother was so upset about being pregnant with you and your father dead she almost wouldn't go with me. I insisted. When I proposed she told me to look at her body—that she was ugly."

"She never was, was she?"

"Hell, no, she was a regal princess. M'wife had drowned six weeks earlier. I never thought I'd find a lovelier woman in this world. I didn't care about her being pregnant. You would be my son when you came into this world. Period."

"I never doubted that you were my dad, either."

"Good. I planned it that way. Your mom was a great educator. You boys have shown it well. Why, I'd have gone to see those Rockies just like you did, but I had her and you, and then Harp to support. When Harp told me where you'd gone I said to myself—I'd have done the very same thing. Good luck to you and Jan. You know she cried when I said I'd give her away?"

"She has a big heart. But she's willing and strong."

"You two will have a great life."

"Thanks, Dad, I sure missed you all out there fighting Indians and no one to talk to."

"Oh, you even missed talking? How did that happen? You don't say two words sometimes."

"Well I missed Harp talking for me instead."

They both laughed. It turned into a grand warm Christmas day.

The newlyweds, after the wedding, went off on the night stagecoach to honeymoon in San Antonio, Janet smiling and talking all the way about how she never figured anything like this would ever happen to her, especially after burying a husband and how proud she was to be an O'Malley.

He felt the same. Immersed in their love.

He took her to an opera in San Antonio. Though it brought back his memory of Rose and her impression of the show, Jan warmed his heart singing a verse or two in the taxi going back to the hotel.

"Only you would think to take me to an opera. My first husband was kind, but he'd never done that. Thanks, Long."

He kissed her and deep in his mind he realized how fortunate he was to have her. In his search for a mate he could have done a lot worse, possibly finding an ungrateful one, a dumb one, or a nagger.

She was none of the above.

CHAPTER 7

When they returned from San Antonio Long learned Harp had chosen Johnny Brooks and Anthony Morales as the two men to ride with him and Jan on the ranch business for the land lock removal or settlements. Johnny was near thirty, but Harp said he was educated and a very steady person. Tough if he needed to be and smiling if things were level. Anthony spoke English and a good Spanish as well. He dressed nicely, spoke well, and yet was tough enough to back Long and Jan with Johnny.

Harp spent some time with Long going over all the notes he had on the owners. Fresh from their honeymoon, the two wore work clothing and began to get acquainted with the two men who would work with them on the ride across the land.

Harp had what folks, by then, called a chuck wagon setup to go along with them. Jimmy Quarles, a great cook, and two young boys who needed a job as camp helpers also rode along. That way they could stay out on the range and not have to come clear in each night.

Long set up for them to go to the crossroads at the site of the Union church on the east side of their new ranch land because there were some landowners around that point. The chuck wagon crew left a day before to find and set up their base. They took some extra saddle horses along, too.

That first morning Long and Jan left at dawn. Cold air iced things and he wore a sweater under his canvas coat. Johnny's horse bogged his head and tried to throw him, but the man rode it out of him laughing. She, of course, wore his great coat and smiled smugly, warm all day in the saddle on the way to their camp setup.

Long didn't mind. With no idea how long this job would take, he set in to handle it. Besides he still felt mellow over their sweet honeymoon in San Antonio.

When they reached the camp setup, Jimmy, the cook, swept his dusty black felt hat off and bowed to her. "Mrs. O'Malley, welcome to my humble kitchen."

She stepped off her horse, handed the reins to Anthony, and laughed. "My name, my friend, is Janet. Jan to you. No need to be so formal with me."

"Then, Janet, good to have you here. What you don't like, complain and I will change it."

She stepped in and kissed him on the forehead. "All I know is the guys say you are a helluva good cook and I need to find a new word for that."

"Not for me, ma'am—I mean Jan."

"I do for my husband. But there is no helping me on the matter of cussing."

They laughed and the way was set to have some fun in camp. Horses put up, they had some tender beef roast and *frijoles* for supper. With fresh bread and peach cobbler for dessert.

"You trying to fatten me?" she asked Jimmy over her dinner plate.

"I figure you'll work off enough riding with them three." He tossed his head at the others seated at the table.

She shook her head. "This business we are doing is not work. It is called hurry up and wait I think."

Jimmy laughed.

Long was about to agree but he just chuckled instead.

In the morning they rode to the Craddick spread.

A bald-headed man came out and spat tobacco aside, then wiped his mouth on the back of his hand at the sight of her. "Morning, what kin I do fur you?"

"We come to talk with you, Mr. Craddick, about your ranch."

"What fur?"

"You have one hundred sixty acres here deeded to you. I can see some is farmland and some is woods and pasture. I would make you an offer of sixteen hundred dollars cash."

A thin woman came to the door and asked under her breath, "What'n the hell do they want anyway?"

"To buy the ranch."

She made a sour face at him. "We selling?"

"I've got cattle branded," he said to Long.

"I'd buy them, too."

The man took out a flat small book. "Forty cows, thirty calves, and two bulls. Plus twenty-five yearlings."

Long added in his head, the cows at twenty bucks and the rest at ten bucks a head. "I'd pay you twelve hundred dollars for them. Round it off three thousand dollars lock, stock, and barrel."

"Write me a check."

"You will have to come to the bank in Kerrville next Monday. I will meet you there and you can sign the papers."

"You ain't sold my cow?" She frowned at him.

"Hell, no, woman. Go get packed . . . he just bought this place."

Long, in disbelief at how fast the deal went through, stepped off his horse and shook Craddick's hand. "Thanks. That's my wife, Janet, and that's Johnny and Anthony. I'm Long O'Malley."

"I knew who you was when you rode up. Nice to meet you. I'll have all my belongings along with me in Kerrville Monday. She's nagged me for years to sell this place and move up on the Canadian River in the Injun Territory. Well thanks to you I've heard the last of it."

"I'm taking your word on that number of stock."

"They're here. I don't lie about anything."

"Could you show them to Johnny tomorrow?"

"No problem."

"Good. I've got a mean bookkeeper I have to please."

"I understand that."

"Thanks."

When they rode to number two on the list, she asked him, "How deep are your brother's pockets in this game?"

"He says deep."

"We buy many of these places they better be."

They reached the R T Bar Ranch near noontime. The owner, RT, was not there but his wife Harriet said she'd ring the schoolhouse bell and he'd come in.

They dismounted and hitched their horses at the rack. Long introduced them and told her they were there to discuss buying their ranch land.

The woman with gray streaks in her hair shook her head. "Might as well ride on. He ain't budging an inch."

"Thanks, ma'am, but I needed to make him an offer."

RT rode in carrying a shovel, and it was obvious from his clothes and gumboots he'd been working in the mud. He dismounted, hitched his horse, and set his shovel aside.

"Ma'am," he said to Janet. "Excuse my mud. I had to unstop a spring today."

"No problem. I know all about ranching," Jan said.

His wife interrupted, "Well that's Long O'Malley and they come to buy the ranch and I done told them no."

He quickly agreed. "We don't want to sell like she says."

"We'd offer you ten dollars an acre today and that offer is only good for thirty days," Long said. "You realize the H Bar H owns the land all around your holdings, and when fencing comes you will be left with a partial section of land here."

RT nodded. "We like this place. We've worked hard to develop water and farmland. I'm forty and not in mind to start over on another one. I know I may lose the rangeland, but we want to stay right here."

"That is your choice. But the offer is only good for thirty days. Nice to meet you." He offered to shake the man's hand, but RT shook his head and folded his arms.

"RT, we aren't out to destroy you. But we felt an offer needed to be made, giving an opportunity for folks to move to more advantageous places."

The man shook his head. "I don't know what'cher talking about. I'm staying here."

"Thanks." He turned to his people. "Let's mount up. He does not want to sell."

Out of hearing, Jan began laughing. "He thought that ten-dollar word you gave him was a disease."

He frowned at her. "It means a better place to ranch."

Johnny and Anthony laughed.

She rode in and pulled on his arm. "Darling, we know the meaning and we won't catch it."

He shook his head at her. "I can see this is going to be lots more work than I thought it would be."

His wife agreed. They headed back for camp.

For the next day he picked two more ranchers' names with deeded land close by to check out.

Jimmy at supper asked how it went.

"One owner agreed to sell, the other wouldn't shake my hand after he said no."

In the morning Johnny and Anthony rode over to count cattle. The two of them went to see Merle Barton on the Five Cross. He owned one hundred sixty acres.

The air held a nippy morning, and the oak wood smoke coming out the chimney smelled inviting. Their property sat on a flowing creek. The house was made from hewed logs and the large winter-bare shade trees made the place look settled. A milk cow bawled for her calf, and a whiskered man came out on the porch and invited them in.

"Don't tell me. You're Hiram O'Malley's son. I met you, your brother, and Hiram at Oak Crossing, I bet five years ago when we tried to get my boy back from them damn Comanche. I'm Merle Barton and this is Hattie, my wife. You must be his wife?"

"Yes. This is Jan. We've been married two weeks. I am Long O'Malley."

"You two have a chair. Hattie is making coffee. Tell me what is the big cattleman and rancher doing down here?"

"You know we bought up a large amount of land over here?"

"I heard about it."

"Well we are offering to buy folks like you out if you want to sell. Ten bucks an acre. Cash."

"Hattie, you wanting to move?"

"No."

"Well that's my answer. I've got to live with her."

"That's right. But some day we may need to fence you off the open range."

"Good. Her milk cow won't get so damn far away."

They laughed.

"Listen we may someday rot up here, but until then we aren't moving. We had two boys.

One died of mumps. The other you know the Comanche stole and we never found a hair from his head of him. Your dad really tried to find him, too. So we'll stay here. This old house is tight and dry. Fireplace heats us. The land provides us deer to eat, and we sell some yearlings enough to cover our bill at the store. So we ain't selling. We ain't got any kin we know about. What say I give you my will? When her and I are gone it will be yours and your brother's?"

"I won't refuse you. But when you get to where you can't get those cattle up and work them anymore, me and some of the boys will handle it."

"That day may come. Thanks."

"Harp has a lawyer. Next time you go to Kerrville stop and see Mr. Lacey. He will draw up the will and you can sign it."

She made them stay for lunch, and after that they rode on south to the 34K and found no one. No sign and by his estimation not a soul had been there in a while. His thoughts were reinforced after entering the cobwebbed house.

"It has been ages since they left," Jan said to him after their inspection.

"Maybe longer," he said when they mounted up and rode back to camp.

"Kind of strange, too. There was someone here when the assessor was here last year."

She shoved him friendly-like, walking back to their hitched horses. "He must have left the next day."

He grabbed her up in his arms and kissed her. "This is long hard work."

"Kiss me again, you big lug. I love you so much—What's wrong now?"

"Stay here. I noticed something."

"No, I am going with you. What is it you see?"

"There is a noose tied in that oak tree over there."

"Oh, do you think—"

"Stay here."

"Hell, no. I am going along."

"Come ahead then, but I suspect someone back then was hung."

"Oh, how can we tell—"

"The damn coyotes scattered his bones in this tall grass, I suspect."

She stopped and shuddered, covering her face at what she saw. "Oh, Long, there is a skull over there."

"I told you—"

"No doubt you're right. They hung someone and no one discovered it."

Long looked around. "I'd bet his name was Harold Terry."

"What now?"

"We'll report the crime to the law and let them solve it."

They rode back to camp. Johnny and Anthony rode in as well, too.

"His count looks close to what he told you," Johnny said. "What did you find?"

She shook her head. "We think someone hung Harold Terry a long time ago. The noose is still up there and varmints scattered his bones."

Anthony looked pained by the news. "Any close neighbors?"

"None on our maps."

"Kind of spooky wasn't it?" Anthony asked.

"We checked the house. No one has been in it in a long time. Then I noticed the rope hanging down. She discovered his skull."

"Scare you?" Johnny asked her.

"Like you two said, it was very spooky." She hugged her arms and shuddered again.

"As for the other ranch we saw, we will inherit that ranch from a couple I'd met years back when we tried to get back Comanche captives. They lost a son to them."

"They're giving you their ranch?" Johnny asked.

"They have no one to leave it to."

"Come eat; it won't be good cold," Jimmy said.

"What's for tomorrow?" Johnny asked.

"Two places west of here. Y-Seven-X and the Tooke's Ranch. I never have been to either I know about," Long said.

Johnny nodded and they washed up after Jan

and they sat down at the setup the cook's crew fixed for them.

Later in their bedroll she asked him if he'd thought any more about the lynching.

"No. All I can think about is my lovely wife."

"You big galoot, you flatter me to death."

They both laughed hard. She was still fun after a long day in the saddle, even though there was not enough progress to suit him. Jobs like this taught him the patience he didn't have enough of. This wife was like frosting on a cake—she sweetened any, especially the worst, deals that came their way.

CHAPTER 8

The next day they found the Y-7-X but no one was at home. People lived there and were either out or gone to town. He left them a note to contact Harp when they went into town, and then Long and his crew rode on to Tooke's Ranch.

A Mexican *segundo* who ran that ranch for the obvious absentee owner met them at his yard gate. The foreman's name was Alex Contreras.

"Señor Tooke, he lives in Fort Worth," the man said. "He seldom comes down here. Tell your wife my wife is inside . . . she can speak some English."

"You hear him?" Long asked her.

"*Gracias, señor,*" Jan said, smiled, and went to find her while the four men settled in the warmer sun to talk some more.

Alex told him he hoped his patron did not sell the ranch. It was his living and also for the two *vaqueros* who worked for him. Long never saw his wife and decided to have their accountant contact Tooke by mail.

Jan rejoined them and they started back to camp on their horses.

"What was his wife like?"

"He just married her she said. Really I think

she was only twelve or thirteen years old. She said something about he sent for her to save face. Whatever that means. I believe she was sold to him, but what can you say?"

"Nothing, but I am very glad I found you."

"Would you want a girl that young?"

"No."

"Good huh, guys?"

"If Long doesn't want you, Anthony and I would have you." The pair were nodding their heads in agreement and grinning while they rode along for camp.

They laughed for a long time about her having both of them. She shook her head at them each time they did. Long rode in closer and hugged her shoulder, then said, "Well, at least I have substitutes."

Another day gone. Maybe he should have had his brother do this sorry job. He was much better at rounding up cattle. That, at least, showed more progress. They were back in camp that afternoon when a messenger from Chaw rode into camp.

The boy, in his teens, spoke to Long. "Chaw said for me to tell you for all of you to come in. Some shooters attacked one of our cow camps last night and told them to leave. He's sent for Harp and told me to come get all of you."

Long shook his head. What next? Trouble already. "We better load up and get over there."

Their upset cook, Jimmy, shook his head at the news. "How do I feed you?"

"Well, we better save our backsides and eat later. They don't know who the raiders were?" Long asked the boy.

"No, sir."

If Jan hadn't been along, he'd have gone looking for them. The business of threatening any O'Malley needed to be stopped right then.

It was after dark when his outfit reached Chaw's place. His wife Calamity came and hugged Jan like they were old friends. She was really glad to have a woman to talk to. Right off Long could see that the rebel in their bunch had found himself that girl of sixteen or seventeen who was a real sweet person. The two women talked for a brief time.

"She has food, men," Jan told them.

"We get unhooked and parked we will be there," Long told her as several of the ranch hands showed up to assist them.

"You all right?" Chaw arrived out of breath.

"I'm fine. What are you so winded from?" Long laughed.

"Last night a bunch rode into the cow camp south of here, shooting. We were on—" He bent over for more air. "Hell, I have three of my best men posted out here so they can't attack the ranch and us not be warned, so they attacked the cow camp."

"Take it easy. I know you are upset. You did the right thing. How are the men in that camp doing?"

"No one hurt serious. They'll be fine. But I knew she was with you—"

"You did the right thing. How many shooters?"

"Somewhere between six and nine. It was dark and they didn't leave anything, but the men were off guard on our own ranch land for cripes' sake."

"We will simply have to post guards."

"Chaw," his wife called out. "Long has not ate. Talk to him at the table."

"We will, honey." Chaw shook his head. "Best damn deal I ever made—marrying her."

"I know how you feel. I feel the same way."

They both laughed and went toward the lighted house. Long's crew was seated and they made room for him. Jan brought him a plate.

"You eating?" he asked her, concerned she wasn't seated.

"When everyone is fed. I won't lose any weight."

Everyone laughed.

"Harp is here," someone said from the front porch.

"I'll welcome him," Chaw said, getting up.

"Hello, brother," Harp said from the doorway.

"About time you got here. Why, I beat you up here by five minutes," Long said, rising.

Jan shook her head at him, busy serving more plates of food to the others.

"It's all right, Jan," Harp said. "I knew he'd be here. He hasn't missed many meals in his life. Did they bother you, too?"

"No. But Chaw was worried and called us in. Not a bad idea since we have no idea who these attackers were."

"Have you eaten?" Jan asked Harp.

"Yes, and I was about to go get some sleep." He stretched and yawned. "Where do we start?"

Long waved at him. "They are up and gone is what I was told. I don't know how to find them. They left no trail they say."

Harp nodded, taking a chair and asking two hands to scoot aside some to make room for him. "Were any of the raiders shot up?"

"No."

"If one of them had been shot, they might go to town to get the wound attended to," Harp said, shaking his head over the mystery of it all.

"We never had a chance," one hand said. "It was over before it really started. They shot things up, threatened us, and rode off."

Long looked around for any of the men in the room to say something else. Everyone nodded that they never had a chance to shoot back.

"Did they threaten any of you?" Harp asked.

"Told us get the hell back to town or we'd die."

"They said next time they'd kill us in our bedrolls if we came back."

"None of you recognized anything about them . . . how they talked or rode a horse?" Long asked again, not believing that someone didn't see something that they could use to trace the night riders.

"It was dark last night. The moon had set. We didn't expect them. Hell I woke and thought they'd already killed me. They appeared to be wearing masks, like Klux Clansmen was what I could see, and I knew they had rifles ready to shoot us. This guy told us to get back to town and not come back, because next time they'd kill all of us." Mike was a tough cowboy in his thirties by Long's appraisal. The raiders caught him and the others asleep, unaware of their presence until they shot, woke them, and imposed their threat on him and the others. It made no sense, but he wanted to hire the best tracker money could buy on the job and quick.

Harp was talking about what they needed to do for their safety.

Long stood up. Harp turned to him. "What do you say?"

"I want the best tracker we can find out here tomorrow to go and sort out their trail."

"Who is it we need?" Harp asked them.

"I know two men who could do that," the horse wrangler Tonto said.

"Who?"

"Jude Crown, he was an army scout, and Red Temple. Jude is a full-blood and Red is half but they know tracking."

"Can you get them up here by tomorrow? We can pay them a month's full wages and our horses to ride," Harp said, nodding about Long's plan.

"I'd do my damndest, Harp."

"Boys, get some fresh horses for them to ride back up here on. We need those two men well provided with good horses and armed to find these no accounts."

"Right," Long said. "No one rides alone. Three or more together and everyone have a loaded rifle and pistol."

Long held up his hands in the lighted room. "No one needs to go back to that camp and mess up any telltale tracks until the trackers have a chance to look at it. We will take a pause and repair your torn clothing, wash them, and be ready to ride at an instant. If we find them I feel they need to be arrested and tried for the illegal threatening of our people."

Everyone agreed.

Harp reminded all of them, "By the way, keep this quiet or we will have black troops all over our ranch. They won't catch any of those men who did this. I want them arrested and tried."

Everyone agreed.

"If that boy, Tonto, can convince them to come track for us we will have a slim chance of finding them."

The crew agreed.

Jan told Long the crew had their tent set up. He checked with Harp to make sure he had a place to sleep.

"Yes. Chaw's wife has an extra bedroom upstairs. Thanks. You two sleep now."

Jan nodded and hugging Long's arm, pulled him along. "We are going to sleep."

In the tent he told her he had spoken to their team a few minutes earlier, and in the morning they were going to circle around the area where the incident occurred. "I want you to stay here until we get a handle on them. I know you want to go, but give me a few days looking for them. It may be like finding a hornet's nest if we catch up with them."

She hugged him. "You know I'd like to go—"

"I know, but I want a wife to come back to."

At that she nodded and kissed him. He squeezed her tight. Good . . . she understood how serious he was about ending this threat business. The issue was settled.

The next morning, early, she and Jimmy made breakfast and coffee before the sun even peeked up. Long kissed her, promised to be careful, and he, Johnny, and Anthony rode out.

"You have any ideas?" Johnny asked him before they began to trot their horses.

"No, but they are people. Someone saw them. Someone knows them. The trackers may find them and they may not. We can't do our job of settling with the landlocked owners until they're stopped."

Both agreed and they set their horses into a trot. Long wanted to look around wide of the camp for places where they might be hiding. There were some places on Horse Creek he knew about, where people camped out deer hunting. That would be the first place he wanted to check. They reached that area mid-morning. They found little trace along the small stream, but the wagon track road was on the hills that ran parallel to the creek and required they ride individually, down off the hill to examine the beach area and then ride back up to the road through the cedar and live oak.

They'd searched several sites riding along on the ridge road when a whiff of smoke found them. Anthony said, "Smoke."

All three nodded.

Long stuck out his hand to stop them. "It might be anyone. No need to tell anyone our business. We are simply checking the places."

They agreed.

As the three rode off the ridge, Long saw someone down there run off through the trees for some reason. He checked the handle on the .45 in his holster and they all shared a nod. He booted his good Comanche horse just ahead of the men and when they reached the clearing, he saw two men with rifles in hand facing them. Long saw there were family members, staying over under a tree-stretched canvas cover, including women and children.

"Good morning," Long said. He hoped these two hard-eyed men didn't plan to try something.

"What are you looking for?" the shorter one demanded.

"I own this land. What are you looking for?"

The two men frowned at each other.

"How do we know that?" the taller one asked.

"Tell him, guys."

"He really owns this land. He asked what you were doing here," Johnny said.

"Just camping."

"You wouldn't know about some raiders riding around here?" Long asked.

"We—"

"Shut up, Grate. He's some rancher's enforcer," the short one said.

"I asked you a simple question. What do you say?" Long demanded.

"No. We ain't seen a damn thing."

"Then I have some advice. Load up and leave here or you will be arrested as trespassers."

"That's bullshit; this is state land."

"No, sir. This belongs to the H Bar H Ranch."

"You ain't threatening us. We've got our rights."

"Listen. There are women and children here, but we are not putting up with your remarks. Be gone in twenty-four hours or suffer the consequences."

That said, Long gave a head toss for them to leave and turned his horse.

"What's your name?" the short one called out.

"Long. Long O'Malley."

The skin crawled on his neck. Would they shoot him in the back? Hardcases, they may or may not be hired guns? One thing he was pleased over—his wife was safe back in camp. Thank God.

On the ridge road again, unscathed, they headed west, discussing the two tough men.

Long said, "I don't know if they worked as hired guns or not."

Anthony agreed, but he seemed amused. "They don't have much of anything but kids."

"There are enough deer around here to feed them, which, no doubt, must make up a big part of their diet," Johnny said.

"Someone rode from the west to that camp recently and then went back." Long pointed to the hoofprints in the road leading in and out of the trace down to their camp.

His men agreed.

"Keep an eye on those tracks. They may tell us something."

"Two horses," Anthony said.

Long agreed. "We may learn something ourselves."

"Are you thinking the men we just saw may have been part of the raiders' party?" Johnny asked.

Long nodded, riding on. "They have no way to make a living up here unless someone is paying them. Maybe they are wanted, too."

"They were pretty damn tough acting."

"I thought something was wrong. They were close to asking for a shoot-out, but with them dead we'd not learn one thing. So I dropped it. The three of us could have taken them out."

The two men agreed.

A few miles farther, they found where more horse tracks went off the road onto another trace that led to the river. Those two could be in this mix of shoe prints.

"Let's stash the horses out of sight and slip down there to see."

They took the horses off the ridge on the far side and hitched them out of sight in the cedars and live oak. Then, armed with their rifles, they went back over the ridge road on foot, being careful not to attract any attention.

Slipping through the trees, they made their way halfway down the hill and stopped. Long could see the camp in his field glasses. By his count there must be two dozen gun hands in that camp.

"We may have found them," Long whispered, and handed Johnny the field glasses. "I don't know a soul from the faces I saw."

"Who could they be?" Anthony asked him.

"Either outlaws or the raiders or both."

"They look tough enough to be both." Johnny handed the glasses to Anthony. "What now?"

"We better go back and get some help. That's more than the three of us can handle easily down there."

"Good," Johnny said. "Though, I figured you planned to bust right down there."

"Let's say I am older now."

"I can see why our boys didn't jump up and fight them," Anthony said. "There are a couple of dozen down there."

"Boys, they have near an army here. Someone is serious about us not taking charge of this land of ours."

They slipped out and carefully retraced their tracks. Close to sundown they were back at Chaw's house, and Jan ran out to kiss him.

"You're safe."

"Unscratched. Where is my brother?"

"Did you find them?"

"We think so."

"Harp and some of the boys, along with the Indian trackers that were hired, went back to the campsite to get an early start in the morning."

Long shook his head.

"Why? What's wrong?" she asked.

"Find a boy to ride over there and tell them to wait until we join them. We know where those troublemakers are at."

"Find Bucky," Calamity said to a hand. Chaw's bride was standing there on the porch drying her hands on a dishtowel. "So, you did find them?"

"Yes, we found the camp. Your boy will give them word tonight, and we will join them early tomorrow."

"Yes, ma'am." The boy in his teens called Bucky had just run up to them.

"We need you to go to the camp where our men went and tell Harp that we will join him in the morning and that we know where the men we are looking for are at. That they are to wait for us."

"Yes, sir."

"You know where that camp Harp is at and know how to find it in the dark?"

"Yes, sir."

"Don't get shot by them thinking you are one of the raiders."

"I'll watch that, too."

"Just be careful."

"Yes, sir, and thank you."

"And you tell your mother she raised a good boy next time you see her."

"I will, sir." He smiled and was gone.

Long was still chuckling about the boy's politeness when he put his arm on her shoulder and let his wonderful wife lead him to the house. He'd have to tell her the whole story about what they found—should have had Harp along to do all that talking for him. No. Not really. He really enjoyed her company and confiding in her. It simply was that Harp had spoiled him all those years growing up by doing all the talking.

"Did you really see them?" Calamity asked him, setting places for the three men at the large table.

"Yes, and they have an army, dang near," Long said, taking a seat after washing up.

"Personally I am glad you didn't try," Jan said.

"You have to be sensible sometimes," he said, filling his plate out of the bowls of food the two women brought them.

"It was a good time to be that way." Jan kissed him on his cheek going by.

"You two guys looking at what I have to put up with?" Long asked Johnny and Anthony, who had joined them at the table.

"Oh, me and Anthony are looking at how real bad you are being treated."

They all laughed.

All he could say was, he was damn glad to be safe, and with her after all he'd been through by going to see the shining mountains and coming back. Maybe in the next days they could round up the ones threatening them, settle that business, and get back to normal ranch life.

CHAPTER 9

Jan's windup alarm clock woke him at four a.m. The skeleton ranch crew was busy saddling horses while the three of them ate oatmeal and drank her good strong coffee. Then they were ready to ride and meet Harp in the cow camp. He kissed his wife good-bye, mounted his horse, and they rode off to war.

Harp and his crew were mounted when they arrived, and they left the camp at a trot. Long explained to his brother and Chaw about the tough guys' camp on Horse Creek and what they'd found there.

"Did they have lookouts?" Harp asked.

"Not when we scouted them."

"Coming from this way we better be careful. This is where they'd expect us to come from."

Long agreed. "There were two dozen or more of them in that camp yesterday and another camp of two men and their families farther up that small creek. The ones with the families didn't offer us their names and they acted real tough. I didn't want the cart turned over so we backed off, but they might have warned the others that we had been there."

"That's a chance we take. I am not familiar with this road."

"It is hardly a road but more a wagon track that goes along the ridge parallel to the creek."

Harp nodded. "These two with us are good trackers if they have already fled."

Long nodded. "This land will make good cow country. There is lots of water in the creek for this late in the year."

Harp agreed. "But it is damn sure a long ways from any place or town."

Everyone was told to be as quiet as possible as they rode in closer. Long and Johnny went ahead on foot to see if they had posted any guards. They found no one at the head of the trail and waited. Most of the O'Malley men's horses were hitched up at the top of the trail. Chaw, Harp, and Long planned to ride theirs down off the hill in case they needed to pursue anyone.

The other men began to spread out on foot to descend the hillside. Wood smoke told them someone was still in the camp. The two trackers said no one had ridden out recently, and when they were certain most of their men were getting close, the three horsemen started off the hill.

They came in at a charge and slid into camp as men were running about trying to set up a defense. Harp shot a man who came out in the open with his six-gun in hand. Both Chaw and Long were shooting at others, when the ranch crew with their rifles joined them to mop up the rest. Then things were silent except for the moaning, wounded outlaws on the ground.

Harp ordered all two dozen of the dead buried and the wounded rounded up.

"Chaw," Long shouted. "Those men at the other camp I bet heard the shooting."

"I'll get Harp's horse," Johnny said, and ran to catch him.

"Let's ride. I want them, too," Long said, and they tore up the hill for the road. Harp could handle the rest; he wanted those two captured, too. They made the trip to the road in fast time, and riding off the hill, they met both armed men coming up on horseback. Chaw shot the tall one who was brandishing a revolver. To stop him, Long drove his own horse into the shorter man's mount, and they both went down in the collision. Thrown from his saddle in the wreck, Long rolled a distance downhill and got up to see that Johnny and Chaw had the short guy covered. He was lying on his back and had obviously broken his leg in the wreck.

Nothing too much felt wrong with his body, so Long stood up and dusted himself off, laughing. "That was a real meeting, guys."

"You all right, boss?" Chaw asked.

"I will be now these bastards are caught."

"He's dead," Johnny said after checking on the tall one.

"This one's broke his leg," Chaw said about his prisoner.

Long shook his head in disgust. "I can see that. My good Comanche horse over there has to be put down, too. His front leg is broken. I hate that happened."

In a flash Johnny rushed over and caught Long's horse's reins, talking to calm him, and undoing the latigos, he stripped the saddle off. "I can do that for you . . . he ain't my friend like he is yours."

The tack taken off, Johnny led the horse, limping, to the edge and shot him in the forehead. The horse went to his knees, groaned, and spilled onto his side in death on the hillside slope.

"Thanks." Long felt the loss. He had been a damn good horse.

"Neither one of them was worth that horse," Johnny said in disgust, and holstered his gun.

"Who are you?" Chaw asked the outlaw.

"Short Taylor. You going to have my leg fixed?"

Chaw shook his head. "You won't need it where you're going. How many women in that camp down there?"

"Three."

"They wives?"

"Two are mine. The other's Caldwell's."

"That his name?"

"Wendell Caldwell."

"What're we going to do with the women and kids?" Chaw asked.

"Get some wagons and send them to Kerrville. Harp can decide."

"I'll go tell him what we've got." Johnny stepped into his saddle and rode out.

Three sobbing young women in ragged wash-worn dresses came from the camp. One held a baby in her arms.

"What's gonna happen next?" the sharp-faced one asked, wiping her long black hair, unkempt and windswept, back from her face.

"They say they're going to hang me," Taylor said, squeezing his injured leg.

She dropped down and kissed him. "I'll pray for you, Short."

"Pray they don't, you dummy."

"I ain't no dummy. You're the one said nothing would come of this business and we'd have some money."

"Who hired him?"

She stood up, red-faced mad. "Tell him, Short. He won't save you."

"I ain't no stool pigeon."

"Then you're the stupid one."

Long said, "I've got fifty dollars . . . tell me who hired them."

Holding out her dirty palm she brashly said, "Pay me. His name's Fargo Jennings."

Short shouted at her, "Damn you, whore. I saved your ass."

She gave him a swift hard kick in the ribs. "You

have me in a worse fix now than when you found me. Broke, pregnant, destitute, and miles out here—" Quickly she counted the paper money Long put in her hand.

Then she curtsied and thanked him.

Chaw asked, "You know this Jennings guy?"

"No. But you can bet good money I will find him." Long reached back and felt his sore hip. His future looked like he'd be hurting for a while from the fall.

Fargo Jennings, he'd remember that name. He'd find Jennings and end his miserable life. That was a promise he'd keep.

When they arrived back to the camp with Taylor, Harp's quietly spoken plan was to string up the remaining raiders, wounded or alive. Then use the three wagons to deliver the six women and children to a church or someplace in Kerrville.

Harp spoke to all the women. Each, when they left the area, would receive two hundred dollars for the promise of not saying a word, except that they did not know anything. Then they must move on to continue their lives on that generous amount of money.

Long knew Harp's offer for the penniless women would be a good start.

Chaw, with three of his ranchmen, had said he'd handle the matter of getting those camp women and kids to his place, rather than someplace strange. Long knew the teary-eyed women and children needed to be moved away before the trial, so, slowly, the three wagons moved out to eventually get to Chaw's ranch headquarters.

Long and Harp went back to the big camp where ten nooses were tied and trees selected. Then four of the raiders were set on horses regardless of their condition, and asked if they had any last words. Most didn't have a thing to say worth their audience's time. They died of broken necks. Six more, including Taylor, met the same fate. The men then buried them all under the trees they were hung from.

After the lynching everyone else rode back to their own places, some passing the wagons on their way.

Long felt really sore from his crash so he borrowed two pints of whiskey from a couple of cowboys, and by the time he reached the headquarters, he was drunk enough to be singing "Sweet Betsy from Pike."

And by then his beat-up body didn't hurt, either.

How he stayed in the saddle had the crew wondering. Harp told Jan about his wreck and the pain medicine he drank. It took both of them to get his boots off and him into bed.

His last words before falling asleep were, "Fargo Jennings, I'll get you."

When he awoke in the morning his head felt

like it was swimming. The pain in his body was sharp. Jan pushed him back down.

"Let me rub your back if that is where the worst pain is."

"In a minute. I'll be right back."

She laughed.

He stumbled outside the tent, relieved his bladder, and straightened. He felt rough. Back in the tent he shook his head. "My back is the worst part."

Facedown on the cot and her sitting on his legs, the cold rubbing alcohol she dabbed on his sore muscles brought goose bumps up on the back of his arms. Then those powerful hands of hers began to knead the stiffness and pain. At first his body resisted her efforts and left him with even more hurting, but soon that sharpness grew less and less. He felt his own body strength drain away, too, until he worried he was too weak to ever walk again.

"Is that better?" she whispered in his ear.

His eyes closed. He mumbled something and was off into a deep sleep.

He woke four hours later, his body able to move. He dressed and still a little light-headed went in the house's kitchen and slumped into a chair.

Chaw's wife, Calamity, poured him coffee and asked what he wanted to eat. She suggested some ham and eggs.

He nodded. "Where's Jan?"

"She's down at the bunkhouse treating a wound a cowboy earned in this last war you had. She didn't like how it was treated and said it must be dressed better to ever heal right. You know she's almost a doctor."

"I know. My back is livable thanks to her."

"They said you had a helluva wreck stopping one of the guys."

"But we did learn who hired them."

"I never heard of him. Faro somebody."

"Fargo Jennings is his name. I'll find him."

Calamity delivered his ham and eggs with a side of hashed potatoes."

"Thanks . . . you're dandy." He smiled at her.

"No, you and Harp are. You gave Chaw this foreman job so he could marry me. I really figured we'd never get married and in the end I'd have to be the third wife of some old man who lost his other two. That's what is so dandy. Me and him married and are having such a good life here on this ranch you all bought for us to run."

"I can see you are a happy wife."

"When he came to Mason and told me we were getting married I did cartwheels in the front yard and didn't care who saw me doing it. Why I'm so happy being his wife, here, and will be as long as we're together."

Busy eating his food, Long grinned at how her outright sincerity amused him. But Chaw was a good person, too, and equally proud of her as well. Like he never knew what he'd do without Jan. Just then she came into the kitchen with a basketful of medical supplies on her arm.

"You better the guy?" Calamity asked.

"Yes. And bandaged the right way this time, too. Calamity, you fed Long?"

"I did. He's doing fine."

"I am not fine. I am much better and can stand by myself. Everyone else all right?"

"Harp said to tell you he's gone to find out more about Jennings and why he hired those thugs."

"The men did a good job and cleaned up the mess in short order. Those won't be back."

"I guess not."

Long was back to being himself in a week, when three white state police showed up in their usual arrogant fashion. At the time, the crew was busy trying out some fresh horses in the home ranch corrals. The first one the boys tried had stuck his nose in the dirt and was trying his damndest to throw the Comanche boy Silver Tom off his back. A regular dust devil to ride. The boy was in the saddle and whacking him between the ears with a quirt to get his head up. There would be no way that pony could throw that boy, so he might as well get over his squealing and bucking. The horse did not agree.

Long was standing on the corral fence,

shouting for Silver to ride him, when a big voice demanded he answer his questions.

Long turned to see what smart mouth was there.

Texas State Police wore large shields for badges. They never wore ranger stars.

"What do you need?" He slipped off the corral to stand at the base.

"My name is Sergeant Callaway. Texas State Police. Three men have been reported missing from around here. Allen Hawthorn, McKendrick Rathbone, and Warren Holden. Do you know the whereabouts of these men, sir?"

"Callaway, I never heard of them before. What did they do wrong?"

"Nothing I know about. Their families reported them missing, and I wondered if you knew anything about them."

"Nope. No one has been around here by those names. But we will look for them for you. Did they say what they were doing out here?"

"No. Working for some guy who has ranches, and their families completely lost track of them."

"What was his name? The guy they worked for?"

"Faro Jennings or Jenks? They weren't sure about it."

"I don't know him." *How about Fargo Jennings? And the men you want are resting under a tree up on Horse Creek.*

"Thanks. Mr. O'Malley, you know that several men have vanished recently around here. If you hear of them contact the Texas State Police."

"Texas is a big place. Cowboys drift through here and are gone. We don't know where they go to."

"But way too many are disappearing in this very area. Enough to make me suspicious."

"Of what? Out-of-work hands don't leave no marks; they simply ride on for another free meal."

The captain swung his horse around and left. His two lemon-sucking deputies followed his lead.

Back when they lived west of Fort Worth, real rangers came by all the time, flirted with their mother, gave him and Harp hard candy, and were part of the family. Those carpetbagger police were like icicles he'd seen on the roof edge during one real cold spell.

Go to hell, Callaway. We won't miss you.

Johnny came by after they rode off. "They're looking for them raiders?"

"I guess I could've told them they were resting under a tree, huh?"

"They won't find them. Those police are afraid of that wilderness we own. That Callaway is kinda like a damn rattler. Rattling some and then squirming off for another day."

Long shook his head. "He's been here before, awhile ago. Asked my dad about some guy we'd planted. Dad didn't know about it but he'd not told that damn Yankee one single thing."

They were getting another bronc saddled for Silver to ride. "Them damn boys sure sent some outlaws for him to ride. Hold up a minute, Johnny." He climbed on the fence.

"Silver, when you go home, stop at the store in town and get your mother a sack of *frijoles* to feed her family and charge them to me. You are doing some great riding."

A big smile on his brown face showed his white teeth. "*Gracias*, she will love you for doing that."

Long damn sure didn't want that to happen—his mother was a typical, fat, many-skirted native woman. Long was just thanking the boy for his effort. "Come on . . . Johnny, I want to study that land map up at the house for where those other locked-in ranchers live."

CHAPTER 10

The next Monday they rode west by southwest again with packhorses to talk to more landowners locked in by Harp's land purchases. Johnny, Anthony, and Jan accompanied him. She handled the cooking chores, and he felt they were better set up to do business this trip.

They met Oscar Beatles, a bowlegged rancher in his sixties. Oscar and three Mexican *vaqueros* ran the Oxbow Ranch.

He and Long sat out under a live oak tree as Oscar spit tobacco and whittled on cedar with a razor-sharp jackknife while Long explained.

"You understand my purpose here is to offer you a price you could live with to sell me your holdings."

"I'm sixty-four. I never intended to do anything but have them plant my bones here when the good Lord or the devil calls me to go yonder. I earned this place in the Texas War for Independence as a mounted cavalryman. I was there when we captured Santa Anna. Bought three more sections for fifty cents an acre with my inheritance—Texas needed money in them days like always.

"Married a woman I met in San Antonio. None of our kids lived. She said she wanted to go home after ten years and four dead babies. I didn't blame her. I gave her some money and never heard from her again.

"I sold grown fat steers for so little that me and the boys that work for me about starved out here for years. But we hung on. This year a man took a thousand head of my steers to Kansas and paid me thirty-five thousand dollars. Can you even imagine that much money? Are those people crazy up there paying that much money for a longhorn steer?"

"My family and I take steers up there, too. He should have paid you fifty thousand. He made fifty thousand for taking them."

Oscar went to laughing. "Why me and them boys went to Mexico and had us a ball charming them *putas*, dancing and drinking. Wow we had a ball."

"Can I take your cattle to Kansas next year?"

"You bet. How about two thousand head? That would clean up my range."

"I can do that. Would you sell it all to me—all this, lock, stock, and barrel—and go live out your life with some pretty *señorita* and one of those drinks with lime in it?"

"Just what would you pay for it all?" He was laughing at Long's offer like he was buying a broke down cart.

"How many cows do you have in your tally book?"

"Nine hundred and forty."

"Heifers?"

"One twenty, and two thousand big steers ready to go this year."

"Four sections of land?"

"Yes."

"One hundred thousand dollars. Half cash now and five thousand a year until paid."

"What do I need to do?"

"Sign the papers. We also want to verify the cattle number."

"My boys and I will show you. Why I couldn't spend that much money in my lifetime."

"You two want some lunch?" Jan came over and asked them.

"Yes. Oscar just sold us his ranch and cattle."

"Well what will you do, sir?"

"Ma'am, you really want to know?" Oscar held a big grin.

"Sure."

"Go to Mexico and dance my life away instead of drying up and dying on this cactus patch."

She laughed and hugged his shoulder. "That sounds like a great way to leave this world. This is a nice ranch."

"Wish my wife had thought so. She left me twenty years ago."

"I would have liked it. The big spring is wonderful. Does it always run that strong?" Jan said to him.

"Yes. That is why I had to claim this place originally."

She nodded and they went in to lunch. "I hope you find happiness and have fun."

Aside, she asked Long what they would do next.

"Go back, get Harp and men to count his cattle. I believe they're here but we need to check."

"It is a nice ranch setup."

He agreed but said nothing else. First, it was over a day's long ride from headquarters. Second, he liked the country up there better and as an owner he would need to be closer to headquarters. He'd find her a place she liked. They had not even looked for one seriously. He'd work it out.

Johnny laughed, shaking his head. "You bought the place lock, stock, and barrel."

"And cattle, horses, and the coyotes as well."

"Wow. Who will be the foreman here?"

"I guess Harp and I will need to pick one."

"Put my hat in that barrel. I'm like Chaw . . . if I had a foreman job and salary I could find myself a wife."

Jan smiled, leaning on her man's shoulder. "Funny how a good secure job makes you eligible, huh?"

"Aw, Jan, you either have to own a working ranch or have a real job to afford one."

She agreed and they went to eat the supper that

she had ready for them. A nice tablecloth was on her table and as Anthony sat, he tucked the cloth napkin in his shirt like a tie and everyone laughed. She filled their tin coffee cups and told them to eat.

Anthony softly asked what they were eating.

"Quail," Long said.

"How did she catch them?" Anthony asked.

"She shot them," Johnny said, and passed him the potatoes.

"With a pistol?" he whispered.

"Shotgun," Johnny said. "Eat. They're good."

One bite taken and Anthony agreed with a smile. "Good. I never ate them before."

Later in their bedroll, Long said, "I guess Anthony liked your quail?"

She laughed. "He ate two of them."

In the morning Long met again with Oscar about the ranch transfer.

"I don't doubt your count, but I feel we must verify it. That would be what my father would call good business practice, and this is a large undertaking."

"You know, God bless them, but I have no next of kin alive I know anything about and I'd sure be angry if any showed up claiming they had a piece of the ranch coming or any part of my business. So I want to include my will in this deal. If I should go to heaven or hell, wherever, then you two won't owe a dime and the ranch is yours."

"If that is what you want to do, Oscar, we'd have no objection."

"I slept on that last night and it suits me. You boys are young and working hard. Why everyone knows you two weren't even dry behind your ears yet and you two took those cattle to Sedalia almost through Yankee lines and brought a widow back her share. Those were some real bleak days in Texas. We'd lost a damn war over secession that we had written in our agreement to join the U.S. I wasn't sure we wouldn't dry up like a cow pie and eventually all blow away. And two big old boys showed everyone there was another way to do things. If I'd had a son could've done that, I'd busted all my buttons over it swelling up with pride when the words came down to me that the boys made it and are coming home with money."

"Aw, Oscar, we did what we had to do."

"Well Texas may never thank you, but I am damn proud you will have this ranch and everything I have, some day."

"We're proud to be the new owners. A week of us counting cows and cattle, and a lawyer will have the papers written up. If you want the deed and your will separate but still in the paperwork, I am certain they can do that, or add it as part of the deed."

"Do that and I won't ever lose another night's

sleep about who heirs this place and where my savings go to."

Long sent for Harp and a counting crew. He had Jan write a letter to his brother explaining all about the deal and with them being Oscar's heirs. How, now, he felt they needed to make a count of the cattle as a part of the business portion of the deal.

He knew when he re-read it, the agreement sounded well founded in business principles and Harp would be tickled. There was some pride in it for him making the deal—obviously he had as much business-savvy as his brother. And it didn't hurt to have a wife who could write fancy, either. He suggested Harp get their lawyer busy drawing up the contract so it could be signed and to have Beatles's ownership inspected by a land expert.

"Beautiful job. Oscar would approve it. Johnny can go find Harp and give him your neat letter, then have him send us lots of help to get through with the cattle counting and on with the purchase."

"Sounds great to me."

"You sound tired. You okay?" he asked her.

She whispered and then seeing they were alone, she repeated, "I am fine. But I may be pregnant."

"Really?"

She shook her head at him. "Hard as we've been trying I should be."

Then she jumped up, hugged him, and they

danced around the ranch house's living room to celebrate.

He stopped and she swept her hair back. "If you are, when?"

"Eight months—September, maybe."

"I should be home from Kansas by then."

"I hope so. But I am a big girl. Kate will help me and your mom—I'll be fine."

"I know but I hate I won't be there to help you."

"I am fine." She bent over, took the letter, and folded the two pages. "It's getting late. Better go find Johnny and get him to deliver it to Harp."

He kissed her to thank her and went off to find Johnny. That was easy; Johnny had his horse saddled and was ready to ride. He secured the letter in his saddlebags and said to Long, "I'll be back with lots of help in two days."

"Just be careful. I want you alive to run a ranch someday."

"I will be and I'm ready to do that job."

"I believe you are. May God ride with you, *mi amigo*."

Anthony smiled, getting up from his seat on the small keg. "He would make a good one, too. When we were out checking on the cattle at that other ranch, he saw things I didn't see, but I am learning from him, too."

"Good. He may need a *segundo*."

"Me?" Anthony pointed at his chest.

"You two might make a good pair."

"Put me down for that. I would love to do that."

"We'll see, Anthony. We'll see how things go."

"*Gracias*. I plan to reset the front shoes on your horse today. Johnny noticed them. I'll do that. You have any other plans for me around here?"

"Not for two days and then we'll have all the work we want counting cattle."

His man laughed. "Plenty of that to do."

The north wind was growing colder. A sure sign they'd have five–six days of cooler weather—no clouds in sight. While it seldom snowed this far south it could blow in some freezing weather.

Jan had a fire in the fireplace and it felt good. He stood at the hearth and warmed his front side to the radiant heat from the split oak wood blazing away.

Could he ever stand to become a leisure rancher instead of having days when he felt he needed to be doing something rather than lounging around like this one? Such non-activity made him antsy as ever, not working, but until Harp and the men arrived, there was not much he could do. So he went in the kitchen where she was making pies from dried apples and raisins.

He looked out the kitchen window. The strong wind was moving any dust it could find.

"You like pie, right?"

"Love it."

"Where did Oscar go today?"

"With one of the boys that works for him. Mica

found a spring stopped up. They were going to check on it." She put two pies in the oven. When she straightened she frowned. "Do I hear horses?"

"Yes." He went and put on his gun belt that was hanging on the hat rack by the front door. Bent over to look out the living room window, he could see a half dozen riders coming hard.

They drew up in a line fifty feet from the front porch. None he recognized right off.

"Trouble?" she seriously asked, drying her hands.

"I don't know what they want."

"You don't have to go out there."

"But I do." He shrugged on his jumper.

CHAPTER 11

"Why look who we found, boys. If it ain't one of them land-grabbing buzzards from Kerrville. The Indian brother."

"State your business or get the hell off this ranch," Long said, coming out on the porch and closing the front door behind himself.

"Well, O'Malley, you don't own this place yet, so you can't order me anywhere." The big man was rocking his large Mexican wooden saddle horn.

"Well I'm buying this place. So I have some say-so in who stops here."

"Boys, we've done come too late to tell the old man not to sell it to them land grabbers."

They nodded their heads and moaned like they were hurting.

"Now leave."

A Winchester action clacked. The horse-mounted men caught their reins and drew them up.

"You don't scare me."

"You should be scared, because my men have orders to shoot you first. Ready to die? Just what in the hell are you here for anyway? To threaten us? Well load up and go home and stay there, because we will shoot you on sight if you intend to trespass and are intent on threatening us."

"We will have lawyers in Texas court that will bar your taking this rangeland from the rightful users."

"Well do that in Austin. The sale was legally made and we own it. Period. If I report that you are threatening me on my own land, the state police and black soldiers will be at your house shortly to take you to that prison camp they have ready for you."

"You're talking big here. You won't be doing that when our lawyers have you evicted. Let's go, men. He will see who this land belongs to when the Texas Supreme Court tells him to go packing."

"Wait. My name is Long O'Malley. I didn't catch yours?"

"Albert Newman. Why?"

"Albert, if you ever come back and threaten me or my men again I'm going to kill you, and I want your mother to know you're dead so she don't pine over your being missing."

"Ha."

"You won't think that when I get through with you. You have till the count of five and my men start shooting. One . . . two . . ."

The open window beside the door showed a black shotgun barrel sticking out from between the curtains. He hoped she wouldn't use it until they were far enough away to only sting them or their horses. The three of them would be hard pressed to fight them. This would not happen again. He'd have a force to back whoever was here until this was all settled . . .

They left, and Long eased down some.

Late afternoon Oscar and his men rode in and Jan had supper ready for all of them.

"How was your day?" Oscar asked, straining his back against the hands on his hips.

"We had company. Albert Newman and some hired guns came by to tell us they are challenging Harp's land deal in court. Told us that the Supreme Court of Texas will trash our purchase when his lawyers get us in court."

Oscar frowned at him. "Can they really do that?"

Long shook his head. "Texas sold us that land to pay some bills they did not have money for. The government didn't have the money to do it."

Jan went by with some food on a tray and asked Oscar if his back was hurting him.

"Oh, some."

"If you can stand a massage I can loosen it," she said.

"I can stand a lot. When you get time I'd appreciate it."

"Eat your supper while it is hot. I can fix your back so you can sleep."

"Thanks."

"She can do it, too," Long told him when they sat down.

"I figured she can. They threaten you?" Oscar asked.

"Some. Anthony had his rifle and she had her shotgun; I wore my gun."

"How many were there?"

Anthony said, "Nine counting him."

"Oh, he had plenty of help."

Long nodded. "They left after the threat he gave me."

Her eyes like slits, Jan said, "Oscar, I wanted to fill his backside with my birdshot."

They all laughed at her words.

"As well as you shoot quail, you'd have him standing in the saddle to ride his horse home."

His ranch hands laughed over that, too.

"They weren't sure how many men I had or we'd had our hands full with that many gun hands. Anthony cracked his Winchester open and shut it. They weren't sure how many more were coming with him."

"You know this man?" Oscar asked.

"No. But I could see he's tough and those men were not kids. We will need more guards down here until things settle down."

"Legally can they do anything?" Oscar asked again.

Long chuckled about the notion. "No. Texas spent that money."

"Who do you think hired him?"

"That's a good question. I doubt even all the landowners inside the area could afford his services. I think someone wants this ranch and wants the O'Malley brothers off it and will try anything to get it done including hiring Albert Newman. I think they heard about our state land purchase too late to stop our man and Harp from closing the deal down there and now are trying to run us off or have a court intervene."

"It won't mess up our deal will it?" the older man asked.

"No. Nor will his shouting in court. They have no real claim."

Oscar smiled. "I am going to enjoy being retired. Thanks."

"I sure hope so. If you want to live here we can fix that for you at no cost to do that."

"I am pleased. I know how short Texans are on money, and it won't get any better fast, either. You two have done many things right and will continue to build on your ranch."

Long agreed and hugged Jan's waist as she came to stand by him. "I told him he could live here if he wanted to live here after the sale."

"Why not?"

"There is no reason for him not to."

"I will get your back feeling better after you eat," she promised the older man.

"I'll be ready, Jan."

Before dawn, Harp arrived and woke Long up. Jan joined them in the lighted kitchen and made coffee while they talked things over.

Long explained how he settled the ranch buyout from Oscar Beatles, and Harper agreed that was super. Then Long told him about Albert Newman and his hired hands. How Newman said he had lawyers to void the sale in court and get the land back for the state.

"I will have our real estate man immediately contact the lawyers in Austin who did this. They are a top law firm. I really checked them out because we'd be dealing with a carpet-bag government and I trust the men who recommended them, though they are outside government because of federal rules. We will have this all checked out. But I am satisfied that everything is good. Who was this Newman?"

"I think he's the chief hired gun and has eight hired gun men to back him. He says he works for landowners around here, but none of them have that kind of money. I think someone rich came along after you made the land deal and closed it, that he wants it for himself."

"Wonder who that could be?" Harp shook his head. "But I don't doubt it. Money is flowing down there to get things done. Our purchase was all done in a very open and legal way."

"Newman said his lawyers would get it set aside."

Harp shook his head. "No way. There are lots of shady deals going on. We were not involved in any. The government needed that money and badly."

Long lowered his voice. "I told Oscar he could live here if he wants to, after he sells to us."

"Why sure. I'll inform our agent and the lawyer in town writing the deed, mortgage, and the will of his desires. I can arrange a large down payment if he needs it."

"Tomorrow, with armed guards, take him into town and get it all arranged and settled. We will have to protect all our operations. This guy intends to bust up our ranch for his boss, and he won't care who gets hurt or killed."

Eye to eye, Harp agreed. "But we won't stand for it. We've fought Comanche. He wouldn't make a wart on a Comanche's ass." Then Harp chuckled and shook his head at Jan. "That's pretty raw for me to say with you around."

She shook her head. "No, that S-O-B was in the yard out there and I had my twenty-gauge pointed right at him."

"I'm sorry he put you through that."

"No, don't be sorry about anything. We are family and families stick together regardless if they are men or women. He isn't getting anything we own."

"Thanks, Jan."

"Don't ever tiptoe around me. I am a big old girl and I'm ready to fight."

Long winked at his wife, then told Harp, "You better get a few hours' sleep, Harp. If you really want, I can take him into town, but you know all about the deal to do it legal. I'd prefer to stay here."

"You may need to send word to the others that we may be under attack," Harp said, shaking his head. "I'll take him to town with some guards. The men for the cattle count will be here before I leave tomorrow."

Jan gave Harp some blankets and told him he could sleep in the second bedroom upstairs.

He thanked her and went upstairs to catch some sleep.

After they went back to their bed she said, "Harp sounds sure enough about the title."

"Oh, I am sure it is good, but no telling what they will do to try to stop us. Newman hadn't been out here long enough to know how few hands we had to support us today or he'd pushed his hand harder, but it saved us and worked this time. We will go armed and ready from here on."

He kissed her and they went back to sleep.

In the morning, while eating breakfast with Oscar and the others, Long felt hungover. He told

Oscar that Harp came the night before and would soon be up.

"I have never met him," Oscar said.

"He's just another O'Malley." They both laughed. "Except he has no Cherokee in him."

"Like I said, I heard lots about the good things you two have done for many ranchers delivering cattle. No one could believe that two boys drove that first cattle herd clear to Missouri before the war even ended. I know I was amazed when I first heard that you two'd done it. I knew you two weren't boys . . . you had met some strong forces and won, and that's why I want to leave it all to both of you."

"Thanks, Oscar. We're going to show Newman and his bunch how damn tough we can be about owning this ranch."

"Him and his bunch wouldn't have given wooden nickels for my ranch two years ago. You boys cut a trail everyone is now taking, and suddenly cattle have a market."

"We aren't the only ones made a run, but yes, it changed lots of things."

"Are you and Jan going to live down here?"

"I am going to be honest. We have a huge outfit, the Diamond Ranch, to run for two older women closer to Kerrville and besides, we have many other ranches. I think we need to live closer to Kerrville because of that. But hey come by, put your boots up, and stay with us there wherever we land. We will always have a room for you."

"I'll consider it. I think your wife is an angel for all the things she does. If I were forty years younger I'd steal her from you. She fixed my back and it hasn't felt this good in years."

They both laughed.

"I bet you'd try."

"Yes, I'd definitely steal her." A mischievous smile spread over the old man's face, and Long decided that Oscar might really have tried back then. He really liked the old man. He only wished they had less trouble over the purchase of his ranch. He had to figure a way to get rid of that damn Newman once and for all. Whatever it required to do that, he'd get it done.

"What are you working on so hard this morning?" Jan asked, bringing him some fresh coffee. "I can tell when you're deep thinking."

He pushed his chair back and hugged her to him. "This whole Newman business needs to be stopped."

"It sure does. But don't worry. My husband's working on it. I know him and he'll figure it out."

"I wish I was as confident of my own skills as that."

She hugged his head. "You will."

CHAPTER 12

The weak winter morning sun shone through the dusty cedars and live oaks, and Long, Johnny, and Anthony were out searching for any sign that Newman and his bunch might be located around the ranch. Oscar said Newman's bunch didn't go south from the ranch, because he and his two men had been that way checking cattle and never saw them.

Harp and two guards had taken Oscar in a buckboard to Kerrville to arrange the paperwork. Harp and Long had decided that Oscar had no reason to lie about the cattle numbers, so the six men that came were sent out in threes, with each of Oscar's men, to check north and west for Newman's camp, if there was one. And they were instructed that when they found it, go back to the main headquarters, get everyone together, and roust them out.

Long's newest Comanche horse had a head full of notions that morning, and he bucked in the chilly air. After being laughed at by his own two men for stopping the bucking, they set out in another direction to find traces of Newman and his enforcers.

By mid-day with no sign of them, they decided

they'd not set up anywhere east of the ranch headquarters and started back.

"Where did he go?" Johnny asked.

"I have no idea. But he has a camp someplace. I'll put out word that I'll pay to know the place they stay, and we'll find some answers."

His men agreed and they rode back. When they arrived, they saw the others were back, too.

"No sign of them?" he asked some of the men unsaddling.

"We didn't find hide nor hair of them," Andy Davis said. "The other teams didn't, either, so they have to be holed up elsewhere."

"Tomorrow all of you head back to your assigned ranches. Harp and Oscar will be back. I'm leaving Johnny and Anthony here with his two men Rico and Donnie. Go in twos. Johnny is in charge here, and until we get things settled everyone watch their back. I have no idea what they will try, but I bet they've got some plans to stop our ranching operations."

Harp and Oscar plus their two guards were back the next day. Jan had her few things packed, but the decision was made to go back home in the morning instead.

Long had told Donnie and Rico they had jobs if they wanted to stay. The two agreed to stay and help Johnny learn all about the ranch's features— water and anything else.

Long and Johnny talked at length about Johnny

making diary entries about things he found needed attention, so when he or Harp came down they could go over them. He was also to make a list of real needs, like how many more hands he might require.

"Also look for land close by that could be farmed. Oscar had no desire to farm, but for a ranch to be self-sufficient it needs a farming operation in my opinion."

"I savvy that," Johnny said. "Did he say if his plans were to live here?"

"He's welcome. The boys, I bet, can find a cook and housekeeper for you. Find one and hire her. I'll leave you some money for small expenses and set up a store account in Kerrville for the ranch. Harp or I will check on you. Need help, send word. Just be careful . . . Newman may do anything to stop us. I don't want our people hurt or property destroyed."

"What else?"

"We'll need a count of all the two-year-old steers we can send to Abilene in March."

"I can do all that, Long, but you be careful, too. We sure need you and Harp safe."

"We will."

Harp and Long had a long visit in the kitchen, heated by the cooking range while Jan was making more pies.

"I asked a lot about this Newman in town. Not much is known about him or who he represents.

The lawyer, Mr. Lacey, wired our contacts in Austin and told them what Newman said, and asked for more information. So we have things moving."

"They have not been anywhere else threatening our people?"

"Not that I learned, but I was really busy getting all the papers signed and done with Oscar. I didn't even get to see my wife or son. It was late but I'll get to her tomorrow. She's fine and so is he."

"Johnny will run this ranch. Oscar's two boys will stay on and Anthony as well. Johnny will need more men to back him and will need more things, but I have him keeping some lists of things he sees he needs as he gets to know the place. I told him to look for future farmland, too."

"I think you did a great job with buying this place. You and I need to go look real close at the Diamond Ranch. I am certain it needs things that you and I will see when we examine it closer."

Long sipped some hot coffee and then said, over the cup's rim, "First time I saw that Diamond Ranch I must have been fourteen. Mom had a book with a dust cover on it. I can't recall the title but it had a painting of a plantation home on it. I swear it looked just like that big house."

"Oh, it's still that fancy a place. I heard one

guy who fought in the South say the Union Army burned lots of them in the war."

Long agreed. "You and I were damn lucky that they needed rangers out here or we'd been in those trenches and watched fine homes burned down."

"I know you are right. The rangers knew they needed to keep the defenses up on the Comanche side, too."

"Not having them now damn sure shows."

"Nothing we can do but be sure not to rile them, or they'll send black soldiers down here to restore peace."

"I agree . . . I sure don't want them. Jan and I still have more folks to see who are inside our boundaries, but let's put it on hold. I doubt many of them are in with the Newman bunch. I bet it is someone wants all of our land, period."

"It would look that way to me. And while I expect more problems, the battle may be fought in Austin in the courts between lawyers."

"I won't be much help there." Long laughed. No need in him even going there; Harp was the talker for that end of the business.

"You will need a new team anyway. Let's go back and we can look at the Diamond and be certain it is going well. Meanwhile, hopefully, our lawyers in Austin can learn what Newman's outfit is trying to do."

Long agreed. So with things set at Oscar's

ranch, they left, Long driving the buckboard with Jan on the spring seat and Harp riding his horse and leading hers.

They made a flying trip back to Kerrville, and she shopped for some things while the menfolk had a draft beer in the Longhorn Saloon.

Near empty, except for the lunch crowd at the lunch counter, Harold Hellmann, the head bartender, took a seat with them and when asked said he knew nothing about Newman.

Harp asked him to put his ears to the situation and told him part of the threat he'd given Long.

"Can they do that? Void the sale in court?"

"We aren't lawyers," Long said. "If it was cow or Comanche business we could tell you, but this land business is all new and we have good lawyers on our side."

"I hear anything I'll send word. You two worked your backsides off driving cattle to hell and back. These worthless dealers wanting your ranch need strung up."

Harp agreed. "But we want it done right and not be involved in some range war."

"But," Long said. "They start one they'll think they have a wild bobcat by the tail."

"And you'll have lots of support. Why, your cattle drives have helped lots of folks around here I can tell you."

They both thanked him and left to meet Jan at the buckboard.

On the sunny winter afternoon, Harp asked him, "You ever regret marrying her?"

"No. She's pretty much my style. She's a tomboy and not afraid to be one. I'm pleased. She's generous, loving, and has concerns that impress me. We kind of fell together. She really wasn't over her husband being killed, but, like your wife was when you found her, she had to realize he couldn't help her, either."

"I've sure never regretted a day since I found Katy. I'm glad you're that happy," Harp said.

"She must have found all she came after . . . she's waiting on the porch," Long said.

"Hey, partner, we are growing aren't we?"

"Between the Diamond Ranch and all this new range we are definitely in the driver's seat to build a great ranch. Harp, I knew we could do it but I didn't expect it for twenty more years. You know two years ago at this time we faced a fifteen-dollar-a-month job driving cattle to Missouri through Yankee lines."

"We'd done it, too."

"Hell, yes."

"What for?" Jan asked, smiling and joining them.

"Oh, two years ago we were going to cowboy for the captain for fifteen dollars a month taking some steers around union troops and get them to the railhead at Sedalia."

She shook her head. "You two have come a

long ways since then. I'm proud to be a part of this train, full steam ahead."

"Right on." He lifted her up on the buckboard and then he went around to climb on and unwrap the lines.

She hugged his arm. "Learn anything?"

"Not really."

"Betty Haycox who owns the Spearhead Ranch may know all about your man."

After he flecked the team to start, Long frowned at her. "What does that mean?"

"I overheard two women in the mercantile talking about Newman staying with her."

"An affair?"

She laughed. "I imagine so."

When they were out of the town and on the road homebound with some fenced fields on both sides, he told Harp to stop.

Harp blinked at him, then reined his horse back to the buckboard. "Is something wrong?"

"Something you need to know. You know Betty Haycox?"

"Sure, she's a widow woman owns the Spearhead Ranch. What about her?"

"Jan overheard two women in the store who were talking about Newman staying with her."

"I'll be damned. Never thought about her hiding him. Thanks, Jan. That may answer more questions I have about him." Harp settled his anxious horse.

Long said, "We need to talk to some loose-tongued men that work for her."

"I bet this Saturday night we learn all about his stay out there. Thanks again, Jan."

Long and his wife were moving again. The sun was warm on the side that shone on him. His back was warm but he buttoned up his jumper. His chest felt cool. What was this troublemaker doing with the forty-year-old widow of Bracket Haycox? He'd only been in the grave a short while when she had an affair with her ranch foreman Russell Macomb, but a few months later she fired him in a violent scandal that the sheriff had to settle. But not before more details were spelled out about her affairs with another ranch hand when Macomb was gone on business.

They needed to get a few Spearhead cowboys drunk this weekend and learn all about what was going on with him. Where did he park his hired guns . . . and find that camp and send those guys packing. Lots to do. Long made the good team of buckskins go faster. Somehow they needed to end this threat Newman tried to put on them.

Things were busy at the ranch when they returned. Harp set up the deal to get the Haycox hands drunk with three of their ranch hands on Saturday night. His mother, Easter, Harp's wife, Katy, and Jan were holding a conference in the kitchen when Long walked in.

"Learn anything in town?" Easter asked.

"Jan must have told you our man is staying out at the Spearhead Ranch."

Easter shook her head. "That poor girl lost her head when her husband died."

"No, Mother, she's had those problems long before he passed away. But they kept it covered up. I simply wonder how those two found each other."

"No idea who he works for?"

"None. No one in town knows much about him but the local women gossips."

They laughed.

"Have you seen your dad?" his mother asked.

"No, is he missing?"

"He and Ira went on a mule-trading trip. Said they'd be back but I guess they haven't arrived."

"Dad's back," Harp said, coming in the house. "They bought four draft mules to pull the chuck wagons; that's what they call them now."

Reg came into the kitchen in his wheelchair. Smiling, he spoke to everyone. "We have the whole crew here tonight I see."

"Hiram will be here shortly then," Easter said. "Everyone sit down."

The women and a Mexican kitchen girl brought out the food. A large sliced prime rib, canned green beans, and *frijoles* with freshly baked sliced bread and butter. There was hot coffee to drink and lots of talking was going on when Hiram joined them.

"Did you find some good mules?" Harp asked his dad.

Passing the meat tray on, Hiram nodded. "Two good teams. Ira and I didn't expect to find two teams that sound and really well broke. They cost a hundred a team, which was a bargain. Closer to herd takeoff time I'd bet they'd cost five hundred apiece. Real good mules are scarce."

"Why, Hiram, people won't pay that for mules."

"Easter, they would if they needed them bad enough. People have lost their minds over this cattle-driving business. I know it is financial salvation for Texas, but there is still reasonable ways to do it."

"How are we doing on getting herds ready?" Long asked.

Harp nodded. "That is why we needed more mules. There are four thousand head at the Diamond Ranch. We have that many of our own now and signed up is near a herd and a half already."

"Six herds?" Long asked, a little awed by their success. "No wonder you bought mules."

"And more ranchland," Harp added.

"This is going to take a lot of hands."

"We will have to hire them now to have any. People who hire them only for the drive won't get very high-quality drovers. We need several good hardworking men and put them on the payroll now."

"How will you do that?"

"Katy and I are going to San Antonio next week and see how many we can hire there. We did good finding them there in times past. Our black cowboys are out hiring some more good hands. They know the good ones from the sorry ones better than I do."

"I sent Hoot and his wife to Mexico. He thinks he can get some tough *vaqueros* out of there. He knows lots of folks on the border and I expect him to find us several hands down there."

"Harp and I think that the cattle market will be saturated and we may only receive around sixty dollars a head this year," Reg, the accountant, said.

"He and I have been following the market close," Harp said. "There are lots of predictions about a lower market. Reg has looked at contracting some sales ahead if we can beat that price."

"Does that mean we sell them before we leave here?"

"If they want to pay a reasonable price, yes. But we get a deposit in the bank so that even if they don't want them we still collect."

Long shook his head at all the complications showing up. "Jan and I will continue to try and settle with landlocked ranchers."

"So far you two have done great. I think Oscar's sale will bring others forward," Harp said.

"There will always be holdouts. But the fear of being fenced in will also help us convince more to take our offer."

"Right. We knew it wouldn't be easy. Shortly we need to start road branding those selling cattle at the Diamond Ranch."

"These new hands going to do that, too?"

"Doug has some day workers coming, and with his own help he thinks he can handle it, but I want him to have plenty of assistance. That is no small job," Harp said.

"Don't it amaze you two any at all?" Hiram asked, shaking his head over the matter.

"How's that, Dad?"

"Well, Harp, two years ago there were only eight hundred steers to go north. And today twelve thousand head busting at the gate to get up there in six herds. Laddies, I can't believe you two have done this much business."

"We've thought about it, Dad," Long said. "In fact we've thought about it a lot." He shook his head—he even recalled the night that Harp fired the cook. That was a long ways back but was what started it all.

CHAPTER 13

Dressing in the morning by the bedroom lamp's light because the sun wasn't up that early, Long asked Jan, "You sleep all right last night?"

"Fair. I am still dazzled by the numbers you all talked about last night."

"It is big business. We are deeply emerged in it. I don't know how but cattle prices could fall away. The economy of this country has not came back to pre-war standards. Some say it is the war debt, others say it is those high-risk takers plunging into things. But things flow in life like a river; it may flood and you have to float or go dry and then you haul water."

"I understand that. Now if I am not with child when the time comes, can I go north with you?"

"A woman in an all man camp is kind of—hell, yes. I wasn't even thinking. It can be dangerous but I'd love to have you along."

They hugged and kissed. Good, they wouldn't be separated for months. She'd spoiled him enough that he knew he'd really miss having her.

At breakfast, Harp said he needed to do some banking business in town that their mom had pointed out needed doing. Harp suggested that Long and Jan go over to the Diamond and visit the "girls."

"We can do that and I can talk to Doug about his plans for the road branding. I expect he has it all lined out, but I want to make sure all the bows are tied on the deal. Take someone with you to town today."

Harp made a face, then agreed.

"There is way too much riding on both of us not to have a guard along. Shame but it isn't the simple two O'Malley brothers from Texas anymore."

Harp agreed.

Long drove Jan in the buckboard with two men along on horseback.

When they drove up to the mansion, Jan elbowed him. "I still would love to live here."

"Someday you and Katy can draw for high card to who gets to live here."

The women and their butler met them at the door all excited, and he knew he was in for listening to lots of chatter and tea. But someday all this would be his and his brother's ranch if they managed to hold on.

After lunch he drove her home. Jan was in a flitter. The girls had promised her, when she got her own house, they had a set of gold-rimmed French dishes and crystal glasses to stock her cabinets with.

"Sounds wonderful," he said, wheeling the horses up his family's drive at the H Bar H.

"Can you imagine me serving a dinner on those plates?"

"No. But if it tickles you it would tickle me."

She fake-pounded his arm. "There you go thinking I am not good enough."

"You are plenty good enough the way you are, and you know it."

"I don't doubt you one bit. But you know a farm girl like me can dream can't she?"

He chuckled. "You aren't hardly one of those now."

"What are your plans for tomorrow?"

"Get on horseback and check things here and up at the CHX place. I just want to see how things are going."

She nodded her head. "I'll stay home and help your mom."

"Good. Thanks for today. Those girls can get to be an earful after a while. You with them let me check that Doug is doing a good job."

She hugged his arm and went into the house. He went by and told Red he needed two men to ride with him in the morning, while he checked some other things out.

"Things going to suit you?" Red asked.

"Yes, I just want to check on things."

"We have lots of cattle to road brand this year."

"We have lots of cattle to ship this year, too."

"Guess that's how we pay the help huh?"

"Yes, it is. Thanks. Those boys did well today."

"I am just glad you didn't need them."

"Things are pretty edgy. Maybe we can learn something from Harp's plan this weekend."

Red agreed and Long went on up to the house.

Harp was back and explained everything at the bank was doing fine. They needed to shift some money to different accounts. The bank was holding Oscar's money in a reserve account that had Harp's name on it, too, in case something happened to him.

He guessed the old man had no plans for it at the present time.

"I'll be riding, with two men, for the next few days to look over things and make sure it's all going right," Long said.

"I need to look harder at the consigned cattle portion tomorrow and be certain how many more we can accept."

"Nice problem to have."

Harp agreed.

In the cool morning, Long found a layer of thin frost in places as the sun peeped up. His Comanche horse bucked hard when he stepped aboard him. Jake and Erve laughed as they accompanied him out from under the gate cross bar.

They were up on Fin Creek when Erve noted several horse tracks crossing the open meadow from east to west.

"Take a look here. Shod horses have crossed

there. Reckon they are the ones that rode with Newman?"

"Let's check it out," Long said.

They crossed the ridge and found some buzzards eating on a fresh large calf carcass. Harp reined up and searched the country. He knew from the evidence, even at the distance, someone had a milk-fat, four-hundred-pound calf. That meant they shot it and took the hindquarters and peeled off the back strap, leaving the rest to the buzzards to feast on.

"Pretty damn fresh," Erve said as he dismounted, sending some of the squawking birds of carrion bounding away and others flying off. "It has our brand on it."

Jake rode his horse around looking for any tracks leaving. Long wanted the guilty to pay for their deed. Sitting back in the saddle he squeezed the horn with one hand—he hated a damn thief worse than most anything.

His inspection over, Erve mounted up. "Follow them?"

"Damn right. Where did they go?" Long asked Jake.

"On west I guess. The tracks go that way."

"Let's find them. That is flat out cattle rustling in my book, and they need to pay for it."

"Damn right," Erve agreed, and whipped his horse to make him run.

Jake had the lead, and Long's powerful

Comanche pony was catching him fast as they tore over the rise headed west. The tracks headed that way, and they rode hard until a hint of smoke struck Long's nose and he told them to halt.

They looked around the open areas between the cedars and saw nothing. His anxious horse circled under him and was breathing hard.

"They're south of us. Go slow. We don't want them to know we're coming," he said under his breath.

Both agreed and checked the load in their Colts, holstered them again, and moved forward at a slower pace. Long felt certain the campfire was just over the rise. They hitched their horses, took their rifles out of scabbards, and spread apart to climb the hill.

Before they reached the top, Long took off his hat and set it on the ground and, carefully in some grass and weeds, crawled up to look at what the next space held. He saw the suspects' unsaddled horses first—grazing in the open. Then he spotted the campfire and the meat cooking on a grill. They were lying around resting. He counted five men but there were six horses. If this was some of Newman's bunch, maybe they should wait. No. This was all of them, he felt certain.

"Erve, work west and come in from that direction. Jake, you go east. There is enough cover there, too. When you two are in place, I'll shoot down into the midst of them. Then I'll shout 'you're covered,' and if they go for their guns, Jake, you shoot them."

"I can do that," Jake said, and headed out. Erve nodded and left. Both had good Winchesters. He waited to give them plenty of time to get in place.

Satisfied they should be there, he rose and fired a rifle round into the camp close to the cook's feet. "Hands up, all of you. We have you surrounded."

"The hell you say," one of them replied, and whipped out his pistol to shoot at Long.

Two rifle shots spun him around. One came from each side and the fight was over before he struck the ground.

Long set out downhill for the camp on his boot heels. His men moved in from both sides and had the rustlers facedown on the ground. Erve tied their hands behind their backs and Jake held the rifle on them.

"Where's Newman at today?" Long asked.

"Who?"

"Come on. Two days ago you rode onto my new ranch with him and demanded we leave. Now you rustled one of my cattle and are planning to eat it."

"We never—"

"We tracked you here."

"What're you going to do with us?"

"Have a trial and hang you like we do all rustlers."

"You don't have the authority to do that."

"Oh, yeah we do. Now tell me what Newman's plans are."

"He said to meet him Friday at Willow Crossing."

"Shut up, kid—he's going to hang us anyway."

Erve gave the talker a hard kick in his gut. Hard enough he grunted and shut up.

"Keep talking, kid," Long said. "What was he going to do from there?"

"Burn you out for starters, he said."

"Who does he work for?"

"I don't know, mister. I just needed work."

Long nodded like he understood. "You simply joined the wrong bunch."

Erve got their names and in pencil wrote them in Long's small herd book, including the dead man's. Meanwhile Jake was busy making nooses from the men's ropes and their own lariats.

"Going to have enough rope?" Long asked, using their cook's long fork to fetch a strip of back strap off the grill to eat.

"It ain't a tall tree. I think so."

"Who does the extra horse belong to?" Erve asked, returning.

"Henson was off taking a shit." The wise-mouth outlaw lying on his belly laughed. "He got away."

The meat tasted good. It drew the saliva into his mouth. They'd get him. There were six gun sets in camp. The escapee didn't have a gun or a horse.

Horses were saddled and three were fitted with nooses, then each outlaw was set on a horse. Erve rode in and knotted the ropes on the thick oak limb, then he reset the knots beside their left ear.

When he rode away, Long and Jake sent the horses off with a hurrah and a slap to their hindquarters. Ropes jerked tight, necks snapped under the weight, and they hung limp. Two more were handled the same way under another tree. The horses driven out. One danced on his neck collar but soon he, too, expired. The last one cussed them out until his neck broke in the fall.

"We better catch the horses, take them to one of our ranches, and advertise them as loose horses. If those ponies go home, Newman might decide not to meet them Friday."

"The one rustler that got away is headed south on foot."

"We'll find him," Long said to Jake. "Erve, can you catch the horses?"

"Sure. Go find him. I'll catch you later and bring the horses."

Long spurred the big horse around and they took off. Two ridges over, they spotted a hatless man wildly running down a meadow. Jake shot his pistol at him.

"Hold up," Long said, slid his horse to a halt, got off, pulled out the Winchester, and laid the barrel on the saddle seat. He took aim at the fleeing man's back, and the outlaw went down with his first shot.

"I'll go see that he ain't alive," Jake said, and ran off in the downed man's direction.

Long jammed the rifle back into his scabbard and mounted up. His man was coming back nodding his head. A few less rustlers on their ranchland.

If he was lucky on Friday, Newman would join them in hell.

It was a damn grim day, but at least they hadn't burned the damn ranch down.

In the yard Jan greeted him wearing a shawl on her shoulders to stave off the cold. "You look upset."

"Some."

"What happened?"

"We found six rustlers today. They were eating our beef they'd slow-elked."

"I understand now why you are upset. Learn anything more?"

"One of the rustlers said they were going to meet Newman Friday to go burn Oscar's headquarters to the ground."

"You will meet him then?"

"I plan to."

She stopped and hugged him. "Long, I love you. I am here when you come home. All this will pass."

"I know. I know. They got what they deserved and are gone now. They didn't have to do that—there is other work—"

"Long, you did what you had to do."

"I know I did the right thing. But it still hurts me—inside."

"It always will. I am sorry."

"Don't be. You are the tree I lean on and I love you."

CHAPTER 14

That evening he, Harp, and Hiram all had a quiet discussion about his day. They all agreed it was the way—not always nice, but it solved the threat.

"There are still four more not with them?" Harp asked.

"Three or four. I'll be set up at that crossing to meet and greet him if he doesn't get word his men have gone to the hereafter."

"Hell all we wanted to do was ranch not fight range wars or court cases," Harp said, shaking his head in disgust.

"It goes with the deal, bro. If you get something, then jealous people want it all for themselves."

"I agree, Long."

"It may take me forever to get these insiders settled."

"You are doing better than I imagined we could do. You are getting a high percentage of them selling you their ranch or willing it to us. I never imagined that happening. And Friday you try for the Newman guy, huh?"

"I plan to get him."

To his force he added three more ranch hands. They drifted down to Oscar's in pairs not to draw attention. Wednesday he took Jan in the buckboard and two men went along. They hauled supplies to feed everyone, making it look more like a supply trip than a reinforcement detail.

The men had searched for any sign of Newman's scouts. Nothing showed up. But Long felt they'd come on the run, attack, burn the ranch down, and leave just as fast.

Thursday night two of his men reported two suspicious groups were camped nearby. Four or five men to each camp. Those, plus the men who would ride with Newman would make a formidable force. But his men were well armed with plenty of ammo and should be able to hold them off.

In the early morning, the ranch horses were moved to the last pasture so they didn't get shot up in the crossfire. Each man had a strategic place to defend with ample protection to duck behind. When they were all ready he fretted over not having enough men, but it was too late to do anything about it. He kissed Jan and made her promise to stay down low in the house.

His men and Oscar's made a strong force to defend the ranch. He reminded her to stay down. He didn't need her shot.

The charge came in mid-afternoon. They rode in, pistols blazing, but the raiders quickly reined up, realizing they were in a trap. Through the gun smoke, he saw someone shouting for them to get back. He couldn't tell who that was, and all the rifle fire hurt his ears. Then, with a break in the smoke, he saw two more raiders. He took them out himself.

Silence fell aside from the wounded moaning and the pained dying horses.

Jan rushed out to join Long on the porch. "Are there any alive?"

"I don't think so. Go back inside and make some coffee. The men can sort it out."

"I knew it would be bloody, but are any of our men hurt or wounded?"

"I am going to check. Make us some coffee."

One by one he was joined on the battlefield by the other ranch hands.

"Anyone get hurt?" he asked.

The round of head shakes relieved him.

"Any get away?" Johnny asked, reloading his Colt.

"I don't know. We have us a big mess. Must be ten dead or wounded horses."

One of Oscar's men went after a team to haul the hurt and dead horses away from the house. They began to shoot the suffering animals. The injured horses destroyed, they dragged away the last of the dead animals. Buzzards were already circling overhead.

Then they drug the wounded men aside. Four were dead, the other five shot up and pleading for their lives.

Newman was not among them. That fact made

Long mad. How many had escaped beside him? He had to make a decision. If he took them to town, then the carpetbaggers' state police might investigate the matter, and he didn't need them snooping around.

He still had not decided the raiders' fate.

"What about the shot-up ones?" Johnny asked him.

"I'm undecided."

"Why don't you and her go back to the home ranch and take two men for guards. We can handle them."

"I hate to do that to you, Johnny."

"I don't. They'd not have buried us. This is our war, too. We need these jobs as well. Take her home. I know she's tough, but I want to learn some things from those bastards before they leave here for hell."

"Harness up the team for me. I'll get her."

In the house she ran and hugged him. "Coffee is ready."

"They will need it. We're going home."

"Why?"

"To be sure they have not struck our other ranches."

"You didn't get him, did you?"

"No."

"What will he do to you next?"

"I am going to try and find out. I want you safe back at the ranch. I can't afford to lose you."

"I'm fine."

"And I want you that way. They will have the buckboard hitched. Two men will go with us."

She buried her face in his jumper. "Your brother bought this land legally. What do they want?"

"To try and take it away from us. Get your bag."

She agreed and he loaded her up. The two hands picked to ride back were ready and he told Johnny and Oscar to keep an eye out—they might try to attack them again.

He clucked to the team and they headed swiftly for home. Leaving Johnny and his hands to finish the situation bit at his conscience, but Johnny was right. There was no need to put her through that.

Newman, I will find you and when I do I'm sending you straight to hell. He clucked to the team and then left.

Long past dark in the near-freezing night they reached the home ranch. The boys told him they'd put up the team. He thanked them, and, her under a blanket to keep warm, they ran for the house.

Hiram with a cup in his hand let them inside. "How did it go down there?"

"We met them. But Newman got away."

She spoke up, "It was very bloody, Dad. He brought me back because of it."

Hiram nodded. "There ain't a war ever happened wasn't bloody m' dear."

She hugged him.

"You two are getting in late," his mother said, just joining them.

"We came real fast."

"Did they raid you?"

"Yes. None of our boys were hurt. Newman got away."

"Jan, come in the kitchen. We'll let the men talk."

Harp came downstairs and frowned at his brother. "Everything all right?"

"All the men are. Nine of Newman's men won't be at church this Sunday, but Newman and maybe a few others got away." He dropped his voice. "Johnny excused the two of us. He will interrogate the four wounded and end their breathing."

Harp nodded. "A good man. Glad he sent you both home. You have any ideas on how to stop them?"

"No. But, after today, when the word gets out about his men disappearing, he will have to pay more to get men to back them."

Harp agreed.

"I expected them to shoot things up and ride off, but they charged in to kill us. We met the charge and turned the tables on them."

"Until ye get the real leader of this business,

ye will have troubles. And it ain't Newman. He's just a paid killer, m' lads."

Long smiled. "Aye, Dad's upbringing is starting to show up."

They all laughed.

The women served hot chocolate in cups.

Things settled down, but Long still wanted the demise of Newman along with Jennings who he'd not heard anything on in weeks.

Plans the next morning were laid out to keep getting ready for the large drives they needed to make to Abilene.

"We are going to leave these ranches short on help. Most of our ranch foremen we'll need heading up herds. So we need to hire several more hands to be here until we get back," Harp said.

Long agreed. Six herds on the road would stretch their needs. "Why not use one of the empty pastures at Diamond to start gathering next year's stock going north?"

"No reason I can see. That would eventually save us labor in the end."

"Yes, that would help us be ready for next year."

"We better get busy hiring. In a month we leave for Kansas."

"We have several *vaqueros* coming. Our team of black point riders have already hired twenty experienced boys from San Antonio. I think with them we will have enough trail help."

"I think Hoot and I can hold the ranch together with some more hands," Hiram said.

"Don't get yourself hurt, or him, either. I hope we have those raiders either dead or run off before then," Long said. "But if not, we'll be back as soon as we can."

"Ah surely. We can get that done, him and me," Hiram said.

"Safely," Harp added.

They all three laughed.

Long asked his wife in bed that evening whether she wanted to go or not.

"I am not with child. Sorry. Yes, I can help the cook and I can herd cattle if you need me. I simply would really hate to be apart from you all summer."

"It can be dangerous. I realize you've done lots of cattle driving, but I don't want you hurt."

"I'll be fine. I won't slow you down."

"Plan to go then."

She rolled over and kissed him wildly. "Great."

He thought so, too. Now if his dad and Hoot could hold it together everything would be fine.

He and Jan rode horses over to the Diamond the next day with a hand along with them. Doug was on his last day road branding the Diamond steers to head to Kansas. Lots of dust-making, bawling cattle were being worked through two squeeze chutes to complete the job.

Doug met them, and Jan rode for the house to visit the two sisters while they talked business. Harp told Doug he was needed to take a herd to Kansas and to pick a man to be his replacement while he was gone. Doug agreed and sent word for Poncho Sanchez to come join them.

Poncho was tall for a Mexican. Smiling ear to ear under his *sombrero* when Doug told him that they wanted him in charge of the ranch while he had to go to Kansas with the herd.

"*Gracias*. I am proud to do that for you. I was raised here and I know every inch of this place. It will be secure for you, Doug, when you get back."

Doug clapped his shoulder. "I know it will be. Long and I have been talking. You know there are some men don't like us owning all the land, so be careful. We don't want any one hurt or any part of the ranch destroyed."

"I understand."

"Hiram will be in charge. He will send help if you need some, and you do the same for him," Long said, and shook his hard callused hand.

"*Sí*. I better get the men back to work. They slack off when I am gone." He remounted his anxious horse and rode off.

"Who all are going besides me?"

"You, Chaw, Red, plus three others we've hired away from another outfit."

"Sounds tough enough."

192

"We have lots of riders but most never have been up the trail. It will be exciting."

Doug agreed. "I had plans to marry a girl from town in June. I may marry her before we go north."

"Fine. Let Mom, Kate, and Jan know. They will help you two get it done. The ranch can buy her a wedding dress. Go to it."

Doug shook his hand and thanked him.

First time he'd heard about this engagement. That was the reason he took the Diamond Ranch job—to afford a wife. Well he'd have one now. The girls at home would be pleased to be asked to help.

Long rode on to the big house. He announced their foreman Doug was going to be married and would also be taking one of their herds to Kansas in a few weeks. They celebrated with tea and lemon cake. The sisters approved of Doug's selection of the acting foreman, and everyone bragged on all the house repairs Harp had done for them. Long agreed the place looked much better, repainted and all the small things fixed.

Riding home Jan asked him who the girl was Doug was marrying.

"I have no idea, but he plans to bring her around to meet you three and I said we'd buy her a wedding dress."

"Yes. That will be great. And you said he was taking a herd north."

"I imagine she will stay here."

Jan rode in close and slapped his leg. "I am grateful you are taking me along."

"I'm even more grateful you're going."

They both laughed.

CHAPTER 15

The home ranch had two herds of large steers. Diamond had two, and there were two herds of rancher-consigned cattle. The number one herd was Harp's with Long as the scout. Number two herd was Red's. Number three was Doug's from the Diamond Ranch. Number Four was Chaw's command for Diamond number two. The fifth herd's leader was Jerry Hall, and Wake Collins headed the last herd. The last two men had experience.

"We have two thousand head down at Oscar's we aren't counting," Long said.

Harp slowly nodded. "How do we do that?"

"Divide them by six. That is about three hundred plus head per herd."

"That's it," Harp said. "Thank God. Long, we need to get them all road branded and up here."

They planned to leave the last week in March, each herd two days apart. Long would scout for the first herd and others would scout for each of theirs. He hurried about checking on many things as the crews were being assembled.

Repeated meetings were held and the herd leaders met several times on things they must handle. All of them had past experience and were becoming experienced with the men on

195

their team. Horses were assigned and wranglers were herding them. The two company herds were being held at Hoot's ranch inside some fenced pasture. Diamond Ranch had enough fenced pasture to hold both of their herds.

Number five, Jerry Hall's, was on some state land west of Kerrville. Number six headed by Wake Collins was closer to San Antonio.

The six chuck wagons were on the herd sites. Each outfit had eighty horses and two teams of mules in case one went lame. Most of the remuda horses were not shod, which saved them money, and most of the land to Kansas was not rocky. Several of Long's mounts were shod since he would need them for some hard riding as the front man.

He and Harp talked out how well the spring rain had fallen and the grass under a warmer sun was breaking dormancy. That was essential to the drive—feed for the steers. That and all the other cattle being gathered to go north would make the alleyway crowded going that way, even as vast as the land was.

Two herds mixed meant weeks lost to separate them and risk mixing with more while sorting. The scouts had to be certain they didn't ever let that happen. Long knew many scouts had never done this job before, and those men didn't realize the full responsibility they held. And some herd bosses wanted to be there first,

196

regardless of the losses they could suffer with such small thinking. He'd lectured all the other scouts about every aspect. But once they left, he'd be up front searching the best path and they would need to make their own decisions each day.

Jan worked on his tight back muscles every night, and he slept well in her arms. They married Doug and Antoinette, a cute young girl who was going to stay with Easter while they were on the drive. Days flashed by and he wondered what he had not done right.

Two years earlier at this time he and Harp were fifteen-dollar-a-month drovers if they managed to get that small herd through to the rail head in Missouri. They did that and had been to Kansas successfully the past year. This was the largest one yet, and it was a real long ways to Abilene when he left the ranch. Under the stars he rode in the coolest part of the early morning northeast to pick the place where they would camp that first night.

He had made arrangements with a landowner but still wanted to be certain there were no problems ahead on the first day's route. Jan would come with the chuck wagon. One thing he appreciated about her, she was a hand with a horse and liked herding cattle. Poor girl. She better like all of it because she had many days in the saddle ahead of her. Still he was pleased she was joining them for this drive because they could use her help.

Lots of things ran through his mind. Some special angel rode on his brother's shoulder, and his as well, to get them through both past drives successfully. He drew a deep breath and set his horse off in a trot. He had lots to do.

Mid-morning he was at the site and spoke with the landowner John Delphi, a German immigrant who met him smiling.

"You said you'd be here early. Get down. Gretchen has fresh coffee made."

Long dismounted and hitched his horse. "Thanks. Cattle will be here about noon."

"There's plenty of grass and water. They will be fine here."

His wife came out on the porch. "Oh, Long, you must be bringing those steers today."

"Yes, they are behind me. Good to see you. My wife is coming with the herd, so she will visit with you."

"She said she wanted to go with you. I bet she's pleased."

"Gretchen, she is very happy to be going along."

"Get in the house. I have some fresh coffee for you two."

Long agreed and started to follow.

John stopped on the stairs. "Any more problems with those raiders?"

"Not so far. We eliminated some of them and

others had not shown their faces before we left. We hired extra men to back ours."

"Good. There's some sorry outfits in this world we live in. Getting worse now the war's over. I thought people would be glad it was done, but they're worse acting now than they were before it started. And black soldiers ordering citizens around. It sure isn't right or good."

"Nothing any of us can do but be quiet, don't upset them, and one day they will leave us and we'll have Texas back."

"When will that be?"

"Not soon, but we will get Texas back. There isn't enough down here to steal to keep them around here very long."

"Can't be quick enough for me."

"John, quit complaining," she scolded him. "Or them black troops will be out here."

"It still makes me mad."

"John, we never arranged how much I pay you for the pasture."

"No need. You're taking two hundred and fifty of my steers. I trust you boys and that will be enough."

"Thank you. You realize that now, every other day, a new herd will arrive. That will make six of them; so for the next two weeks there will be lots of bawling going through."

Gretchen poured his coffee first. "It will sound like money to us."

"They say cattle may be cheaper this year up there."

"How much cheaper?" he asked.

"I am not sure but twenty to forty dollars a head some say. I don't know anything certain, but we will sell them for all we can get."

"I understand markets and I trust you two men. I won't complain either way. Gretchen and I are out of debt and have money held back. Not a lot of people our age are that well off in these times."

"And God bless the O'Malley brothers for getting us there."

"We try, Gretchen. We really try."

The chuck wagon and remuda arrived, and Long went with John to show them where to park.

Jan arrived and hugged him. "First day went fine. I love helping. I'll help Jimmy get the food ready. The cattle aren't far behind us. No problems whatsoever."

"I'll put your horse up."

"Good. John, tell Gretchen after we get the meal ready I'll be back to see her." She half ran for the chuck wagon being set up.

"She'll love that," John said, and they went to put their two horses in his corral with hay and water.

He had three more scheduled nights to stop. Then he'd have to start locating places for them to stop in on the day before they arrived. Some places he knew where to stop. Others were farther apart. They liked to make ten miles a day, then water the herd and let them graze all afternoon to maintain weight on the steers, but eight to twelve miles were the usual limits. Barriers, like fenced land, detoured them. Some places the new grass hadn't had enough rain to be up tall enough. It was all a risk.

Both Long and Harp didn't want all their groups to be the last cattle to reach Kansas. A flooded market was not any fun, and there were many rumors flowing down to Texas this year that this might be the lowest priced market yet.

The first few days of any drive had extra hands ride with each herd to keep the turn-back rebel steers who didn't want to go in the herd. But after a few days they'd give up and follow the next tail. The social order was settled by then for the most part.

Fighting upsets cattle drives when two animals try to decide who is boss, in an angry head-pushing for the status of lead steer.

Stampedes can be tough, and this would loom in Long's mind all the way to Kansas. But these cattle were not as wild as the first ones who had been put into a herd right out of the Texas brush.

Everyone in their crew ate at the same mess tent. Several black cowboys were riding with the six herds, and they ate with all the rest. Long realized that rule cost them some cowboys who refused to eat meals with them, but their outfit paid the highest wages and his men had jobs after they got the cattle sold. Most of the outfits only paid wages till Kansas and no return money.

Long and his brother felt anyone that proved good enough to herd was good enough to eat with everyone else. Their own two point men on the first herd were black and taught the rest their skills. There was to be no fighting on the job, no matter what. Both would be fired. For teenage boys that was a stiff rule. But it kept down any trouble.

They made each stop he had set up and were well up the road. The Colorado River crossing was made on the coolest day so far, and there was a light rain. They had Hiram's great lead bell steer to take them over. He went out in the river and swam across. Jimmy, the chuck wagon, Jan, and the two camp helpers took the ferry and went on to the next campsite.

Long had taken the ferry, too, to find the site he wanted and to be ready, so he missed the actual crossing. He did some hard riding north and found one herd in the way. They'd need to detour around to reach his place.

That left him in a quandary about how to flag their place as taken, then ride back to get them around that loose herd stumbling along. He cut some saplings and tied his ranch flags on them so the area was claimed for his usage. Then he topped some others about waist high to tie his flags on them.

He mounted his horse, hoping the other outfits recognized this as a valid identity to say the place was taken. Then he pushed his horse to go back to warn Harp of the herd in his path.

Harp was on the north shore, and when he got to him he was bragging on the whole crew. No one hurt, no cattle lost—a perfect crossing. He was proud of the entire bunch.

"There is a herd ahead, which is why I came back. We need to swing west and go around them. They are a sloppy bunch. I have my spot posted, if they even know what that means."

"Is there enough open country west of them?"

"Yes. We need to hurry the herd up and then send some hands to deflect them away from our place."

Harp went and talked to the two point riders. Long rode back telling riders to get ready to move around the other herd ahead. He knew that to get the cattle moving faster the two on point had to close the gap between them.

Long rounded the tail of the drive and told those men the plan that they were hurrying the herd. Then he spurred his horse up the left side telling those riders the same thing. By then the cattle were trotting hard, moving left enough he felt certain they would miss the herd lollygagging along before them. He reined up and headed back for the right side to do all he could to keep the herds separate.

Dust rose from cloven hooves, and the bawling cattle were hard on the move. Grateful for the stout horse between his knees pounding the ground, he pushed him. He and the herders ahead and behind him were shouting and waving their hats or beating their leather chaps with rope tails to keep the right side moving farther to the left.

Long could see their passing stream set the other herd moving to the right, shocked by the commotion of their sudden appearance. He began to feel certain they'd make the pass by and not mix herds. He spurred his hard-breathing horse up beside some cattle in their herd who acted interested in the ones they were going by, ready to shut off their escape.

In and out of small dust storms, he knew the worst was over and they could soon slow down. But the plan worked and they'd be ahead of that bunch from there on. He saw their mass begin to slow—no doubt Harp had the two point riders loosen the distance between them apart. They soon were down to a fast walk, and at that point Long reined in his horse and he began thanking the riders for their great job.

To most of them it was all in a day's work. A few riders laughed.

"Hell it was all part of my job."

"Well you did it right," Long shot back at them.

With a dusty large kerchief around her neck, his wife showed up riding near the rear. "Hey, Long, that woke us all up."

"I guess we didn't lose anyone."

She shook her head. "Wonder if that bunch we passed lost anything?"

"I don't care. They were tottering around and stood in our way."

"Well it was exciting for a while. Love you."

"You just be careful. I only have one wife."

She laughed and said, "That's all you need."

He nodded his head in agreement and rode on to thank the others.

When they were in camp, Harp was drinking water at the barrel on the side of the chuck wagon.

"It worked good," Harp said. "I could tell you had things in hand at the rear."

"Just riding with them. Everyone did a helluva good job."

"We might make drovers someday, you think?" Harp teased.

"I'd hope so." They both laughed.

Jan came walking up in her boots and divided skirt—with the quirt hanging from her wrist.

"You all right, Missus O'Malley?"

"Fine. Curly offered to put up my horse. I agreed. We did make a real smooth pass around that other bunch today."

Harp agreed.

"You two do that often?"

"No," Long said. "But sometimes you have to do things and there isn't much time to plan. You simply do it and hope it all holds together."

She kissed his cheek, dust and all. "I know it's the pure D old tomboy in me, but I sure thank you two for letting me herd them."

"You do a good job."

Long's arm on her shoulder, they headed for the chuck. "I kinda like having you along."

"Me too. I'm seeing lots of country I never would have seen if I hadn't got to come."

"Plenty of it out here to see."

"What were the Rockies like?"

"Towering tall and even in summer got snow on them, or so I hear."

"Someday take me there. I'd love to see them."

"I promise to do that. Jimmy, how was your day?" he asked the apron-wearing head cook.

"Fine as frog hair. You boys skinned by them lazy peckerwoods today?"

"Slick as a whistle."

The three of them laughed about it.

Later, Harp and him talked about the "passing."

"If we hadn't had some experience we'd never done that," Harp said, holding his coffee cup up to drink.

"I thought the same thing. And we have five more herds behind us who will have to make like decisions."

Long nodded. "And we have heard lots of tales about outfits losing all their cattle in tornados, river crossings, rustlers, and outright thievery."

"Remember that story you told about running into Pinkertons looking for some drovers who took the money and ran?" Harp asked.

"And I never heard they found them, either. You could bet if Pinkerton found them, every newspaper would have had a front-page story on the recovery."

"I agree. Be a sad day for the folks at home who gave them their cattle to sell and were waiting for the money."

"They said a cowboy wired for money to come home, or they'd not known about it for months."

"Who can you trust, Long? Ever since the war there has been lots of cutthroat deals happening. Maybe the war taught folks the wrong ways to go."

"You hear any more before we left from the Austin lawyers?"

Harp shook his head. "I am convinced it is all bluff, but it still eats at me they might get something done."

"There is always that worry isn't there?"

"Two years ago we worried how we'd get through with a pittance of the cattle we have today and we made it. How I will always wonder."

Long was chuckling. "Jan, he had this fistfight with a man from a posse sworn to kill us all up there. He knocked him on his butt, and then he hired him and the whole posse to help us load cattle. We had lots of help in Sedalia."

She smiled. "You two won't ever forget it will you?"

"No. But things have changed a lot."

Long said, "Now you have to rush by slow herds and have real big herds to manage."

Harp spoke up, "Jan, I sure expected to have ulcers before we ever got to Sedalia. They say you can worry holes in your stomach, and I knew we'd been challenged. And with the captain dying and I'd never sold eight hundred steers nor ever been close to that many."

She smiled. "And this year you have twelve thousand."

He nodded. "And more worries to boot because I have less hold on those others and what they can get into."

She shook her head. "Aw, guys, you two will make it fine. You are both professionals."

"Thanks. Someone needs to remind me of that every day."

Jimmy came over. "The boys said Alex was sick. I'm going down and check on him."

"Need my help?" Jan asked.

"Not right now."

"He the boy from Haleyville?" Long asked.

"Yes, Alex Thornton. Good worker." She sat back down. "Wonder what he's got?"

"No telling. We can wait until Jimmy comes back and find out."

"Oh, I bet he has an upset stomach. Jimmy can cure that. Get some sleep while you have the chance," Harp said as the sun dipped low.

So they left him and went to their bedroll outside the camp.

"I really miss taking a bath," she said on her knees working to smooth out the blanket.

"We get somewhere we can go take one. We'll do that. Fair enough?"

"I didn't really expect one short of Abilene."

"Aw there will be a private stream or creek somewhere up here."

"That would be nice. But I am not nagging you."

"No, you aren't, and I am damn proud you are here. I am spoiled to death having you along."

They were kissing under the covers.

She said, "You spoil awful easy."

CHAPTER 16

Daylight cracked and they were eating breakfast in the cool morning air. The wrangler had his herd in the rope and an iron post portable corral ready to select the horses the cowboys needed. He'd already cut out Jan's, Long's, and Harp's mounts for the day. When Jimmy came by with the large coffeepots, she asked him about Alex.

"He's riding in the chuck wagon today. Got a fever and he's dizzy."

"No idea?"

"I don't have much medical training."

"If I can do anything, tell me," Jan said.

"Maybe resting some will help him. I just fear it is a deeper thing. He's no crybaby and has a really high fever."

"If you need me call out," she said.

But nothing stopped the fever that consumed him. By that mid-afternoon Jimmy shook his head when he met Long with the chuck wagon at the night's site.

Mid-day in north Texas, the spring sun shone hard. The tender new grass blades waved in the eternal wind.

"That boy ain't doing good." He reined up his mules.

"I hate to hear that," Long said, hitching his horse to a small tree sprout.

Jimmy looked around. "Ain't no sign of a town is there?"

"Probably not short of the Red River. We're two to three days' short of there."

Jimmy shook his head. "He won't last that long. And I doubt a doctor could save him."

"My wife will hate that."

"No more than I do."

"I agree. Sorry I am not a medicine man, either." He kicked a pile of horse apples. There were things in life beyond a human's ability to repair them, no matter how hard they were to swallow when they happened.

"He won't last through the night." Jimmy tucked his upper lip over his mouth and shook his head. "I guess we can pray God accepts him?"

"Yes."

They both dropped to their knees.

Long began, "Lord, we are some cowboys who have a good friend about to be delivered to you, sir. His mother is a widow and we will help her, but make him at home in your big meadow and hold him in the palm of your hand. He is a great person, generous and polite—in Jesus' name we pray. Amen."

"Thanks."

They helped each other up. He could hardly stand the sorrow he knew his wife would feel when she learned what was happening—God bless her.

CHAPTER 17

They buried the boy after sundown. In the orange glow of the coal oil lanterns, many wet faces stood in the circle. Alex Thornton was interred on the north Texas prairie. His mother could never visit his grave. The crude cross they marked it with would be stamped away by the oncoming waves of thoughtless bovines. He held Jan in his arms to comfort her as her tears soaked his shirt.

"Darling, he's out of his pain."

"I know, but he had such a strong leadership quality in him. We will miss him. He got things done and could accomplish what most his age stumble over."

"I know we lost a strong soldier. We will support his mother. But we, the living, must go on. He is in God's hands now."

"I'm sorry I am so sad, but it really gets to me when such a great young person is stolen from us."

They ate supper in silence and everyone talked soft. Despite Jimmy's great dry apple–raisin cobbler dessert they loved, they remained silent.

The days ahead they had crossing the Red River were troubled, with the herd having to cross on high water. Two hands were nearly lost save for the effort of two cowboys who got out into the cold water among steers circling in the current. Harp had shed his boots to go in but was restrained by the men.

Each lifesaver grabbed a hand or collar and pulled the men into shallow water. Saved their lives, all happening within a few minutes of tension. Long saw the dripping four cowboys standing on the bank when he rode his horse out of the river with the last steer. Good. They were all right. He only saw part of the wreck but could tell they were unharmed. Good deal.

They brought him a blanket and his bundle of clothes and gun.

"We have a good fire to warm you up on top of the bank," Chuck Matthews told him. "Let me have the horse."

"Thanks. Those two boys saved Tim and Bucky didn't they?"

"Yeah."

"See what color that one saver was?"

He nodded sharply. "Harry's black. Murray's white."

"They're both heroes."

"Oh, yeah they never hesitated going to their aid."

"I'm going to the fire. Next time I want heated water to cross that damn river."

"I'll turn the heat up next time, Long."

Harp had his boots on and met him. "I recalled us saving the captain all over again."

"Me too. Those four boys lost their hats. Get their hat sizes and send someone across by the ferry to buy them new ones."

"Good idea. I might have them go pick them out themselves. We can rest tomorrow and catch up."

Long agreed. "There is plenty of grass off to the west. Nice idea. We have been pushing hard. I'll let you settle the hat deal."

He looked up and saw Jan coming on her horse off the high bank. Most of the boys were dressed or wrapped up and waved at her. She didn't mind. They were like him anxious to get warm again.

"Where we going?" she asked.

"When I get dressed, you and I are taking the ferry back over to the store. Take a bath, wash our clothes, sleep in a bed, and eat a meal at a real table."

She smiled and turned the horse around. "You know there are times I think I really did marry a great guy."

"Quit thinking."

"You had an incident in the river today?"

"Two boys that didn't swim got in a merry-go-round with some steers circling. Two boys, one was black, swam out there and snatched them out of harm's way. Harp is buying them four new hats over at the store on the Texas side. Everyone is resting for a day on the bank, so you and I are taking a holiday."

When he was dried out he dressed and they brought him his horse to ride with her back to the farside by ferry. He'd told Harp his plans and his brother sent them packing. Laughing he shouted after them, "I'm jealous."

CHAPTER 18

The next morning they left their overnight room to ride back to the herd. They crossed on the ferry and reached the camp mid-afternoon. The men were mostly lying around trying to catch up on their sleep. Jimmy was resting in a canvas-folding chair and rose to his feet to welcome her.

"You ready for another couple hundred miles of dust and bawling, sister?"

"I am. I am. I lost ten pounds of dirt, but the cooking was not as good as yours."

"We missed you, too."

"Well, I am back to help."

One of the hands came to take their horses.

She thanked him and asked what Jimmy had for supper.

"Irish stew."

"Well your helper is back and I may live to make it to Abilene."

"I am sure planning to dance with you when we get there."

"We will do that, Jimmy. Maybe have a high-land fling."

"That suit you, boss?"

"Fine. I'll be that glad to get there myself."

Jan gave him a shove. "Better get our bedrolls . . . we'll be up in a few hours."

Long left laughing, recovered their big bedroll, and they headed to a secure place nearby to spread it out for the night. The day off had been fun, but she was a treat for him to be around all the time.

Making ten to twelve miles a day on an average with the herd was his goal. That gave the steers enough time to eat the new rich grass, which was slicking them out as they went north. When a big steer reached way back to lick an itchy spot and left a shiny circle in his new hair, it was gaining weight. Pounds were what they sold at Abilene. Larger and fuller the steers were the more they brought up there. New feed was popping up fast now with the passing showers and warmer, longer days. No severe weather had hatched since they left home.

Springtime on the plains could sweep some powerful storms armed with tornadoes, scattering cattle herds all over or stampeding them off a bluff to their death, and injuring hundreds of head.

The ex–Texas Ranger Charlie Goodnight had used a plan he had in some bad storms that swept his herds the year before and it saved them. He'd shared his plan with others when he got up to Kansas and, over the winter, his plan "to get them moving" swept all over Texas.

He and Harp had gone over the plan with all his lead men. In advance of such a storm the person in charge gets all hands mounted and the cattle moving in a trot, forming a chain behind the lead steer. If this operation can be started soon enough, there is no stampede, but Long knew it would have to be sheer hell for all the men involved at keeping the cattle together while being battered by the raging storm.

Harp and Long knew that most of such storms happened at the end of the day, or later, sweeping the plains at night. Running beside cattle guided by lightning strikes was damn dangerous. A horse could go down or the rider could be struck by that lightning. When Long pulled the covers up that evening . . . the entire notion made his belly cramp. *Lord save us from that.*

Each morning Jan helped Jimmy and the boys serve breakfast, then she would ride with the herders or go with the chuck wagon to the next site. He checked his rifle loads, shoved it back in the scabbard, and left for that afternoon's site in a short lope.

They worked through and around the hills of the southern Indian Territory and then the lands of the Cherokee Strip, that wide band of rolling prairie given to his father's people that spanned the top of the territory. He had no idea where his father was killed, but the lush bluestem grass was a cattleman's dream. And the mileage left was soon down to two weeks. That was after they crossed the lot less threatening Arkansas River than the first crossing they made two years before in the Indian Territory west of Fort Smith. Back then there was lots more current and the water higher.

In Wichita saloons and doves lined the muddy ruts the cattle rumbled over. The girls were challenging the cowboys to stop and visit them. Skirt in hands, some ran alongside the cowboys on horseback who were trying to keep the longhorns in the herd. They would shout "Stop and love me!"

One shouted back, "Darling, I'll be back in two weeks and have money. Save it for me."

Long was chuckling as he pushed some more steers back to the herd. *That boy probably would be back*, *too*. He swung the Comanche pony after another breaking stray and soon had him back in the fold. Damn steers must not like crossing into Kansas. He did. They were that much closer.

There were cattle buyers in their camp that evening. They did that last year. Came to try to buy their cattle at less than market prices . . . told them big tales of being swamped with cattle at Abilene and a bottle neck was holding it all up. One even said the Mississippi River Railroad Bridge was down and wouldn't be fixed for years.

Harp was not budging. He thanked them for coming, refused a free bottle of whiskey, and that was that. Before they rode away they told him he'd be begging to take a lower price when he found out the truth about the market.

That night in the bedroll, Jan was upset by their words.

"They're liars. They want our cattle and they will resell them for twenty more than they paid us."

"Really?"

"Really."

"Good. Kiss me and I will forget them."

"Darling, that is easy."

He loved having her along. Damn he wished he'd found her a long time ago.

CHAPTER 19

The beef-shipping capital of America was a sleepy cow town called Abilene, Kansas. The town was full of saloons, pickpockets, con men, people looking for a way to swindle away a fortune, wanted criminals, ex-cons, and prostitutes that ran the gambit of fifty cent Indian squaws, ex-female slaves, Orientals, teenagers, and very fancy expensive beautiful women of the trade.

Whiskey and beer flowed like a river every night in the bars, and one person said it was bright as daylight at midnight because the cowboys shot so many holes in the sky every night. Card games went on for days, and the smoke in those places could be cubed and resold to smokers. Horse races down Main Street happened as often as the scheduled ones at the county fairgrounds.

Gun fighting and bareknuckle fights broke out among the cowboys quite often. Give a sixteen-year-old boy a six-gun in Texas, and by the time he gets the herd to Kansas he thinks he is the toughest *hombre* on a stallion, and on earth. All that adds up to is that he is a target for the lecherous criminal men and women on the lookout for his pay.

Long made sure he talked to the men with the herd before they reached Abilene. "Men, Abilene is a pirate nation. They cheat at cards. Don't play. They will take your money. Most of the whores are diseased. That means if you climb into their bed you will be infected and may die from it. They will get you drunk and then roll you for everything down to your underwear, and they may steal that."

The crew laughed.

"It is not funny. It is the truth. To take your money home, let Harp keep it for you. Stay out of fights. These are not like the fights you have fought in Texas at a dance. They will cut you to pieces or their friend will hit you over the head while you are fighting the other. Go in pairs or more, and cover each other's backs."

"It don't sound like fun," Rooster Gilbert complained.

"I have been here and seen it all. You boys have a life ahead of you. Don't ruin it in Abilene for some small thrills."

"Yeah, but you and Harp got lucky and made it rich."

"We also didn't let some damn thief rob us or some woman of the night poison us, either."

"How am I going to do that on cowboy wages?"

"Get off your ass and put a drive together yourself. We took eight hundred head to Sedalia through the Yankee defenses."

He saw the men had begun talking to each other. Maybe, just maybe, he had reached them. Damn he hoped so.

Harp and two hands rode for Abilene the next day. They only moved the herd five miles to better water.

Harp returned after dark and met with them.

"Cattle prices are ten dollars per head lower than last year. I was offered seventy dollars a head. They know what kind of cattle we bring. I can sell three herds. They want to see how the market holds—I sold the first three and hope we can make a similar sale on the last three. I think it is the best we can do."

"That is over four hundred twenty thousand dollars," Long said.

"How did you do that? Figure the amount?" Jan asked him privately.

"Six thousand steers times seventy dollars per steer comes to that amount."

"I would need a pencil and paper to ever get that figured." She shook her head and squeezed his arm.

Long asked Harp, "What will the markets do before we can sell the others? You get any information?"

Harp shrugged. "Maybe another ten dollars down. No one is sure. There is some resistance at this price. I sold ours today so we had that money and let them grumble. We topped last year's prices because some of the outfits wanted to resist them. We will have this bunch sold. Half the job and they will work to get the rest in when they have a price. These guys have to make a living, too. They know we bring sound cattle."

"You did good, brother."

Harp nodded, but Long knew his brother would be worried about the last of all the sales until he had them. They were the Diamond's second herd and the rest of the consigned cattle. Lots of people depended on them, and Harp carried a strong conscience for the people who gave them their cattle to sell. If the market broke some more, Long knew Harp would feel the effect. He had no answer. They needed to sell these cattle but were at the whims of the market.

They did lots of work to have six herds and to reach Abilene before many even crossed the Red River.

"It still is iffy isn't it?" Jan asked him in their bedroll.

"Harp wants to do the best he can. Yes, it is shaky. But we will be fine and can buy more ranchland and fix the ones we have."

"You two are what do they call them—Die-coons."

"The word is Tycoons. Means big business-men."

225

"Yes." She laughed quietly. "Exactly. Did Easter teach you all that?"

"She did."

Jan snuggled against him. "Can we go see the Rockies after we load the cattle?"

He tickled her until she made him stop.

"Hell, no. Why do you need to know about how they look?"

"Nothing, silly."

CHAPTER 20

Loading the first cattle began four days later. Things had gone smoothly aside from a rogue steer having to be roped and dragged to the rail yard after he had a wild party of horning hitched horses, chasing honest women off the street screaming, fighting some town curs, and wrecking a horse watering trough and two hitch rails. The ex-bull was being dragged by two cowpony riders to the loading pens with a lariat on his right leg attached to the third cowboy's horn to hold him from charging anything else.

Long, who rode up at the end of it all, laughed. It took three of them to bring him to submission.

"Thanks, guys . . . our bill for repairs won't cost you over eighty apiece."

The hands shook their heads and rode on past him and Jan on their horses.

"You really won't charge them for the damages will you?" she asked.

"No, and they know it."

"Good. I never saw any men as hardworking and determined as your outfit. Many are hardly more than boys but they do work, and loading all these cattle with no more outbreaks than that one is a miracle."

He agreed. They should be shutting the door on

the last cattle car for that first herd that afternoon. He sure hoped so anyway. Harp was to meet them for lunch at the Cattleman's Restaurant. Katy sent him a letter that everything at home was fine and neither his father nor Hoot had mentioned any more trouble since they left for Abilene.

Herd two had arrived and so had three. The only serious occurrence was the one cowboy from herd two who had drowned at the Red River crossing. His body was not recovered and Long knew Chaw was upset.

Harp was there with Frank Ransom and Justin Coble from the National Cattle Buyers, Incorporated. Both men wore suits and derby hats they removed for Jan when they sat down.

Frank made her welcome and asked if she really enjoyed the trip up.

"I really did. I have worked cattle all my life, and it was a great adventure."

"Most women would run away from such a task."

She shook her head. "Before Long and I met, my ex-man and three cowboys, in sixty days, gathered and branded five hundred mavericks out of the south Texas brush. Now that was real work. The drive up here was a sleigh ride. I never rode in one, just heard about how smooth they were."

"My, my, I am impressed."

"No need in that. A gal just does what she has

to do in Texas. This was my opportunity to see the Indian Territory and Kansas. A little cow chousing never hurt me none."

"Jan is a Texas cowgirl," Harp said.

"Well, Mrs. O'Malley, I am pleased to meet you, be assured, and so is Justin."

He nodded.

They turned in their food order to the waiter.

"Frank told me this morning the last three herds could be sold at a five-dollar discount from the first. I sold them," Harp said.

Long agreed. That wasn't as bad as he had thought it might have been, ending up lots lower. Good. They had them all sold. When they got the second herd loaded, he and Jan might head home with some of the men.

The bunch back in Texas was spread way too thin if trouble began to brew again. And he felt certain that it would. The herds were now all in Abilene and it was a miracle that they had only had two deaths. Sad, but still, a miracle.

"Will you bring this many herds next year?" Justin asked as they ate their chicken-fried steak, green beans, mashed potatoes, and yeast rolls with coffee.

"We hope to."

"They are talking about moving the loading spot next year south to Cottonwood Falls where the railroad track will be by then."

"Save us a few miles," Harp said.

229

"Oh, hell, it won't be the same," Justin said. "And we just got Abilene up to being half pleasurable. What is that town's name? Anyway it is some dried-up farmer's village."

"Winfield I think."

"Won't be the same."

There was lots of talk of more and larger processing packing plants in Chicago gearing up to do more slaughter business. Frank thought Chicago would be a much larger market in the future than St. Louis. Long didn't give a damn what they did, but expansion meant more markets so that pleased him. These two were all right, but they had such airs about themselves they really got under his skin. Lunch with them was enough. Leave the rest to his brother. He liked straightforward talk like he got at home from ranchers and storekeepers. He almost laughed with their haughty talking about some big businessman inviting them to his mansion and what they served. And, oh, how his old French wine was so superb.

Going back to the hotel room he and Jan had, he slapped his knee laughing. "Did you get a little tired hearing about Crabtree and the fancy meal he served them?"

"Heavens, Long, I'd take a real Texas mesquite barbecue to any of that junk."

When they reached the boardwalk on the farside, he swung her around and kissed her with a "Me too" on the end of it. Right there in downtown Abilene under the bright Kansas sunshine and he didn't care who saw them do that, either.

They went laughing all the way to the hotel.

They hadn't been back to the room very long when a knock came on the door.

Hat in hand it was Kirby Drone, one of the hands, and out of breath.

"Mister O'Malley, they've done shot Boone Allen and may kill the rest of them boys behind the corrals at the rail yard. I didn't know who to ask for help. Clerk said you were up here." He was still deep-breathing.

Long reached for the coatrack and gun holster, strapping it on while Kirby leaned on the door-jamb to recover his breath.

"How many are against them?"

"A bunch."

"Harp is at the cattle buyers' office. Can you get him?"

"I can, sir. But I don't know about—"

"I'll see to him. Get Harp." Then he turned and told Jan to stay there until he came back.

He silenced her with a kiss and tore out behind the man. They scrambled down the stairs and out into the street. He spotted one of the men riding by and shouted, "Bring me that horse. They have some of our boys treed behind the loading pens."

The boy reined over, jumped down, stuttering what could he do?

"Get more boys." He bolted in the saddle, tore the horse's head around, and dodged him in and out of the street traffic. He arrived behind the pens in a sliding halt and reined the horse to the right.

He saw the smoke of a pistol being fired at him by someone standing there. He whipped out his .45 and returned fire. The shooter had missed him, but Long didn't and the man went down.

The horse slid on his heels getting sat down. And several of the gathered were running away in all directions.

"Who did this to you, Boone?" he asked on his knees, looking over the obviously shot youth.

"Those bastards—you remember when we passed their herd back down there in Texas."

"They found us huh?"

"Yes, sir, and they ain't getting paid to go home, either."

"That bullet hurting you bad?"

"Bad enough." Boone nodded, tight-lipped.

"We need to find you a doctor—" Long turned at the sound of a man's voice of authority.

"What in the hell happened here anyway?" The man talking to him had a big mustache and a badge.

"Some lowlife shot one of my hands. We need a way to convey him to a doctor."

The lawman's face formed a frown at his words. "Injun, where did you learn to talk like that?"

"Half Indian. This boy works for my firm and needs medical care. My name is Long O'Malley and I am part of the O'Malley Brothers Land and Cattle Company. That dead man over there I shot in self-defense—he was shooting at me."

"Hickok is my name . . . most folks call me Bill or William. You got any name on the rest of those shooters?"

"I'll find them. Right now this boy's medical attention is more important."

"Skipper, get us a wagon to carry him to Doc Proctor, he's the best at gunshot wounds. His house is only a block and a half away. See me afterward, O'Malley. Boys, let's all of us settle down. Things will be fine."

Then Hickok told the guy he called Skipper to load the dead man in another wagon headed for the undertaker.

Harp and Kirby were there by then. Skipper found them a wagon and they lifted Boone into it, his pal Kirby going with him.

"Tell them your bosses will pay the bill," Long shouted after him.

"I can handle it, sir." Kirby jumped on the wagon to go along with Boone.

Harp asked Long, "What happened here besides Boone being shot?"

"Those boys from that herd we passed down in Texas shot him, I guess, for passing them."

Harp shook his head in amazement. "Guess folks hold grudges."

"They do. Anyway I see Jan coming. We'll handle the doc business, but we better warn the others about this threat."

"I will do that tonight. Is he real bad off ?"

"He was bleeding. It was in his left shoulder."

"We can talk later; go on down there. You kill a man?"

"He shot at me. I told them it was self-defense. They didn't act like they had time for it and packed him off."

"Reconsidering the whole thing, you may face a grand jury or revenge from that other outfit. I am sending two men to back you at the doctor's office. Don't say no. These are desperate times. Jan and I need you."

She frowned. "I dang sure do."

Long laughed and shook his head. "I'll be fine."

"I am going to be damn sure you are. Watch him," he said to her, and turned on his heel.

"I will, Harp."

They headed for the doctor's office under the heating-up sun to check on Boone.

"This was over passing that bunch down in Texas?" she asked, hurrying along beside him.

"Boone said it was. He was the one they shot."

"People have gone crazy."

He agreed and led her across the traffic-crowded street. On edge that those shooters weren't through—he eyed everyone in the crowds and on the sidewalk hurrying in case there was someone looking for him. When he shut the door of the house where the yard sign said DOCTOR HALE PROCTOR, he felt better to have her out of harm's way.

A woman in white met him.

"You have my cowboy Boone here?"

"Yes. They are removing the bullet. Will you have a seat in the living room? Doctor Proctor will tell you all about it when he finishes."

"Fine. Thank you."

Behind his glasses, the gray-headed small man introduced himself as the physician. "Your employee should be fine in a few days. We have the bullet out of his shoulder. Barring an infection he should be back to his work in six weeks. He is a very tough young man."

Long agreed. "Should one of us stay here?"

"No. He will be fine. I had them give him some painkiller to sleep. Rest will increase his recovery."

"Will the damage cripple him?"

The doctor shook his head. "He may never know they did it."

"Good. He works for us and is a valuable man."

"We will get him well."

"Thanks. Some of us will be by to check on him tomorrow. Good evening."

He and Jan lost no time heading for supper at the Cottage. They were there early enough to get seated and had turned in their food order, when a man in Texas-style clothing stopped at their table. He had an expensive-looking, weathered felt hat in his hand. "Ma'am, excuse me, but my name is Clyde Nelson and, well, I live in the same area down there in Texas you all live at. I wanted to introduce myself. I own some land inside your new ranch. It was my grandfather's and he earned it in the war for Texas Independence. It is a full section. We have not used it for years, but they say you are buying land inside the borders."

"Have a seat, Clyde," Long said.

"No. I've been in the saddle a lot—"

"Don't worry about that," Jan said. "Haven't we all?"

"Yes. Thank you, ma'am." He took a chair.

"After you introduced yourself, I remember seeing the name on my map. You don't use the place?"

"It is very isolated . . . my brother and my wife wouldn't consider it. My grandfather loved it and died there. My mother told my father if she had to live down there she would not marry him. He built a ranch west of Kerrville. And he and I talked about selling the place."

"There is no ranch headquarters left?"

"Oh, I was there three years ago, and the house was boarded up and it is in good shape. Corrals are not. But it does have an eight-acre natural lake, which is why he took up that land. It is an unusual feature."

"Very unusual. Six thousand dollars."

"These cattle drives have raised the price of land haven't they?"

"I would say so, Clyde. When Harp and I took eight hundred head to Missouri two years ago, you'd have had to pay someone to take it off your hands."

Clyde raised his hat brim with a finger. "You are right. When I get back home I'll talk to my dad and brother. I think you are making a fair offer. We'd like to buy some more land out our way; we can see prices soaring with this cattle money coming home even at a lower price than last year."

"Exactly why Harp bought the big parcel when it was on sale. I didn't get home until Christmas and he had already bought it."

"Long, your brother is a real businessman. People all over say he may be the smartest man in west Texas."

Clyde ordered his food.

"Harp is a smart guy. But two years ago we were near Sedalia, Missouri, facing an army out to kill us. He whipped up on their big man and then hired him and his men to work for us to deliver the cattle."

"I'd not heard that story, but I knew you had plenty of opposition going up there. The war wasn't over was it?"

Jan shook her head. "You two were at Fort Worth when they said Lee had surrendered?"

"Captain thought since the guard in the west was pretty thin we could skirt Van Buren, Arkansas, and get around the army and go on to the railhead."

"Boy, you were lucky Lee surrendered."

Long put down his fork and smiled before he sipped his coffee. Then said, "No, we were dedicated to do that job. There won't ever be a force like them. Captain was going to pay us fifteen bucks a month if we got them through."

"Cheap help."

"Not really. There were no jobs at all in Texas, no money, nothing down there. It made the two of us tell Mom why we'd be rich coming home."

"I see."

"Those two have come a long ways, haven't they?" Jan asked him.

"Yes, and I am honestly jealous because I could have done it if I'd seen the pot of gold at the end of the rainbow was in Sedalia."

"It was for us."

"How did you find her?"

"You want me to tell it or you do it?" he asked his wife.

"I was married to a good honest man. An old man who lived up around Waco decided I needed to leave him and be his slave. My husband became so angry, he went off to find them and shot two of them—they killed him. Some ranch hands and I tried to hold the ranch together. They ran them off and came by, kidnapped, and doped me. I pretended to be more doped than I was and managed to escape them. But I passed out. Fell off my horse. He wandered off to Long's camp who was just passing through. From there Long planted three of the old man's boys and had him and his other sons arrested. Then deputies shot them."

"Wow I never heard that story."

"We've been together ever since."

"Nothing comes easy, does it?"

"No, but I'm lucky. Not only for finding her, but our first cattle drive. Sure we broke some new ground, but I don't think we'd ever be where we are had the captain not hired us to help drive his cattle to the railroad site at Sedalia."

"I savvy that. Someone had to do it to show us all how. Why a longhorn cow prior to that wasn't worth nothing."

"Damn little and our dad must've saw something. We were branding mavericks hard—people almost laughed at his effort. Turns out they are all worth money."

"Hey when we get back home I'll contact you."

"I've got your supper," he said. "Nice meeting you."

"I guess you could afford it."

"We'll manage to do that."

Walking back to their hotel room, Jam mentioned how polite their new friend acted toward them.

"He sounds real levelheaded. I want to see that lake he talks about."

"You've never heard about it before?"

"No. But it will be neat to go find it."

She agreed.

That night he wondered about the lake some more. They were a rare thing in his country—he and Jan would need to go see it. Oh, well, still lots more cattle to load, but financially things looked good for him and Harp.

CHAPTER 21

Why did the trip home to Texas end up being twice as long?

Harp sent Jan and Long home with the boys that were hurt along with Rex Neely, whose mother, they learned, was bad off and might even die before the cowboy could get back. Shade Clements had his once broken leg reset by a real doctor in Abilene and put in splints. He had crutches and was recovering. Ivy Martin had his arm in a sling from a horse wreck. A few healthy boys went with them to drive and hitch teams. The Chinese cook, Low Me, handled cooking and Jan helped him.

Besides the chuck wagon, they had another team and wagon that the recovering Boone Allen drove filled with hay and grain—so the animals they rode and drove had feed and they could go all day making thirty to forty miles. The move and graze made for a slow train back, and Long wanted to get back as fast as possible and see how things were going in their new empire.

Nothing in the mail that had caught up with him in Abilene indicated anything had gone too wrong, but he still felt a need to be back and be sure for himself that things were all right. Jan stayed in good spirits riding with him while they detoured around many northbound herds. Everyone knew him, stopped him to talk about markets.

He told them the price might be shaky, but when he left they were not that bad. That was all he knew. With the waves of cattle going north each day—he was damn glad they had sold early. Texas might have sent too many head this summer. He shrugged it off. They were going to use the ferry to cross the Red River with wagons, horses and all.

"You thought any more about a home place for us?" Jan asked, approaching the river.

"Oh, some. What have you thought about?"

"I don't want to sound jealous but I'd like the Diamond Ranch house."

"Why if wishes were like that they'd be fishes and the lake would be full."

"You crazy guy. A gal can want can't she?"

"Yes. But we have never been shown the sisters' will and have no idea how that will work. At least Harp never said, except they told him they had it figured out. If you want a big fancy house, we can go to San Antonio and see an architect who can plan one you like."

"I'd hate to be the greedy witch."

"No one said a word about that, girl. I can afford to build you a house."

"Fifty-fifty. Your money and mine."

"I wasn't going to spend that on us. If we ever

have any children, I'd like that to give them a start."

"With my luck at that, it will never take place." She shook her head at him.

"We better get ready to settle with this ferry-man."

He dismounted and went in the ferry's shack.

A bald-headed man wearing spectacles asked him how many he had.

"Two wagons and teams. A dozen horses and six riders."

"Take three trips. Be seven fifty."

Long frowned at him over his high figures. "Your prices have gone up since I was here last."

"That is the charge to cross going south. North may be cheaper."

"All right, but folks will buy a boat if you get much higher." He paid the man as the ferry bumped the dock, and the man in the buggy under the shade nodded at Long going by him.

He didn't know him and waved to Robbie Boyd driving the chuck wagon to get on the ferry. The wagon chained down, they loaded his and her horses and then the signal was given to start the team on the farside to begin pulling the thick rope. Water slapped the side. The day's heat was building and the south wind swept his face. It would be good to be home. The river thudded the side of the ferry as they moved for the south bank.

They stood on the floor beside the chuck wagon with Robbie who was keeping an eye on his mules. The tobacco-spitting man in charge spent half his time spitting brown juices in the muddy stream.

Long wondered if the ferry would work without him—probably would.

"How much longer will we be to get home?" Jan asked, squeezing his arm in the brilliant sun reflecting off the water.

"Oh, two weeks I imagine. What do you say, Robbie?"

"About that long, sir."

"What are you going to do when you get home?"

"Go fish and hunt. I think those damn steer bawling in my ears is never going to quit."

"Harp never offered you a job?" Long asked him, wondering why his brother had not encouraged this sharp young man to stay. He'd never mentioned anything he saw wrong with him and even picked him to head up the returning party and look out for Long and her both.

"I never asked. He said he wouldn't pay me until I got back home. I figured I had that much time left on this job and you all won't need me."

"No. You misunderstood him. If he didn't want you, he'd never sent you home as a bodyguard for the two of us."

"I understood you had rules someone had to

ride with you on the ranch because of some close calls you two had."

Jan laughed. "Why I almost shot him myself when I found he had my horse. It got away from me and it was a dark night. He was going to find me first light. But I had the drop on him."

They laughed.

"Long, I am glad you guys are who you are. You guys aren't run off by anyone. And I came looking for work when I heard you paid both ways. Bunch of cheap bas—I mean people, ma'am. When they said they wouldn't pay us to come back home I said I wasn't going north."

"We need good men to keep this ball, that we have started down home, rolling. Figure that you have a job at the H Bar H Ranch. So make the hunting and fishing trip short."

"I may not even go."

The three laughed.

The mules and chuck wagon went up on the hill, unloaded, and they started a fire to fix lunch for the others soon to arrive in camp.

After the meal, Harley Callis played his guitar and Phil Combs played the mouth harp. Both were a couple of the able-bodied men. Phil asked Long if he had a job when they got back. "I don't see a reason in the world why any of you seven guys won't have a job."

They shouted and tossed their hats in the air.

The next day they reined up, because there was

a woman, with a little girl, sitting at the side of the road crying.

"What's wrong with her?" Jan asked.

Long dropped off his horse and handed Jan his rein. "I am going to ask."

"Ma'am, you hurt?"

"That no-good Kenny Cooper dumped me and Missy off last night. We ain't got a penny. And no way to go nowhere."

"She your daughter?" Long was down on his right knee talking to the woman.

"No, she's my sister's girl, but she was bad sick and said she was dying and I needed to take her with me. I told her I was going to Fort Worth with Kenny, and she said well take her with you. But he got so mad about it that he made me get off the wagon and drove away."

"Were you married to him?"

"No."

"What do they want?" little Missy asked her, sounding upset.

By then Jan was there and their procession had stopped. The wagon and teams secured beside the road, the men came on the run.

"Is she hurt?" Phil asked Jan.

She shook her head. "Not physical that I can tell."

"My name is Long O'Malley."

"Gladys Norton."

"Where were you going in Fort Worth?"

"I don't know. He does day work—"

"I understand. Let's get you out of the sun. There are some trees over there."

He and Jan helped her up, and with the little girl they walked them to the shade. Robbie had the others move the two wagons and set up a canvas shade for camping.

Jan found out the two had only one day-old biscuit to eat that day. She ordered oatmeal for their empty stomachs. One of the men brought drinking water and a dipper. Jan held the little girl and had fed her two pieces of hard candy. Long considered it bribery, but it and Jan's kindness settled her down. The little girl was pleased at the attention.

He stayed back. The men fixed her some water, soap, and a towel to wash her face and hands. What sort of a man leaves a woman off on such a stretch of unused land of stunted oaks and cedars? He'd kick him in the butt if he crossed his path. And that poor little child abandoned way out here. Damn. Some people were absolutely worthless to have no more sense than to do that.

They cooked the rest of the leg of beef they bought three days earlier up at Denton. Kept cool under a wet canvas it was still good enough to eat, and they would eat the rest for breakfast along with the pinto beans that didn't get done until sundown. They were eating under the coal oil lamps.

Gladys had recovered from her tears, and Long heard her tell one of the boys she was eighteen. He still knew little about her and her story except about taking her niece from a dying sister and herself no more than eighteen—if that was true—and already living with a man. She never said she was his wife.

Oh, well, what could she hurt? They knew her story—or did they?

In their bedroll, he asked his wife what she thought.

"Poor thing," she whispered. "That guy Kenny was thirty."

Long bet he promised her the moon. Obviously, from her own words, he had a bad temper and she was better off without him.

"Do you believe this story that her sister gave her that girl?"

"That was hard to swallow, but we may never know the truth."

"You won't just dump her?"

"No. But listen close. I fear we have not heard the truth or all the story."

She snuggled to him. "Long, I will sure be careful and keep you informed."

"We will see."

"Yes. And you know what? I appreciate your brother sending us home early. I love you."

He was happy they were going home early, too.

248

CHAPTER 22

This Kenny never showed up. They arrived in Fort Worth. The two of them stayed at the Houston Hotel for two nights. He paid room and board in a lesser hotel, in the stockyards area, for the boys and another for Gladys and the little girl. They promised to protect her. Jan gave her a small amount of money that she said the girl needed for necessities.

Awake, standing at the third-floor window, Long saw the early sunshine spread over the sprawling city. Damn, he was lucky to be an O'Malley and not some illiterate bum working the alleys begging for his meals and sleeping in a trash pile. Nor a reservation Indian trying to raise crops in dry dirt—Hiram O'Malley saved him that twist in fate.

She was hugging his waist from behind and sleepily rubbing her face on his bare back. "What are you thinking?"

"Jan, I am so lucky to have you, Harp, and my parents. That I am not some drunk wrapped in a blanket outside some western fort passed out."

"Oh, Long, that sounds so bad."

He turned around and hugged her. "It is bad but it shadows me. Many men and women like me do not fit into either side. They are not white men, they are not red."

"I understand, but I never thought you'd worry about that."

"Not worry. The word for my concern is reflective."

"What does that mean?"

He looked at the high ceiling for his answer. "I am looking in a mirror and seeing me as that defeated person."

"Your mother found that word?"

"Every day, even Sunday, we had a big word to look up in that thick dictionary."

"I will remember that if I ever get to be a mother."

"I thought, at the time, what a drag when I'd rather be out shooting crows or catching catfish, but yes, it had made me think a lot."

"Well I am glad that you aren't a blanket-wrapped Indian."

"So am I."

"Tomorrow we move on south. Ten days we will be on Mom's porch and dancing again."

"That was so neat. Dancing in the yard when we got there the first time. I knew I was welcome and not as the woman who stole her son."

"Irish are a fun-loving people. They are much like the Indians. They came to America for real freedom after the potato famine, and they rode the wave of America to the West."

"Before you are through, I will know more about things than most folks I know. Thank you, Long O'Malley. I want you to know that your words never bore me."

"We better get dressed. Those boys will be here for us ready to move south."

"Yes, and I will be ready. I love and appreciate Texas and especially our real estate down there. Can we go look for that lake we talked about?"

"I promise you we shall, since I am going to buy it when Clyde Nelson gets back home."

Gladys and Missy were up on the wagon seat with Boone in the street, Missy shouting for *Janny* to come see her new dress. They got organized and rolled south. Long felt pleased in the late afternoon when a nice shower settled the dust. They were out of Fort Worth headed south when the showers rolled over them. The sheets of rain were not too angry, and the fresh smell on the wind, with a cedar aroma, tickled his throat.

But like so many ranchers and men of the soil, he gave the good Lord a big thanks for all moisture that fell, big or small, and even if not on his own land but for all the receivers. After supper the cool wind, with some moisture still in it, swept across his face as he stood in the doorway of his tent. He was close to where he wanted to spend the rest of his life . . . on his ranchland in south Texas.

His men, all the way home, were spoiling

251

Gladys and Missy. Nothing turned up from her past. Boone told him she heard nothing from that Kenny when they were in Fort Worth.

Her new dress improved her appeal to the men, he decided.

He asked Jan if Gladys had contacted her dying sister when she was in Fort Worth. Jan shook her head and turned up her palms. He shrugged and rode on.

They really pushed hard going south and arrived on the home ranch on a late hot August afternoon. However they must have been seen by some hard riding teen on the outlook because Long heard the bell pealing.

The closer he came to the ranch, his horse began a prancing sideways walk. It was like when he'd heard the Mason German Marching Band playing and marching. His mount did the same thing when he heard the bell pealing. He was never certain why it was with the bells or music, but he smiled at his wife who was frowning at his former Comanche mount being so stirred up.

"He can't help it."

She shook her head. "I am excited, too, but you don't see me jumping around."

His mother came on the run to hug Jan as soon as she dismounted. "You two made it?"

"Hells of course they made it," Hiram shouted as he hugged Long. "Damn. You lads are really cutting a big rug selling all those cattle for near a million dollars. It ain't believable. M' God I still don't believe it happened."

"It happened. And we had a good run, too. I want you to meet Gladys and Missy. A man abandoned them on the road. They are family."

"How was Harp?" Katy asked, just joining them with her son in her arms.

"Hobbling around. No. Harp is fine. He told me to get Jan home and I did."

She and the baby boy hugged him. They laughed. Hiram shook hands with the returning cowboys and thanked them.

Long told them, "Men, I know Rex has already gone to see about his sick mother. Why don't you all take three or four days off and then come back." He handed them each twenty dollars. "Have a good time and I want all of you on our payroll."

They thanked everyone, flew into their saddles, and left waving hats and hollering.

Long turned to his father. "You and Hoot holding it all down?"

"So far we are. We are getting lots of gossip that the Comanche plan a great raid this fall. Maybe the largest one we've ever seen. These black foot soldiers are not mobile enough to stop them, and their state police are jumping around suspicious we are going to fight the war over again . . . they are worthless."

"Have you seen any sign of the Comanche scouting things out?"

"Yes. But we've only seen sign they were around. No one has actually seen one. Or they'd have probably shot them. I think they are scouting a way to do the most damage and face the least opposition and get the most loot and horses. A Comanche counts the number of horses he has like you and Harp do your money in the bank, so I expect that will be their goal, and, Long, it will be bloody and revenge filled."

"What can we, as ranchers, do?"

"You two men come into the house. We're fixing a meal. You can talk cows later," his mother said to them.

Neal Hogan joined them—an older man Harp hired to be supervisor while Red was on the trail. Short, with a slow smile, Neal shook Long's hand and hugged him. Neal was a small rancher who had agreed to do the job only while they were gone and that he'd go back to his own place when they got back. He was a man with a level head and knew the ranch business well.

"How are the men that went up there? You look good."

"Fine, thanks. We lost one man, and a boy as well, but we had the least wrecks and troubles of any drive. Market was softer but we did well. Harp will be back in a few weeks. He sent Jan and me home with a few hurt boys who are mending."

"Well, Hiram and I held it together with binder

twine. Now you're back things will go much smoother."

"I hope I can keep up with all you've done with Dad here."

"Oh, I am sure you'll beat us ten times. Who is that girl with the child?"

"A stray we found abandoned. Her name is Gladys and the little girl is her niece, Missy. Some worthless guy abandoned them north of Fort Worth on a stretch of empty land on the road south. She said she has Missy because her sister was dying and wanted her to have care. I think all of that is right."

"You know the guy who dumped her?"

"No. She is polite and acts like a lady, so, other than suspicions, I have nothing nor know any more than that."

Neal shook his head. "In my time, I'd have found him and horse-whipped him until he wouldn't forget for pulling that stunt."

"I guess he's gone. She said she never married him. Nor mentioned the rest of her family. She's a good worker . . . she always makes herself busy and helpful."

"You be right. There be a story there, the likes of which we may never know."

Long smiled. His father's accent came through in his speech when he talked about things that happened, or he was upset. His mother said he'd lost most of it since they got married, but it was still there, the last sign that he was Irish.

Jan was dabbing her eyes with a hanky when he found her standing around the corner in the living room.

"What's wrong?"

"Nothing. I guess I got carried away about being home. I mean, in my home, after all this time and your lovely caring mother, Katy, and Lee. I should be laughing and having fun but instead I melted into a crybaby."

He hugged her and reassured her everyone had a crying moment. She could have all she needed . . . she was at home and among folks who loved her.

She agreed and squeezed him tight. "And still not with child."

"That will be what God does. We've done all we can."

"Long, thanks. I am proud I found you and more pleased I didn't shoot you."

"Everyone all right?" his mother asked.

"We will be fine. Being home kind of swallowed Jan."

"I understand. Food's ready. Come eat. And since Harp is not here, Long, you say the grace for us."

"I will." And he did.

With Neal on his right he listened to the man talk. "We've worked quite a bit on the placement of those new shorthorn and Hereford bulls you two bought that were delivered while you were gone. But Hiram and I learned that for them to compete with a rank longhorn they need to be older and more powerful. We have three in the pens. I had the boys drive them in and put them on feed. The longhorn bulls had them treed and wouldn't let them out of their sight, so we cut a few of those worst fighting bulls and that helped some."

Long shook his head. "Nothing in change comes easy, does it?"

"That's for damn sure."

Jan was doing better, getting over her sadness, and his mom's *frijoles* must have soothed her some, too.

Things were in good shape on the ranches. He'd found how well most things were going. That took the strain off his mind, worrying all the way home how some deals might have fallen into bedlam while they were gone.

He finally slipped off and took a nap.

Before he went to supper with Jan, he stood at the upstairs window and let the hot wind blow the curtains by him. Being a large landowner was lots different from being a cattle drover for fifteen bucks a month. Lots different.

Supper went well and during it he talked to the young man, Reg Hoffman, who from his wheelchair sat and did the ranch books.

"The money for the cattle is already in the

bank, and I have the shares figured out on paying the people when Harp gets here. It really was a highly successful trip."

"The O'Malley brothers win again."

"Do you have more plans for next year?"

"I imagine we will continue those drives as long as it makes money or we find a new way to market cattle."

"I have heard lots of stories from guys my age who went north. Can you swim?"

"Yes. My father taught us how to swim before we even left Arkansas. My mother, too. His first wife drowned, and he said he won't let it happen to any of us."

"Is swimming fun?"

"In nice warm water on a hot day—yes. On a cold one it is like running around naked in a snow storm."

"Oh, I wouldn't like that."

"Early in the spring on a cattle drive it is no fun."

He laughed.

"What is so funny?" Easter asked him, coming into the room.

"Long said swimming in a cold river was like running around naked in a snow storm."

They all laughed.

It was good to be home where you didn't have to be on your guard all the time. There were lots of people in the outside world who might, for no reason at all, become a biting dog.

After the meal he read some back issues of the newspaper. He found nothing on carpetbaggers leaving Texas, which was what he was looking for. They were not going anywhere soon.

Several small reports were written up on Indian raids in the country west of there. Most were attacks on isolated ranches. Rewards for kidnapped children being returned were also reported on. Why offer rewards? Those Indians who had them couldn't read.

There were auctions listed. Some had large cattle herds in estate sales. The O'Malleys would need more cows. Well, when Harp came back they could talk about it.

"You going to see the sisters next and report to them on the sale?" his mother asked him.

"I better hadn't I?"

"You are the co-manager."

"I prefer Harper to go have tea with them."

"I'll go along and you can talk to the manager while we have tea," Jan said, having just walked in to join him.

"No poison in the tea. I am certain we will inherit it."

She laughed. "I could hurry it up."

"You are bragging now."

"I really enjoy them. They are sweet and like some people I knew up by Waco—well I never had tea with them. You know that tall girl in ragged overalls looking inside?"

"I understand. So having tea is feeding that little girl's past."

"You were a boy growing up. Your mother made sure you had pants and a clean shirt to wear. I bet you wore boots when you became teens."

"Dad bought us boots instead of brogans. He told Mom we were in Texas and Texans wore boots."

"Well when I had shoes they were off the pile of brogans piled on the counter and never fit."

"Darling, you fit very well in society today after having such a horrible start."

"And I like it." She kissed him.

No one realized, growing up, how students thought about things like that. Harp and he rode good horses to school. Kids who rode burros or plow mules must have felt like her about them. Someday . . . I will do that . . .

CHAPTER 23

Two days later Hoot sent word there were parties of Comanche roaming around down there and for Long to send him some backup men. Hearing that, Long rode into town and found the boys or had others round them up. They said that Rex's mother was improving so he'd be joining them.

He told them to find four more good tough guys for him to hire and they would ride to Hoot's place and back them against any attack or whatever those red devils were up to. The men he needed had to be able to fight and shoot a Winchester or Colt. They would be paid twenty bucks and would be given a bonus for Indian fighting.

Long had a beer in the Longhorn Saloon and free lunch off the bar while he waited. Fresh rye bread, with sliced ham, cheese, and mustard. A big thick delicious sandwich washed down with draft beer. He had barely got the first bite down and they were back with four young men ready to ride.

He wrote down their names in his logbook so he could keep them straight.

Mickey Carr—freckles.

Heft Davis—face scar.

Tootie Morgan—always smiling.

Webb Yancey—big guy, stoop shouldered.

"Get lunch and a beer. We will head to the ranch afterward. Get a load of supplies, cooking gear, and packhorses and head out in the morning. My man down there says he has Comanche like some folks have ticks or fleas. We are there for Comanche control. It will be hard, fast riding. No place for the weak of heart. Anyone want out?"

They all shook their heads.

"Good. Eat well. It may be the last decent meal you have for weeks."

The new ones thanked him. There was always day work around, but a salaried job was a real good deal to have in those uncertain times. He understood the reason the four men were excited.

Long hired a buckboard to take two of the new men, with their saddles and gear, to the ranch. The other two had horses the ranch would pasture. All were there at the cowboy supper that evening, and he told them to be up and have breakfast by sunup.

After supper, Boone and Rex got their supplies out of the adobe warehouse where they were stored. Low Me wasn't going with them, so the cooking chores were to be divided up. They might not be able to get a wagon through some of that brush country they might have to go through to chase down the enemy.

Long felt good when he turned in—he had the men and the equipment to run down escaping Comanche. Action came next.

CHAPTER 24

Worst part about leaving—in the cooler morning air—had to be him kissing her good-bye. He'd miss her and she'd do the same about him. However this move was necessary. Stop the Comanche before they struck . . . and he hoped his lightning force was fast and strong enough to handle the matter.

At the moment they had his complete faith. They would meet their painted red faces and turn them back to where they came from. Time would tell, and by late afternoon they were at the well-guarded South Ranch. Hoot came out to meet them wearing his large gray Boss of the Plains Stetson hat.

"Well they didn't swallow you in Kansas. How are you, Long?"

"Great. We had a successful trip north. No big problems. Lost one cowboy, and a young boy who came down with a fever."

"That may be a record ain't it?"

"Might be. What are the Comanche up to this morning?"

"One of the men shot two of them three days ago at a watering hole."

"How was that?"

"We knew they had been drinking there. Ross Durban laid low up there. He wanted a shot at them. The boys even took his horse away so they'd not see it. Three of them bucks came to water about daylight. They were stripped to the waist and had yellow and red war paint all over their bodies.

"One was on his belly getting a drink, one on foot. The third on a horse. Ross shot the horseman, reloaded his single-shot sniper rifle with another bullet and managed to get the drinker. The other one got away, but those two were dead. His fifty-caliber Sharps put them both out of their misery. He ended up with two good war ponies he caught. Rode one of them back and he led number two to the ranch. Things have been slower since then."

"I can imagine. But can we still use a force to sweep our ranges of them?"

"Tomorrow Ross can show you some other places where they've been. Wash up. My wife will feed you all at the house."

"What about your men?"

"They will eat the next shift. They aren't back yet."

"Okay, we'll get our horses unloaded and we will be there," Long said.

"Good. She will love to see you."

"Men, unload and put the horses up. Wash up. Food's on at the house."

They thanked him and took Long's horse. Then Long and Hoot started for the house. "How is your wife?"

"Pregnant again. Mexican women can get that way at the drop of the hat, but she loves the big house and loves having babies, so who the hell am I to complain. You know I thought I'd live out my life in Mexico. I had no fortune, no big ranch, and a few years ago when there were no markets, hell there was no need in having cattle. Figured I'd get me a *hacienda* and eat *frijoles* until I died."

"But Dad got you off your rump, out of your hammock, and made you come help us?"

"He damn sure did. I never believed the cattle business would be this damn good this long. You had to own a thousand of them and they barely paid expenses. I thought he'd lost his mind branding all them worthless mavericks with you boys. That old son of a buck knew damn good and well it would change. Now who in the blazes told him that?"

"Intuition."

"Aw, who in the hell is that?"

"It ain't anyone. Something in his head told him that and it worked."

"What else will do that same thing then?"

"I don't have any of it. He has it and Harp and I are working it hard."

Hoot took his hat off and beat on his dusty

chaps with it. "I want a better explanation than that."

"That is simply what it is."

"Sounds like ammunition."

"No. It might blow up but it is not real explosive. It is like you seeing something in mesquite beans to market and know they will be best sellers and you corner the mesquite bean market."

"How do you get it?"

"I guess study some things until you find a winner."

"I hated studying when I was a kid. Like why know what six times seven amounts to? I don't give a damn. I know it and never used it in my life one time. And the teacher rapped me on the back of my hand for saying, 'I will never use that in my life.'"

Long was laughing washing up on the back porch. He dried off and followed him inside.

Hoot's wife's welcomed him with a hug and then handed him a cup of coffee.

"It is hot but it is your brand. I am glad you buy that brand for all of us. How is your lovely wife?"

"Jan sends her best to all of you. We are hitting the brush so she stayed at home."

"Good idea. These Comanche have us all upset."

"You're safe here. They want defenseless people and to kidnap their children."

"Why do you think they do that?"

"A professor once told me Comanche women rode horses and lose them. They have a very low birth rate so they steal young white and brown children to raise them as Comanche."

"I would hate to live with them. They smell bad."

Long agreed.

Hoot shook his head. "You should teach school. I never knew what intuition was. I also never heard them redskins had a low birth rate."

"Listen, when I was a boy I wanted to shoot crows with a twenty-two rather than study."

"But today it stuck to you, that is all that matters."

One of the house girls brought him a plate with browned beef and corn on the cob. She then brought him some fry bread and a bowl of *frijoles*. That set down before him she asked if he needed anything else.

"No, and thanks. It smells wonderful." He turned to Hoot seated across from him and not eating. "We had no mesquite fires in Kansas to cook beef over. Maybe you could cut down mesquite and sell it to them. I missed having it up there."

Hoot made a painful face. "Won't be me cuts it down."

They both laughed.

That night he met Hoot's Indian hunter, Ross

Durban. They talked about Comanche and where to find their camps to attack them on a hit-and-run basis. Durban shared his thoughts on where they might find them. The man was past his twenties, had shoulder-length brown hair, mustache, and a beard. After a short conversation Long considered him to be a damn good tough scout, and, with his skills, they might actually send the Comanche packing from their country.

Fight fire with fire his father told him several times, and that meant making a surprise raid on them in their camp, so in the morning they were going to try to run them down. The tough men Long brought would ride with him and Durban, aiming to find and make a hard raid on the Comanche secreted in the hills of ranchland the family owned.

"I feel we will find them in the drainage of Wooly Creek and Kennedy Branch," Durban told Long. "That's the country I found the most signs."

"You know that country better than any man. We can head there. Taking only three pack animals with us will make us mobile, but we will need to be resupplied on the third day."

Durban agreed that if they were not resupplied, their efforts would be shut down or weakened.

Hoot said that they need not worry—they would be supplied.

Before he undressed, Long stood in the dark bedroom and stared out into the moonlit yard. He felt the risk they planned would work, if they could manage the surprise. They simply had to do it right.

CHAPTER 25

It proved to be another hot late summer day when they made camp. All the signs of Indians they found were old, but Durban said they were still short of the country he'd found the most fresh sign. Long had a night guard schedule, and his men all knew the big dipper time clock to tell them when to go wake their successor—that made Long smile—they'd never call for him. *Get up. It's my time to take a turn.*

They were all ready before dawn. Horses caught, a quick meal, and in the saddle on the move. By afternoon Durban began to point out fresh sign. Several barefoot horse prints and scattered horse poop, signs that were looked for. They split into two groups with plans to relocate at a spot nearby before dark.

Shade Clements could track and he carefully listened to Durban's description of the land they'd find before taking the men on their hunt to a place Durban called Lost Hats. If they found something they were to come back. "Don't be stupid. You see a handful of Injuns, there may be more just around the corner."

Both Long and Shade agreed that made sense. They split up and Shade led half the crew on the dim road headed west by southwest.

Long decided the road had not been used for a wheeled vehicle in many years. Some of this land had been widely settled much earlier, but with pressure from the warring tribes and a lack of market for anything they grew, made them move back to more populated areas.

In a land of cedars and live oak patched with grassy meadows and beds of prickly pear, they rode on. Long and the others were craning their necks around all the time—in case they spotted a Comanche.

A shot rang out. Long took charge. After not seeing the telltale smoke of a rifle or pistol, he pointed to the cedars ahead. They busted into the cover, unlimbering their rifles and handguns on the way.

"Two hold the horses. The rest get down and try to see who is shooting at us."

Rex held over half the horses. Ivy had the rest all crowded in the tall cedars. Nearby, Shade was on his belly under the cedars shooting toward the way the other shots had come from. Long was beside him. He spotted something red, took aim, shot, and he knew that there was one less Comanche in the world. Ejecting the casing, he wondered how many more there were out there.

"Go easy on our ammo," he told them. "This could go on for a while."

Rex soon joined them on the ground under the pungent bows. "The horses are hobbled."

"Good thinking," Long said.

"Anyone has seen who it is?" Ivy asked.

"Can't you smell them?" Boone asked.

"No."

Just then two war-painted armed bucks came riding by, yipping like coyotes and wildly shooting at the thicket. For a moment they were there. Then a wall of bullets sent the horses to the ground, and their riders were thrown to the grass screaming in pain.

"Wave one," Long said. "I have fought them before. That is the testing of what we can do—I expect much more shortly."

"You really did this before?"

"My father, Harp, and I held them off on several occasions trying to recover captives."

It wasn't more than a few minutes when another, larger, wave of fierce bucks charged them. The horses were, again, shot out from under them and the raging screaming riders jumped free to stand with smoking guns cutting through the boughs of the cedars, but their action was short-lived. Accurate shooting soon wilted them all down. Long had had no doubts that his men could fight, and they were sure answering the call.

Long mopped his face with his kerchief. It was as hot as hell in that cedar grove waiting for another wave. The Comanche ponies, wounded and in pain, were limping around or were dying, lying on their sides in the dried grass among the corpses of the raiders.

Sweat—or was it tears?—masked his vision, and his eyelids couldn't clear the moisture fast enough to suit him. This place under the evergreen needles was not a place he wanted to end his days. He had a lovely wife, a bigger ranch than he'd dreamed of ever having, and a life he found interesting.

The sharp smell of the spent ammo was burning in his nose. Belly down once again and he wondered how many more wanted a one-way trip to hell. It was amazing. His men had already held off two waves of them—obviously the Comanche had underestimated his small force's ability to fight back.

Time crawled by as slowly as a caterpillar covering a road to reach the other side. Then he heard more shooting to the south of them. What was that all about? He rose to his knees, holding his palm out for them to be quiet and listen.

There were several horses coming their way.

"Men, get ready. I think Durban and the other have some Indians on the run, and they will come right by us."

A cheer went up from his men.

Everyone frantically reloaded their weapons to be ready. The shooting was ear deafening, and there were enough horses shot to cause a jam-up. A billowing cloud of gun smoke became a dense fog as the desperate braves were being slaughtered, if not injured, by the crashing horses.

Then Long saw Durban and the others come riding hard in pursuit with smoking guns that assured him they would all see another sunrise. What a day in the Texas brush . . . he hoped the surviving tribal members would go back to their tepees and tell the others they found a hornet's nest down there in the Texas brush and know to leave the ranch area alone.

"Is everyone all right?" he asked Boone.

"A few got skinned. Nothing serious. We're fine."

"Our horses all here and sound," Ivy said.

"Hey, what have you guys been doing?" Durban shouted as Long beat the sticky needles off his hat and chaps.

The two men embraced, and Long thanked him and the rest of the men. "We did very well, men. The smallest army to ever whip the Comanche besides the Texas Rangers. You did a great job."

The men congratulated each other . . . a real grateful feeling between them all of a job well done.

The group counted the number of Comanche and sent any of them not gone on with their brothers to hell. Sixteen Comanche braves were not breathing. They managed to catch six sound horses. With all this done, Long felt that the

Comanche would go somewhere else, gather their forces, and raid. Anyway he hoped so.

There were enough supplies to hold one man for a few days, so Durban decided that he would take a packhorse and the rest of the supplies with him to search more of the ranchland for signs of Comanche. Long shook his hand before he rode out and thanked him for taking the job, and to get back to the ranch fast if he saw more. Obviously the man liked the job and would be a good lookout. The rest rode back with Long to Hoot's headquarters.

Back at the ranch and kitchen table, Hoot listened to Long's description of the battle. "We had no idea the size of the force. We were pinned down, in good cover, but how we all came out unscathed I will never know. Except God must have saved us."

"He must have. That Durban is a helluva scout isn't he?"

"Yes, a great one."

"He told me he had been kidnapped by them and lived among them for many years. They never treated him right. One day a sub chief kicked him around as that *damn white boy*. He said it might have been over his talking, earlier, to his daughter, but the beating made him so mad he left them and swore revenge."

"I'd say it was to our good fortune. Keep him on the payroll."

"Oh, I plan to. Long, thanks for handling this. They may get out of our hair after this."

"Or seek revenge."

Hoot nodded, a very serious look on his face. "They are vengeful."

Long missed his lovely wife more than usual. "Well, I'm headed home in the morning. Harp should be getting back. I have more ranches to buy. You ever see an eight-acre lake off in the southwest on some private land?"

"Is it in our block?"

"Yes."

"I bet some of my men have found it. I'll check around and let you know."

"I met the son of the owner of that section up in Kansas. His name is Clyde Nelson. It's isolated and he told me they'd sell it when they get back home. I'm going to go find and look at it. It is on a section in the southwest."

"I think that's funny. You found a lost Texas lake in Kansas."

"Things are under control here for now. Are there any mavericks left to brand?"

"We keep finding a few, but they are almost all gone."

"I guess everyone found they'd better brand them or someone else would do it."

Hoot agreed and shook his hand. "That spring you two went to Missouri. I should have branded a few thousand and I'd be rich today."

"Dad had us doing that every chance we got."

"Him and I argued about it. Me telling him why do that . . . they aren't worth the effort."

"I almost felt that way, too." They both laughed.

"When you sold that first herd, what did you think?"

"It struck me, when we got back home, that we had thousands of dollars because of those cattle."

Hoot shook his head. "It's been unbelievable hasn't it?"

Long agreed. His whole life had been unbelievable ever since. He thought he'd found his woman in the captain's widow, but she wouldn't have him. Then some women came and went. Like fog, they were gone in the morning. Then Rose came into his life, and losing her left him alone and sad. He'd worried, headed for home, if being a breed was his problem with women, but then he found Jan. She didn't care about his origin, and now he was sure anxious to get back to her.

The next day he and his crew hurried home. Hiram met him. One of his men took Long's horse and they walked to the main house as Long told him how they sent the Comanche packing.

"I'd liked to have been there and gave them what for with ye."

"I thought about that, with five of us denned up in the cedars and my men busy mowing them down. Then this tracker Durban brought the rest of the men on the run to support us. Not one man was more than scratched—"

Just then his wife, Jan, shedding a straw hat, came on a hard run for him and jumped into his arms. "You're back in one piece."

She smothered him with kisses as he swung her around in a circle like she was a feather. "Damn right I am, girl, and am I glad to see you."

When he set her down she looked a little embarrassed.

"Don't worry . . . I missed you that bad, too."

"Oh, Long, I was so worried you'd been hurt or shot—"

"No way. We beat them at their own game and sent them packing."

"I can't say how excited I am to have you back in one piece." She pressed her forehead up against his.

"Damn, Jan, I really miss being with you when you're not around."

"That makes two of us."

"What would you like to do?"

She glanced around and, satisfied no one was close, said, "Let's go get lost in our bed."

"Good idea."

CHAPTER 26

They got up the next day and went down to breakfast. Harp and Katy were down there at the table.

"It's trying to freeze us outside," Harp said.

Long scooted the chair under his wife. "Is it that cold?"

"Water left outside is frozen."

"That is cold down here. I have always been glad winters were not as hard down here as when we lived in Arkansas as boys."

"We had lots of snowball fights up there. I miss that here."

"We'd get behind on busting stove wood and have to do it on the coldest days of the year."

Harp laughed. "That was serious."

"Has anything else happened while I was gone?"

"Nothing important. I think you can go back to buying those ranches that are included in our original purchase."

"We'll start back in two days. I want to study the maps more. And I'll need two more guards. Johnny and Anthony are going to run that last operation we took over."

"Boone asked to do that the next time we need a new rider for you. What about that boy broke his arm?"

"Ivy Martin's good but Robbie Boyd has lots of qualities that, I think, make him a better choice."

"I thought he was just a cowboy?"

"He thought you didn't want him after the drive. Jan will tell you he's a guy that gets things done."

"You say he will work, then we'll get those two set up."

Long nodded.

"We don't need a cook and crew," Jan said. "I'll do that. We'll take packhorses and be able to make more places. There isn't over a half dozen left."

"I didn't want to burden you."

"I'm as tough as those men, but thanks anyway."

After breakfast and alone, she asked him if she sounded too bossy.

"No. He was being thoughtful of you."

"Good. My way, I think we can get this job over a lot quicker."

He hugged and kissed her. "I'm like you. The sooner we get through this deal the more work we can get done on other things."

A cold morning faced them when they rode out. She looked warm in her wool-lined coat with a scarf and a knit wool cap. In his long johns and layers of clothing, Long rode beside her warm enough to survive. Boone and Robbie Boyd were outfitted for the cold, they assured him, and breathing steam they laughed when one of the packhorses tried to buck in the four-horse chain.

They had a planned route to take to the last of the ranches. The HKC Brand outfit belonged to Cash Burnett. Long had met the rancher in Kerrville on several occasions in the past. He was a wiry short man who was very quick about things that concerned him and how he wanted a situation to begin or end. Burnett's wife remained unseen in public—there was talk that she was yellow, which meant she had black blood in her.

No one who worked for him ever answered questions or even spoke about her. Burnett must have threatened their lives if they did. Long considered the issue as he rode in the cold air headed southwest with his crew. Both men were excited to be his new aides since they had only heard rumors about the man who had all *vaqueros* for help.

They camped that night on a creek they discovered. This pleased Long. Water in the west was critical to any ranch operation. They rode across country after he decided the two-track road was too long a route. He was seeing new country, and even bunches of mavericks that he marked down and counted as theirs. When they got back he'd send men down there to brand them.

They reached the ranch, and the stock dogs

sounded mad they'd come. Long observed as, wrapped in a blanket, the hatless Cash Burnett came out of the adobe house. He shooed the dogs off with a few curt shouts at them.

"Morning, Cash." Long stepped off the bay horse.

"What the hell—oh, hello, Mr. and Mrs. O'Malley. What brings you down here?"

"You know my brother bought a large part of the land around you?"

"I heard that."

"We want to offer you a fair price for your place."

"I am not interested in selling out."

"Fine, but sometime in the future it may be we'll have to fence the land."

"We will see about that."

"Know that we have title to all the land around your section, and if you're shut down to six hundred forty acres, you will be out of the range cattle business."

"So you came clear out here to tell me to get the hell out of here."

"No. I came here to give you a hand to go find a larger place with less restraints that can hurt you down the road."

Cash shifted the blanket he wore. "If you rode all the way out here to tell me that, O'Malley, you wasted your gawdamn time."

"My offer is good for thirty days. We can work

out any problems you have to move if it is your desire."

"I won't be interested."

Long felt he had the man's firm decision.

Jan booted her horse forward. "Tell your wife I am sorry I did not get to meet her."

He never answered her. He turned on his heels, shifted the blanket up on his shoulders, and went back to the house.

"Come on, boys. He's set and we won't change his mind. We have other places to see about."

There was a squatter named Hernandez west of there that he planned to tell to leave. There were several such squatters that had to be moved. Lots of them merely stopped and set up a place to exist. Some like Hernandez came from Mexico and hoped to claim a free farm.

"Do you wonder what his wife looks like?" Jan asked, riding in close to him.

"I never saw her."

"He never answered me about meeting her, did he?"

"He had to keep his security of hiding her."

"I wonder why?"

"We may never know."

"How far is this next place away?" she asked.

Long twisted in the saddle and asked Boone, "How far away is the next one?"

"A day's ride. The cowboys drew me a map."

"Do we have all the landowners now?" Jan asked.

"The rest are squatters. But Harp and I discussed moving and helping them get resettled."

"What do we know about this next guy?"

"He and a few others are farming small plots along a creek and have a spring fenced."

They camped that night in a nice valley and spotted more unbranded cattle that ran off with their tails over their backs like spooked deer.

The sun had warmed the day, and the fire that was cooking the beans radiated more heat as they relaxed—seated on blankets—waiting.

"Hey, I think you two are great aides, but you have noticed the number of mavericks still unbranded out here?"

"I told Boone we needed men to round them up and brand them," Rob said. "He agreed that a good crew could make a good showing of rounding them up, and drive the branded cattle off the holding."

"I have a spare notebook in my saddlebags. Start a list of what you need, and when we get back, if you want, we can get you two going with a team to do that."

Boone said, "I told Rob yesterday we could show you what kind of foremen we'd make."

"I chose you two because I saw foreman qualities in both of you working as a team.

Before we're through moving folks off the ranch, we may find a setup for you two."

"Sounds good to me."

"Boone and I have been talking about Gladys, Jan."

"What about her?"

Rob kind of ducked his head and then said, "I know you didn't think much of her. But she takes good care of Missy. They say she works hard for Long's mom as a helper. She ain't ugly and she kinda shocked us as being respectable. I'd kind of like to court her."

Long heard what was said. "Jan and I don't care, but Mom might not want to lose her."

"Well—my intentions right now are honest ones. I'm not afraid of that guy who dumped her coming back."

"Well, good luck," Long said.

"Yes, we hope something works out," Jan said. "Those biscuits in the Dutch oven must be done."

"I can get them," Boone said, and told her to stay seated.

They ate supper and went to sleep. Someone shouted for them in the night.

Long, with the pistol in his hand, sat up in the blankets and pressed her to stay down. "I don't know who it is."

The intruder in Spanish said, "I must talk to the patron."

"He must mean you, Long. You savvy him?"

285

"Keep your guns ready." He rose and went to see what the man wanted.

"The *señora* asks you come back to the *ranchero*. A bad thing has happened. Our patron has taken his life."

"Cash killed himself?"

"*Sí, señor.*"

"Oh, Long that is terrible. What will she do? What can we do for her?"

"Right now I don't know. One of you stay here with our camp. The rest of us will ride back and see what we can do for her. Whoever stays needs to load up and join us there in the morning."

Boone said he'd be along with their outfit.

Long thanked him and horses were saddled. The man who came told them his name was Randle. He led the ride back to the ranch under the stars.

Around the house, the *vaqueros*, their wives, and children were wrapped in blankets praying and crying in the starlight.

Randle had the ranchmen hitch the horses, then Long, Jan, and him made their way to the house and inside the door where the silent Cash had entered several hours earlier.

Another *vaquero* rose from his knees on the living room floor. Cash's body was laid out under a blanket, and a woman stood wearing a black veil beside him. Long could not tell anything about her.

"I am so sorry to call you here, but I don't know what to do. My husband has taken his own life despite my pleas not to do it. He spoke so bitter that you had told him to move—"

Long shook his head. "We didn't tell him to move. We told him we'd buy him out and help him move. We told him he might be fenced in by fences on his boundaries in the future."

"I could not change his mind. Now what can I do?"

"My name is Jan. I am Long's wife. Would you rather talk to me? We did not come today to make him that wrought up."

"My name is Eve Burnett. I have a marriage license from the Indian Territory signed by a judge. I was born a slave in Mississippi, ran away, and made my way as a teenage girl to where the Seminoles lived. They took me in and I met Cash up there. He promised me no one would ever find me on his ranch in Texas. Up till a year ago, agents of my owners could've taken me back. I was grateful to have lived here in seclusion."

"They can't come get you now."

"Cash was afraid Texas had a law against marrying a black woman."

"I don't know anything about that." Jan shook her head.

Long said, "If you wish to leave here we will move you and help you get settled, pay you for your ranch, and get you into a new life."

"But, Eve, you can stay at our ranch until you feel ready to meet the public."

"I am not good at business."

Jan hugged her. "We will help you."

She squeezed Jan's hand on her shoulder. "I will be brave."

"Do you want him buried here?" Long asked.

"Yes, he would want that. Why did he get so worked up?"

Long shook his head. "That we may never know."

Cash was buried. All the *vaqueros* and their families were told to remain. He told them Boone would stay there while they found a place for Cash's wife. He would be there and Rob would come back, and they would be the bosses and the ranch would pay them.

He told Rob he should make a list of anything he and Boone would need. They would be on the ranch list as the buyers from there on. They should verify the pocketbook they found on Cash, which stated the numbers of cattle and horses he owned. He wanted them to look for farmland to put up hay on. This place was so distant from everything that sometimes they would need reserves of forage to support the cattle during droughts or unusual snows.

Boone came the next morning and Rob told him all that had happened.

The two men were excited about their new job

and thanked him. Boone promised him he'd have the men start counting cattle in the morning.

"If you could hire a dozen *vaqueros* down here, could you round up those mavericks?"

"Damn right," Boone said.

"I bet the guys here could get us a crew in a week," Rob said, equally excited.

Long herded the two of them aside. "Rob, what will you do about Gladys?"

"I told Boone I'd ask her to marry me."

"What did you say, Boone?"

"I told him to do it. I have a gal, Marsha Kelly, up at Honey Springs who will marry me now I have a real foreman job. Rob and I can share the house."

Long was laughing. When he caught up with his wife she asked what was so funny.

"I caused two weddings coming down here."

"Who?"

"Rob is going to ask Gladys to marry him. Boone has a girl up at Honey Springs he's going to ask to marry him now he has a foreman's job."

"You and Harper are going to have lots of married foremen."

"We will also have some hard workers in place."

"I think you guys are lucky to find these men. You get to test them and I bet those two do a great job."

"First, we take Eve back to the ranch and then

find two more men to guard us. We still have squatters."

"Eve is a lovely woman, and he didn't want her taken back to slavery did he?"

"Just like me. I wouldn't let them take you away, either."

She was laughing. "You may be getting over being so stoic."

He laughed some more. "Yes, I am. How did you—"

"I am taking a word a day to catch up with you."

He hugged and kissed her. "Now I have competition."

They headed home, with Jan driving the buckboard and Eve beside her. Long led the packhorses.

Things were going right again.

CHAPTER 27

Eve wore a veil as they rode through the main street of town out to their ranch. Long knew some people saw her, but he didn't mind that—she could be the mystery woman.

At the ranch Easter saw they had a passenger and hurried out to meet her and welcome her.

"Mother, this is Eve Burnett. She is Cash's widow and needs some support." Easter and Jan got Eve off the buckboard and got her inside as Harp arrived.

Long headed him off. "We had a tragedy out there. Cash Burnett committed suicide over our offer to buy him out, so we brought his widow here with us."

"You didn't threaten him?"

"Harp, I explained all the details. Stay, do what he wanted, but she said he was so upset he took his own life."

"That is bad news for us. Word will spread that we threatened him, and it will put the remaining ones on their guard."

Long shook his head. "The rest are squatters. They may have homestead claims, but he was the last one who owned the land inside that block."

"Hey, you two have been busy and I wasn't complaining," Harp apologized.

"We have been. The lady is black. I think that was his secret. He married her in Indian Territory. She is his heir and wants to sell to us. I made my two aides the foremen for that place. They are counting cattle and then gathering all the mavericks. It's pretty isolated, but I bet there are a thousand head of unbranded cattle there. We saw lots of them when we were coming and going."

"That was a helluva job you two got done."

"We still have the squatters. They won't be easy. This suicide made me do lots of mind searching, brother. But I never threatened him about it."

"I believe you. The sisters, again, left this year's cattle money in the ranch account that we handle for what they said would be repairs."

"Whew. That's a hundred sixty thousand. They say what they want us to do?"

"Keep up the good work. They have that much money and much more. They call it the 'repair the ranch fund.' "

"Could we use it to buy another place?"

"I never asked but that with the money already in there we could buy another large ranch in their name for them."

"Are you and I going to present a plan to them? And, brother, we need to look hard at this cattle drive business for next year. We need to do it, but we also need to separate our cattle drive business from our ranching."

Harp agreed. "Ranching is too important to take our leaders away north every summer, and while we have not had any big losses while gone we are exposed."

"I love to go but it is not something a foreman can't handle. One of us can go up and sell the cattle when they get there."

"Long, you've done lots of thinking on these trips of yours."

He smiled and nodded. "You get a mountain to move, you need to start shoveling."

"Hey, we can get a job to drive some steers to Sedalia this next year. Pays fifteen bucks a month if we can get there."

"It was a job all right. Right off you got to be night guard boss. And I recall saying they could shove it."

"We have come a long ways."

"Harp, did you even dream we'd get this much done?"

"No. I couldn't have thought that big. I'll run into town and talk to our agent about another land deal. He sent me a note there were two men to talk to, and we can plan something maybe with the sisters?"

"I think it is time to strike while the iron is hot. Places are increasing in price fast enough with all this cattle money available."

"I agree."

After lunch Long went and talked to Red about

who would be his new guards. Not because he felt threatened but he'd promised everyone he would not go around alone. Red wanted to sleep on it.

"I sent you the best two guys I had and you hired them to run that ranch." Red was laughing hard and pounding him on the shoulder.

"They really were good, and now they are both looking for wives."

"I heard that. I wish them well and will help them."

"Good. They are two smart guys. I learned that on my trip home."

"If they need help on the roundup of those mavericks, I can spare them some men."

"Red, they may hire some *vaqueros* out of Mexico. We'll see. There's plenty to do up there."

Red agreed and they parted. So many of those guys who went to Sedalia turned into good managers. He recalled the guys who lived around there who told him he was crazy trying to run the blockade with that herd, and to this day they still had nothing. He realized the ones that went along had guts and a desire to succeed. Anyone could sit on his butt at home, but it took back-bone to tackle an untried deal and then make it work.

A couple hours later he was headed for supper. He hung his canvas duster, hat, and gun belt on the hall hook and washed up. The house was warm from the crackling fires in the big fireplaces that his father built in the house. His mother said it was exactly like he had across the waters. Long could remember himself, as a boy, using a crowbar to pry the huge flat rocks up, then teamed with Harp, loading them into a wagon to haul back to the new house site. They gathered way more than their dad needed because he insisted he needed them. They made walks and even garden walls with the leftovers.

Before he could get angry thinking about all the extra work his dad made him do, Jan ran over and kissed him in the hallway.

"Have a good day?"

"Yes. How was yours?"

"We measured Gladys for a wedding dress and she sobbed all day. Said she never had one and no one ever worried about her having one. Missy is as excited as she is. We also found out about Boone's choice, and when he proposes to her and she accepts he will tell her we will sew her a wedding dress."

"Sounds like you are handling it all."

"Harp is going to be late. He's been doing some investigation regarding a large ranch that might be for sale," Katy said, walking down the hall with them toward the dining room.

Jan looked at him to see if he knew anything about that.

He shook his head.

"The food is hot and ready. Everyone, take a seat and we shall say grace. Long?"

He said a quick thanks and everyone said amen. Then they passed platters and bowls around. Hiram was talking about a new colt born that week and how great he looked.

Easter came around with a coffeepot to fill cups. "I think he just rode in."

Katy stood up. "Excuse me. I'll tell him we are eating and to come on."

"Fine. He may have news for us," Hiram said.

Everyone agreed. She went out on the porch to summon Harp and soon returned and took her place. "He's coming."

"Hi, everyone. I rode hard and fast. It has been a stirring evening. I went to see our land agent today. He had two lawyers in his office, and I was ready to leave since he looked busy. Instead he came out and stopped me. Now this is a secret. You knew Rupert Glass, who owned the Three Star Ranch, died six months ago?"

"His place is larger than ours, isn't it?" Long asked.

"Yes. And that doesn't count his ranches in Mexico."

"How much is down there?"

"Two large operations."

"What is happening with the family?"

"His wife Juanita is running it now. His only son by his first wife is a drunken playboy. His name is Scot Glass. She wants to sell all of it."

"For how much?" Long asked.

"Three hundred thousand. But she will take payments from us."

"That sounds too cheap," Long said.

"She wants to live out her life in the main house. We would have to keep it up for her, and when she dies it will be ours. But we will need to protect her from anything happening to her. She thinks he had enemies and she wants our protection. People told her we were real doers and good businesspeople."

"What about the Mexican properties?" Long asked.

"I think they are rundown from the bits and pieces I got from the lawyers today."

"Who runs it?"

"Some nationals."

"I would have thought so. Mexico is in financial ruin just like the States. They are fighting wars among themselves. We might be in the path of some homemade general, and he might destroy the ranches if we took charge."

"Hell, Long, the Union Army at Arkansas on the Butterfield Road could've done that to us."

"Or killed us south of Sedalia if we'd let them."

"Yes. I am thinking the sisters might help us. I want us to go talk to them as investors."

"How soon do we have to decide?" Jan asked.

"Not over a week. She is very nervous according to the lawyers. I offered to send her some protection now."

"What did they say? The lawyers?"

"They have hired some men, but lawyers are not leaders of such a force."

"One of us needs to go up there if we buy it."

"Yes. Draw straws?"

"No. You have a son and a wife. Jan and I can go. She gets along with women. I can figure out if her threat is real or imagined. At least we can put her fears to rest since she will be our ward. Has she sold any cattle in Kansas?"

"I think that needs to be organized. Some trader took fifteen hundred head scraped up on the place according to his lawyers. She got less than thirty thousand. Those two lawyers knew I knew all about cattle sales."

"Hell that was only twenty bucks a head."

"That is why she wants us to take it over."

"Stop now. You boys, eat supper. Everyone is missing their meal over this conversation," Easter scolded them.

"Yes, ma'am. Mom, we'll talk later. This is a monumental deal, but, like going to Missouri, I believe we can do it," Harp said.

"Like your father said, that whole task was insurmountable for two Texas ranch–raised boys in their teens to deliver cattle past the Union lines."

"He never told us that," Long said.

"I doubted you would've listened," Hiram said.

Long shook his head. "We didn't expect to have to take over, or we'd probably not gone, especially if we'd realized we'd have to do it all. We inherited a mess. The good guys were not back from the war. We thought if we got paid fifteen dollars a month we'd be rich."

"Boys, at that time anyone paid fifteen dollars could hire the best labor in town. No veterans were home. The war was still on."

Harp agreed. "And no one had fifteen dollars to pay anyone."

They all laughed.

Plans were made to talk to the sisters the next day, taking their wives along, hoping to get permission to use their fund to buy the Three Star. Or a portion of that money.

In bed that evening, Long and Jan whispered about all the things that could happen or not happen with them getting this large a ranch. He fell asleep, his head whirling about the purchase of the Three Star outfit. When he awoke, he sat on the edge of the bed, his mind still spinning.

"You ready for the war?" his wife asked.

"I have no excuse not to be."

They both laughed and joined the others downstairs.

Harp, still taken aback said, "I never thought about that ranch being in our reach."

"You know his wife?"

"No. She must be in her thirties. Her parents were Mexican and that may be how he got those Mexican ranch holdings. Hey, before we went to Missouri we were like the rest of Texas—poor farm boys. They were the rich folks."

Jan smiled. "Well you two have moved rather fast into becoming big businessmen."

"The way I figure, we still have lots to learn, but we are doing real well."

"Today is the day it all starts."

He hugged and kissed her. "Wish us good luck."

After breakfast they took the two-seat buckboard and went to the Diamond Ranch with Harp and Katy. Red sent along two hands to cover them.

Mid-morning Long reined the team up the driveway and told the two guards their business might take some time. The men took the team up to the stables and told him they'd be ready whenever to go back.

The sisters were excited about the visit and ordered tea and small cookies.

Settled at the dining table, Harp spoke in a very businesslike way to them.

"We are here on a mission. A very respectable large ranch is up for sale at a very low price because of conditions. You knew Rupert Glass who died about six months ago?"

The older sister said, "He was a good friend of our father."

"And we went to his ranch for his second wedding to Juanita. Ten years ago?"

"About that long ago."

"Her lawyers came to us and asked if we would be interested in the property. It sounds like the place is badly mismanaged. She is concerned for her safety and wants to live out her life there. She would have the main house as long as she desires but is willing to sell it for three hundred thousand dollars on the condition we look out for her."

The older sister nodded and her sister did, too. "She is right where we sat before you two took over our ranch management."

"Thanks. We have been buying lots of land. In time we could absorb that ranch, but facing more cattle drives and ranch expenses we wondered if you would agree to us buying it using your ranch-upkeep funds?" Harp asked them.

The pair looked at each other. The younger one asked, "Is there enough money in it?"

"Certainly," Harp said.

"Well, if you run short in that fund you tell us, and we will replenish it."

Harp looked across the table at Long. "Bro, we will own the Three Star and their Mexican holdings by dark."

"So quick?" big sister asked.

"The deal will be sealed anyway."

"Can't you stay for lunch?"

"Long and I need to meet those lawyers. I promised them an answer today. Thank you very much. Ladies, you stay for lunch. Long and I will run into town, and the men will see you back to the ranch. And again, thank you both."

They hugged both women. On their way to the stables, Long was shaking his head at the ease of the agreement they reached.

"That was a tough job over," Harp said.

"I expected it. It was very generous for them to do that."

"You and Jan ready for Three Star?"

"I want those two boys I left down on the Burnett place. Wives and all I need them. That wouldn't leave you too stranded would it?"

"No. Has Boone proposed to his girl?"

"We can speed all that up. I am going to need some tough support, and those boys are the kind of men to do it."

They took their men's saddle horses, told them to drive the wives home when they got ready, and lit out for Kerrville in a gallop. It was past 3:30 p.m. when they reached the hotel and found the two lawyers in the hotel lobby.

Harp introduced the bald-headed one as Anthony Cripps and the heavyset gray-haired one as Curtis Taylor. They shook hands, drew up some upholstered chairs in the lobby, and talked in quiet voices.

"How does she expect the money?" Harp asked them.

"A hundred thousand down. She has some bills to pay. Twenty thousand a year at five percent interest."

"Four percent," Harp said.

"Four percent," Taylor agreed.

"Pay off any time no penalty," Harp said.

"Yes."

"Will we own the Mexican properties as well?"

"Yes. They are included. All the deeds will be free of any attachments."

"Does she know the names of the parties threatening her?" Long asked, sitting forward on the chair and searching both men's faces.

"She is not sure. But several people were at odds with her late husband."

"What did he do to them?"

"He was not in his right mind the last six months of his life. It may have been business plans he made and then didn't do what he said he would."

"Have they threatened her?"

"Yes. That is why we hired guards for the place."

"No idea what it was exactly?"

"A contractor named Colgate was one she said had threatened her. The other is a Mexican national named Florence somebody."

"That is his last name?"

"This is all that we know. We are lawyers not sheriffs or Pinkerton men."

"I savvy that. But knowing who they are would help me stop the threatening."

"You two have the power to handle this sale?" Harp asked.

Cripps nodded. "When can one of you take over this guarding business of her?"

"Three days," Long said. "I will have some men with me. Are the men you hired worth anything?"

"They are supposed to be. Two were former lawmen. Deputies I believe," Cripps said.

Hell anyone could be an ex-deputy. Long figured to go armed and supplied. That was why the lawyers wanted one of them there—they had no faith in their hires. This might be a bigger mess than the first herd deal they had run.

Harp wanted his local lawyers to read the final agreement, and their land man needed to look the contract over as well, before he'd sign it.

Long wanted to gather some men, immediately, and go north to the Three Star, which was a good distance from the H Bar H. The new place was north of Junction. He left Harp and rode home. His brother could handle the paperwork . . . he needed to see when he could get Boone and Robbie to go up there and take over the ranch.

Red could find some men to take care of Cash's ranch. This was a lot more important. He found

304

Red down at the blacksmith shop watching the work being done on repairing a wagon wheel.

"We need to talk outside."

"Sure. I'm not doing a damn thing here but chousing him on."

Once squatted on their boot heels in the warm sunshine, Red asked what he needed.

"Robbie and Boone. Harp and I are buying the Three Star Ranch and the two Mexican properties. They have some big problems up at the Three Star, and I need some real tough hands."

"How soon?"

"I need to be up there in charge in three days."

"Wow, that's fast."

"Yes. I know there is not much time."

"I can send the guy who ran the Diamond Ranch while Doug was gone on the drive. Poncho Sanchez is a good man and speaks Spanish. He should get it all done at the Burnett place."

"The house is usable and we can help him move. I think he has a wife and family."

"I suppose I better send someone to hold it down until then. Get these two up here, fast."

"I do need them. They can still get married but this widow of Glass is real worried for her life, they say. The lawyers hired some guards, but I don't think anyone knows how good they'd be if they came under fire."

"I'll send two men to run Burnett's until

Sanchez can get down there. Rob and Boone should be here tomorrow night. You can leave the next day or if you need to go up there. I can cut some men out to back you and they can meet you up there."

"I know this is all fast, but keep it all under your hat."

Red shook his head. "Wasn't it yesterday when Harp fired the cook?"

"Bet you never figured, in this short a time, you'd be heading up our main ranch, either."

"Hell, no. I was worried if I'd even draw them fifteen bucks a month he promised us."

"Thanks. I see my wife is back so I better help her pack. She's going with us."

"You're lucky. I don't know anyone's got a good hand for a wife as you."

Long agreed and went to join her.

She had a million questions to ask him.

Where would they live up there?

What would she have to do up there?

What would be his position up there?

He promised her she'd like it, and they were going to run that ranch and the other ranches Glass owned. Period.

With all the fussing and fury, they had all her belongings and things they'd need packed and tarped down in a strong farm wagon. A hand would drive it up there. His men would arrive from down south the following evening.

306

The next evening he, Jan, Robbie, and Boone sat at the dining table. He explained all he knew about the Three Star and what he wanted from them. They didn't need to cancel any plans. They'd just get married in a different place. But, first, he wanted them to ride up there with him and secure the place.

"Two days ride huh?" Boone asked.

"About that. It is north of Junction," Long said.

"I want to go see Marsha and tell her my plans. I am sure she will be fine, but I can join you tomorrow on that road?"

"That will work. I think in two weeks we will have things under control and you can marry her."

"Good."

"I guess Gladys is at the house?" Rob asked.

"We told her you'd be here today."

"Good. What time will we leave tomorrow?"

"Daybreak."

"I'll be ready. Excuse me," Rob said, and headed for another part of the house. Boone saluted them, left, mounted his horse, and rode off.

Long and Jan came out and sat on the bench in the warm sun.

"New adventure huh?"

"I been having lots of them lately. Found a wife. Bought some land. Fought some Injuns and now have a new adventure. The Three Star Ranch next. No telling what we will find up there."

"But my husband will straighten it out."

"Glad you have that much faith."

She clapped his leg against her. "I do. You saved me from the impossible."

"Oh, that was no big deal."

"Four men shot and killed. I was impressed. What did you and Harp talk about?"

"Things I might face and need to do. Get a list of the employees. Try to solve that messed-up cattle deal they got into last year. I can't understand that cattle sale. That was robbery. And I don't know what they scrabbled up to make the drive. And I have to figure out what to do this year. Learn how many cattle they have. Solve this threat she is so upset about. Lots of things going on."

"I can help listing the help and those things."

"I am counting on it. I may need an accountant, too."

"I guess we have all that to learn. It's a two-day travel from here?"

"Yes." Long really felt he should be there already. He needed the backing. Rob and Boone would be that. It was the unknown bothered him the most.

The next morning they were headed for the Three Star. Two more of Red's ranch hands were bringing the loaded wagon. Gladys and Missy were there to send Rob off. Hiram was there nodding his head and grinning. Easter told them at breakfast she was cheering for them. They'd pick up Boone around mid-day near Honey Springs, and plans were to camp north that night, about forty miles from home.

His paint Comanche horse was excited, so he rode him around some, held close to set him down if he considered bucking. The horse calmed, and they were soon on the road. He, Jan, and Rob rode together up front in the pink crease of dawn on the horizon. There was a touch of silver frost on the grass, and they were all breathing steam into the cold.

Noontime Boone met them on the road. A pretty brunette girl sat in a buckboard; Jan rode over and spoke to her.

"Everything all right?" Long asked him.

"Oh, we're fine. Marsha says she can wait. She thinks the Three Star will be a better place to live than Cash's ranch way down there."

Long laughed. "It might be. Jan's coming. We better ride. We still have miles to make today."

Jan joined them. "You have a lovely future wife, Boone. She said you told her about the dress we'll sew for her."

"Her folks are excited we are going to be closer to them."

"We have lots to do."

"Oh, I figured that. I told Rob we'd have a real job up there."

Long nodded. "The four of us can cover a lot."

That evening, they camped beside a small stream. Everyone helped her fix the evening meal. Toby Carpenter and Rowdy Peabody were the younger hands and excited to be in on the trip. They reminded Long of him and his brother headed for Sedalia—lots to learn.

They avoided contact with people in settlements they passed through, and Long told them the less learned about them the better it might be. Noon the next day they were at the base of a hill looking up at the huge, redbrick, two-story mansion above them.

"Wow," Jan said, reining up her horse. "Now that is a mansion."

"Big house."

"How many people live there?" Boone asked, holding his saddle horn and rising in the stirrups to stretch.

"I don't know where his son is. The lady, his widow, lives there."

"It would take all day to just check the rooms," Rob said.

Long booted his horse on. "I was thinking the same thing. Let's go see what we have."

At the circle drive, he dismounted and then waited for Jan to join him at the door. He'd not seen any security checking on them.

A butler answered the door and asked for their card.

Long frowned at him and Jan spoke up. "Mrs.

Glass is expecting him. His name is Long O'Malley and mine is Jan. I am his wife. We are the buyers her lawyer sent."

"Wait here. Who are those armed men out there?" the butler asked.

"Employees of mine. No threat."

"I can't be too careful."

"We understand—that is why we are here."

"I will tell Mrs. Glass you are here. She may be indisposed at the moment."

Long nodded and looked around the entrance. He laughed. A butler had put him down. He recalled riding into that camp of buck skinners and getting into the ax-tossing contest—at least they welcomed him.

The butler returned. "She asked I show you to the living room. She will be there shortly to talk to you." The living room was a long one furnished with couches and drapes from floor to ceiling. He went to the front windows. He couldn't see the operating portion of the ranch from any of them. There was a lawn surrounding, big enough to pasture a herd and obviously trimmed by a large flock of sheep brought to do that, and then returned to their pasture.

"Would you desire some coffee?" the butler asked them.

"That would be fine." Long looked at Jan, who nodded, examining a book on the table.

He strode over there.

"Photographs of them."

There was a photo of a man with a jaguar that must have been shot in Mexico. He'd seen Rupert Glass back when he was a boy and recalled he always wore those pants that ballooned out and German riding boots. He carried a quirt that he used to point things out and had a monocle in his left eye.

His second wife looked like a teenager in their wedding photos. Long thought she couldn't have been any older than fifteen when Glass married her. His son was from his first marriage. That woman died suddenly and, some said, conveniently for Glass to marry Juanita. This led to his inheriting those Mexican ranches.

"Oh, I am so sorry I have kept you waiting." He decided the woman wearing layers of white lacy gowns rushing in the room was Juanita Glass. "I have been so upset about my situation. But I see you are here."

"I am Long O'Malley and this is my wife, Jan."

"Yes, I have been told. They are bringing you coffee. Have a seat. Did you have a nice journey up here?"

"It was all right," Jan said, taking a seat on a sofa close to her choice of a chair.

"I will have my foreman show the ranch, Mr. O'Malley, when you two are settled. Perhaps after you have rested today and tonight."

"Mrs. Glass, I brought four men with me. Direct me to the ranch operation and I'll introduce myself to your men."

"Oh, I wanted to let you rest after such a distant journey."

"No problem. We are all right and ready to inspect the ranch."

"I don't know where Mr. Doogan is this morning."

"How far is the ranch operation from here?"

"Two miles. That is why the house is here. Too much smelly fecal stuff and dusty animals always bawling. That is why Rupert built me the house here."

"Has anyone threatened you since he died?"

"Yes . . . they came with torches, and masked, and told me to leave."

"How many times?"

"Twice."

"Have they been back?"

"Yes. I was worried they'd burn this house down."

"Did the law do anything?"

"There is a justice of the peace at Thorny. He said he would have the deputy sheriff investigate. But he only makes monthly trips over here. I told my lawyers I feared for my life, so they hired some men to guard me."

"Where are those men at?"

"Oh, over at the ranch operation."

Long was on his feet pacing back and forth. "Mrs. Glass, those men need to be stationed here if they are going to save your life and house."

"Oh, Mr. O'Malley. They smell like horses. No. Not in my house."

"Mrs. Glass, that might be better than smelling smoke or bleeding to death."

"What do you suggest?"

"If not in your house, then in a tent and guards around the house. Two miles away they may never get here in time. I will look into that."

"I understand you and your brother are much respected men who could help me. I know nothing about the ranch business. Rupert handled all that."

"One more thing. Who handled your cattle sale?"

"I was assured that Mr. Bell was a very honest man, and I told him to get some cattle—we had lots of them—and take them to Kansas."

"Well, you got robbed but we can't do anything about that now. Who is the man in charge at the operations?"

"Mr. Doogan is the superintendent. He is a very honest hardworking man."

"I will go meet him. You don't need to go along. Jan?"

"Oh, I will go with you. Nice to meet you, Mrs. Glass."

"You won't stay down there. It is usually dusty

and smelly down there. I cannot stand it. You can come up and stay here, in the house."

"I was a widow and I had to run my own ranch for some time. I am used to it."

"Oh, my dear, and you are such a lovely woman. I don't see how you remained with such a fair complexion under those conditions."

"Thank you. I have to go with my husband. We can talk later." Jan excused herself.

Outside, Long took his rein from Rob.

"How is she?" he asked.

"A snob. More later. We're going to the operation. It is two miles away"—he lowered his voice—"and see just how this ranch is run."

"Who lives in that house?" Boone asked, still sneaking looks back at it.

"Just her and maybe the butler. She is obviously a rich girl, and the cattle bawling and the dust upsets her."

"Smells like money to me," Rob teased them.

"I asked why her guards are not up here. 'Oh, they smell like horses,' she said."

"Boy you've got a real winner."

Jan was laughing. "She's a widow, guys. A rich one, too."

Rob shook his head. "I'd have to sleep two miles away so she couldn't smell me. What will we do?"

"If she is so worried what can we do?" Boone asked.

"Set up a tent. And give her a twenty-four-hour guard."

"Will she smell it?"

"I don't give a damn what she smells," Long said. "We are going to stop those night raiders or anyone who aims to hurt her."

"And I am not living in that house with her. So find me a tent, too."

Long was laughing. "Whatever gave me that notion?"

"You can put up with her. I don't have to." Riding along with them, she was shaking her head, repulsed at the thought of living in the house with Juanita Glass.

"So much for part one," Long said, checking his horse to go around a chuckhole in the road.

"Bet she never drives down here or that hole would be fixed," Rob said, sliding his horse over on the other side. "We're going to suit her?"

"I don't care if we do. We will see she is protected. But that is all I am doing."

"What else did you learn?" Boone asked.

"I asked her who made the cattle deal. She said she trusted the man, a Mr. Bell."

"I figure that means they drove some cattle in and took them to Abilene."

"I think Rob said it. The only cattle you can sell are large steers to go in feeder pens for fattening. They don't want cows, calves, or bulls."

"So they rounded up some cattle, whatever they were, and drove them to Abilene?" Jan asked.

Long nodded his head. "I bet that's what happened."

They found the operation headquarters and stopped a man who looked like he worked there.

"Where can I find Doogan?"

"I don't know. I ain't seed him in two days."

"Who runs things when he isn't here?"

"Oh, Sam Rogers. He's up around the dairy barn."

"Thanks." Where was Doogan? The worker didn't know. Not a good thing.

He saw an operation that might be a dairy. Several Jersey cows were in the pen.

He dismounted, and a large man in a plaid shirt came out of the doors. With a speculative look at them he asked, "What'cha need?"

"Rogers?"

"Yeah, that's who I am."

"I'm Long O'Malley and I just bought this ranch."

"The hell you did. I talked to Juanita two days ago, and she said it was not for sale."

"It was sold. And I am down here to see what all it needs."

"Okay. I don't reckon you'd lie about that. What do you want now?"

"Do you have an office where we can go and talk?"

"Doogan locked it. Told me no one was to get in there."

"Where is he?"

"I don't know. Said he'll be back in a day or two."

"Show me the office. I am going to open it. I don't have two or three days."

Rogers shrugged. "He may have a fit."

"I own this ranch. I can handle Doogan."

"It's that building over there."

"Let's go over there and open it up. Where are those guards her lawyers hired?" Long asked, looking around at things.

"Sleeping I guess. She asked we not be up there."

"Where do they sleep?"

"In that cabin over there." Rogers pointed to a building.

"We can check on it later."

On the porch Long found there was a padlock on the door.

"You have a hammer or a crow bar?" Long asked.

"Toby, get that pry bar from the wagon," Boone said as the rest were looking around at everything.

The youth quickly got it and put it under the lock bar and ripped it off.

Long walked inside the room. It had an office desk piled with papers and receipts, and it stank.

"That's a dirty socks' smell," Jan said. "Every-one, find them and throw them outside."

So their search began while Long searched the desk. He opened a leather-bound book and flipped to the back. It gave a head count from almost eighteen months earlier and it was crossed out—in pencil. "NOT RIGHT."

With some concern, he closed it. He'd inspect this later.

The men had pitchforks and were gathering dirty underwear and socks and throwing them on the porch. Rob was building a fire in the woodstove after lugging out two pails of old ashes. The windows and doors were open. Both younger hands that came along, Toby Carpenter and Rowdy Peabody, were proving to be real workers.

"Get that mattress and all those blankets out on an ant hill," Jan told the men while she swept up the floor with a broom, Toby holding a shovel to scoop it up.

"You know where he kept his books? That is an old head count."

"I guess in that safe."

It was obviously closed. "Did he need a combination to open it?"

"Turn the dial to the left a quarter turn," Rogers said. "That is all he ever does."

On his knees, Long gingerly turned it a quarter turn, then pulled on the handle. It opened with a creak. He shook his head at what he discovered—there were piles of bound currency and sacks of coins. His first thought was worthless Confederate money—southern rich people lost fortunes when the South gave up. He shook the dust off one bundle—he could not believe his eyes. These were very good one-hundred-dollar bills.

Long could not hardly fathom the value of the treasure in this old safe. *Harp, there may be enough here to pay for this ranch.*

Stunned he sat down on his butt. Jan settled down on her knees next to him.

"That real?"

He simply sat there and nodded. There were all kinds of implications to this find.

CHAPTER 28

The office was cleaned, the stinking old clothing and bedding were removed, and the trash taken out and burned. Long had carefully closed the safe, and the ranch people began to gather outside and talk among themselves about what was going on. In the living part of the building, Jan had her things set up and Doogan's were put in another shed.

Long had Rob and Boone sorting things of obvious value, putting them apart from things they would not need. Mid-afternoon, that done, Long addressed the gathered workers and spoke to them.

"My brother and I have bought this ranch. We are cattlemen. We took cattle to Sedalia before the peace was signed, but we are Texas ranchers and we need people to plant crops, raise livestock, and keep up a nice ranch. If you had a job with the Glass family, you will have a job here.

"My name is Long O'Malley. I am not a patron. You call me Long. Over there is Boone. Stand up. He is one of my *segundos*. The other is Robbie Boyd. Call him Robbie. If I am not here you can talk to them. Tomorrow we will want your names and talk about what you do here and if you want to stay."

He looked them over as the sun began to dip for the day. "We are proud you are here and will try to keep all of you working for many years. Does anyone have a problem?"

They all shook their heads.

The men hired to be guards were rounded up by his four. They met him in the office, and Rogers went along.

"I want a guard of two men set up to secure her house every night. The purpose of hiring you was her safety. If she is not protected, why haven't you?"

"She didn't want us down there," one shouted.

"I do. I want a signal bell, too. So the rest of us can come help you if you are challenged. Do we have such a bell?"

"It is set up down here."

"Tomorrow we set a tent up there. Move the bell and when it rings everyone will get a gun and come to back you. You men on duty can sleep in the tent. If you can't live with this plan, load your things up and ride out."

He felt none would quit. The pay scale was forty a month for guards. Everyday cowhands were paid twenty-five to thirty bucks a month.

"Who's in charge of you?"

"When Doogan ain't here, Carter is. He's checking cattle today. Then me," Sam Rogers said.

"Sam, come back here after you set up who will

be the guards for tonight. We need to discuss the job you have here and how we can make it work better."

"I will set it up and be back. Doogan did all that."

"That rule is out. You will answer for these men as their boss, and I expect my orders to be kept or I will find a new boss."

"Yes, sir."

"My name is Long."

"Yes, Long." The man stood there before him in the bloody light of sundown. Holding his hat in hand, he turned to go gather his men to the side.

"Much better. Anyone of you hear where Doogan went?" Long asked his four men.

"They say he drinks a lot."

"They also say he likes women and isn't married."

"Well, I am not afraid of him unless he gets violent. But I am certain he will be in an uproar over what we have done so far. I am not Harp. My patience is very thin. If he gets out of hand I'll slap him on the ground, disarm him, and hold court."

"You going to hang him?" Boone asked, amused.

"I may have him charged with some crimes and sent to prison. Rob, you and Boone put up some drapes on the windows for Jan. When things quiet down, we need to count and verify the money. I have no idea how much is in there."

Jan and the two young cowboys fed them supper. Long and Jan would sleep in Doogan's room now that they scoured it out before moving her bed and their things in there. It had a back door to a row of outhouses in a line. The men would sleep in their bedrolls in the office until he got them quarters.

One of the mess cooks brought her some freshly butchered beef to cook outside, with rice and beans and fresh Dutch oven soda biscuits. Plus a pot of Arbuckle coffee to wash it all down with.

Lamps set up, after the meal they began to count the dusty money. They shook each bundle of bills over a bushel basket to loosen the dust, then counted, keeping score of what by writing it down. Boone packed each bundle into the new wooden box that he and Rob made down in the shop. They had drilled holes for the string rope handles held in place by large knots. It had hinges and two lock rasps on the other side to hold the lid down on the money.

The counting went slowly. There were several bundles of large bills, like hundreds and five hundreds. Boone's eyes got real big when counting the thousand-dollar ones.

"Where do you figure he got all this money?"

"They said Glass's family made fortunes with

ships at sea. This money was printed in this century and it's not counterfeit, either." Long had to find a safe place to put it.

"But down here in the foreman's office?"

"Outlaws would never look down here."

They all laughed. Jan finished adding it up. "Two hundred thousand, eight hundred and fifty-six dollars."

"Men, mum is the word. Let's get this put away. Let anyone who knows about it think it is still in the safe. In the meantime, under her bed," he whispered as two of them carried it by the handles into their bedroom.

What next? He had found near a quarter of a million dollars in an old dusty safe on his newly purchased ranch. How did the money get that dirty? He was thinking it had been buried somewhere and in haste to get it all they just left the dirt on it. Maybe left it that way to go find more. No telling. Did Juanita know about it? He'd bet good money she had no idea it was there. Glass probably never told her about it before he died. This foreman, Doogan, might now be the only one to know it was there.

How did Rogers know how to turn the handle? He must have seen Doogan open it but didn't recognize it was full of money . . . it was that dirty.

More things for him to worry about. Jan pulled him into their bedroom by the sleeve. "Those two guys are tired. We need to let them sleep."

CHAPTER 29

Long left the outhouse in the gray light of the foredawn. Several people with jobs were moving about. A horse hustler was bringing in some fresh saddle horses from up the road. On horseback, he was slapping his chaps with the end of his lariat and had a sharp whistle to get the attention of any herded horse he suspected was ready to break from the bunch he was bringing in. Good horse hands were indispensable for the operation of a ranch or cattle drive—especially on the road with cattle.

Long waved at the youth taking the horses by him. He'd know his name next time. It was his business to know the men. Every man had his own world, and knowing something about it meant the boss cared. He slipped in the back door.

Jan was already out front cooking oatmeal and coffee.

Where was Boone? "Boone go somewhere?"

Rob nodded and moved closer. "He said one of us needed to check on the chuck served here. He'll be back."

"Good idea. The wrangler who just brought those horses in looked to be a good hand."

"His name is Cole Henry. He checked with the

two of us and asked if you'd need horses today. I told him we might need four. He will have them in the pens for us if we need them."

"At least someone really works around here."

Rob agreed.

They ate breakfast inside around the unfired woodstove. Boone came back picking his teeth and nodding. "Those cowboys had a good breakfast. Sammy the cook said he would feed us at dinner and supper tonight. I told him we'd sure eat with him. He had scrambled eggs, fried homegrown ham, biscuits light as a feather, and grits for everyone along with coffee. It was all damn good."

"Send word we will eat with him. What was his last name?"

"You ask him. I can't say it. Chinese."

"Thanks."

"Even without his last name I will like him," Jan teased.

"Oh, the man in charge of cattle under Doogan is coming to see you. I think he can help us on cattle numbers. His name is Heath Carter."

They were winding up their oatmeal when a short bowlegged man with gray temples showed up.

Long got up and shook his hand. "Long O'Malley. Nice to meet you, sir."

"I would have come down last night, but no one told me you were here. What can I show or tell you? Your young man was very polite explaining your family had bought the ranches."

"Have a seat on one of our kegs. We're the O'Malley brothers. Yes, my brother Harp and I bought the ranch. Harp is nine months younger than I am. We are the ones that took a herd of steers to Sedalia two years ago and formed our business. We were sought by Mr. Glass's widow to protect her and to buy the operation."

Carter shook his head as if disgusted. "Those night riders were just trying to get in their bluff. They won't harm her."

"She told me she thought her life was in danger."

"Mr. O'Malley—"

He used his finger to point at his chest. "My name is Long."

"Long, I am afraid this widow is a woman quickly driven to hysterics. Even before his death she had problems. She accused a gardener of trying to rape her."

"She convinced her lawyers about her fears."

Carter threw his hands out. "You want my resignation now or later?"

"Carter, I'm not stupid. Of course I want you to remain. You know this ranch like the back of your hand. But I need some answers. Tell me about the botched cattle sales."

"More of her hysterics. Doogan and I talked about a cattle drive. This slick cattle trader caught her alone. Told her we were doing nothing to sell her cattle and she should hire him and he'd take care of all of it. He didn't want us doing any part of it . . . told her we'd take too long gathering them. Him and his town cowboys rounded up everything they could find on the north side—cows, calves, and bulls—and drove them away.

"We both knew it was a wreck going to happen. But she silenced us any time we tried to explain the mess they had made. He was a cattle businessman and we were mere ranch foremen."

"I had wondered how that had happened," Long said.

"Is she leaving the ranch?" Carter asked.

Long shook his head. "We agreed to protect her here."

"Well I guess we can ignore her."

"She can live in the house, but if she ever moves out or dies it belongs to us."

"Well, at least she won't be running the ranch."

"Right. Where is Doogan?"

"He said he was looking for a new job. I have no idea where he went. As I said, I am sorry. I would've come and talked to you last night if anyone had told me you were here."

"I met Rogers and he and those men are now guarding her house."

"He worked for Doogan, not me. To be quite frank there was no need for him and those men."

"Let's talk cattle numbers."

"We have near three thousand mother cows. Fifteen hundred bulls. All are half British blood or greater. Close to two thousand calves this year. They need to be worked and weaned. We have five thousand large steers . . . mostly longhorns but some are partial British."

"Those we need to get road branded and ready to go north in sixty days."

"We will need to hire help. Rupert was dying so we didn't get the cattle on the ranch worked last spring. She didn't want us to leave. When he died she started this business about them being after her, so we were barred from leaving the base to go do that or to hire more help. It really is not our fault."

"That makes sense to me. You know when Doogan will be back?"

Carter shrugged. "He never talked much about himself. He was real cheap and never spent any of his money, even on soap. You living in there?"

"We scrubbed it down and threw his old socks out."

Carter laughed. "I won't lie to you—this job would be hard for me to leave. I am pushing fifty. My wife has arthritis. We don't have a big amount set aside, but I can pack and go if you say so."

"Where did Doogan come from?"

"Why?"

"I want you to tell me where he came from . . ."

"They say he was a sea captain. Worked for Rupert's father, and he wrote Rupert years ago that he wanted off the sea and would be his ranch foreman. That was twenty years ago. Rupert told him he could have the job. I was a young cowboy then. Doogan didn't know anything about a cow, so when he got here he told me to handle the cows and I'd get to be cow foreman."

"So that was how it worked? Okay. I want you to take my men and start showing them the steers that we need to get to Kansas. I can pay this place off with that many head of steers.

"I want all other things slowed down. Get started and hire all the men we will need. My two young men will need your knowledge. You can stay as long as you want, but I want them to drive those cattle to Kansas or to wherever they set up this year to buy them. And I will need you here to run the ranch."

Boone and Rob, hearing all this, went to rubbing their hands together and smiling at each other.

"Rob, we each have a herd," Boone said. "I'll bet you a hundred dollars my herd brings more money than yours."

"Hold up. Each of you has plans to get married. I am tying you up. Now how can we settle that matter?"

"Long," Carter said. "Let them two go get married. I will hire several cowboys in town and start gathering. This country isn't as tough as down where you come from. When they come back we'll have it all set up and enough experienced hands to pick from. I have some empty *jacales* we can get repaired so their women can have their own places when they come back."

"Well I like that plan. What about you two?"

"Hey it sounds great. Gladys I am certain will marry me and move up here," Rob said.

"That goes for me, too. How long do we have?" Boone asked.

"Two weeks. Jan and I will help him get ready to gather the steers. We have time."

Jan was shaking her head. "How will we furnish the houses that Carter gets fixed?"

"I think you can handle that."

"My wife Edna would love to help you," Carter offered.

"Edna and I will furnish them."

"Hear that?"

"Yeah. Thanks, Jan. Hey we can be halfway there if we leave right now," Boone said.

"You know what to tell Harp, Rob?"

"Yes. You have this place under control, and have five thousand steers we are going to drive to Abilene or wherever they buy cattle. Boone gets one herd. I drive number two. Boone and I have two weeks to get back with our wives to move into what will be furnished houses when we get back."

"Ride careful. I know you will take care of each other."

"You need that box sent back?" Rob asked.

"Naw. I'll take it back myself when I go home."

They waved and ran to get ranch horses ready to ride.

Long turned to her. "Are we going to eat at the mess hall?"

"You bet. After that I am going to meet Edna and get ready to see those houses we will furnish."

Carter laughed. "How long you two been married?"

"Since Christmas last."

"Oh, by the way you two think together, I thought you'd been married for years."

"It seems like that," Long said.

"Long."

"Well we got married before—" She was shoving him around slapping his shoulder.

Walking together, he hugged her. Sam S., as the cook was known, because no one could pronounce his name, met them at the door.

"They're newlyweds, Sam," Carter said, and went past them going on inside.

"Where big cowboy named Boom?"

"Boone. Him and Robbie had to go home, get married."

"He just come."

"Yeah. Two weeks he will be back here with his new bride."

"You big boss he tell me is here?"

"Yes. This is Jan and I am Long."

"You plenty long."

"When my dad saw me that is what he said. And that is my name."

The oriental bowed and shook his hand. "Welcome to crazy ranch."

After the meal, Jan bragged on his food and promised they'd be back for breakfast.

He noted Toby and Rowdy were getting lots of attention from some of the Hispanic girls working for Sam.

"Long, you need us tomorrow to look at cattle with you?" Toby asked.

"Yes. First thing in the morning, have that wrangler, Cole Henry, bring in my Comanche horse to ride."

"We will. Before he left, Boone told us the plan. We can ride guard on you."

"I will go see that Miss Priss is all right in the morning, and then Edna and I will start shopping for furniture."

"Need money, holler."

"Have you figured out how that money got here?"

"It is not her money. I'd bet it's Doogan's money and he will be back for it. He had all that money when he quit being a sea captain and brought it up here with him as his retirement. As a sea captain, I bet he saved it and hid it, afraid of being robbed. Then dug it up from the beach and brought it for his retirement when he got the job out here. I guess he was so cheap he never spent it."

"Carter or Rogers know?"

"No. Doogan kept it secret."

She was undressing sitting on the edge of the bed. "You and Harp both can step in a cow pie and come out not smelling, and big-time winners."

"I thought that when I got you."

"Long O'Malley, if you are talking cow pies, I am going to whip you."

CHAPTER 30

Three days passed and Doogan had not returned. On Friday a cowboy named Shirley Hanks came in and looked up Long and Carter. He said he had found out why Doogan never came back. Shirley was cutting across country on his horse and found Doogan. It appeared that the horse went down, broke his leg, and later died. When he threw Doogan as he went down, the fall broke Doogan's neck. He didn't suffer like the poor horse.

The three rode out there, wrapped up his corpse, and sent some boys back to bring it in. He was buried at the operations center. That night, in bed with his wife, he read Doogan's will that he'd found in the safe: *I here bye bequeath my fortune to whoever owns the ranch and finds this money.*

Under blankets, pulled up to their chins in the cool night despite the stove, she asked, "Do you think he found a shipwreck?"

"No . . . he murdered two old maids in New England who had won the money in the Irish lottery."

"Long O'Malley, you're crazy."

He threw his arm over her and said, "Good thing 'cause I really love you."

Dawn, Long and Carter rode out to look at

some of the cattle in the frosty morning. Sun coming up promised to warm the day.

"We never missed having spring roundup before this year. But we never had a hysterical spoiled woman for our boss. Rupert was a spoiled rich guy, but he knew how to make money. He sold cattle and even collected gold from the Confederates. He was in their high society before the war, too. Then when fall came and the screwworm flies were gone, she still wouldn't let us do it. Hard to run a ranch like that and be successful. I told Edna we'd just roll with the tide."

"After we get these steers rounded up, you can keep those men on the payroll and get things straightened out around."

"Thanks. I hate the way we have been trying to hold this place together."

"I fully understand what you have been through. Tell me more about Doogan."

"Rupert tried to be the ranch foreman when he assembled all this land. While he could wheel, deal, and make money he was neither a cowman nor a good boss for the day-to-day of a ranch. Doogan was an old sea captain and though he might've ran a ship, he didn't know anything about ranching, so he made me cattle foreman and listened to me. He was a tough boss but he realized this was different than running a ship. Cowboys were not sailors. And there were not many men left to work cattle after the war started. The rest were pressed into being soldiers for the Confederacy."

Long nodded. "Things did change overnight. Texas had the cattle, and the captain I worked with told us all the chickens and hogs had all been eaten up during the war. And they had."

"You and your brother got on the train and kept right on going."

Long agreed. He liked the country up here, the forage, and some good live creeks made for real cattle country. There was some rolling country, too.

If he sold five thousand steers this coming season at the railhead, he'd have the ranch debt completely paid off. He better start putting things together—two chuck wagons, teams for them. How many good horses did they have? Where were the point riders? The cooks? Lots to do and he had to do it—Jan would help.

Carter was no fool. They could do it. Harp could manage the home deal. He'd probably have six herds set to go north. Two herds from H Bar H. Two from Diamond. Plus Oscar's herd. Then two more from their consignments from small ranchers.

This was unbelievable, but it would happen. On the way to mess, he picked up Jan and they went, hand in hand to go eat. Neat to have her . . . good things were happening in their lives together.

"Would you live in a house built right here in the dust and smells?"

"You thinking about doing that?"

"Yes. If we have this place paid for next summer, why not we stay and run it?"

"What will Harp do? I think he counts on you to help him run it all."

"You may be right. How is the widow doing?"

"She doesn't like the tent in front of her house."

"The tent can be a white one. But those men will stay and guard her."

"Rupert really spoiled her or she came that way."

"I suspect she was brought up spoiled."

Jan squeezed his hand. "You think?"

After supper, they went back to the office. He stoked up the stove with wood and they got ready for bed.

"I like this ranch. It is a kingdom. Whatever you want to do I will support you."

"Thanks, Jan." He hugged her. "And I treasure your advice. Help me get this cattle drive together. You know things I may forget. We need to get it set up right."

The effort was under way. Carter went to Fort Worth and he found several hands. Over thirty more reported for work at the ranch after hearing they had openings.

Long and the horse wrangler, Cole Henry, who he liked so well, went through the horses. They would need a hundred more for the trip was the decision. Carter agreed and they put out word for what was needed.

Long was amused. Carter put Cole in charge, and traders came with strings of horses to sell them. Cole had four teenage boys on his team who could ride to try them out. They were damn tough hands. A bucking horse was not cut from the list, but a dead-headed plug was given the thumb to go away. The better horses were better because Cole knew his reputation hung in picking the right horses. The teenagers Cole used also knew their coworkers counted on them to pick horses with heart and depth. Strong enough to turn a stampede in a helluva rainstorm.

Long recalled the sorry ones they'd rode to Sedalia. These boys should be grateful they'd have real ones between their legs. Things moved on. The blacksmiths and carpenters fixed the two chuck wagons so any cook would drool to have one like it. The tarp covers and tents were bright and new. They'd go north looking sharp. Pride in an outfit helped them do things— he knew that was what got them to Sedalia and what got them back to the market the next summer.

Sometimes it took a setback or a wreck to bring up the souls of the crew. Somehow he needed to instill that in both crews, and when his men got back from their honeymoons they could start heading the crew that way.

Then it struck him. They would choose teams and start the competition during roundup and build on it. Carter had the men busy. They had started collecting the steers to go. In the future, Long promised himself, they would build a pasture enclosure to hold the steers they intended to ship. This year they'd have to herd them up and riders would be needed to keep them together, but it would work out. Just more help was on the payroll than a fenced place would need. He was working toward a real working ranch.

It was bound to happen. At breakfast a fistfight broke out between two of the men over some little thing. Four others egged them along. Long stopped it, not too gently. He busted one of the fighters over the head with his pistol butt. He went down like a polled over steer and the other fighter threw his hands up looking wall-eyed at the muzzle of Long's .45.

"We don't fight with team members on this ranch. Absolutely no fighting. You four over there, get over here. You encouraged them. So the six of you will shovel manure out of the barns and sheds for the next two weeks and spread it over the fields. You start at six a.m. and don't quit until dark. If you don't work together and help each other, I will fire all of you. I will decide if you have done it all right and worked hard.

You won't do that, load your stuff and get off the ranch right now."

"We're sorry," one of them said.

"I am not accepting that. Fourteen days of shoveling shit is your sentence or leave right now."

They all nodded.

He looked to the rest of the men to see who would oversee them. Hugo Salazar agreed to do it, and Long told him to make sure they worked hard at it or fire them.

Still steaming when he reached his wife, he slid onto the bench next to her.

"I don't think I ever saw you that mad, even when you straightened out my problems."

"You have to stop fighting right off at the start."

"Well obviously you did that."

One of the girls brought him a plate of scrambled eggs, bacon, and biscuits.

"You want oatmeal?"

"No, this is plenty . . . thanks." He reached for the butter and fixed both biscuits.

"I doubt they'll fight anymore."

He stopped. "I intended it that way."

She elbowed him. "You damn sure did that."

He set the biscuits down and turned her face toward him, kissed her, and received applause from those that saw.

Everyone laughed.

The two honeymooners arrived with two

wagons of their things. Harp had written him a long letter. Before Long opened it, he welcomed them and explained how hard his wife and Edna, along with the ranch workers, had worked to get the two houses ready and while all the sawdust had not been swept out they could move in.

The new residents smiled at the remodeled facilities and furniture bought for them and thanked him. Long packed Missy on his hip during the inspection. She had many important things to tell him. Rob promised her a pony. Harp gave her a doll as a going away present, and Katy said if she didn't like it there, she could come back to them and play with her boy, Lee.

Gladys was shaking her head, and Long said it didn't matter, he understood.

Later the two men sat down with him and Carter and talked.

Boone started in, "Harp told us that the deal up here sounded exciting."

"How is he doing?" Long asked.

"He will have six herds. He said he had them set up and would miss you. He said two herds from this ranch first year would be a good deal and to congratulate you."

Rob added, "Several of the top foremen gave us some pointers."

"It all will help."

They agreed.

He opened the letter alone in the office.

Dear Long,

Sounds like you have that operation working. Thanks for explaining what happened to the ranch's cattle sale in Abilene last year. You have my best getting along with the widow. We knew she might be a problem, but the ranch is ours no matter what so you have my backing for however you handle it.

We have to make the whole thing work and pay for it. Your plan to move two herds to Abilene unless they move it south of there like they talked about—I think it is too late this year to move it but in the future they will probably have a new point to load cattle.

Tell Jan that Katy is expecting next year. This was not to upset her but Katy wanted her to know. Still having some rustler problems but we are managing. And the Austin lawyers don't think we have any-thing to worry about regarding a court case over the land purchase. Once done, it will be good to have it behind us. No word what those troublemakers will try next.

I will keep you informed.

We all miss you but understand that this ranch needs leadership, and I hear you are doing great with it.

Your brother Harp

Long told Jan about Katy's pregnancy.

She started to cry, but he cheered her up by his hugging and holding her tight.

Two more letters arrived for him in the next week.

The first one was from an undisclosed sender and originally was mailed to Camp Verde, Texas, and hand-printed out. The postman had forwarded it.

Long—
Those two bastards you want are up around Ruby City.
An <u>amigo</u>.

Long stood for a long time wondering who sent the letter, and how did he know about them—he had to be someone who had worked for them.

Carter found some experienced hands who had been to Abilene that last year. They asked if they would be paid coming home, and Long told them they would be, and possibly be paid for a month's work if they stayed.

Long said, "Yes, many outfits only pay for going north and the job ends in Abilene."

"Hell I saw why they were upset."

"We can afford to pay wages coming home if they stay and work."

"Whew, I never heard that before."

"Lots of things are happening and fast," Long said.

"They brought that slick wire back you ordered."

Long said, "I sent a boy to town to look at a setup I heard they were doing in a blacksmith shop on how to make barbed wire."

"Yeah, I've been running around and never heard what he said."

"He is pretty sharp for an ex-slave. I am not holding him back because he's black. I believed him when he told me about the wire. That wire is to make barbed fencing wire. He says he can do it. There is big demand for it. Shops all over are making it. So we will see."

"You going to have to have this place surveyed, huh?"

"To fence it, yes. And next year we will have some fenced acreage to hold our sale steers. We have eight ranch hands out there herding them now."

"I bet surveying costs a lot."

"It will have to be done. I'll go to checking on it."

"Do you see all ten sections fenced in?"

"Yes. Maybe more than that, as good as things are going right now."

Carter took off his cowboy hat and scratched his white hair. "You are what folks call a mover and shaker."

"We need to strike now. Things will keep getting higher and higher."

His foreman agreed.

CHAPTER 31

Long talked to Jan about surveying the place, so the next time he was in Junction he spoke to several people and got some names and addresses. She would write and ask them to bid on surveying the perimeter of the ranch.

Things were shaping up fast for the drive. His two head drovers were getting more confident about the operation.

Cooks were hired. Steers were still being found and driven in. Having that holding pasture next year bore on his mind. The bids came in explaining in order to survey his ranch perimeter they had to start the survey, and they estimated it was twenty-two miles in the northeast corner of the ranch. The estimates ran from fifty thousand down to twelve thousand if they had no troubles.

"What troubles are they talking about in this lowest bid, Jan?"

"How would I know? You choosing them?"

"I don't want add-on charges. That is enough money to survey the whole of Texas."

"I don't understand the point to start?" Jan shook her head.

"They have to have a known place to start

347

a survey from and then to get to where our northeast corner is. Then they go from there to the next point and so on."

"Twenty-two miles?"

"Yes. Ask them to list what they call troubles."

"Anything we do is lots of trouble isn't it?"

"Not everything we do."

She shook her head. "I will write. You are a devil at times, you know."

"I know that."

"How is Simon coming with making wire?"

"It was harder than he first thought, but he is making progress. For a man who can't read or write he is a craftsman and how you can do that without those skills impresses me."

"I don't think Juanita is happy up there in that big house. She thinks, now, there are wolves going to attack her. Rogers said they were coyotes and he would try to move them off or shoot them."

His wife shook her head. "You need to move that widow off the ranch. She is a pain in the you-know-what. They have to boil all the water she uses, even her bathwater."

"You and the new wives are getting along?" he asked her.

"Oh, yes. We're sewing clothing for all the workers' girls every other afternoon."

"That's great. I saw you taking one or the other, in turn, each time you go to town."

"I want them to think they are wanted around here."

"Good. Things are shaping up better all the time. It looks like we will have more than four thousand head to ship in three weeks."

"How many?"

"They are estimating close to five. Those men can handle twenty-five hundred each. This is another good thing coming our way."

"So five thousand at sixty dollars is three hundred thousand dollars, and that is what you paid for the ranch," she said.

"Hey, your math is getting better."

"I have a good teacher."

He hugged and kissed her. "This is all so surprising. But my conscience bites me at times that I am not helping Harp more. I hate it."

"You can't be two places seventy miles apart. I think you are doing a superb job here."

"New word, huh?"

"You betch'em."

He hugged her tight. "Jan, things are going good for us up here."

"I bet your brother is getting it all done without you. He has lots of great hands."

"The only thing we still need to do is form two businesses. One for ranching and one cattle driving. We will be using all our foremen to make the drive, and that makes us too thin at all the ranches."

"He never mentioned any problems he was having."

"No, but there are more people hate us down there for just being ourselves."

"You may be right."

"I'm going down to the blacksmith shop and see how progress is going. Meet you at lunch."

In the shop that reeked of burning coal he and Simon squatted down and talked.

"That wire you done got us has flaws in it. Places thicker than I need and places so thin it breaks."

"I savvy. Poor quality. I will have the store people buy us better wire."

"I have made two twisters. They are getting better. Last trip into Junction, Jonsie told me his secret. I am building one like his." He turned up his calloused palms. "All I can do."

Long clapped him on the shoulder. "I understand. You are doing good work. We will whip this business."

"Amen, boss man." He smiled at his boss's confidence in his project.

"Thanks. We'll get it done."

Long had things all ready to go north. The weather warmed. The rains had been generous and new grass blades waved in the wind. They had a final send-off for his two men and their crews. Boone went first with his bunch. He and

Rob both had good lead steers, probably one of the most expensive parts of the drive. They made river crossings and herding go much smoother. Their bell ringing summoned all the steers that it was time to get up and move. They cost four hundred apiece, but they were leaders. Boone had a red roan-hided longhorn. Rob's was blue colored.

Rob left two days later. Long rode out on the first day with both of the herds.

After parting with Rob earlier, he told Jan that night in bed, "Things went too damn smooth."

"Good," she said, and hugged him hard. "You deserved it."

CHAPTER 32

In their letter, the survey company listed the many things that would cost more money.

Raids by hostile Indians

Too many rattlesnakes gathered in one area

Vigilantes stopping work and threatening workers

Harassment by people opposed to surveying

Mad bulls charging survey crews

Prairie fires

Tornados and bad storms

Long said, in his return letter, he accepted their terms and would meet them on the first day at the point where they would start. Long went to town and mailed that off. Next the mercantile. Mr. Garner, at the mercantile in Junction, told Long he had ten spools of smooth wire coming from a recommended supplier, and also apologized saying he had no idea people even made poor-quality wire. Long thanked him.

When he got home that afternoon, Jan and Carter were in his office waiting for him.

"Hi. What's going on?"

"Juanita wants to move to San Antonio," she said.

"Good news huh?"

"She expects us to move her there."

"Rogers can do that and once off the ranch she can pay him not us."

"She doesn't know how much she will take along, but it will require three or four wagons," Carter said.

"I will gladly hire them to have her off and gone. When she is gone, do you want to live up there?"

Jan shook her head. "That is not a warm house for me."

"It must be for all the wood she burns up there." Carter agreed, almost grinning.

"That is not what I mean."

"I know. But once she is gone we can do what we want to do with all those rooms." He could still hardly believe it was that large.

"Let's get this going. What do we have to do?" Carter asked.

"Get a date she will leave. Tell Rogers the plan, and she will be told if she wants him, she must pay him."

"She is so afraid of a shadow she will keep him," Carter said.

"My thoughts exactly. I'll handle it in the morning."

"How did your day go?" Jan asked.

"Like I expected it to go. I am pleased that Rob and Boone are running the two herds from here. I know they will get them there barring a big storm."

"You were lucky to find them two," Carter said.

"I put them in charge of another ranch and when they thanked me, they told me they could now afford to get married. Once I saw this place, I knew if I was ever going to get this ranch going right, I would need them here with me."

"Damn good move. I'm tired. Good night, Long." He chuckled and left them.

They went into the bedroom and climbed into their bed.

"Aren't you excited?" she asked him under the covers.

"Yes. Two cattle drives smoothly out of here and Juanita leaving is a big load off me."

"Did I sound too bossy, in front of Carter, telling you that I didn't want that house?"

"No. I didn't know if you'd changed your mind. This office is kinda shabby."

"No, not if you're here."

That's why he loved her so damn much.

CHAPTER 33

Long had his meeting with hell about nine a.m. the next morning.

Juanita's ranting and raving was loud.

"I am a poor widow, and no one understands I lost the man I loved. He was a god. And I am living in the backwoods. None of his would-be friends come to see me out here. Oh, mercy, I am so sad. So neglected. My lawyers say they have me a house in San Antonio. Maybe there I can find a life."

Hat in hand, Long stood up. "Rogers will take you there in the surrey. He will continue to be your protector when you get there. He costs fifty dollars a month. His men thirty-five apiece and their food and lodging."

"Oh, so much money. Could you pay them for me?"

"No, ma'am, when you leave here you are no longer my worry or obligation."

"But I gave you my ranch."

"No, ma'am, I am paying you for it."

"But-but, oh, my head hurts." Her hand gripped her forehead like she was holding back the pain. What an actress she was in this melodrama she was playing.

"The wagons to haul your things will be here Thursday. Have everything packed and ready to go."

"You sound so much like other men bullying me."

"Juanita, I am doing what I am prescribed to do. I am paying for your moving."

Hands on her hips wearing that Roman-style many layers of white lace dress, she spat words at him. "Long O'Malley, you are simply the bastard son of a squaw, and you have no business talking to me like that."

"This conversation is over. Be ready."

When he walked down to the buckboard, Jan sat waiting on the seat.

"How did it go?"

Without a word, he took his place beside her and picked up the reins. "That damn woman can go to hell. Carter can handle her from here on. I came close to killing her. You know what she called me?"

"No."

He made the team trot. "The bastard son of a squaw."

"Long, I'm so sorry. She isn't worth a dime. And for her to say that makes me mad as well. You have been defending her from the rest of us from the beginning, and she says that to you."

In town he hired the wagons to haul her things

to San Antonio. That handled, he had another letter from Harp and also from the survey company.

After he read the surveyor's letter, he told her they needed to wire and confirm the date he'd meet them at the survey start point.

The letter from Harp told him he would sell the Three Star Ranch cattle for him. He said he was fixing to head out with the first herd and had everything under control and ready to head to Abilene.

It was a crazy day, running around town. Jan picked up material and supplies for the sewing parties. He sent the survey company the date to meet them. Then checked with the blacksmith, who asked how his man was getting along on his project.

"Simon's doing great. When we get the new wire I think he'll be better. Thanks for your help, and if you ever need anything, holler. We'll surely help you."

"Thank you, sir. Tell him I wish him good luck. We are covered up with orders for rolls of the wire ourselves."

Jan joined him and they had lunch in a café. A couple living southwest of them introduced themselves. He was Lloyd Hudson. His wife Abigail was about thirty. He, ten years older. They had two boys ten and twelve. His brand was the Rocking H, and he told them he had shipped three hundred head of steers with Garland McCoy earlier.

"How many did you ship?" Lloyd asked him.

"Two herds made up of five thousand head this past week."

"Wow that should help all of our range. I have some Three Star cattle on my place."

"I will send my men down to get them. The woman who owned the ranch before me wouldn't let the men hold a roundup, but we are bringing it back to being a ranch now it is our place."

"Where did she go?" Abigail asked Jan.

"Thursday she's moving to San Antonio."

"I bet you won't miss her. Nice to meet you two. Come by sometime."

Jan said, "Yes, and you do the same."

"I guess you will move in the big house now she's a-leaving?"

"Oh, we'll see."

They left. Jan turned to him. "She seemed to like it; maybe they'll rent it."

Both of them chuckled over the notion while finishing their meal.

They rode back to the ranch, and on Thursday Juanita walked out of the house for the last time, climbed onto the surrey, and Rogers drove her away. The seven loaded wagons had rolled out ahead of her. He figured that she'd taken lots of the valuable things, but that didn't bother him that much. He had no need for them.

Jan joined him and together they went up the hill and through the door she'd left open.

"She left all of his books. Bet she couldn't read English anyway."

"She packed and took all the dishes, the women told Carter."

"Wonder where this door goes? It has no knob." It was a plain door in the hallway on the right going into the kitchen.

After a search Jan said, "Here's a glass knob and the stem is on it. That should open it." She brought it to him.

He inserted it and tried to twist—well it must not have been opened in some time. It didn't budge an inch. Next, two-handed, it moved some. How long had it been closed?

Then at last it opened, and he discovered a steep set of stairs right before him. "Where does that go?"

"Damned if I know. But I want to look."

"Hmm, there may be snakes down there."

"If I had a light, then I could see them."

"I see a lantern she left. It still has kerosene in it."

"I have some matches." He lit it and set the wick. Now he had some light. "Stay right up here. I'll go look."

He descended the stairs, fighting bunches of cobwebs. At last he reached a hard floor, gritty under his soles. He swept some more webs away and held the lamp higher. A once green six-foot-tall two-door safe faced him.

"What did you find?"

"You will never believe in your life what is down here."

"Is he down there?" Carter asked, coming into the kitchen.

"Yes, and he's made a discovery. What is it, Long?"

"A huge safe. Bigger than most banks have. Carter, you know anything about it?"

Carter was down the steps and took the lamp. "No. I never knew it was even here. It was built inside the house, wasn't it?"

"What is in it?" she asked, joining them.

"I imagine it's locked."

"You know the combination?"

"No. I bet it went to the grave with Rupert."

"Well try what opened the other one."

"Here goes." He set the dial back to the left and then forced the handle down.

It creaked and she screamed. "You did it again."

It took both Long and Carter to swing the stiff heavy door open. The light Jan was holding shone on gold bars that were stacked like bricks from the floor to the ceiling of the vault. Both men fell back in shock.

"There is a damn fortune in here," Carter said.

Jan was gasping for her breath. "My Lord what is this?"

Long was wrestling to get the second door open. It finally gave and screeched open like it was in pain. Canvas sacks were piled in that part of the safe. He cut a cord on one and shoved his hand in, and came out with a fistful of twenty-dollar gold pieces.

"You know he had this here?" he asked Carter.

"No. But I bet it cost the men who stacked it in here their lives," Carter said.

"I was told that when he was building this house, they had a terrible Comanche raid and all the workers on the house were killed and buried north of here."

Long agreed. "I bet he and some gun hands killed them and blamed the Comanche. It would have taken several men a few days to pack it down here and then stack it."

Carter collapsed, sitting on the stairs. "He never ever told her this was here or she'd never have left this house. How much is here?"

"Maybe a million dollars and she has no claim to it. She left and it is ours. Whew. I can tell you right now, Carter, I will give you enough so you and Edna will have a small ranch to retire on when you are ready to retire."

"You don't owe me anything. I work for you two."

"No, Carter," Jan said. "Long John O'Malley

owes you a ranch to retire on. Now let's close the doors almost shut, climb upstairs, hide the doorknob, and figure out what to do next."

"My exact orders."

She wrinkled her nose at him. "It is stuffy down here."

Once out he closed the hall door, and she used a broom to sweep the cobwebs off of the two of them.

He hid the doorknob. Carter swept the webs off her. Then they sat on the simple chairs she had left in the kitchen.

"We need that in a bank vault in Junction," she said.

"Yes, we do. Carter, go buy a stout ambulance and a team of big draft horses. Make sure it has bows and a canvas cover. We will also need canvas to cover everything we put in the bed, too."

"That all will weigh more than a ton." Carter shook his head still in disbelief over the discovery.

"I bet you it will, too. Buy the horses tomorrow and have one of the boys along to drive them back.

"Sunday we will load it up and cover it. We'll have two men guard it at night. Then Monday we will take it to Junction with four riders along acting like they are going to town to raise some hell."

"That would be slick enough."

"I'll pay them forty bucks apiece for keeping quiet."

They separated, and Jan told him, going to mess, "You should make it eighty for everyone. Then if they wanted they could buy a new saddle or whatever else they need or want."

"I'd have to pay the cattle crew that, too, when they came home."

"I agree. We can certainly share, considering our haul."

"I heard he was rich, and I wondered where his fortune went. It is much more than I even dreamed. Now I want more answers, especially of how it got there."

"I don't care about that. I will be happier when it's in that bank."

"Amen. Start counting employees. I will pay them in gold coins."

"There are a dozen men working on things around the ranch headquarters. At the blacksmith shop there are four. A dozen hands worked the ranch. Twenty-four cowboys on the trail and two foremen. Two cooks and they each have a helper. Two horse wranglers and five house workers up at the big house who kept it for her. Sixty-five to pay. Eighty times that comes out five thousand two hundred dollars."

"You are getting good on figures. I can pay it."

"What did that foreman say to the teacher about some figures like six times eight?"

Long laughed. "He got rapped on the hand with a ruler because he said he'd never need it becoming a cowboy. That was Hoot."

"You whipped out an answer on me one day, and I made my mind up I could do that, too, so I have been practicing."

"It will never hurt you, either."

"So we move it all to the bank on Monday?"

"And Thursday I go up and meet the surveyors at the place they start at."

She put her hand through his elbow and hugged his arm. He stopped. Why, he could see she was about to cry.

"What's wrong?"

"All this is happening, and I can't give you a baby."

"Stop worrying. We can't help it."

"Oh, Long, I do so want to have a baby."

"I love you. I can't do anything else but love you."

"I know. But it is killing me."

"It will work out. We found a million dollars today. One good thing. Others will happen. Stop crying and brighten up, please."

"I will try. I don't want to bother you with this."

"You don't bother me. I just can't stand you crying when there is nothing I can do about it."

When they walked in the mess hall, everyone

stood up holding their cups and someone shouted, "Here's to the best boss we ever worked for and now we have the whole ranch."

"Hurrah" came from all around the room.

"Thanks. Jan and I are pleased that Mrs. Glass has left and the entire ranch is now ours."

They broke the news to the crew that all the cowboys would be needed after lunch Sunday for a big project.

That morning Carter drove the big team to park at the front door of the mansion. They used caulk blocks on the wheels to hold it there. The men were issued leather work gloves and the gold bars were brought up. Another crew took them to the truck, and the third crew stacked them in the wagon. There were several questions asked. How did Rupert get it? When did they find it? Long told them to just load it. He would explain more later.

Carter told the curious to stay away. It went faster than Long ever imagined. The sacks proved heavier, but soon it was all laid in the wagon and covered. They pulled the caulks, and the stiff-legged team of horses went down the hill slowly, and wagon and horses were soon parked and hitched out in front of Long's office.

Long finally explained. "This is our treasure and will be transported to the Junction bank tomorrow. In appreciation for your help and for not talking about it, every worker here will get eighty dollars to do what they want with. Don't spend it wildly. If I was a cowboy I'd buy me a new saddle or at least a better one than I have now."

That drew a round of applause.

"We leave tomorrow before daylight. Carter will tell you who goes. He will tell you now who will guard it in shifts tonight. And thank you all."

It was all set. He did not sleep well. In the cool morning he and Jan rode their horses alongside the wagon. The four men chosen to ride into town acted like they'd be having a big time.

At ten in the morning Carter parked the rig in front of the doors of the Texas National Bank in Junction.

Long went inside and asked for a bank official.

"Sir may I help you?" A young man in a suit met him.

"You the president?"

"No, sir. My name is Grant Thomas."

"The president here?"

"Yes, sir."

"Ask him to join us?"

"But sir—"

"Ask him to join us. I am going to deposit near a million dollars in your bank."

"We don't have that much money—"

"We want to deposit it. Not steal it."

"OH—sure, sir—"

"Are you and those cowboys out there here to rob us?" the big man demanded, coming out at a run from his office. "My name is Lawrence Hobbs."

"My name is Long O'Malley. I own the Three Star Ranch. I have a large deposit to make in your bank. You do take deposits? Then come with me."

"Sure—well—I must say I am glad to meet you."

"Drop the tailgate so he can see."

Hobbs stared in disbelief. "Was—was this stolen?"

"No. This is my gold and I want to open an account in my name and place this all in your vault. Some of my men can help. They don't all need to stand guard."

"We certainly can take care of it."

"Men, get him the wooden trunk."

They carried the new lumber box back by the rope handles and set it down.

"That is cash." He unlocked both locks and handed them to one of the men. The lid was lifted.

Hobbs swallowed hard. "May I ask how you acquired all this gold and money?"

"They are a part of the assets of a ranch, the former ranch owner's legal heir sold to us."

"Do you have a copy?"

"Jan, show the man the copy of our deed."

Hobbs read it quickly. "It all seems in order. The money?"

"That is ours."

"You realize I need to be careful in this business."

"But at the sight of the crowd gathering, you are telling everyone you have a very rich vault huh?"

Hobbs frowned, then he spoke to his man. "Thomas, tell the marshals to move the crowd back."

"Yes, sir."

"I hope we didn't get off on the wrong foot with you, sir?"

"No. We know this is unusual. But I am anxious for you to get all of this inside."

Two men showed up with wheelbarrows, and things speeded up. It took over an hour to empty the bed. They gave him a receipt for the bars. They were still counting the cash.

The bank was closed for the day while the exchange was made.

"May I buy you and your wife supper at the hotel?" Hobbs asked.

"Certainly."

"My cashier will bring you the receipt for the money. The value of the bars will be what the gold sells for."

"I understand that."

"Madge, my wife, and I will meet you at the hotel in thirty minutes. I have sent for her. I am very grateful for your business."

"I think we will get along fine. I am glad it is your obligation to guard it."

The rest went easy. Long felt all the eyes on the two of them walking the two blocks to the hotel with Carter, Jeb and Collie Burns, the two brothers that were his guards for the day, coming behind them.

That's the guy with all the gold bars he put in the bank.

CHAPTER 34

On the next Thursday he met the surveyor at a grassy point north some twenty miles east of his place. Arthur Miles was a thin man but he looked wiry. He wore shorts and a tan short-sleeve shirt. Long considered it too early to trust the weather though it was warming every day. But the man was not a warm person to talk to—like this survey was all beneath his worth.

Jeb and Collie Burns rode with him and waited while Long finished his business with Miles.

Miles said, by his calculation, they would be at the northeast corner of the ranch in three to four days. They would use strips of cloth to mark the ranch line as they went for any fencing activity to follow. That satisfied Long. Section corners would have brass markers. He promised to have one of his crew to check on them twice a week to see whether they needed food and supplies.

The surveyor never said when he expected to have the survey completed. No matter. It was being started. The next morning he shook Miles's hand and they rode home.

Ira and Collie commented to Long about the man.

"Now that was a damn real stiff shirt—short sleeves and all."

"He was colder than a long icicle," Collie added.

"But he drawled too much to be a Yankee."

"Hell, bossman, even Yankees wouldn'ta had him."

They had a good time trotting their horses in the fast greening world of spring. Long thought it might be a bluebell spring. That was when those flowers carpeted the entire rangeland and made it so pretty, painted blue.

Later he told Jan and Carter about the short-sleeved, stiff-shirted surveyor.

"Of course that doesn't mean he isn't accurate."

"Well for what he costs he needs to be accurate," Jan said.

"I need to go to town and straighten out some things one day this week."

"Good. We need more material for our sewing projects. Be sure to take those two men with you," Jan told him. "I think I am keeping Rob's and Boone's wives busy sewing clothes, so they are not fretting too much over their men being gone with the herds."

"Neat idea."

Carter and Long talked about fence post procurement. There were plenty of cedars, and cutting them down would improve the range as well. Carter felt some private contractor could handle it.

"What will we fence first?"

"I think the west line. You have to send riders over there all the time to get cattle back."

"It is a long ways out there, and we don't know when it will be surveyed."

"Miles will do it. Thanks, Carter. Find the post cutters." They parted.

He found Jan in the sewing circle, told the women hello, and motioned for her to come over to talk.

"I just realized we didn't tell Harp about our gold before he left with the cattle drive to Abilene."

Jan looked at him. "I think you are right. We were rushing around like chickens with our heads cut off, shipping cattle ourselves just before then."

He hugged her. "If that's all we forget it will be a miracle."

"He will be surprised."

"Yes, but it will be a good one."

The next morning, in the early cool pre-dawn, he left for Junction, Ira and Collie with him. Collie's horse walked on eggs the first half-mile, but Collie never let him buck.

"Your wife's sewing sure is popular among the womenfolk on the ranch."

Long agreed. "I guess if you were a female and all you had to wear to school were secondhand overalls, you'd think a lot about other children's clothing."

"You kidding us?"

"No. Jan had a broken family and lived with a widowed aunt who was poor. All Jan had to wear to school were some hand-me-down overalls. The aunt didn't do that because she was mean— it was all she had."

"I never would have believed that. She always dresses nice."

"Collie, she looked to people around her as rich. Those girls who had decent dresses. It made her pretty tough. I suspect her first husband was equally as tough. When some old man came and told her she needed to be his concubine, her husband went and shot two of them. The others in the family killed him. She cussed worse than a sailor when I first met her. I told her that would not help her, and she quit. I mean she quit cold."

"I never heard her swear."

"She doesn't."

"Yeah," Collie said. "When I went to school in east Texas, there was a girl there wore her older brothers' used overalls. But she wasn't near as purty as your wife."

"Collie, I never saw her back then, but I bet boys said that about her. She said boys never dated her."

"Them boys up there by Waco needed glasses," Ira said, and they laughed.

In town he went into the bank and spoke to

Lawrence about his money, the gold, and other financial matters.

"The price of gold goes up and down like going over those mountains in the West. To change some of that gold to money on the high market will make you more money."

"I'd risk, say, one-tenth of it. That works, we will see about more. But I want a good earning or I'll keep it in the gold."

They agreed and he signed the papers on the deal.

He was walking on the boardwalk down Main Street in the warming sun, when three men began to close in on him. A big man with a walrus mustache stopped him almost face-to-face. Long looked him over—from the ivory butt of the Colt to the silk-wrapped brim of his Stetson hat.

"You one of them O'Malleys?"

"My name is Long. What do you want with me?"

"Howard Burke. I'm against fences on Texas rangeland. I understand you are considering fencing some open range."

"It is not state land. I own it."

"No, it is rangeland. See, you don't understand. This puts small ranchers at a disadvantage."

"You own any land at all?"

"That isn't the point."

A rifle action unmistakably clacked. "Mister, you want to go on living you back away from my boss." Ira was sitting his horse right behind Long.

The three men backed up as Collie joined Ira, also on horseback.

"I can see our conversation about fencing is over." Long touched his hat brim. "Good day."

"You better not stretch a single wire," Burke said through his teeth. "You try, you will die."

"Better say your prayers if you come after me. I'll send you to hell."

"You will see. You've been warned."

Long turned on his heel and spoke to his men. "I am going to meet Jan up at the Silver Spoon for lunch. Meet you two up there."

"We will just mosey along with you," Ira said, booting his horse forward. Collie did the same.

Many people had crossed the street to avoid the obvious threat. Others had scattered, but many were craning their necks to see where they went and who they were.

A waitress was holding the door open. "Anyone shot?"

Long looked back and shook his head. "No one hurt I know about."

"Good. There's some crazy people in this town."

"There are crazies all over," he said.

"You in trouble?"

"No. My men are coming. A man by the name of Howard Burke stopped me to give me advice not to put up any fences. He doesn't like them."

She shrugged and shook her head. "Good thing you had backup. Your wife is sitting over there."

"Thanks. And my men handled it."

"May I take your order?"

"Soon as two of my cowboys get here."

"Okay, I'll be back."

"Thank you."

"Who was that guy?" Jan asked.

"The president of the 'don't fence' club."

"Come on."

"I never saw him before. He said he hated fences and threatened me not to fence any rangeland."

"You think he will block your survey?" she asked.

"That S-O-B might do anything to prevent a strand of wire to be strung. This no-fence-deal in Texas has been in the newspaper."

"Really?"

"Sure . . . if I had no rangeland I'd say don't fence it. I'd want to graze free grass, too."

"So it is a big deal?"

"For some. But if they try to stop us, I will end their worrying about it."

Ira and Collie walked in and sat down with them.

Collie shook his head. "I knew he wasn't a friend."

"Thanks," Long said.

"He was damn overbearing," Ira said. "I saw him coming at you. We untied our horses and thought we'd do better on our horses if hell broke loose."

"Perfect job."

"That's our job." Ira and Collie nodded.

They gave their order to the waitress.

Long noticed there were lots of folks talking behind their hands, probably about the issue.

"They make you think about not fencing?" Ira asked.

"No. We have lots of range. It needs to be rested from time to time. Like selling all these steers. Our neighbor pointed out that was a lot less grass eaters up there, but under a fence the regrowth is ours, because we'll soon have more cattle to eat it."

Ira agreed and wrapped his hand around a coffee cup to sip.

"You ever have any squaw boots?" Ira asked Jan.

"No."

"Long, did anyone ever talk to you about shoes for them wives and kids?"

Long shook his head.

"If we can get some leather, needles, and strong thread, I think I can get some of the boys to take a footprint and make them some. Be better than them old store shoes."

Long winked at Jan, then he reached over and shook Ira's hand. "You have a deal."

"I bet they'll love them in the winter," Collie said.

Long agreed. Lunch arrived.

He shook his head. He had a real ranch family. Making barbed wire, herding cattle, and dressing the children, women, and now making them boots.

"Let's pray."

"Yes, we have lots to thank for," Ira said, and they laid down their utensils and bowed.

"Lord, we thank you for our people on the ranch. Thank you for providing this meal. Be with our herders on the way to Kansas, and look after them and all of our family down at Kerrville and here. Amen."

Both men quietly thanked him.

On the ride home, they had to put on their slickers as a shower spilled precious rain on them and irrigated the bluebells. Dismounting in the barn alleyway, Long felt blessed by the rain. His wife, still in her slicker, waited, ready to hurry for their office-house. The air was clean and fresh. His men told him to go on, that they'd unsaddle the horses.

They ran for the office holding hands and once inside hugged and kissed.

"Neat day."

"Aside from that Burke guy who didn't want me fencing."

"How bad did he threaten you?"

"Not much, with the men there. I expect that kind to show up. I have had bullies like that get in my face all my life. I used to knock them out. Harp told me to just ignore them. I tried, but I still blew up if they got my goat."

"Hey, I lost one guy who got mad and went to find bullies. I don't want to lose you."

Carter came in the office dripping. "Hey, Ira said—"

"Those boys did good. The guy hates fences."

His foreman put his hat and slicker up on a tree hook. "I am pleased you were not hurt. Randy found the survey crew and he says they are making progress on our north line. They asked for a list of food items since there are no stores. He said we would send it with the next guy who checks on them. They will be fine according to him."

"That's good."

"We will handle it," Carter said.

"Your post cutters coming?"

"They will be here in a week. I have saws and axes coming, too. We have enough tents and cookware. And I selected a ranch butcher and two helpers. Between our headquarter crew, the post cutters, and eventually the fence crew we will need someone to deal with getting them meat."

"Sounds good. Oh, and Ira said he had some cowboys who would make squaw boots for our people."

"I bet they would. That is great news."

Things settled in. Both Boone and Rob sent him a short letter that they reached the Indian Territory. Things were going smoothly so far.

Infrequently, he and Jan attended the Methodist church in Junction. They drove in on Saturday afternoon, ate supper at the hotel, slept overnight, attended services, and drove home after a lunch on the grounds of the church.

Quietly, he paid to have the parsonage reroofed and set up what Reverend Clark called the "widow's fund."

Jan laughed at how they were like the German farm families who traveled every weekend from their small town homes in Mason to attend Lutheran services. He agreed.

"Going home and seeing those bluebells starting to bloom, it is sure peaceful," he said, making the horses on the buckboard move a little faster.

"Did you ever think that there was a special plan for you to go see the Rockies?"

He nodded. "And how I just happened to be in that area up by Waco and found your loose horse."

She arched her back and nodded. "One night about dark you found a horse."

"An hour shift in my time and I would not have found you."

"Exactly. I guess fate sent me"—she hugged

his arm—"and I am grateful. I spent my early life feeling left out, and look how it turned out."

"If you don't want that big house maybe the church would want it for homeless children or a school."

"That would be fine with me."

"Then we will try to do that, and then we'll go to San Antonio and find plans to suit you for your house."

"That isn't being too bitchy?"

"No. I am so proud of you. What you do for the ranch and me. I could not have found a better mate."

"Good. When you can go, I will have my bag packed."

He laughed. "We will do it when the men get back, or if I see a break, to run down there. Maybe you can draw something you like and we'd have that to show the architect."

"I can do that. Good idea. There are many times, here in Texas, where we can entertain outside on a covered patio so if it rains, it doesn't ruin the fun. And I'd like a breeze through the house in the evening. Oh, and the white limestone can be quarried from on the place, can't it? And thick cedar shingles on the overhanging roof. And some fireplaces in some of the rooms to warm the house."

He laughed at all her plans, agreed, and told her, "We'll put a windmill up that will put water in the attic, and the pressure at the faucet will give us running water for baths, showers, and toilets. They even have water heaters in the attic that can send hot water down to tubs, showers, and sinks. We can afford it all."

"Good. I want it."

"We'll get it. As for the ranch, when we get the survey complete and a perimeter fence up, we will cross-fence and need more windmills. We'll develop more springs and dam some creeks that will give us more water in the dry years. I want several hundred acres of hay meadows to put up for dry times and hard winters."

"I thought people just turned cows out. They would find grass and then the ranchers would go find them when they were ready to sell."

"That was the old way. Now you have to plan more, and do more, and those people will make more money."

"And my cowboy husband born in Arkansas, who moved to Texas, is going to build me a real ranch house?"

"Trust me. I will get it done."

"I know. It's all part of this storybook life we lead. Money, ranches, cattle drives. We are one large business."

He hugged and kissed her. "Not bad for two kids."

"I bet you were grown up a long time ago. A lot more than most kids."

"My father's Irish dedication to get kidnapped children back from the Comanche was strong. We never talked about the Comanche we killed. Dad said don't count them. It would weigh on your mind. Count the children we brought home. We freed them from a slave life among heathens."

They hugged and held each other tightly in the dark office.

Jan said, "We better get to supper. They hold their breath for us to be there."

"I'm ready. I get flashes of those two men of mine on the trail and hope they aren't in trouble up there," he said as they went on to supper.

In the hall they were joined by a cowboy and Carter.

Harry White told them he'd checked on the surveyors and they were headed south. He said he couldn't believe the ranch went that far west.

"Long, that Rocking H headquarters may be on our ranch."

"We met them. I hope not. I don't want to upset them. They are hardworking people when I was out there one time. Surely our ranch land doesn't go that far?"

"Hopefully you are here, but if you are gone and we do take in their operation, we will assure them we will adjust the border so it doesn't harm him."

"Correct. Keep an eye on it if I get busy."

"I will. With all this land we can be generous, right?"

"Exactly, Carter. And we will be if it happens. Soon, I need about seven days to go to San Antonio and find Jan an architect, have him make some plans for a house from her drawings, then come back. We would like to donate that mansion to a church for a school or orphanage."

"I bet one of the churches would take it."

Long nodded. "I hope so. I knew she didn't like it."

They sat down and Carter told the girl he was only sitting there and wasn't eating.

He turned back to Long and Jan. "Hey I heard there is a guy who did well drilling, Lance Grey. Had two setups and was working seven a day. I understand his partner, Ted Hanson, crawled into bed with Grey's wife, then convinced her to run off with him. They took the company strong box and left the country. Lance fell off the wagon over it and has been dead drunk ever since he learned she was gone. Your banker had to take both rigs to protect his loan on them."

"Men do that. It is easier to be drunk than face reality."

"What can we do?"

"I can go see my banker, find out what he owes on them, and then, maybe, try and sober him up."

"You ever did that?"

"My father saved a man in Arkansas who was a

drunk. It was not nice. But he never took another drink. I think it is why Harp and I don't drink. Dad tied him up in our barn, and we had to hold our hands over our ears because of his screaming. But when he dried out he went home and minded his own business. And he later cried when we moved to Texas."

"Boy, I've heard about folks doing that."

"Get me two hands and we will run into town in the morning and see what we can do about a drunk with two well drilling rigs."

Ira, Collie, and Carter rode with Long to town. Jan stayed home because she had sewing plans. They arrived mid-morning at the bank and Lawrence met him in the lobby. They stepped to the side and Long asked him about the rigs.

"You want them?"

"Maybe. I'd like to see if I can sober him up."

"For you, on the rigs, seven-fifty each. The business of making him sober, I bet will be harder."

"Charge them to me. I will sign the papers when I come back to town."

"No problem. Good luck. I think even the ministers gave up on him."

"Draw me a map to his house."

"Grant, draw Long and Carter a map to Lance Grey's house. Long is buying those rigs. All he needs is a harnessed team to pull them out to his ranch."

Grant Thomas nodded. "That is how I repossessed them. They are both at the livery stables."

Ira nodded he heard him.

"Here is the map, Carter."

"Thanks."

Outside, Carter showed the map to the others. Ira knew the place. Back in the saddle, Ira asked him if they'd better get the drills. Long told them it could wait until they talked to Grey.

"We have anyone in our crew to run one?"

"Yeah, Jud Aikens worked as a helper for three years on one. He said last night, with a little guidance, he thinks he could drill with them."

"We may need him. My banker thinks the ministers gave up on this guy."

They rode out to the weed-grown adobe place. Long dismounted and with Carter walked to the open front door.

A small Mexican teenage girl carrying a baby in a sling asked what she could do for them.

"I am Señor O'Malley. I need to talk to Señor Grey."

She shook her head. "He is sleeping."

"Is that his baby?"

"*Sí*. I am a cousin of his wife. She left the baby with me when she left him. There are two more small children. She left them all and ran away."

"Bad business. And he drinks because she is gone?"

She nodded.

"What is your name?"

"Wanda Robles."

"Wanda, I am going to send a couple of cow-boys and a wagon to get you and the children. And if they have to hog-tie him, they will bring him along. My foreman has a house for you and we have plenty of food. I will pay you to care for and watch the children for him. I aim to dry him out."

Tears ran down her brown cheeks as she nodded. "My prayers have been answered. *Gracias, señor.*"

"Can you buy some goat's milk for the baby?"

"*Sí.*"

He gave her a few loose dollars. "We have milk goats at the ranch. The ranch women will help you clothe the children. And they will help you when you need it.

"Ira, go in there and see how many men you'll need to haul him home."

He came back. "Two of us can hog-tie him and load him in the wagon."

"You have much to move?" Long asked the girl.

"Some pots and some blankets. The crib." She shrugged.

He got out a pocket-size book. "Your name is Wanda Robles?"

"Yes."

"What are the children's names?" That was what Jan would ask him right off.

"Gloria, the baby. The girl is Stella and the boy Drake. They are napping."

"You can bathe them, and they will be given clean clothes at the ranch."

"Oh, I prayed to the Virgin. I have done everything. Thank God you have found us."

He gave her his kerchief. "Quit crying. Tomorrow you will have a better place for you, the children, and him."

She shook her head. "I will care for the children. I fear he is what you say pickled."

"We will try."

She impulsively hugged him.

Not many things got to him, but the squalor and what she didn't have stabbed his heart. That passed-out drunk had shed no tears for his children when his wife left him.

"Get four men to do it tomorrow, Ira."

"We can handle it."

"I'll have that empty *jacal* cleaned out and ready for when they arrive," Carter added.

"Sounds good."

"Damn right. This was sure sad to find."

"But we can try and sober him up. With Ira dealing with the girl, children, and the drunk, Collie, you are in charge of a team to haul the drills back to the ranch."

Collie spoke up, "I aim to get both of them out to the ranch tomorrow. Someone might steal them if we don't claim it."

Long laughed and shook his head. *Way to do it.* Men like Ira and Collie grew into foremen. He liked to see people who saw things that needed to be done and did them. It was how men rose up to better jobs—men like Boone and Rob. Riding home with Carter he looked north at the blue horizon. All he could do was hope those two were making their way to Abilene without any trouble. Harp too.

"What did you find?" Jan asked him, joining the returning men.

"A drunk. A sister—no, a cousin—to his wife had their three children dumped in her lap when she ran off. He drank because she ran off. He was passed out when we got there. I gave her some money, and Ira will head a crew tomorrow to bring them out here. They can use that empty *jacal.* Carter's going to get it swept out and will put some furniture in it. That poor girl was even left with a baby. Oh, and we bought two well drilling rigs."

"Who will run that?"

"Ira has a cowboy who has had some experience. The first well we'll do is the one you want for the new house."

"Up on the hill. So I can look over the headquarters and get a good breeze."

"Got'cha, ma'am," Carter said, taking their reins to put them up.

Long and Jan walked to the office.

"I want to run to San Antonio, take your drawings, find that architect, and have him draw plans so we can build this house before Christmas if possible."

Inside the door she drew him back to her and kissed him. "And one more thing. It may not happen but, right now, I think I am two months pregnant. I wasn't going to tell you since I had so many miscarriages, but I really wanted you to know."

He hugged her. "Wonderful news. I know you are pleased. Should you stop riding horses?"

"The doctor told me at three months I should since I am so risky."

"No worries. It sure pleases me."

"Carter's wife, Edna, told me she lost all of hers after birth. So having one isn't the only challenge. Tell me more about this cousin."

"She is in her teens. A Mexican girl who has been stuck with three small children and their drunken father. I promised you and the entire ranch wives would help her."

"She just—"

"Tomorrow she will tell you all about it."

"Fine. Have you eaten?"

"Supper is soon. I will be fine. I charged those rigs at the bank. They cost seven fifty. Mark it down somewhere, please. It has been some day, but now it is a special one. I am so glad we have a chance at having a baby."

"I'll write it in the ledger when we go back to the office. They'll feed you early. Let's go to mess."

"That must have been Doogan's word for it. Sounds like a sailor's slang."

"Just think. You never had to put up with him."

"I am certain I'd have fired him. I want to check on the surveyor tomorrow."

"I won't ride with you out there."

"Good idea."

"Aren't Ira and your men going to move the girl and children here by then?"

"Yes, they are. All I need is one man to ride along with me. There is little threat west of here."

"Pick him out tonight."

"I will."

"Then you have no excuse to go alone."

"Yes, ma'am."

Easy enough, maybe he could see if the line was going this side of the Rocking H Ranch headquarters. That niggled him, too—the chance of running into their operation.

He drew an elbow in his side for that.

The cook crew welcomed him and said they'd have them a plate soon. The biscuits were done.

He and Jan took their place and steaming coffee came in cups.

The cook, Sam, came out of the kitchen and thanked him. "That butcher very good. Thank you for him."

"You need something, holler. We can fix it."

"I quit but not now. I proud of this ranch."

"Sam, you have not seen anything yet."

"Good. I will love it."

Their steaming food came. The men were coming in and the dinner bell—a schoolhouse one—was pealing. Suppertime on the Three Star Ranch was ready.

"Will you have a cook at the new house?"

"Do you want one?"

"Maybe one to run the kitchen?"

"Maybe. But I am not the witch. I can cook, but I like this system and it puts us closer to the crew."

"Fine. I will check with you again later on that. For now, I am thinking that we can go to San Antonio after I get back from seeing the surveyor. By buckboard, I think we can reach there in two days and find an architect. I have names to check out."

When Carter came by, Long asked him to find Harry White. He wanted him to ride with him out to the survey crew in the morning.

"I can do that. You need two?"

"No, we'll simply run out and see where that line will go."

"Harry will be here for breakfast and have two

horses ready. Long, are you expecting trouble out there?"

"No, but the fence line might crowd out our neighbors. Harry mentioned it and I want to check it out.

"Thanks." He turned to his wife, "Good luck with the girl, tomorrow."

"Yes. I will have a nice welcome for her and the children when she arrives."

"That would be great, Jan."

"We can show her we are going to help her."

"Edna will be here, too. She is coming about ten."

Jan spoke up, "They won't be back until mid-afternoon. Let her come, then she won't miss a thing."

"Anything else you need?" Carter asked.

"Jan and I want to go to San Antonio the day after tomorrow."

"Collie and Ira will go along with you two. Ira will be back tomorrow. I will have the buckboard ready. I still think another man tomorrow?"

"Harry and I will be fine."

"Good to see you, ma'am."

"Thanks, Carter." She put down her fork for some coffee.

He tipped his hat at Jan and left to go back to his house and the meal waiting for him.

When he left she said, "He is a real good man."

Long agreed.

● ● ●

The next morning, at breakfast, Carter was there to make sure all was well.

Long kissed her and headed for Harry and the horses.

"Busy man, isn't he?" Carter asked Jan.

"He stays that way," Jan said, amused.

"Well it damn sure is a better ranch than before he bought it."

She agreed.

Harry White sat a bay horse, and he had a saddled dun horse with a few white patches on his side for Long.

"They said you liked him," Harry said, handing him the rein.

"Comanche are damn fine horse breeders. I've learned that living closer to them than most folks. This is one of their horses."

"I've heard that, too."

"Where did you come from?"

"Georgia originally. After serving in the war I headed west to find a place wasn't burnt down. Got a job to go north last year with a herd, came back, and learned that Carter needed more hands."

"Nice to meet you. I want to be sure we don't cut the Hudsons out at the Rocking H by our survey. I guess he told you it concerned me."

"I planned to see about it when I went back out there with supplies."

"Good. I don't like surprises that can be prevented."

Harry agreed.

They rode along at a trot and made good speed, so by noon the working crew was in sight. He reined up, and Arthur Miles, in his shorts, met him. His bare legs bore some scratches, but he seemed unbothered by them.

"Back again," Miles said to Harry.

"Yes. We're collecting your needs. I will bring them back next week. Long is concerned about finding out if the next ranch is going to be inside our line."

"I made a projection. We are going to be a quarter mile east of them, and I think their headquarters are north of the line of the land they own. They are not on your property."

Long said, "I imagine that is Texas rangeland and that they can buy it."

Miles nodded. "Your man pointed it out so I ran a fast survey. They will be west of you."

"Without surveys it is hard to know, isn't it?"

"It is like throwing darts blindfolded. Do you want lunch?"

"No. Harry and I brought some food. Thanks again. I appreciate your effort and concern. In the next year we will have the exterior fenced."

"That will be amazing."

"I thought so, too." Long shook his hand and they rode back.

But he felt better—one matter not hanging. When they galloped back, they flushed several prairie chickens and jackrabbits. He'd be glad to be home and with his wife.

Visions of him and Harp driving those first cattle up the hill street, past the Butterfield Hotel in Fayetteville, Arkansas, came to him. The big green hardwoods lined the street still showing artillery damage from the war. And he was riding a plug that day northward to Sedalia.

What a change, compared to riding, at a gallop, on this powerful horse through the grass and low brush of his large ranch. It sure was different. He dreaded the next day and the drudgery he faced driving a buckboard all the way to San Antonio, but he promised. And Jan would be with him.

CHAPTER 35

Dodging a few of spring's rains, it required three days for the four of them to reach San Antonio. They ate supper in the nice hotel restaurant, and Long said they'd visit the architect's office in the morning.

"We will be ready for breakfast," Ira said to her as they split up.

"It is a long ways from our ranch to here."

"It didn't hurt you, did it?"

"No. I am simply tired."

"Good. So am I."

In the morning, they were at the most recommended architect's office. The men waited outside in the lobby. Long and Jan met Jim Fountain and his two assistants, Earl and Norman.

He looked at her drawings and nodded that he could make her a house plan like that.

"We want pressure water and one of those water heaters," he said.

Fountain nodded. "Five bedrooms enough?"

"That would be more company than I need."

He laughed. "Seat twenty for a meal?"

"We may have that many sometimes."

He nodded. "Do you have limestone on the ranch that can be quarried?"

"Yes. It was used in another large building," Long said.

"Timber."

"No."

"We should have this plan sketched in six weeks. You can look at it and make any changes you want. Should we mail it?"

Long said, "I think that would work. We are three days away each direction."

"Okay, we will mail it, but we will need your comments before we do the final plans."

"Thank you," Jan said.

They left his office, and Long felt sure they had the right man. Time would tell.

"It is not raining. Let's grab lunch, check out, and go home. We will be a half-day closer to home by sundown."

Everyone agreed. He thought about his family west of there at the H Bar H Ranch. Two days west from here. He thought about going there, but he needed to get back north and keep his section under control. Besides, he'd heard nothing had gone wrong. With all that was going on with all the herds, everyone was spread thin, but so far no bad news. It was unbelievable, all that had happened to him and his brother, in what was now going on three years.

He could see while traveling north that Jan being pregnant had sucked some of her strength out of her. Simple things, but he needed to take more care of her. He wanted this to be a wonderful experience for her. She had waited so long for this to finally happen. He knew he would worry about her.

Their arrival two and a half days later brought cheers from the workers.

CHAPTER 36

Ira's man, Jud Aikens, must be drilling up at the house site. Long heard the thud sounds of the drill when he was still a quarter mile from operations, and knew the driller must be poking a well down in the earth.

"They're drilling your well." He kissed her. "I have to see this."

The buckboard parked, he, Jan, and his guard hiked up the rise to where it was set up. A bareheaded cowboy in leather gloves held the cable so as to quickly stop the reel if the drill bit hung up. If the tool got hung up in the rocks, his failure to hold the cable might break the drill. His man was smiling over the roar of the steam engine.

"We are forty feet down," he shouted.

"Great work. Where's the man, Lance Grey?"

"Let me shut down and we can talk."

"I hate to stop progress."

"Oh, we can catch up. This rig is in good shape. He is napping. He's still really drunk, but managed to tell me how to use this one. We borrowed some whiskey. Gave him one drink. It stopped his shaking, but he is exhausted. I had some experience doing this, so I can make it work—save having a big problem."

"I will double your wages if you make it work."

"Oh, I will make it work. The last guy paid me half cowboy wages and that's why I left him."

"He must have been a damn fool."

"I know for a fact he's had six guys since me."

"You need to keep drilling. We have a lifetime job for you drilling wells on all our ranches."

"Sounds great."

"How deep will he have to go?" Jan asked, going back downhill with him.

Long turned his hands up. "I have no idea."

She shook her head and grabbed his arm. "My husband knows all things."

"No. How do you feel?"

"All right. I had a little nausea but it passed."

"We have lots to experience in the months ahead."

"I am looking forward to them all."

"Darling, I agree."

Carter met them at the mess hall.

"I went up and saw your driller. He's doing fine," Long said.

"Another ranch hand did well drilling for two years. He sounded interested when I said he could double his pay."

"Is the other drill ready?"

"That was the one his partner ran. It needs a new cable."

"If you think he can drill, get it fixed and put him to work."

"Did you think that guy down there can design a house to suit you?"

Long told him about the architect and the plans.

Jan smiled. "Oh, he and I talked about it over my sketches. We have final say before he completes the plans."

"Carter, he asked about quarrying limestone on the ranch."

"They used lots of it in that big house. I wasn't here then, but the quarry is north of here and I know there is a lot of exposed limestone to use."

"I had seen it riding by. I think that answers our question."

"Harry said next week the survey crew would start surveying east. No changes out there needed."

"Good. We are moving on."

"I had twenty-five purebred shorthorn bulls offered to me. They are sound, two years old, and they would be delivered here by the seller."

"How much?"

"Four hundred apiece."

"Would he take less?"

"Want me to offer three fifty?"

"Money is still short. No one is back from Abilene, yet, with pockets full of money. Offer him that. And make sure they are sound."

"Oh, yes. I will try."

"If he has more we'd take a hundred sound ones at, say, three or three and a quarter."

"I will try for that."

"That would shed us of all the half-breed longhorn bulls?"

"It should."

"Handle it."

"We have enough money in this account?" he asked her.

Jan nodded, rocking her head back and forth. "Drill wells, surveying, building fence around the world, and we buy a hundred bulls."

"And we have money for the new house?"

"Yes. I am teasing."

"We will have one of the best ranches in Texas."

"I don't doubt that."

The three laughed.

The next afternoon his neighbor Lloyd Hudson from the Rocking H came by to see him. He and a cowboy dismounted, and Long left his desk, trying to find a better way to keep track of the cattle numbers, and greeted him.

Hudson was looking around and shook his hand. "You must be well drilling?"

"That is for my wife's new house."

"Didn't I hear his widow left the mansion?"

"Yes. Come on in. What suits one woman might not another. I offered it to the Methodist church as a school or training place."

"I understand. I came to thank you for surveying. They told me when I bought the land that I had nearly a mile of land when I built my house. Well yesterday I found out it was barely a quarter mile inside my place and a portion of the corrals are in the next Texas section."

"I went up there and discussed how it was with the surveyor. He said there was some land north of your line on the section next door."

"How did your brother buy that land you two have?"

"He had a lawyer and an agent in Kerrville do that. I bet that agent would help you."

"Ten bucks an acre is the going price?"

"I understand that. It means sixty-four hundred dollars. If you can buy it for that I'd loan you any part you can't pay, and you can pay me back over ten years."

"That was my big concern."

Long clapped Hudson on the shoulder. "When you need it, just holler and we will loan it."

"I will write your agent and get started. Your man made a description of it, so if I bought it that would be the right one. I sure appreciate the help."

"I am glad it worked out so well."

"It will."

"How is your family?"

"Oh, they'll be fine after today."

"You had lunch?"

"Oh, Mark and I just rode over to talk."

"My cook, Sam, will whip you up something. Get your cowboy and we'll go over there."

"I didn't come to bother you."

"No bother. Food is over in the large tent."

Hudson said he couldn't believe he fed everyone every day.

Long told him it made them all family.

Jan came over from her sewing circle and told him to bring his wife next time.

He agreed, and after a meal they rode home.

Long went back to his project at the office. Soon they would need to do this on all the ranches they bought around Kerrville. Get everything under one brand.

He heard the shouting and ran outside.

"Long! They've got water up there."

He ran hard. The water was blowing fifty feet into the air. It looked like a gusher. Jan would be pleased. It would mean she'd get water pressure without a windmill set up.

Nearly out of breath, he was high enough up and able to see the drilling crew dancing around under the falling water. What a day this turned out to be.

CHAPTER 37

The next day he was back at work figuring out how to cross-fence this ranch in a way to manage it the best. He had lots of trips to make, to draw the water sources on his maps. Someone rode up hard in front of his office.

Jan came through from the house area to join him.

A hatless teen boy, out of breath, stood in the doorway waving a yellow wire. "Mr. O'Malley?"

"Yes. What do you have, young man?"

"An important wire for you, sir."

His heart stopped; they had a wreck on the cattle drive. Oh, dear God . . .

The paper straight, he began to read.

> Long, I had no one else to call on. We had a bloody raid on the CKH Ranch. Hoot was shot and two cowboys are dead.
>
> Three more are wounded. I am strapped. Everyone is north and cannot be reached.
>
> You are my last hope to lead a force to stop them. I am gathering the men now. Many will follow you.
>
> > Your father,
> > Hiram.

"I wonder if Hoot is all right," Jan asked.

Carter was there. "I heard most of it. What will you do?"

"I have worried about something like this—we're spread out too thin."

"What will you do?"

"I need to answer him, Jan, then line up a team and go down there to stop them."

His wife closed her eyes. "I expected you to do it, but you must be careful."

He hugged her. "How many men can you spare, Carter?"

"How many do you want?"

"At least four."

"I am thinking since we seem to have no armed threats here, I can get you six."

"I want them armed with good rifles and pistols. Ammunition enough for a war, camping and cooking equipment. Load the packhorses. We can get fresh horses down there. We leave at six a.m., and I have no idea when we will be back, but we will settle this matter."

"I can hire some day workers until you get back."

"Thanks."

Workers had watered the exhausted boy and his horse.

Long told one of the men, "Take that young man to the mess hall. Sam will feed him, and have some boys cool down his horse so he's ready when he wants to go home."

The worker and boy left.

"I am wiring my father that the Three Star Ranch is sending a team to help and for him to get his men ready to ride."

Jan and Carter stayed in the office with Long.

"Ira, Collie, Harry. That makes three right?" his foreman asked.

"Yes."

"Allan Jules?"

"Freckled-faced strapping guy?"

"Yes. Reed Walls?"

"He's the older short man?"

Carter nodded. "Guy Holt?"

"He should work."

Long might not have taken Holt, but Carter knew the man better than he did. If he had his reasons, Long felt sure it would work. The thing he hated the most was how his father would be feeling—that he had failed to stop the raid. Whoever they were, Long would find them and punish them for what they did.

Jan packed some clothing into his bedroll. It was now hot Texas summertime, so he'd not need a jacket. That job wrapped up and tied, she turned and asked him where he would start.

"The H Bar H to learn how many men Dad has lined up to ride with us. I will get all the information I can. I hope the raiders have not shot any more of our men."

"Lots to do."

"I will need some men who know the lay of the land. I also have to find out who is leading the raiders, and hopefully find out where they are hiding out. Then close in on them."

"You just remember Carter and I need you. This baby in my belly needs you, too."

He hugged her tightly. "You know I can handle myself. No one else can help my dad. They are up in the Indian Territory. That's why they raided— to test our strength—and I aim to shock them."

"I wish I could go along and help you."

"Number one is the child. I fear I can't protect you there. Stay here. Work on the house plans and I will return."

He gave her his kerchief to cry into. That cut him to his heart. He had grown so close to this cowgirl. Loved her and enjoyed her efforts to make life better for both of them more and more.

He and his crew left in a long trot in the pinking dawn. His plans were to be there in two days. They pushed hard, taking short breaks. A horse went cripple but he stopped at a ranch, bought a fresh one, and they rode on.

The men were in good spirits and laughed most of the day. At sundown they camped by a stream. The crew cooked the meal and turned in. The night was short. Day two was a hard push, but they reached the home ranch by dark.

His mom, and the wives alongside of her, fixed them a big meal. Hiram's stable help rubbed down their horses and promised him fresh ones in the morning.

He answered his mother's questions about his wife and her pregnancy. Yes, she was, all seemed good, and they were planning a Texas ranch house of her own design.

Quietly he told her a little about the money and gold in the bank. Her eyes opened wide and, holding her hand to her chest, asked him, "Really?"

"Really. I will tell you the whole story when we get time in private."

She swallowed, hugged him, and kissed his forehead. "Will this help you realize all your successes with Harp?"

"It seems that things are falling into place, and we were there to use it."

"I lived in a log cabin in western Arkansas. If we saw fifty dollars in one year we were thinking we were rich."

"Times change. I need to talk to Dad about what we can do. How is Hoot?"

"He's going to be all right. He's still laid up at the doctor's office, but he is showing signs he will live."

"Good news."

Long and Hiram went outside onto the porch to be alone and talk. The night bugs were loud, and the day's heat finally showed signs of falling.

"There are rumors that Newman and Jennings

are the source of these raids, but they also know how to keep hidden. Sheriff Coker sent ten deputies out there, and they found nothing. We have a camp of those black foot soldiers set up south of town, and they just marched around and quizzed the innocent folks. Several men said they'd join a posse if you led it."

"We must locate the men and get one of them to spill his guts."

"Friday and Saturday night let's get our best cowboys into town buying drinks. Hopefully someone will be drunk enough and talk, and that way, I think, they will find us a lead."

"Maybe? What else?"

"I am taking three good men and do some scouting. If any of us, or the boys in town, can find a lead I bet we can buy or force information out of one of them. There is someone hiding them, and it can't be that big a secret. If we find the right person, we can learn their whereabouts."

Long divided his men up. Two pairs of his Three Star men went with the best two men selected by Hiram. He wanted them to circle around the sites of the attack. On the ranch maps he gave them areas to examine closely. He selected an area in the far corner for his own team.

Long, Ira, and Collie, along with one packhorse and some food, went the back way and were far down in the ranch acreage by noontime. There was no activity on Horse Creek. They circled

Oscar's ranch and by late afternoon found the eight-acre lake Clyde Nelson spoke to him about buying while in Abilene.

Before they came over a hill to see it, they heard voices. Long waved his men back immediately. He hoped the ones down there at the lake hadn't heard or seen them. They hitched their horses back down the hill. Long grabbed his saddlebag.

Ira shook his head. "We find them?"

"Either that or some hell-raisers. I hope they were so busy they missed us."

Things had quieted down by the time they, on foot, had climbed back up the hill to see.

"They did not hear us," Long said.

At the top of the hill, he brought his field glasses out of the saddlebag and crawled, hatless, on his belly and began to search through the trees and down to the lake. Were those men swimming and wading in the lake the raiders?

He hoped so. They all looked under thirty. He counted seven of them.

"You think that's them?"

"Yes. We need to get back to the horses and quietly circle this valley and come in from the west. We don't need to be discovered. I want them alive and so we can get information out of them."

"It will be dark by then."

"Yes, Ira, but while I don't know the terrain, I think we can still sneak up on them."

"You don't own this section?"

"No, Collie. It is so isolated no one wanted it. It was claimed by the Nelson family. His grandfather lived up here, but after he died, no woman in his family would live this far out."

Collie shook his head.

The men chuckled, remounting.

Long felt success might be coming as the sun set, and under cover of the darkness, they'd reached the heights west of the place. Guided by the campfire below that the men must have cooked on, Long and his men eased their way down the steep slope with only starlight and the fire's flames guiding them. Ira lost his footing, his butt hit the ground, and he slid about ten feet down the steep slope.

They regrouped almost snickering.

"You hurt?"

"My pride."

They moved on slower until they were at last on the flatter ground behind the house. Long eased up to sneak a peek at the men around the fire and listen to them.

"Yeah, Newman promised us some Mexican women. I ain't seen one of them yet."

"Hell, I bet he brings some tomorrow."

"He coming—"

Long counted eight of them, the same number that earlier were wading in the lake.

He gave his men a head toss.

With Ira and Collie, their guns drawn, the three stepped out and he ordered the men to put their hands in the air or be shot. One of them jumped up. Ira shot him and he went facedown. The rest obeyed as the gun smoke drifted away. One by one they were disarmed and told to lie facedown on the ground.

Ira went and found some rope.

None of his crew answered the question the men on the ground kept asking. "Who are you?"

The prisoners secured, Long told Ira to build up the fire.

"I know you men ride for Newman. A week ago you killed two of my cowboys and shot my foreman and left him and two more wounded men on the ground. I want the name of the man heading this up."

No one spoke.

"Men, take one of these outlaws down to the lake and keep his head under water until he names their leader and where to find him. If he dies, leave him for the fish and come back and get another."

They picked up an outlaw and he screamed, "I'll tell you. I don't want to be drowned."

"Talk."

"His name is Albert Newman. He lives with a ranch widow and he works for Fargo Jennings who lives in Dallas. They have a big boss pays them that they won't name."

"Is Newman really coming tomorrow?"

"Huh?"

"I heard someone say he was bringing women tomorrow."

"He promised us some."

"Did he say when?"

One said, "We don't know to tell you."

They lowered their prisoner back down on the ground.

Long waved his two men over.

In a low voice, he said, "We may waste a day hanging around here, but I'd like to have him."

"So would we."

"Tie their feet. We will share the guard shifts tonight. Put them in the house and wait to see if he shows up."

"We're willing."

"This guy they mentioned was in Dallas, you knew about him?"

"I didn't know where he went, but I knew Jennings was in this mess. That leaves the big man in Dallas who pays them. We get Newman, we'll get who their real boss is out of him."

"We can do that easy," Ira said, rubbing his hip, obviously hurting from his earlier slide.

"If Newman doesn't come tomorrow we'll ride back."

Both men agreed, and the prisoners were allowed to relieve themselves and then their feet were tied. They knew that any effort to escape meant their death. He felt they were awed enough not to try. His men then brought their horses and packhorse down to the corral.

Not much sleep for him and his men. The shot outlaw died in the night. Long wasn't concerned about that.

Two of their prisoners buried him the next day. Then the seven were held tied up in the nearly fallen-in barn. The day ticked away slowly. Long paced across the bare dirt floor in the living room. Collie guarded the prisoners. Ira had been scouting from the hillside using Long's glasses. Long turned when his man quietly slipped into the house from the back door.

Long knew he had found something from the grin. "They're riding in from the south. There is a cocky-acting guy leading them in. Three guys and some *putas* riding mules."

"If he breaks shoot him. That is Newman."

"Got'cha. I didn't tell Collie. But he will hear them."

The sound of the mules braying made Long smile and nod. That miserable killer Newman was only seconds away from being taken or shot.

He and Ira were ready when Newman shouted, "Your women are here like I promised. Where the hell are you at?"

"Right here . . . get your hands in the air or

416

die." He and Ira had them covered. Gun in hand, Collie stepped out of the barn to back them.

Long went down the porch stairs, rifle raised ready to shoot him. When Long reached Newman's horse, he jerked him out of the saddle and facedown onto the ground. Then he stepped on his arm and disarmed him. His six-gun in his waistband he stepped back, lowering his rifle but still at the ready. "Didn't Fargo come?"

"I don't know any Fargo. Who are you?"

"Long O'Malley."

"Son of a bitch how did I not kill you?"

"Who pays you and Fargo?"

"No one."

Long asked him, "You see that lake? You can tell me who he is or drown in it."

"I ain't telling you anything."

"Then you will become fish food. Tie those three up."

The three Mexican girls huddled defensively, holding the reins of their mules.

Long walked over there to them. "We won't hurt you, ladies. These *banditos* have seen the last of their days. I will pay you and you can go home."

They nodded woodenly.

He walked back and put his rifle muzzle to Newman's head. "Undo that money belt and don't try one move."

"How?"

"Get on your knees. Know my hammer is cocked."

He tore open his shirt and snaked the heavy belt out.

"Drop it."

"They're tied up," Ira said. "Let me and Collie get that information out of him."

"I want to know where Fargo is and who the man footing the bill is and where he lives."

One on each of his arms, Ira and Collie hauled Newman to the lake. They dunked him, once, twice, and then him sputtering, they pulled him up by his hair and he couldn't get the words out fast enough.

"Fargo is up at Mason on the Burgess Ranch," he gasped, and vomited.

"Who is the man furnished the money?"

"This will get me killed."

"Tell me. He may miss but I won't stop short of drowning you."

"His name is—John Q. Blaine."

"He wanted this ranch. Why?"

"Years ago he was on a deer-hunting trip and saw the lake and tried to buy it, but the state wanted too much money. He kept trying to buy it, but your agent struck a deal with the carpetbaggers to buy all the land around it. The lake area was empty."

"And?"

"Fargo said we could run your asses off the land first, then take the lake."

"Newman, we are the O'Malley brothers, and you should never have messed with us."

"I agree."

"Tie him up. I may strangle him barehanded."

Long grabbed up the money belt. He took out several twenty-dollar bills and gave it to the girls. "Go home. Say nothing. Those mules are yours."

One crossed her forehead and bowed. The other two threw him kisses. Then they climbed on their mules and galloped away.

"I seen prettier ones," Ira said.

"I'm sorry."

"No, I did not want any one of them."

Long laughed. "We have Newman and his men. Before the word gets out, we need to arrest Fargo up at Mason, then ride to Dallas and get that Blaine fellow. I need to talk to a prosecutor about swearing out a warrant for him."

Still holding the money belt, Long turned to Ira. "I don't know how much money is in this belt. Split it with Collie. You guys have taken all the chances to catch them." He handed the money belt to his man.

"Well thanks. You don't have to do this."

"I know what I have to do. You two earned it."

"You know, I bet that big man in Dallas will have some high-priced lawyers."

"Even in occupied Texas, the law is upheld."

"Maybe," Ira said.

"Oh, it will be."

"Tomorrow we'll take these prisoners to the ranch. Then we need to go find Fargo before he runs off. So we really have to move. We should be proud. Three cowboys have caught a gang of killers and found the guy behind it."

"Damn good deal," Collie said. "That belt I mean."

"You two have any women you might want to marry if I raised you both up to foreman wages when we get home?"

Ira blinked at Collie. "By damn, Long, we can find someone."

"Find yourselves one."

Collie threw his Stetson in the air and howled. "We damn sure can do that, boss man."

The trip back to the main ranch the next day was slower than he wanted, but right after noon the other posse members found them on the road and took over the prisoners. Everyone was excited and had to know how they were found.

"Boys, have any of you seen that lake down in the southwest corner on the border of our ranch?"

Some had.

"A real rich man saw it deer hunting some time back and decided he wanted it. Someone else owned it, but I met the man who owned it and he wanted my brother and I to buy it. We were starting to talk about it. The man who wanted the land thought we already owned it, so he hired Newman and Fargo to make trouble so we would sell it. We have Newman and his men. Fargo is next, and we need to be at the house where he is hiding by morning and we still have to park all these prisoners at the ranch, then ride all night to Mason."

The man in charge of the second group said, "We'll get fresh horses at the ranch for you. We wondered why you didn't come in, and we've been out looking for you."

"I know. We stayed out overnight because, once we caught the original gang, we overheard them say Newman was coming the next day. He showed up and we arrested him and three more of his men. He told us, after some dunking, where Fargo is staying over at Mason. I want him, too. So we will hold these prisoners at the ranch until we get Fargo into the Kerrville jail, then we'll bring these guys in, too."

"Who is this big rich man hired them?" the cowboy called Carlos asked.

"John Q. Blaine. He lives in Dallas."

"Will these men talk?"

"Some of them will. They are facing murder charges for killing two of the ranch hands, but I will need a sworn statement from Newman or Fargo to go up and arrest Blaine. I think we'll get it. And congratulations to everyone. This should stop the problems of the raids on our ranches."

They hurried on toward the ranch as the sun was setting.

When they arrived several hands and the armed guards swarmed them to learn about the tied-up outlaws.

"Six of us need fresh horses. Carlos, pick two more men to ride with us three. We need to go up to Mason and arrest the other leader before daybreak. Anyone know where the Burgess Ranch is up there?"

"Sir, it's on the road goes north out of town. It's a big brick house on the right on the first hill after you leave town. What did they do?"

"They are hiding an outlaw named Jennings."

He watched as the prisoners were taken off their horses. One of the hands said they had a tight place to jail them.

"Take any knives or objects off them and take their boots off so they can't run away," Long said. "I want them held for the law."

"The cook has some apple pie for us to eat. The men are changing your gear to fresh horses. They will feed the rest in a while, but pie is all he had right now," Carlos said.

Long nodded. All was going well.

The cook and his helper fed each of them two pieces of pie and apologized.

Collie laughed. "Hell, I'd rather eat your pie."

Long agreed. When they finished and mounted up, Carlos told him Ted knew the ranch's location.

They set out in the dark for Mason. Long decided the stars would shed enough light until the moon rose in an hour to help them navigate. They made good time and rode through the empty streets of Mason, waking a few dogs, well after midnight.

The big brick two-story house looked stark under the tall pecan trees. Long's mounted riders surrounded the house.

Two rifles were shot in the air to break the night. Long stood in the saddle and shouted, "Come out, hands in the air, and you won't get shot. But if there is any resistance we will shoot everyone and burn the house down."

One woman opened a second-story window. "Give us time to dress."

"You can save that. Tell Fargo to get out here."

"He isn't here."

"He better not be or you all will go to jail for harboring a criminal."

"Cut the talking," a hatless man said, coming out the front door pulling up his suspenders.

Long set down in the saddle smiling. "Gentlemen. Meet Fargo Jennings."

Two of his men dismounted quickly and brought him to Long's horse.

"What are you doing here?" Jennings asked. "They told me you were up north of Junction."

"I came home to stop the murdering that you and Newman have been involved in."

"You don't have any witnesses. How can you do anything?"

"I have about a dozen cowboys facing being hung that will testify against both you and Newman, for better sentences."

"I'll have lawyers that'll talk rings around any prosecutor you have."

"No, Jennings. You better start praying a lot. If you walk out of that courtroom free, I will gun you down in the street for killing my men, and that's not a threat. That is a promise.

"Boys, put a lariat around his neck. We're riding, him running behind. If he tries anything or falls down along the way, drag him till he's dead."

"You can't do that—"

Long moved his horse closer. "You better know how to run, because we will be trotting our horses all the way back to Kerrville."

"No!"

Ira dandled the reata that was around Jennings's neck, then around the horn of his saddle and started out. His action jerked Jennings into the dust.

Long rode over as the man gagged and tried to loosen the rawhide-braided rope.

"Jennings, you better listen or you won't live to make it back to Mason. Now start jogging . . . we're heading out."

"I-I—"

"All you have to do is jog and not fall down. Go ahead, Ira."

He made it the short distance back to Mason. They gave him a short breather, and Collie went to rent a horse from the livery. Obviously, on purpose, Collie chose a horse with a high backbone for him to sit on bareback. It would be a rough ride.

"I paid five bucks for the horse," Collie said, riding by Long. "Didn't have time to dicker."

"I'll reimburse you."

"No, he's my gift. Now we can trot and I, maybe, with all this done, can find that gal you talked about."

"Which one?"

"The one you told me to marry."

"Good." Long laughed.

The Bexar County jailhouse in Kerrville was the Texas arm of the law in that widespread county. The only other county west of Bexar was Mason. They had to have enough citizens to set up a county. For the rest, they didn't have enough people so they did county business at some outside posts of Bexar or went to San Antonio as the headquarters. The jail accepted Jennings as charged with two murders and armed assault.

The deputy said he didn't have the funds to ship him to San Antonio or feed the rest of them when Long would bring them in.

"How many leg irons you got?"

"A dozen."

They had ten men, and Newman, as prisoners at the ranch. Jennings made the twelfth.

Worn out, he told the men that one of them needed to take the leg irons to the blacksmith and have leg irons welded on each one four feet apart. Then he wanted extra rivets to lock them on their legs.

Exhausted, he finally sat down.

"Long?" Ira said. "Let's lock this smart-talking bastard in the jail. We'll figure out who takes the leg irons to the ranch. He'll put them prisoners in leg irons and bring them back in a wagon while the rest of us sleep. Add Jennings to the chained ones and then we can haul them to San Antonio."

"That is good planning. I agree . . . who will take the legs irons?"

"I'll take them and then I won't be back. Someone else can drive the wagon back. I'm going to sleep two days."

"A driver and an armed guard to bring them back? That works. The rest of us will be sleeping at the livery. Tell them to wake us up when they get back with the ranch prisoners."

"I sure will. And I'll send fresh horses for all of you."

"We will need them. Thanks."

They stuck Jennings in the hoosegow, then Long and his bunch went to the first café they came to, ate steaks, and then wandered back to bunk in the livery. No one had to rock Long to sleep, and when they woke him it was dark. He had not slept for long enough, but he wanted this job over.

On fresh horses the ranch crew brought, the wagon was loaded with the dozen in irons, and they set out under the stars. At dawn, they found a roadside café and a good-looking blond woman waited on them. He ordered oatmeal for the prisoners.

She asked him if he wanted raisins, sugar, and cream.

"None of the above. They are prisoners. Oatmeal in a bowl and a spoon."

He and the somewhat refreshed six-man team had ham, scrambled eggs, syrup, and pancakes with coffee.

At dark the next day, they were close to fifteen miles from their goal. Ira, scouting ahead, found a woman living on the side of the road who agreed to cook a big pot of beans with ham in it and a Dutch oven peach cobbler for twelve dollars. He told Long that he paid her twenty.

"Is she good looking?"

"Not that good."

"Just asking?"

They both laughed.

The poor woman ran out of bowls and pots, so some ate their food from coffee cups, but they all bragged on her. Long decided that was because they didn't have to cook it. But her peach cobbler was wonderful, and there was lots of it.

Collie told him if she started a café she'd be busy when folks found her.

However, Long could see his men didn't consider her bride material.

They camped there for the night, and she cooked oatmeal for them at sunup. They all thanked her.

She told them to stop anytime and thanked them for their generosity.

Mid-afternoon they set the brake on the wagon in front of the courthouse. Long and Ira went ahead to find the sheriff and the jail.

"May I help you?" a desk officer asked.

"I have a dozen prisoners that committed murders, raids on innocent people, and other crimes."

"You a deputy?"

"No. I am a private citizen from up by Kerrville and I have these killers in irons out in a wagon. The sheriff sent ten men up there, but they never found them. Us private citizens did and we brought them here."

"Your name?"

"My name is Long John O'Malley. I am an owner of several ranches and very tired of these outlaws running over my ranchers. Will you accept them? Decide or I am going to noose them and toss them one at a time out of the wagon and drag them back to Kerrville for burial."

"Wait. Let me get my boss, Under-Sheriff Cal Newton."

A man in a suit and a badge emerged from the back office. "Mr. O'Malley, what can I do for you?"

"It's what I can do for you. Your sheriff sent ten men up to our ranch to find raiders and killers who murdered two of our men and wounded three more. They found no one. We have the two top men that ordered the raids, and ten more of the outlaws that did the deeds. We brought them here for trial, since your deputy in Kerrville had no money to ship them to you."

"What evidence do you have?"

"I have four men ready to testify to what they did and who their bosses were."

"This arrest is highly unusual."

"Go get your boss. He promised my father, Hiram O'Malley, that he would back us if we found the raiders."

"He's in Fort Worth this week."

"Wire him."

"That is not a policy of this department."

"That means you are turning me down to accept them."

"Yes. You have no authority to do what you did."

"I am going to the state police and tell them

you declined to accept felons. I have witnesses who saw they shot and wounded three of my men and killed two on my ranch land."

"Wait. I will jail them. But you must meet with the prosecuting attorney at nine a.m. here."

"Good. Accept no bonds. This gang has some rich supporters. Bring them in, Ira."

"How would they know we are holding them?"

"Word travels fast. People can see them being brought in here."

"They will still be here in jail in the morning when you come in."

"Fine. Make me a receipt for delivering them."

The man turned to his deputy. "Make him a receipt."

"Ira, bring the prisoners inside."

"Yes, sir, boss man."

There was something wrong here, but Long couldn't put his finger on it. Why would the man refuse a citizen's arrest of criminals? The sheriff, his boss, told Hiram he'd back him. Why was this first man refusing them?

There were lots of unanswered questions inside this room. He and his men needed a meal and some sleep. What did the prosecutor need? He wished Harp was there. He was the talker in the family.

Outside in the hot night, Ira asked the same question. "Why wouldn't he accept this bunch of worthless outlaws?"

"I guess if I knew that I could also tell tomorrow's weather."

"I would like that. Damn hot again."

Long laughed. "It might be that in there come morning, too."

An hour later at a Mexican restaurant, while eating supper, in low voices they all questioned him about the cold-shoulder treatment.

"Tomorrow we will learn more."

"Is it turn the outlaws loose?"

Long shook his head. "I won't allow them doing that."

He didn't sleep well that night, but they had breakfast at a nice sidewalk café and reached the jail before the time to meet the attorneys.

Long walked into a heated shouting match by three men he considered must be lawyers. They were arguing with a different deskman about posting bail or seeing the judge about some of the prisoners' release.

"My orders are not to take any bond for the individuals on your list—it's signed by the under-sheriff."

"They have not been charged. Who arrested them?"

"You can't hold them."

"Excuse me, do any of you gentlemen represent John Q. Blaine?"

"Who in the gawdamn hell are you, cowboy?"

"My name is Long John O'Malley, and I am the

citizen who brought in, for trial, these felons you obviously want out of jail."

"What are the charges?"

"Murder. They killed two of my men. Wounded three more and one or two of them may not live. They are raiders as well."

"You are all wrong. These men have alibis and witnesses to prove them innocent of all of that."

"That dog won't bark."

"Wait till we confront Judge Arnold. He will allow these family men to go back to their lovely spouses and children while we prove them innocent."

"I really come from the old legal way. You know, most folks keep the country west of here free of culprits by way of something called Judge Rope. They don't escape prosecution by phony lawyers like you. And tell the man who hired you, he'd better enlist someone smarter because I am going to try and see him hang, too."

The senior attorney told the others to shut up, gave a head toss, and they went out the door.

Ira slapped his knee. "You got them with a red hot poker right in the gut."

Probably raised the bounty on him being dead by a thousand dollars or more, too.

Two prosecutors arrived and they, Long, and Ira went back into a private office. John Hammer and Toby Goodwin were the attorneys for the State of Texas. Gatsby Fellows was their stenographer. Long would have called him their secretary.

Hammer started off, "You have brought in a dozen men accused of murder, raiding, and making a range war?"

"I don't know all the legal terms, but, yes, these men are guilty of murder. Separate them and they will spill their guts not to be hung. These are the men who raided our ranch and shot Hoot, our foreman. He is expected to recover. Two cowboys were killed outright and more wounded."

"Who planned this?" asked Goodwin.

"We know that John Q. Blaine is the man hired them to make us quit an area he liked in western Bexar County."

"O'Malley, are you serious?"

"They told us that was the deal. My men and I heard the story that Blaine was on a guided deer hunt for a huge buck and fell in love with the place. My brother and I bought a package of sections. Part still belongs to some other people, but Blaine didn't know that and thought it was in our package. Most of that land has not been surveyed, so who knows what Blaine thought. They did raids to try to scare us off the land, but we found and caught them. Newman and Jennings must have left to go back for more money to hire more men to force us to sell, or we'd die."

"Blaine is a very powerful man in the

community, even before we lost the war. He will be difficult to convict. But that is not to say we won't try to. You say split the men up and don't let them talk together?"

"Exactly."

"Long, we will separate the prisoners and begin interrogating them. That was a neat way you figured out how to squeeze this out of them," Goodwin said.

"We can do this with your help. Were you ever in the Confederate Army?" Hammer asked.

"No, I was a Texas Ranger."

"Would you wear a U.S. Marshal badge?"

"On my shirt?"

"Not necessary. But if we could call on you from time to time to help other lawmen in arrests and investigations?"

Goodwin spoke again. "For instance, if you are on duty, you could hire your man here to be a posse member for a dollar a day. The U.S. Marshal office would pay him. Arrests are ten dollars alive. A dollar a day to feed prisoners. Twenty cents a mile out and back."

His partner intervened. "Let me tell you we need smart men like you to put down crime or we will never get out of this federal occupation. The congress says we have too much crime in Texas, and until it goes down they won't even consider us for statehood."

"Like you, I want Texas free and back to being

run by Texans not carpetbaggers," Long told them.

"I am going to undertake getting you that commission."

"I would take that commission if you would let me arrest Blaine when you have the evidence."

Goodwin added, "And if we could prove Blaine crossed a state or territory line planning this raid, we could have him arrested him on federal charges and the sentence would be tougher."

"That is called an interstate crime."

"I am liking this better."

"How soon could you get down here if we needed you?"

"Two to three days. One more thing. I am suspicious of the under-sheriff. He almost didn't accept them last night. I had to threaten to call the state police. That needs to be looked into."

"It does."

"Some lawyers were here trying to get Newman and Jennings bailed out when I first arrived here, and when I asked them if they worked for Blaine they fled the courthouse."

"What were their names?"

"The desk man will know them."

"We will check on them." Goodwin shook his hand. "Be careful. We wish you a safe trip home. We will try to find out about this Blaine and his involvement in all of this."

Long thanked them and left the room. He met

up and shook the hands of the ranch hands from the home operation and gave them meal money to get home with. He and his men from the Three Star Ranch rode north and west, ate in cafés in small towns, and slept under the stars.

On weary horses, they were home in three days. Jan ran out of the office to hug him. Yes, she still was pregnant.

She shouted after the men that she was glad they brought him back. Then she turned back and asked him, "Did you get them?"

"All of them but the guy who hired them. He's in Dallas."

"Why not him?"

"It's still not over." He told her how the under-sheriff in San Antonio, at first, wouldn't accept the prisoners.

"The prosecutors want to deputize some people as U.S. Marshals. They say the crime in Texas is too high to allow Texas to come back as a state. And they feel having more smart U.S. Marshals would help suppress crime."

She nodded and smiled. "Did you raise your right hand?"

"I told them when a warrant to serve Blaine came up I'd take the badge and go arrest him."

"Do you think they will let you?"

"Yes."

"The plans for the house came. I changed a few things, but I like it. He wrote back that we should start quarrying and gave me the dimensions they need. He has three contractors to bid on the house. We may have to set up tents for them. Did I do the right thing?"

"Yes. You do not need my approval to do things."

"It's better, having you home."

"So far so good with the baby?"

"Oh, yes. I pray a lot."

"I will, too."

"Let's go eat. Nothing bad happened here."

"Good. It is so fine to be home. I have elevated Ira and Collie to foreman status. They were fantastic rounding up those outlaws by the big lake."

"Was it pretty?"

"That's why Blaine wanted it. I am telling Harp to buy it from that family when he comes home this fall."

"When they get a road in there I want to camp down there in the spring or fall."

"We can do that. Where are the well drillers?"

"Carter had started wells to put in windmills and tanks for better grazing."

"We get that finished, and Harp will have plans to use them down there."

"Your bare-legged surveyor had a close brush with a diamondback but only got a scratch. He was sick for a few days and now wears leather pants."

"We all learn. Sam, how are you?" he asked the cook.

"Better now you are home. This place always better when you here, boss man."

"Well I sure missed your cooking."

"I have good steak cooking for you. God bless you, Long O'Malley . . . you and lady make this best ranch in Texas to work at."

"Good. We'll just keep it like that, too."

First sip of his coffee and he smiled at his wife. "Arbuckle's the only brand made worth drinking."

"Oh, I forgot the best news. Your brother wired you he sold your five thousand head for eighty bucks a head."

"I know you figured it out when it came."

"Four hundred thousand dollars less expenses."

"That is a shocker. You know that."

"Not one man lost. Your two outfits are coming home."

He remembered all his concerns, worrying about them. Hire good men and you get good work. Now, over the winter, he and Harp would have to divide things up. Make those two companies. One for ranching and another cattle marketing.

"Carter's coming. I know he has some things to tell you."

"I came on the run. The men told me you caught those killers," Carter said.

"Have a seat . . . I don't want everyone to hear. We arrested them in a sweep. Even Newman and Jennings and had to haul them to San Antonio ourselves. The under-sheriff tried to turn us down in taking them. And the big guy behind them had lawyers there demanding they get out on bail in twelve hours. I was preparing to lynch them, but I figured we needed to give the law the chance to handle it."

"What happened next?"

"Texas prosecutors are now handling it. But I am not too sure the lynch law wouldn't have been better. Ira and Collie were a great help. I raised them both to foremen status, so you need something, you can confide in them."

"Less work for me. Johnny Consuela has his crew stringing a fence from the northwest corner to the southwest corner. Now the men are back I will have them search that country west of the survey line and get all our stock back on the ranch. I am fencing some bull pasture. I have those hundred shorthorn bulls coming. Simon said to order him the steel and he can make the frames to attach the windmill guts to it. He has four men making barbed wire now."

"Supply keeping up with him?"

"That is why he wants steel to make windmills, to keep his men busy."

"Order it."

"You heard what the cattle brought?" Carter asked.

"She told me and they did not lose a man. How is the adobe housing stacking up?"

"What for?"

"We now have two more foremen looking for wives and will be wanting houses."

"I will deal with that. Oh, and the well drill man has almost completely recovered. He is not drunk anymore and is teaching those two cowboys everything he knows about drilling. He is now running that operation."

When Carter brought up Lance Grey, Jan nudged Long. "The sober driller wants to marry the girl who has been looking after the children. She is willing so I told him we'd buy her a wedding dress. We were waiting until you came back to set the date."

One of the girls brought him a tray with a large slab of prime rib on it and smiled. "Sam said you needed this to get your strength back."

"*Gracias.*"

"Can you believe this?" Long asked, shaking his head at the size of the meat.

"Yes. But all I care about is that my husband is home."

"Damn glad to be here, too. Let's pray."

His wife nodded as he began, "Heavenly father, thank you for our success here on the Three Star Ranch. We've had a good year, and we all will have a good life in the palm of your hand. Protect our men coming home, all the ranch help, and workers. Bless this food, Lord, and be in our hearts. Amen."

Carter stood up. "I am going to let you eat. I'll get on the house building right away for those new foremen. I bet I have enough adobe bricks for two, but we will need a better one for the driller and the family. Better than they have now."

"Carter, we get busier all the time. Do it."

"I tell you there were times I wondered why I stayed here with that crazy woman and Doogan, but I am glad I did. I have had more fun accomplishing things since you came than I ever had in my life."

Carter left and the men coming in to eat all stopped to thank him for coming back.

"Will you have to go back?" she asked.

"I imagine. To testify at their trials."

"I am just so glad you are back sound."

"No more than I am."

"The man we hired to quarry the limestone for the house is telling me he is having more expenses."

"He bid it to get the job. If he won't do it for that he can hit the road. I am not paying him more than what was decided. I'll handle it."

"Didn't mean to upset you."

"No. This is business."

"The preacher thinks the church wants the mansion for a boy's school. There are some officials coming to look at it and to see how it would work for them."

"Good."

"I bet you're tired and your back is stiff."

"Yes. I need one of those back rubs you give so well."

"Hard to believe we've only been married a little over a year."

He agreed and stopped Sam going by. "I have eaten all that I can and not spit on it. Someone else can eat the rest."

"Always hands come back late. I feed to them." Sam took the tray and left.

Long and Jan walked hand in hand back to the office. It was nice to feel that they were still on their honeymoon. Long smiled at the thought.

CHAPTER 38

There was lots to check up on. To keep that year's crop of heifers as cows they'd need more grass, so Long planned to talk to the land agent about other land around him for sale.

How much steel did a windmill require, that plus the works to make up the pump? He sat making notes on an Indian Chief tablet of the things he must do.

Ira came by still looking tired and asked for a week off.

"You find a girl?"

"Well I want to see if she is still available."

"You need money?"

"Half that money belt you gave me will do me for a very damn long time. We got paid well for doing that, I figure."

"Carter is going to build you a house if you stay."

"That's good. I ain't going nowhere else. You go somewhere, you make sure to take a good man with you while I am gone."

"I will. Ride easy and good luck."

The next day, Harry rode with him. The cowboys were hauling supplies to the fence builders plus posts from the cutters and wire from the blacksmith. The place buzzed.

The surveyors were nearly to the southeast corner. That would mean the ranch was half fenced.

The two men trotted their horses to town. He stopped to see Lawrence at the bank who stood up and shook his hand. "Your money from Abilene arrived this week."

"Four hundred thousand?"

"Real close to that. You knew about it?"

"Harp wired my wife it was coming. You have any large ranches you have foreclosed on?"

"I do. You want more?"

He noticed that Lawrence had lowered his voice. "Yes."

"I have a hundred forty thousand on one place we had to foreclose on."

"Many cows on it?"

"Not enough. That's why he can't pay me."

"How big?"

"Thirty sections."

"Nineteen hundred acres. Is it good grass?"

"It hasn't been grazed. He went too far into debt buying it to get any more credit. He had a small herd he branded to get started. But to get a steer to go to market he has to be two years old. I warned him."

"What would it cost me if I want it?"

"One hundred sixty-five thousand."

That made it around eight an acre. Less than Texas prices. "Lawrence, draw me a map and I'll look. Hold it. Unless it is real broken-up country I will buy it."

"It isn't. I will hold it. Not a word."

"No, not a word."

He stepped out in the sunshine and saw a man on horseback go for his gun, swearing, "You fence-building son of a bitch."

Too slow. Long had his short pistol out of his holster and shot him in the chest. He fell off his horse.

Harry came running down the boardwalk to help him. Spooked horses at the hitch rack broke loose and traffic blocked the street. Two marshals blowing whistles were trying to get through all the folks who ran out of the stores to see what had happened. Downtown Junction was in a mess Long decided.

Lawrence caught him by the shirt to drag him inside the bank for safety.

"Hold up. I shot him. He ain't hurting anyone."

"Well thank God you're all right. You knew him?"

"He's an anti-fencer."

"Why?"

"I guess he grew up hating barbed wire."

Harry said, "I was getting a new cinch and saw him go by. There are sure a lot of people in town today."

"I'm fine. I don't think he is."

A man walked into the bank and right up to

Long. "I'm Marshal Cline. What in the hell is going on here? It's against the law to discharge a weapon inside the city limits."

"He was fixing to kill me."

"You know shooting with all these women and children in town today could have caused more deaths?"

"I do understand, Marshal Cline, but when he swore at me and went for his gun I had to decide if it was him or me going to the pearly gates. I decided he could go first."

"What is your name?"

"Long John O'Malley."

"You own the Three Star Ranch?"

Lawrence shook his finger at the lawman. "And I saw it all. He was about to be shot by that man, and Long shot him instead."

"How is the shot one?" the marshal asked his partner, who had been standing with the body lying in the street but had now joined them in the bank.

"He's dead."

With a wry look on his face, he turned to Long. "He beat you there, sir."

CHAPTER 39

The justice of the peace held a hearing and spoke to Long, who was on the stand. Then Lawrence, a gray-headed woman, Harry, and the two lawmen were questioned also. He summed it up as, "Justifiable Homicide."

Jan had come to town with him, Harry as their guard, for the hearing. The three went to eat lunch at a café and after the meal, they went and looked at Lawrence's wall map showing Ralph Bowman's ranch that had been foreclosed on.

Lawrence told him Bowman was moving off and he only had two hands who were leaving to help him move to his brother's up north. He'd left his herd book, which Lawrence had secured in the foreclosure.

"I gave him the twenty-five hundred dollars from an undisclosed source who wanted him to have a stake. Which was very considerate of you."

"I have Harry here. Ira and Collie are going up there to look at it and what needs to be done. We haven't seen it all, but it is a cow ranch. Shame he didn't have what it took to make it."

"I shake my head every time I think about what you two boys have done."

"We've been very lucky, but you need to

447

make hay when the sun shines, Dad always said. Considering the state of the U.S. economy and the war debt, I still see problems ahead for all of us in the future."

Lawrence agreed. "Will you live on this one?"

"No. We are building a home on the Three Star," Jan said. "I hope by Christmas we will have an open house for you and your wife."

"Don't you have a mansion?"

"Tell him, Jan."

"We deeded that to the Methodist church for a homeless boys' school."

"Oh, I see."

They left the bank and Harry asked, "We surveying it?"

"Yes. I'll talk to them and you can supply them."

Harry smiled and nodded. "I know how to do that."

Long clapped him on the shoulder. "We have lots to do. Move our heifers up there. Survey, then fence, and those guys can drill some wells. Bowman's corrals are too small for our usage. We'll need to build new."

"I'll enjoy it anyway it goes. Working for you and the missus is the best I ever had it in my life."

"Me too, Harry," Jan said.

Two weeks later Harp and two of his men stopped by the Three Star Ranch headquarters on his way back home.

"Damn, brother, I had to open gates and couldn't believe all the work going on here. What's going on with the big house?"

"We deeded it to the Methodist church for homeless boys."

Jan took him out on the porch and pointed to the construction on the hill.

"I wouldn't have lived in that place, either." Harp laughed.

She agreed with a nod.

"Your boys are a few days behind me with the wagons. They are anxious to get here for a reunion with their wives."

"We will have a real one for them."

"Oh, and thanks. Dad said you solved the raiders' problem, and have got all of them in jail."

"It wasn't easy. We need to get past our wanting to deal with it ourselves, using Judge Rope. Texas has lots of crime and we needed to do this right. Once we get one more of the main ones in jail, I'll be satisfied. Oh, and I bought thirty sections north of here for eight dollars an acre in a foreclosure deal."

"Is it Four Star now?"

They laughed.

That evening he and Harp talked about forming two companies. Ranching and the other a separate company handling the cattle.

Harp agreed. "We need to be full-time ranchers and have a separate cattle-gathering deal."

"Remember I told you about Clyde Nelson, and the far southwest section that has a lake on it that he wants to sell? You need to buy it."

"I'll do it."

"I mailed you the information."

"Long, I am amazed at you and what you are getting done. You were the guy who told me they could stick herding out of sight."

"Sometimes you have to grow up. I cut out and went to see the shining mountains, something I needed to get out of my blood. When you talked about Katy waiting for you at that store and not knowing why, but it working out the way it did. I wanted that for me."

"Oh, yes, the afternoon of our lives—mine anyhow. Why they sold her in her early teens to be a wife because she was alone, a survivor of a fire, I'll never understand. But I am glad I have her."

"And for me—they had Jan drugged up, but she had fallen off the horse and escaped. I found her horse in the dark, and then she found me and nearly shot me, but passed out, falling on top of me. The orphan girl who had been dressed in boys' overalls to go to school. Just think. One hour's difference I might not have found her horse or her."

"Dad said, either the haints or God did that to people."

They both laughed. Jan brought them out coffee.

"Neither of you drink do you? Every man I knew, and God bless my first husband, drank. How come you two don't?"

"Probably how Mom raised us. Every time I see a blanket-wrapped Indian drunk, I say that could be me. I have nightmares about it."

"The time most of the boys drank was after we got done riding with Dad after Comanche to get hostages back."

"I am not disturbed by it. Simply wondered. And I love how both of you ended up with Katy and me, both of us women with really tough back lives."

"We got the pick of the litter."

"This day that Lincoln put on the November calendar count on us being down for Thanksgiving and Christmas, too. Next year we will have the events up here in my new house."

"Did you ever expect to have a house like you're building? I saw the plans."

"I had hungry days back then. We didn't have much. Some neighbors fed me and my aunt or we'd have starved."

"Long finding you and me finding Kate was fate. But we started riding these waves when I fired the cook before we moved that small herd a foot." Harp shook his head.

Long added, "For a while I thought he'd done the wrong thing. We had to cook after that."

She refilled their cups. "Nice evening. Good to have you two together. It has been a long summer."

"Amen," Harp agreed.

With lots of things settled, Harp rode home the next day.

CHAPTER 40

Jan wore a nice dress on that cold day in November on the second floor of the Federal Building in Dallas, Texas. Someone held her lined winter coat as she stood beside him while they swore Long in as a U.S. Marshal. He finished the oath and thanked them.

"May I kiss my bride?"

Others in the room laughed. He did it, anyway, after they pinned the silver shield on his coat.

Then he reached inside his coat and took out the warrant for John Q. Blaine. It was a secret grand jury warrant for him to be arrested and held without bond for his involvement in the ranch raiding and murders in Bexar County, Texas. A slow smile crossed his face. He had the badge and the warrant.

Three more marshals were to meet him at two p.m., outside the Lone Star Bank, which housed Blaine's office on the second floor. U.S. Deputy Marshal Long John O'Malley would make his first official arrest in three hours. He could hardly wait.

Dear Readers,

I stay pretty busy writing my yarns about the West.

I thank you for supporting my books.

My e-mail is the best way to catch me. You have a question I can answer, shoot one down the line. If you don't get an answer in four or five days, resubmit the e-mail. I answer them pretty quick and it should have been answered.

In my next yarn about the O'Malley brothers of Texas, Harp will have to deal with the Mexican ranches south of the border that came with the Three Star Ranch that they bought in this deal. Until our next ride, hold on to your hat and don't let that horse duck his head.

God Bless you all,
Dusty Richards
dustyrichards@cox.net

Center Point Large Print
600 Brooks Road / PO Box 1
Thorndike, ME 04986-0001 USA

(207) 568-3717

US & Canada:
1 800 929-9108
www.centerpointlargeprint.com